THROUGH DARKNESS

Jenna-Lee Brown

Tellwell Talent

www.tellwell.ca

ISBN

978-1-77302-735-7 (Paperback)

Acknowledgments

First and foremost I would like to thank my very talented editor Marg Gilks of Scripta Word Services. You have been so patient with me over the years, and I am so grateful to have found you. I could not have picked a better individual to work with me on my book.

Reha Sakar, thank you for making the vision I had for my cover come to life. You are truly an amazing artist.

I want to thank my parents for raising me right. Without you I would not be me, thank you for everything you both sacrificed to give me a better life.

And lastly, thank you to my mom community; I truly would not have made it through the last couple of years without you. The support I have received from all of you has helped me more than you know. I love you all.

Dedication

I am dedicating this book to the people that are the lights of my life and are my reason for living every day with purpose.

Jed, Logan and Clara.

CHAPTER ONE

I LIE IN BED and listen to the rain. The storm seems to have passed for now. I can faintly hear my mother's sobs as the echo of thunder rumbles in the distance. It pains me to hear her like this; she has cried every night since the sudden passing of my father four years ago. I learned a long time ago to let her be. How would I ever understand her grief? I was certainly not that close to my father; in his eyes there was only her. They were so in love.

My dad was killed in a hit and run accident while he was crossing the street to buy my mom flowers. He bought her flowers every Wednesday. "A little treat for the middle of the week," he would say. She had a sparkle in her eyes for him that would glow whenever they looked at each other, a sparkle that disappeared along with Dad's spirit the day he died.

They would often talk about how they met. How fate brought them together, the usual crap. It was more them talking between themselves than actually retelling the story to me, but I had heard it often enough for it to be embedded in my brain: Mom had recently been dumped by her boyfriend at the time for some reason or another—he probably found someone better; she never really went into detail about it—and she was feeling sorry for herself. Her girlfriends had invited her to a carnival that was in town for the summer to get her mind off of the breakup. One of the friends had brought along her older brother as a chaperone. Mom never thought much of him; he was older by a few years and had already graduated from high school, and was not in her usual clique. They were all having a good time when Mom spotted her ex-boyfriend with another girl; panicking, she grabbed the hand of her friend's older brother. She begged him not to let go, to please pretend to be her boyfriend to save her from embarrassment, to stick it in her ex's face that she had moved on. George—my dad—said that it felt as if electricity shot through his hand at the moment their skin touched, and he knew at that instant that he would never let her go. It was always Denise and George, ever since that night. After Mom graduated from high school they eloped, and a year after that I was born. You would think that after having a child, they would spread the love evenly among us. I wish that had been the case; I was always placed second. Don't get me wrong, my parents loved me in their own unique way—Mom still does—but since Dad's death she is even more distant than when he was alive. A part of her died the day he did.

I break from the memory and reach for my cell phone to see the time. It's 3:00 a.m. and I have an exam in the morning, the last one for grade eleven—thank God it doesn't start until ten. I have my alarm set for eight; hopefully five hours of sleep will be enough. I'm going to need a ton of makeup to conceal the dark circles under my eyes.

It's been a really good year at NorthBerry High. I've been there since grade nine, when Mom and I moved to NorthBerry Hill. Starting a new school was terrifying. The thought of having to explain why we moved, and trying to get people to like me scared the hell out of me, but somehow I lucked out when I was asked out by the most popular guy in school. I don't know how I pulled that off—maybe he pitied me. Whatever the reason, I am grateful that he did, because I've had it really easy since then.

I close my eyes and daydream about Shane—or would that be night-dream? He definitely takes my breath away, along with that of every other girl who sees him. He has a smile that melts you, and the darkest brown eyes that give nothing away. Tall, dark, muscular, and handsome—that's my Shane. We've been going steady now for almost three years. I wonder if we will have the love my parents used to have. I can only hope.

The light rain hitting the window and the image of Shane's mesmerizing smile in my head lull me, and I drift off to sleep.

oOo

I'm on a raft on the ocean; the waves are crashing over me. It's freezing and black, so very black. My heart pounds against my ribcage. I'm going to fall off, I just know it. I can't hold on for very much longer. A foghorn moans in the distance, the sound getting closer. Where is it? I can't see a ship anywhere. Oh God, I'm falling! I brace for a splash into the black nothingness, but—why haven't I hit the water yet? The foghorn is right in my ear now, sounding faster and faster. "Stephanie!" I hear Mom shouting.

"Stephanie, wake up!"

I bolt upright in my bed, almost smacking Mom with my head. I am covered in sweat that's now cooling on my skin, and confused by a sound—my cell phone! That damn alarm; why I would pick the "Ocean" option to wake up to is beyond me. I make a mental note to change it.

"Are you okay?" Mom asks.

"I'm fine, Mom, just a little nightmare."

Mom sighs and shakes her head. She looks worse than I'm sure I look this morning. I draw a deep breath and fall back onto my pillow.

"Sorry, I didn't mean to scare you," I say with a small smile, all I can muster.

She nods and leaves the room. I groan loudly and sit back up again. There's another alarm on the other side of my room that is set for five minutes after the cell phone to make sure I get up, and that one makes a loud buzzing sound. I love my sleep. I am definitely *not* a morning person.

I get out of bed and slip my feet into my fluffy black slippers, then dart from my bedroom into my own bathroom across the hallway and close the door behind me. It's still too early to look in the mirror, so I step past it. I really do not need that sight until after my morning coffee. I turn the shower on. The water in this old house takes a while to heat up.

We had to move from our really nice townhouse into this piece of crap after Dad passed away. He did not have life insurance and we were in debt before he died. The funeral cost put us further behind. Mom spared no expense on that. I tried to tell her to get him cremated, knowing that funerals are expensive and we could not afford it. The only response I got to that was a slap across the face; I never voiced my opinion again after that.

I guess this house has character. I mean, who doesn't like the adrenaline rush of never knowing when you are going to fall through the floorboards? Okay, I probably make it out to be worse than it actually is; thank my over-active imagination for that.

The steam seeping around the shower curtain prompts me to strip off my oversized t-shirt—one I stole from Shane—and slip out of my cozy slippers. Pushing the shower curtain aside, I climb into the claw-footed bathtub, my imagination again conjuring typical horror movie images involving shower curtains. I shudder and shake the thought away. This house is creepy enough without me putting bad images into my head.

My whole body relaxes as the water beats down on me. I stand there for a few minutes until I am fully awake, then wash myself, turn off the faucets, and reach out of the shower for the towel hanging on the rack. Nothing grabs me. I laugh at myself for being so childish. I dry off and wrap my pink cotton robe tightly around me. Avoiding the mirror again, I stride from the bathroom.

The hardwood floor creaks as I walk slowly down the hallway. The walls are covered with abstract art that Mom started collecting after Dad died. It's not cheerful; I find most of it depressing. It really darkens up the place. The art is meant to signify finding light through the darkness, which I can understand, but I think Mom sees it differently.

I pass Mom's bedroom door on the left—closed, as usual. I never go in there. I was surprised to see her in my bedroom this morning. She usually never steps foot in my room. I think it's too colourful for her—unlike the hallway, everything is bright: off-white walls, sun streaming in a window in the far right corner, a white wicker chair below that. Next to that I have a small bookshelf holding various romance novels. Even my queen-sized four-poster bed is white. No fancy canopy or drapes; I was never really Daddy's little princess.

With all the white furniture and walls I needed something to brighten the heck out of the room, so I bought the brightest pink and orange bedding I could find. Without it I am sure the room would have looked like a hospital ward. There are two bedside tables with wicker lamps on them, the shades pink with orange polka dots, and there is a chest of drawers across from the foot of the bed that has the alarm clock on it, and many photos of Shane and me. I also have a huge, shaggy pink area rug on the floor that

I love curling my toes into. My closet is a bearable size, but not quite the walk-in that I used to have. My bedroom is all mine to do with as I see fit, and I think it counteracts the dreariness of the rest of the house well.

I make my way down the steep stairs and walk through the small living room with its black leather loveseat, antique coffee table, and of course, where the TV should be—more abstract paintings. It's not like I would watch TV in here, anyway. Sometimes I catch Mom sitting on the edge of the loveseat, staring blankly into one of the paintings. I glance in that direction. This particular painting is all blacks, reds, and mustard yellows melting into each other and dripping down the canvas like an open wound that is still bleeding.

Maybe that's her heart, I think.

The hairs on the back of my neck rise. I never stay too long in any of these rooms if I can help it. This house is gloomy overall. I have been living here for just over three years, and I still hate it.

I finally reach the kitchen and put the coffee pot on. I sit at the small pine table in the centre of the room and look out the window. The sun is struggling through the clouds. At least the rain has stopped.

The coffee machine beeps, letting me know the coffee is ready. I grab my favourite coffee mug with its picture of my old cat, Charlie, on it. I miss that cat. He ran away when we moved to this house—or maybe he was eaten by a coyote, who knows. He was fatter than fat, and orange. He reminded me of an even grumpier version of Garfield. Charlie hated everyone he met; sometimes I think he hated me, but at night when I lay down to sleep he'd jump up on the bed, flop next to me, and knead my shirt with his little paws. That was the only time I heard him purr. He did love me, as I did him.

I break my gaze from the mug, head to the coffeemaker, and pour myself some of the good stuff. I add two sugars and two oversized scoops of coffee whitener, then grab my coat from a hook by the door and slip my feet into my floral gum boots. Coffee in hand, I head outside. I could go out the front door and have my morning coffee on a rickety old swing bench on a decent-sized porch—if I had a death wish, which I don't, so I've found another place to have my coffee. I cross the unkempt lawn, pass through a drape of weeping willow branches, gingerly walk over four big stepping stones, and duck into an old gazebo hidden among the trees. Its roof looks like it was made out of a large, ancient satellite dish. Under that, a wooden bench curves around the perimeter, and a raised, red brick fire-pit is in the centre.

I sit on the bench and lean back against one of the posts. I put my feet up on the bench and stare through the trees at the distant lake. I never bring anyone here, not even Shane. It is my private little escape from the world—and more so...from Mom. I love it here.

A rustle in the bushes behind me makes me jump, leaving my thoughts behind. "Shit!" I cry as my mug slips out of my hand and smashes on the cement floor. I look into the bushes and see a squirrel. It hisses at me and scampers away. I had no idea squirrels hissed.

I look down at the remnants of my mug, which draws a pout to my lips as I bend over to gingerly pick up the pieces. I saw comfort in that old mug. There is a small portion of ceramic that contains Charlie's face, still intact. I smile as I place the fragment on the bench, grateful for that keepsake.

I rise and drag my feet back toward the house.

Mom's car is gone. My heart skips a beat. *Crap, what time is it?*

I rush into the house. The time on the microwave says 9:00 a.m. I have to be at school in an hour and I still haven't braved looking in the mirror.

"Bye, Charlie," I say as I throw the pieces of mug into the trashcan. Then I run upstairs and into the bathroom. I groan as I finally look in the mirror. The bags under my eyes are huge. I look as if I haven't slept in weeks. I pick up my concealer and foundation and get to work. Then I sweep brown and purple eye shadow onto my eyelids to bring out the hint of green in my hazel eyes, and finish it off with three coats of mascara. I was not blessed with long eyelashes. I take a brush to my hip-length, mousy brown hair; it's dead straight, as usual. I've tried curling it before but it doesn't hold.

There, that's better, I think, and grin like an idiot into the mirror.

I leave the bathroom and rush into my bedroom, almost tripping over the shag rug in my haste. *Clothes, clothes, clothes—what to wear, what to wear?* "Ugh, why does this have to be so hard?" I say out loud as I stare at the mess of colours in my wardrobe. I really need to sort it out someday.

I glance at my alarm. *Twenty minutes—crap! I haven't even heated up my car!*

I snatch up my favourite distressed jeans, a white tank top, white flip-flops, and a purple button-up hoodie. Not really what I had in mind for the last day of school, but it will have to do. I dress like there's a fire in the room, then grab my car keys, the black satchel that I use as a school bag, and my purple aviators. I do not have time to make sure I have everything. I run through the house and leave without locking the front door.

There is frost all over my car.

"Double crap!"

I open the car door, put the keys in the ignition, and turn it over. The car coughs at me then, with much struggle, starts. I switch the heat onto the highest setting and get back out of the car. It's so much colder in there than out here. I worked really hard last summer, looking after bratty children, to pay for this vehicle. It is a pretty sexy car, though—a 1987 Red Fiero coupe. I was determined to learn how to drive a stick shift and, thanks to Shane, I am now a pro. The car has a four speed transmission, no power steering, and no electric locks or electric windows, but I love it.

I lean in and look at the clock in the dash. *Ten minutes. Mr. Clarke is going to be pissed!* I get into the car and use my sleeve to wipe away the condensation on the windshield. *Good enough.*

I release the clutch, put my foot on the gas, and I'm off down the steep, curving driveway.

Minutes later, I pull into the school parking lot. Apart from the many cars, there is not a person in sight. "Holy hell, I am so late," I say to myself as I scan the lot for an empty spot. Mr. Clarke is definitely going to have a fit. Heart racing, I swing into an empty space, grab my bag, and burst out of the car, almost knocking the door into the black car next to me. I scan the school grounds. Empty. *Please don't tell me I am the only late student.*

The red brick building looks desolate. It was built in 1917 and is the only high school in NorthBerry Hill. Only two of its three floors have classrooms. The basement holds the library and the cafeteria and is called Floor One. It's a different setup. It used to be an old hospital, back in the day—which is really disturbing, to realize we eat lunch right next to where they once kept dead bodies. I usually go outside during breaks. I hate going into the library especially, as that's where the actual morgue used to be. They have totally transformed it into a pretty good library, but I still find it dark and dreary.

I glance up at the third storey as I cross to the doors and see my best friend Melissa—Milly for short—frantically waving at me from one of the classroom windows. Even from far away her beauty radiates. She has shoulder-length, wavy auburn hair and dark green eyes. If she could be a cartoon character she would be Jessica Rabbit, without a doubt. I wish I could be as sultry as her. For now, I push such thoughts aside and sprint toward the school.

Moments later I reach the classroom door and hear Milly arguing with Mr. Clarke.

"She's only fifteen minutes late; you have to let her in—have a heart!" Milly exclaims.

"Sit down, Miss Shepard, before I ask you to leave," Mr. Clarke replies. His voice sounds controlled, as if he's trying to control his fury.

Boy, he sounds angry. I cautiously knock on the door.

It feels like minutes before he swings the door open and steps into the doorway, blocking my entrance. "Miss Martin, you are quite late." He reminds me of an ostrich. His neck is too skinny and he has beady, almost black eyes.

I take a step back and find my voice. "My car wouldn't start," I lie.

He stands there staring at me. Is he trying to be intimidating? Because if he is, it's working. I feel like I'm four years old. My palms get sweaty, but I refuse to be the first one to break the stare.

Milly appears behind him, her hand on her hip. "Mr. Clarke, if you haven't noticed, everyone has stopped writing their exams, and you are now wasting *our* time. Just let Stevie in so we can get on with it." She raises her eyebrow, challenging Mr. Clarke. I am surprised she doesn't start tapping her foot impatiently.

Mr. Clarke breaks his stare and steps aside. He motions with his hand for me to pass. I duck into the classroom and give Milly the hugest smile. God love her. I sit down in the first row. That's what I get for being late, the seat right in front of Mr. Ostrich.

He shoves the grade eleven mathematics exam onto the desk. "Do not think for a second that I will be this lenient next year, *Miss Martin*," he hisses.

I fight the urge to talk back to him. Instead I grab a pen from my bag and start the exam.

Although I was late for class I am one of the first people to finish the exam. There is still half an hour left when I stand and gently place my paper on Mr. Ostrich's desk. He looks up at me and I give him a mocking, in-your-face kind of smile. His ears turn red. I hear a snort behind me and know it's coming from Milly. I turn and face her and she puts two fingers up, letting me know she's almost done. I leave the classroom to wait for her at my locker.

I walk along empty hallways, passing lockers and closed doors on my way to the second floor where my locker is situated. *Am I seriously the only one out here? Where is everyone?* It's eerie to be walking the halls by myself. The only sounds are my breathing and the slap of my flip-flops against the soles of my feet.

My shoulders feel like targets, as if someone is watching me. I try to shake off the feeling. *Why do I have to be so paranoid all the time?*

Then I jump at a loud *bang-bang-bang* as something hits the steel of a locker somewhere, though I can't tell what direction it's coming from. I swing my head around and look behind me.

No one.

Then I instantly think, *Is this the part in horror movies where I look forward and someone is right in front of me?*

Dammit, Stevie, stop scaring yourself! I put on a brave face and turn back around. *No one...*

A nervous laugh escapes my throat. I stifle it and round the corner into a short hallway containing a few lockers on either side and the stairs at its end that lead down to the first floor of classrooms, or Floor Two, as the school calls it.

All of a sudden I am grabbed and lifted off my feet. I scream. Whoever has a hold on me has pinned my arms to my sides with one arm and the other rises from the right, cupping a hand over my mouth to stifle my shrieks. I stark kicking and struggling, all in vain; whoever has me is a lot bigger and stronger.

I look down at the arm wrapped securely around my stomach and see the same watch that I bought Shane last Christmas, its silver tone bright against his caramel skin. I bite down on the hand that's covering mouth and now it's his turn to shriek. He lets me go and I spin around to face him.

"Dammit, Shane, you scared me half to death!" I exclaim, pushing him in the chest.

He erupts in laughter and takes my hand to pull me closer. "God, you are fun to scare, Stevie," he says, grinning down at me. "I've been following you for at least six minutes; you make it way too easy."

I scowl at him, but can't keep a smile from creeping across my face. "You are such an ass!" I yell, but there is not a hint of anger in my voice.

Shane picks me up and I wrap my legs around his waist. We kiss way too passionately for these surroundings.

"Get a room, you two," Milly says as she rounds the corner. "You guys will have plenty of time for that at my parents' lake house."

I blush as I relax my legs from around Shane's waist and slide to the floor. We have been planning this trip for months now. Milly's family is really well off. They have agreed, after much deliberation, to let a small group of Milly's friends stay in their luxurious vacation home. We leave tomorrow.

Milly is bringing her boyfriend Bradley. They've only been going out for about a month. He's from a couple towns over. They're kind of opposites. Milly usually goes for guys like Shane—muscular, tall, athletic, and sexy as hell—but Bradley is different. I guess she was running out of options. She's pretty much dated every guy in a fifty kilometre radius. Milly is all boobs, curves, and ditsy, whereas Bradley is tall, lean, and actually has a head on his shoulders. I believe he's studying to be a psychiatrist or something, which for Milly is great; she has her head in the clouds most days. They do complement each other in an uncanny sort of way, and they seem happy so far.

Shane's sister Sara and her boyfriend Calvin will be joining us as well. I get along with her wonderfully. We've become really close over the years. She's a few years older than Shane and just as gorgeous, in a feminine way, of course. She reminds me of a twenty-one-year-old Beyoncé. It's a pity her voice doesn't come anywhere close to Beyoncé's or I would have let her ride with me for the three hour trip to the lake. Sara pleaded to go in my car for the drive and I begged Milly to come with me. There are only seats for five people in Shane's truck and there was no way I was going to suffer that length of time with Sara's high-pitched squealing while I tried concentrating on the winding mountain roads. I love her to bits, but I think she's tone deaf. *Good luck with her, boys.*

"So Shane's going to pick us all up tomorrow around eleven and then we will be at your house around eleven-thirty, okay?" Milly says, breaking my train of thought.

"Yeah, sure," I say, and smile.

Shane and Milly are so lucky that they live on the same street.

"Don't be late," I joke. "Oh, and Milly, thanks for earlier—Mr. Ostrich can be a real asshole."

"I agree," she says. "Well, I have a bunch of packing to do so I'll see you two tomorrow."

"See you," Shane and I say in unison as Milly walks away.

Shane pinches my behind, making me squeal, then takes my hand. "I'll walk you to your car," he offers, and I beam at him.

We stop at my locker on the way out so I can shove my shoulder bag into it. I retrieve my sunglasses, wallet, and keys and put them in my hoodie's front pocket, absently perusing the collage of pictures in my locker. There's Milly and me at the beach, me looking way too skinny next to her. I need to borrow some of her boobs and maybe a little of Sara's ass, then I'd be happy. There is a picture of Shane and me. I look tiny compared to him. We're hugging in the picture and I barely come up to his chin. He makes me feel so fragile. Then there's a picture that Shane took of us cuddling. Half my head is cut off, but he looks so dreamy I just had to put it up. That one was taken last autumn, before he decided that a buzz cut would better suit him. I miss his hair. Shane is lucky, though. He could have a four-foot afro and still look hot.

The nice thing about this school is that you get to keep the same locker until you graduate, so I don't have to take anything down at year end. It's going to suck to remove it all next year when we leave.

"Are you ready?" Shane asks patiently.

"Yeah, sorry; got lost in the memories," I say shyly. "Let's go." I close the locker and we walk to the front entrance hand in hand.

"Want me to stop over later?" Shane asks as we get to my car. There's a mischievous gleam in his eyes.

"Probably not a good idea, Mom's been extra weird this week," I say honestly. His face falls. "Shane, we will have two whole uninterrupted weeks together, and I've really been thinking about what you asked me."

"Really?" His face lights up.

"Yes, I think it would be good to take our relationship to the next level. I don't want to be the only virgin in grade twelve," I scoff.

Relief floods his face and he embraces me tightly. "Only if you want to, Stevie. I don't want to push my luck or pressure you. We can do other things if you're not ready. Are you sure you don't want me to come over later?" he says eagerly.

I laugh and teasingly shove him away. "I thought you said you didn't want to push your luck," I joke. "I will see you *tomorrow*."

"*Fine*," he says, mirroring my tone. He gives me a peck on the cheek, winks, and walks to his truck. I watch him get in. I could watch him all day.

I get my keys out of my pocket and unlock my car door. I am about to get in when I hear footsteps behind me. I am stuck awkwardly half in and half out of the car.

"Miss Martin?" I hear from behind me.

I back out of my car, turn, and straighten. I am face to face with Mr. Ostrich. "Mr. Ost—er, Clarke?" *Crap.* I stifle the urge to burst out laughing.

He is staring down at me. His eyes feel like they're tearing a hole through my soul. I shudder. The urge to laugh vanishes instantly.

"You finished your exam early; it would be a shame to see you rush a very important final so you can flirt with your boyfriend," he says smugly.

I'm speechless; he has obviously been watching us. He extends his long, skeletal arm and rests his right hand on my left shoulder.

What the hell? I cringe. Oh God, I need an exit strategy badly. His touch feels so wrong. I can feel the coldness of his hand penetrating the thick material of my hoodie. *Think Stevie, THINK!*

I pretend to see someone behind him and try my hardest to put a believable smile on my face. He swiftly removes his hand and turns around. I take that opportunity to jump in my car and close the door behind me. I push the locks down and take a sharp breath in. I reach to start the ignition.

Shit, where are my keys?

I realize at that moment that I left them in the car door. I scold myself for being so dumb.

There is a knock on the window. Mr. Creepy-as-hell has my car keys dangling from his long, stick-like fingers.

Fuck. I roll down the window. I feel my face burning at my stupidity. I must be as red as a tomato.

"I didn't mean to startle you, *Stephanie*." The sound of my name on his tongue gives me instant nausea. "Have a good summer," he says as he drops the keys onto my lap. He looks satisfied and sardonic at the same time.

What the hell was the point of that? God, he's creepy. I watch him in my rearview mirror as he walks back toward the school building. I don't take my eyes off of him while I start my car. I don't need anymore surprises today.

oOo

The car moans as it climbs the steep driveway toward my house. Mom's vehicle is still gone. I never know when she leaves or returns. Sometimes she's home the whole day—her car is here, but she's nowhere to be seen; hiding in her room, most likely. I don't know what she does up there.

The old two-storey house looks lost among the many trees. The only houses in the vicinity are acres away. Behind the house are miles and miles of forest. I never venture too far into the woods. I've seen many different animals roaming in our yard—bears, coyotes, and deer—so the thought of being alone with them scares the heck out of me.

I don't think even a fresh coat of paint would make the house look any more cheerful. The brown shingles on the exterior are in dire need of replacement. The white paint on the columns around the porch is peeling off in chunks. The green shutters on the side windows are still intact, but also desperately need some TLC; I worry that if the wind blows too hard, they'll fly off. When we moved in the interior looked as if it had been ransacked—the cupboards were all open and there was garbage all over the floors and holes in the walls. Maybe teenagers or homeless people trashed the place while it was standing empty for roughly five years before we moved in. It took weeks to make it livable. You can tell the yard used to be really beautiful at one point in time, but now only remnants remain— weed-infested flowerbeds and window boxes holding nothing but dirt.

I park my car just off the driveway, gazing at the house through the passenger side window as I get lost in a memory—and it's not a pleasant one.

oOo

Hoping to bring a smile to Mom's face, I'd decided to surprise her by planting flowers in the garden near the front steps. I waited for her to leave for the day, then walked to one of the neighbouring farms and bought a selection of flowers with all the change I could gather up. I hid the flowers near the gazebo and spent the rest of the afternoon fixing up the garden.

I decided to wait until the next morning before school to plant everything, thinking it would be a nice surprise when she woke up. All went as planned and I left for school. I was so happy that I could do something for Mom. She never smiled anymore. I missed that.

When the school bus dropped me off at home that afternoon I ran up to the house to see if she had enjoyed the surprise. I was shocked at what I ran into: Mom sitting on the front step, covered in dirt, streaks on her muddy face where the tears had rolled down, and bloody fingernails. And the garden—well, there was nothing left of it. She had torn it all up.

Mom's eyes were unfocused until she saw me standing there with my mouth hanging open. I have never seen her move so fast. She grabbed a handful of my hair and dragged me toward the house. She shoved me into the garden face first. "How could you, Stephanie? How could you do this to me?" she cried.

Mom had my hair wrapped through her fingers and I couldn't move. My mouth was full of dirt. I couldn't speak; the words were there, but I couldn't for the life of me get them out. It all seemed like a bad dream.

"Do you know what these are, Stephanie?" she shrieked. "How could you be so hurtful? How could you do this to me? Have I not had enough pain to last a lifetime?"

She let go of my hair and I crawled like an infant in the dirt. I turned around and saw her clenching a handful of daisies. She was holding them so tightly that her fingernails were digging into her palm; blood trickled down her wrist.

"Your father—how could you be so stupid—your father..."

I finally coughed, spat out the dirt, and found a voice that sounded too small for me, the voice of a child. "Mom, I don't understand," I whimpered.

"These flowers, Stephanie." She held the crumpled daisies toward me. "These flowers were on his grave!" Her eyes searched mine frantically.

I saw her expression change in front of me. Realization hit her. Realization of what she had done.

"I—" Her voice cracked. "I'm so sorry, Stephanie. I don't know what came over me. I saw the flowers in the dirt and had a flashback of his grave, and I-I lost it." She got up slowly and walked back into the house without saying anything else.

I sat there in the dirt for I don't know how long. I was embarrassed. I was ashamed. She was right, I was stupid. How could I do that to her? I couldn't believe that I'd forgotten what flowers he'd had on his grave.

οΟο

I tried many times to apologize to her over the weeks that followed. I think that's why she started avoiding me and hiding in her room in the first place—to get away from me.

I force myself to break from the memory, and my brain fades back to the here and now. My stomach growls and I realize I haven't eaten since yesterday. I don't think I can afford to lose any more weight, at five foot seven and only one hundred and eighteen pounds. Can people live off of coffee alone? I think not.

The front door is locked so I know that Mom has been home. I don't know how she times it so perfectly to be here when I am not. I have a really bad habit for leaving the house unlocked. I am way too trusting. The way I see it, we live in a house that obviously does not have expensive things in it. Anyone that looks at the outside can tell, so why would anyone even bother to break in?

I unlock the door and go straight to the kitchen. I drop my keys and wallet on the kitchen table and head to the fridge.

I swing the door open. *Yay, food!* Although Mom is, for the most part, detached from the present, she still manages to go to work, pay the rent, and put food on the table. I am grateful for that. I do most of the cooking and cleaning. She works at a small art supply store in town. I think the owner, Greg, is totally in love with her. He pays her well and gives her time off whenever she's having a bad day. I'm quite fond of Greg; he seems like a decent guy. He knows about our past and has assured me that she has a

21

job there as long as she wants, and that I have a job there if I want it, too. I think I will stick to babysitting, though. I remember the look on Mom's face when he offered me part-time work. She looked as if she was about to have a stroke. I kindly turned him down; art isn't my thing. It's nice to look at, but I really don't know anything about it.

I select salami, mayonnaise, mustard, and spinach, and grab four slices of white bread from the breadbox, then load up a sandwich for myself. Eating this way, you'd think I'd be a lot heavier. Thank you, fast metabolism. I make a much lighter sandwich for Mom, wrap it in plastic wrap, and put it in the fridge along with all the fixings. I never know if she eats what I make, but the food seems to disappear, so I suppose she does. I hope she eats while I'm away for two weeks. Thinking of that reminds me that I really need to pack. I get a plate from the cupboard, place my sandwich on it, and carry it upstairs.

I eat while I'm packing for the trip and collapse on my bed when I'm done. It's four o'clock. This day is dragging on. I am so tired I don't want to move. *Hmm, what involves not moving while still being proactive?* I wonder what Milly is up to. I decide to call her.

"Hey!" Milly answers on the third ring. "What's up?"

"Just finished packing. Oh my God, you will not believe what happened," I say, remembering my weird encounter with Mr. Clarke.

"Oh, what?" she asks, and I go into full detail.

"Someone seriously needs to put that asshole to sleep," she fumes when I'm done. "Thank God we don't have to deal with him for a couple months."

"I know, it was bizarre. So what are you up to?" I ask, trying to change the topic. You do not want to get a redhead angry. I'm afraid she'll go down to the school and rip him a new one. I laugh at the thought.

"What are you giggling about?" She sounds annoyed

"Oh, just the thought of you going bat-shit crazy on Mr. Ostrich."

"Hah, maybe one day. That would be a sight." She snorts and we both burst into laughter. "Stevie, I have to go—call waiting, I'll see you tomorrow, okay?"

"Sure, see you," I say, and hang up.

I look down at my phone: 4:15. "Seriously?" Maybe I'll try Shane.

The line rings once and then I hear "Call forwarded to voice mail." I roll my eyes and groan. Well, I'm not trying Sara to ask her to get Shane to call me. I don't want to seem like *that* kind of girl. I reach out and place the phone on the side table.

I blink and my room has gone from light to dark. Did I fall asleep? I fumble for the bedside lamp and switch it on. I pick up my phone at the same time. The small glow from the lamp illuminates the bedroom enough for me to see the area around my bed. I push the button on the top of the phone to turn it on. Dead. "Dammit," I moan.

I look at the red glow from the alarm clock on the opposite side of the room. Eight p.m. How the hell am I going to fall asleep? I stare at the numbers on the clock and count. Okay I must have slept for about three hours. I should still be able to sleep later. Maybe a hot shower and camomile tea will help.

My eyes slowly adjust to the darkness in the room and out of the corner of my eye I see the outline of someone sitting on the wicker chair near the window. My heart feels like it's constricting and I struggle to take a breath. I can't make out its face. Can it see mine? Surely yes, with my bed lamp on. That draws a thump from my heart. Maybe my mind is playing tricks on me, I tell myself. I blink hard and reopen my eyes.

Shit!

I jump up and make a beeline for the door.

My foot twists in the comforter and I overbalance and fall on the pink shag rug. The comforter is now wrapped around me. I'm a tangled mess. "Ahh!" I scream, thrashing desperately to free myself.

A series of thumps vibrates the floorboards—footsteps, running across the room toward me. I scramble to get away.

For the second time today I am lifted off my feet as if I weigh nothing, and tossed onto the bed. I roll around frantically, trying to see my attacker. I go giddy with relief, which quickly turns to anger. I leap off the bed.

"For fuck's sake, Shane!" I yell, and hit him in the chest as hard as I can.

He takes a step back. "What the hell, Stevie?" he says, confused.

"What do you mean, 'what the hell, Stevie'?" I say, exasperated. I am not laughing this time. "*You're* the one who scared the *shit* out of *me*."

"Stevie, chill out. I didn't mean to scare you."

"What the fuck are you doing here, Shane?" I snap.

"Jesus Stevie, you didn't answer your phone so I came over. The door was unlocked and Denise's car wasn't here so I let myself in. I came up here to find you sleeping and I didn't want to wake you. So I sat in the chair and must have passed out. I woke to you screaming and freaking out on the floor, all rolled up in your comforter like a burrito." His mouth curves slightly in a smile at the memory. "Look, I'm really sorry, but I did try calling and you had me worried."

How can I be angry at him now? He's gone all doe-eyed on me and it's making me melt. "Shane, you are so lucky I was trapped in that comforter or I would have beaten the crap out of you." I can't keep a straight face. A grin stretches my lips.

"You really should consider locking the front door; I could have been a creep, for all you know," he says.

"Who says you aren't?" I quip.

At that comment Shane pushes me to the bed and lies on top of me, holding me down with his weight—all one hundred and eighty pounds of him. "I guess you're right," he teases, and forces his mouth onto mine.

I wriggle my arms out from under him and wrap them around his back. I can feel his muscles rippling under my fingers as he grinds on top of me. The kiss intensifies and we are both panting. The room feels like a sauna. We have made out before but this is way more heated, way more intimate. Shane moves his hand to my hip and slowly runs his fingers across the waistline of my jeans to the front button. He unbuttons it effortlessly.

The front door slams.

Shit, Mom!

Shane groans and rolls off of me.

I've sunk into the soft mattress and it takes me a few tries to push myself up. "You should probably go," I say, "even though I really don't want you to."

Shane turns onto his side and pecks me on the cheek.

Seriously? After that episode I get a peck on the cheek?

"Two whole weeks together," he whispers in my ear, which sends shivers through my entire body.

"Yes," I say, feeling flustered, "two weeks."

"See you tomorrow." He brushes a kiss over my lips and he's up and out of the room.

"See you," I murmur after him. I listen as he runs down the hallway and down the stairs. Hopefully he can avoid Mom.

The front door opens and closes. I get up and go to the window to look out. Shane turns to look at me and I wave. He gives me a gorgeous smile and gets into his truck. I turn as I hear the engine start up and then the truck drives off. I guess he made it past her.

I am wide awake now.

Great... I decide to shower. Maybe I'll make some tea and read one of the boring romance novels I have. Those usually do the trick. I'll be asleep in no time.

It's going to be a long drive tomorrow and I need to be fully rested. The winding mountain roads might be slick from all of the rain we've been getting, and Milly already doesn't trust my driving skills.

oOo

My hair is still wet from the shower and it smells like oranges. I'm sitting in the wicker chair with my feet up on the low windowsill in my room. I'm not in the mood to read any of the books on the shelf. Not after what just happened with Shane. I don't want to distract myself from that memory. Looking out into the darkness, I can see my reflection in the window. I grin at myself and take a sip of camomile tea. *Mmm, this tastes good.*

I contemplate sneaking into Mom's room to steal one of her sleeping pills, but she's in there and I'm sure the door is locked. How am I going to get to sleep? Maybe I'll read a book after all, I decide.

That does the trick: after an hour I can't take it anymore. My eyes feel heavy. I pull the comforter up off the floor and make the bed, leaving a corner turned down. I reach under the bed for the phone charger. The damn thing always falls off the side table. I plug in my cell phone and set the alarm for 9:00 a.m. I consider changing the "Ocean" option to a cheerful "Birds Singing" tone. *No nightmares tonight,* I hope as I lay my head down. The pillow still smells like Shane's cologne. Yes, this will do; definitely no nightmares tonight. I inhale his scent on the pillow, curl up, and fall blissfully to sleep.

CHAPTER TWO

THE ALARM CLOCK BUZZES, rudely interrupting a very good dream I was having about Shane and me running hand in hand on a white, sandy beach. "*Why?*" I whine, and pull the pillow over my face.

It's five past eight in the morning. I should read romance novels before bed every night; they make my dreams wonderful. I wish myself back into the dream, but I can still hear the muffled sound of the alarm through the pillow. I huff and kick the comforter off my legs.

"Okay, I'm up, I'm up," I say to the alarm clock as I take the pillow off my face. I rise and walk over to the clock and pull the cord out of the wall. "Hah! I don't have to listen to you for two months," I say proudly, and poke my tongue out like a child.

I move to the window and look out. There's not a cloud in sight. That's good. Mom's car is gone. That is also good. I won't have to deal with her today. I'm in a really good mood and I don't want her bringing it down.

I rush to the bathroom feeling as if I might burst; drinking tea before bed is never a good idea.

I look in the mirror after as I wash my hands. *Damn, I look good today.* My hair is a little messy, but it looks sexy—I blush, remembering Shane and I entwined. *We need to do that more often.* My heart starts to race. I am suddenly nervous as Shane's words echo in the back of my mind: *"Two whole weeks together..."*

Am I ready for this? What if I'm not? I have already led him on. I don't want to be known as a tease. *Oh God! Calm down, Stevie.* He did assure me that it's fine if I'm not ready. Didn't he?

"We can do other things..." What did he mean by that? The only thing we've done is make out, and he's gone to second base. What else is there? I really need to talk to Milly. Thank God we have a three hour drive in which to do so. I can bombard her with questions then. Sometimes I hate how innocent I am.

I push those thoughts out of my head and focus on the most pressing matter: the amazing aroma of coffee drifting up from downstairs. I need to deal with that.

The coffee pot is still on when I enter the kitchen. It looks like there is just enough for one cup. *Thanks, Mom!*

Usually Mom leaves the house early and the machine will turn itself off; she must have left within the last hour. She usually starts work at nine, but it's a Saturday and she has weekends off. Where could she be? *Not my problem. Not today—not for two weeks!* That thought alone makes me feel relieved.

I walk to the cupboard to grab my favourite mug. *Oh right...* I assume a melodramatically sad face and grab a plain old white cup and fill it up. I take a sip. The coffee doesn't taste quite as good in this cup. My mood depreciates a little.

I turn my gaze to the window. Not a cloud in the sky. The weather report said it will be hot for a few weeks. I never trust that, though. They always change their minds. I glance at the clock on the microwave. I have a couple of hours to kill so I decide to take my coffee to the gazebo.

It's a brisk morning outside. The sunshine is glinting off the leaves and there is frost on the grass. My gumboots make a crunching sound as I walk. As I push my way through the weeping willow tree, droplets of water run down my face. I really should cut a better pathway through here—but then again, I prefer this place to be hidden away. I cautiously cross the stepping stones, mindful of the frost, and enter the gazebo to skirt around the fire-pit and sit down on the wooden bench.

"Ouch!" I squeal as I sit on something sharp. I hop up and hear something clink on the cement floor. Looking down I see the piece of ceramic with Charlie's little face staring up at me.

I reach inside my pajama pants and feel around to see if the fragment drew blood. I pull my hand out and look at it. No blood. Good. I don't want to have scabs on my butt the first time Shane sees me naked. I laugh anxiously at the thought as I bend over to pick up the little piece of ceramic. I scan the bench to make sure there is nothing else I can injure myself on, then sit down.

I fidget with the bit of mug, then hold it between my fingers to look at it. "Oh Charlie, I miss you. Even though you are still a pain in my ass." I grin. I need to put this somewhere where I can see it so we can have coffee together every morning, like we used to do when he was still alive. Somewhere where it won't be a danger to me. I've been really accident-prone lately, which is unusual for me. I look around. I'm sure this gazebo has a cranny somewhere. I can see a few nooks in the wood posts, but none that are the right shape to angle Charlie's face toward my favourite spot to sit. Maybe I can glue it somewhere.

I look down toward the brick fire-pit, six rows of red bricks high. The pit itself isn't very deep. There's a crack between two bricks that looks like it might work. I rise and crouch down next to the circle of red bricks. There's not just a crack, but a hole between the bricks. I squat lower and look into it. Blackness. *Spider* comes to mind and I quickly pull my eye away from the gap.

I hold the piece of mug up to the hole; it's a perfect fit. I balance it against the opening, trying not to make it tip backward. There is no way I am going to stick my fingers in there to retrieve it. Insects freak me out.

You are such a girl.

"Shush you," I say to myself.

Satisfied with the angle, I carefully push the fragment into the hole with a stick I find on the ground, just enough so it's secure, not so far in that I can't see it. I toss the stick into the bushes. Maybe it will hit that squirrel. I giggle at the thought. Stupid thing would deserve more than that for making me break my mug. I move back to sit on the bench. Looking down, I can see little Charlie's face once more. *Perfect.* Feeling very pleased with myself, I take a sip of my coffee. It's cold. I scowl into the cup.

I guess I should be getting ready anyway. I still need to shower and shave. I do not want Shane to feel any stubble on my legs. That would be embarrassing. If this weather holds up it would be nice to swim in the lake. I have a skimpy bikini that I've been dying to wear. Shane's going to have a heart attack when he sees it. I smile at the thought.

"Up and at 'em," I say as I rock off of the bench. I pour the cold coffee into the fire-pit as I walk by.

A short time later, all showered and shaved, I wipe condensation off the bathroom mirror with my hand and regard my reflection. I decided not to wash my hair. It still looks pretty good. I can't believe the steam from the shower didn't flatten it. I lightly comb it with my fingers and ruffle it a bit more, then look at the result. I never really thought of myself as the sexy type, but standing here with my hair tousled and a black towel wrapped around me, I actually look sultry. *Yes, sultry! Take that, Milly!* I can be sexy too. Who needs all those curves? Actually, I still wouldn't mind some. The towel has barely anything to hang onto.

I open the bathroom door to let in some fresh air. The switch on the ventilation fan doesn't work, and this bathroom doesn't have a window. I wipe the condensation off the mirror once more and start my makeup. I decide to go with bronze and dark brown eye shadow. I apply black eye-liner, a bit thicker than usual, and pack on the mascara. I finish it off with pale pink lip gloss. I study my reflection. *Wow, I look good.*

I head to the dreaded closet, wishing now that I'd figured out what I was going to wear today *yesterday*. That would have been the logical thing to do. I stand gazing into the closet for a few minutes, mentally putting clothing options together. I need something comfortable for the drive. I settle on my very broken-in white denim shorts with the frayed hem. They make me look like I actually have an ass. I turn and check myself out in the long mirror attached to the inside of the closet door. Scanning the shelves once more, I find a navy blue spaghetti-strap top that has ruffles near the bust; they give the illusion that I have boobs. "Boob mirage," that's what Milly calls it. I roll my eyes at the thought. Shane knows that part of my body well, so I don't need to worry about him thinking I have more than what I actually have. I make another turn in the mirror and smile at myself.

I hear honking outside. *Crap, they're early.* For Shane to be early, he must be really excited about the trip. *Or other things...*

"Shut up, you!" I say to myself in the mirror.

"That's not a very nice way to greet your bestest friend forever, is it?"

I turn to see Milly standing in the doorway, grinning at me. "You look great, Stevie. Did you blossom overnight, or what?" she says, gaping at me.

"Just a good night's rest, I guess," I say, blushing. "I didn't hear you come in."

"I said hello, but you were too busy eyeball screwing yourself to notice."

"I was not!" I say, shocked.

"Well, hurry up. I'll wait for you outside. Shane is driving us all mental. I think he's had way too much caffeine today."

"Okay, *okay*," I say with my hands up. "I'll be right down."

Milly turns on her heel and I hear her bounding down the hallway. I take one more look in the mirror then grab my suitcase, keys, sunglasses, and wallet.

Downstairs, I meet Calvin. "Hey, Calvin!" I say as he walks toward me and gestures for my bag.

"Hey, Stevie." Calvin grins. "Sara ordered me in to get your stuff. Just one bag?"

"Yup just the one," I say, handing him the suitcase. "Tell them I'll just be a second. I want to write my mom a quick note."

"Sure thing. I'll load this up in Shane's truck. He's busy making room. Milly packed her entire wardrobe, it seems," he says, shaking his head.

I roll my eyes. "That's Milly for you."

I run to the kitchen and pull a pen and paper from the drawer, and write:

Mom,

I was hoping you would be here this morning. I thought you might forget I am going away with Shane and Melissa for two weeks. Please eat! If you need anything just call me or ask Greg, okay? He knows I'm away and I've asked him to check up on you. I hope you don't mind.

Stephanie xox

There, that should do. I doubt she will call, but I like to leave the option. I put the note on the coffee table where I hope she will see it, and I leave the house, locking the door behind me this time.

Shane looks over from the truck and winks at me. He has found a place for my suitcase. The truck is almost overflowing with hot pink bags. Milly really did pack her whole wardrobe. I hope nothing falls out.

Sara spots me and skips over. "Stevie!" she says as she embraces me.

"Hey, Sara," I say. "Wow, I love your dress." Sara is wearing a gorgeous blue and green floral summer dress. It hugs her curves on the top and flows gently down her thighs. She has her hair tied back tightly in a long ponytail.

"Not too shabby yourself, Stevie; you look hot!" she says, eyeing me. "I am so sad I don't get to ride with you today." She pouts.

"I know. I'm sorry. Maybe on the ride home?"

"Yeah, that sounds great! I made a new CD I am just dying to play," she says happily.

I can't keep the smile off my face. "I'm sure the boys won't mind, will you, Shane?" I call over.

Shane jumps off the bumper and looks at us. He does not look impressed. "No, not at all," he says as he walks over and gives me a squeeze. He leans in to whisper in my ear, "You owe me for this one."

I poke him in the ribs and it makes him jump. The poor boys really are going to have to endure Sara's torturous singing for the whole drive. I smile sweetly at him.

"Let's get this show on the road, people," Milly hollers.

I give Shane a quick peck on the cheek. "Drive safe, okay? It's not a race."

"You wouldn't stand a chance at beating me in *that thing* anyway," Shane says, nodding toward my car.

I stick my tongue out at him and smack him on the behind as he turns away. He looks back and gives me a cheeky smile.

"Let's go, people," Shane says boldly.

I notice Bradley sitting in Shane's truck and wave hello to him. He nods in return. I wonder what his problem is. I dismiss it and get into my car. Milly has already made herself comfortable.

"Everything okay with you and Brad?" I ask.

"Had a misunderstanding," she replies without any emotion on her face, and I know this topic is closed.

I squeeze her leg and start up the beast. "Do the boys know where they are going?" I ask, changing the topic.

"Yes, I put the directions into Shane's navigation system; they should be fine."

"Cool," I reply. "Ready?"

"Yes," she says coolly.

"Let's do this," I say, wiggling my eyebrows at her.

Milly laughs. Job well done. I mentally pat myself on the back. Somewhat-happy Milly has returned and we can have the fun-happy-chatty drive I was hoping for.

Milly's very quiet for the first hour or so of the drive, but I refrain from pestering her with questions and instead blast music on the stereo. Shane insisted on buying me one last Christmas. He even installed it for me. I smile fondly at the memory of him contorting in my car to get under the dash. I'd enjoyed watching him work with his nimble fingers.

I am really grateful that it's not raining. I don't mind driving in the rain during the day, but if it's dark out and raining, forget about it. I'm a little night-blind.

The scenery is beautiful. I'm finding it hard to stay focused on the road. Milly's driving on the way back, so I'll have a chance to really appreciate the view then. We are at a pretty high altitude right now, with a mountain rising on our right and another on our left, off on the far side of a deep canyon with a river running through it. I lost sight of it a while back but now that we're higher up, I glimpse it now and then. I can't see Shane's truck anymore, though. He passed us on the long climb up the highway—my car hates going uphill. I told him it wasn't a race, but I guess boys always have something to prove. I scoff out loud and it makes Milly jump. "Sorry," I say.

"It's okay, I was zoning out," she replies.

I turn down the music. "Hey Milly...is there anything you want to talk about?"

"Not really; you?"

Dammit, she really does not want to talk about what's crawled up her ass. I guess I won't probe. "Well, since you asked, I do have a few things I want to talk about, like Shane and 'other stuff.'" I glance over at her nervously.

She's all ears now; I think her mood actually lifted a little. She never turns down a friend in need—or gossip. "So...?" she prompts.

"Well, Shane came over last night and we started making out and it was almost leading to something...a lot more, but my mom came home and we stopped." I pause, waiting for her to say something. She doesn't. "Anyways, I'm nervous. You know. We haven't gone further than second base and I've told Shane I'm willing to take things to the next level."

Milly exhales and I can see her looking toward me from the corner of my eye. "What do you want, advice or something?" She sounds annoyed for some reason. Where did her improved mood go?

"Well, yes. You know me, I have no idea what I'm doing half the time, and the other half I'm in la-la land. Advice *would* be good. I just don't think I'm ready to have sex. I get so nervous. He says he won't push me and I should take all the time I need, but on the other hand he says we can do other things and I have no idea what he's talking about. I don't want to disappoint him. I've already waited this long. I'm scared he might break up with me if we don't do *it*." I bite my lip. Maybe this was a bad idea. She is clearly going through her own crap right now.

She finally breaks the silence. "Oh Stevie, look, if you don't want to have sex I'm sure he will understand. Maybe just tell him how you feel. He's gone this long without it. What's a few more months—*or years*?"

"What do you think he meant by 'other things'?"

Milly replies with something that sounds like a snort. "Are you serious right now? How can you *not* know?" she says sarcastically.

"Well, it's not like I research this stuff. I don't have a computer at home, and I can't very well look it up at the school library," I retort. "Just forget about it. I shouldn't have asked." I am so annoyed with her right now. Milly never acts this way with me. What happened between her surprising me in my bedroom this morning and her attitude now? I was in such a good mood. Maybe Sara *should* have driven with me.

I can feel Milly scrutinizing me. It's times like this I wish I had a better poker face. I show every emotion that flies through my head. It's very frustrating. Minutes go by. I am trying very hard not to let my feelings get the best of me. She is supposed to be a friend but she's acting like a total stranger right now.

"Look, Stevie, I'm sorry, okay?" she says, sounding contrite. "I had a fight with Brad this morning."

Finally she talks! I sigh and push my anger aside. I guess I can try to help. I take a deep breath. Maybe I can actually *be* a friend right now and make her look like a fool, or at least make her regret her callousness.

"What happened?" I ask, my tone sympathetic.

"Brad wants me to go to Mexico with him, for like three weeks," she sounds exasperated. "He bought me a ticket without even asking me beforehand, just expected me to say yes."

"And...? What's the problem with that? I thought you liked him." I lift my eyebrows, perplexed.

"I *do* like him; I just don't want to go away with him this summer. I told him that and he got upset with me. He's really hammering down with studies next year for his psychology classes and we won't have a lot of time together, so I'm thinking, what's the point of going away with him if he's just going to dump me in September?" she says.

"Milly, I doubt he is going to dump you. He really likes you."

"Well, you asked, so that's it. Can we drop the subject? I don't want to think about it anymore."

"Sure, whatever you want," I say dryly.

We're silent for a few minutes. I hear my cell phone beep and welcome the sound to break the tension. "Can you read that, please?" I point to the glove box.

Milly retrieves the phone and finds the text. "It says 'We have stopped at a coffee shop with a big grey duck on it. Take Exit 46. Meet us there, slowpokes.' It's from Sara."

I could not be happier to get out of this car. The awkwardness between us is killing me. I take Exit 46 and drive a short distance; lo and behold, there is a small coffee shop with the most disgusting blown-up duck balloon-thing on it. I couldn't care less; coffee and a moment without Milly will be heavenly.

I park the car in the dirt lot and get out, stretching and walking around to get the blood circulating in my legs. My ass is a little numb. I look over at Shane's truck and from the look on the guys' faces I can tell they need the break just about as much as I do.

Sara leaps out of the truck, happily singing a song I don't recognize. I grin at her as she runs up to me, takes my arm, and yanks me toward the coffee shop. I glance at Shane's truck and see Milly talking through the open truck window to Brad. I hope they sort their shit out. We still have about an hour and a half to go and I really want the drive to be smooth. I'm seriously contemplating telling Milly to get in Shane's truck so I can just go home, but I don't want to break Sara's heart.

"Come on, Stevie, stop *dragging your feet*," Sara croons as she pulls me into the coffee shop.

Saying the place is rundown is an understatement, but holy hell, I have never had such a good cup of coffee. I bask in the gloriousness of every sip. I glance around the coffee shop. Shane and Calvin are braving the old fifties-era dinner booths—those things are more rickety than the porch swing at home—and are deep in conversation about Jet Skis. I think Milly's parents have a couple at the lake house. I might have to get Shane to take me for a ride. Sara is playing with a jukebox that, thankfully, looks broken. She is still dancing to a tune that must be in her head. I need to borrow some of her enthusiasm, and her moves. I can't dance; I feel like my arms are too long and I don't have enough curves to really shake what my mama gave me. A vision of me with skinny orangutan arms comes to mind and I laugh a little too loudly. The pudgy waitress gives me a quizzical look and I turn away to look through the window, hiding my reddening face. The window still has Christmas decorations up: spray snow with faded painted snowmen. I assume it never gets wiped off. The twinkle lights are in need of replacement; most of the bulbs are burned out.

Milly and Brad are still talking outside. He's out of the truck and has his hands on her shoulders. His expression is sullen. I can't see Milly's face.

"Hey you." Shane grabs me from behind and nuzzles my neck. "What's up with those two?" He nods toward Brad and Milly.

I didn't realize he had risen from the booth and snuck up behind me. His touch is always welcome, though. Sara has taken Shane's seat and is now playing footsies with Calvin under the table. It's funny, how Shane and Sara, whose mother is white and their father African American, both found such pale partners. Calvin has a little more of a tan than I do but his hair is strawberry blond. He is handsome in a boy-next-door kind of way. They would make gorgeous babies.

"Do you know?" Shane nudges me from my daydream.

"Something about a trip that Milly doesn't want to take with Brad for some reason," I answer. "I don't even know why she doesn't want to go.

Milly turning down beaches and tanning...I don't get it," I say with a frown that Shane can't see.

"Maybe she's not that into him," he says matter-of-factly.

"How would you know?" I snap.

"Jesus, Stevie, it was just a guess."

"Sorry; I didn't mean to bite your face off. Milly has not made the ride as pleasant as I had hoped for, and I'm feeling out of sorts."

"Maybe I should talk to her," he offers, letting me go and spinning me around to face him.

"No way; let them sort their own crap out. I really don't want her knowing we're talking about her. That would piss her off more."

"Yeah, I guess you're right," he says, and frowns.

"I'm going to go find a washroom. Can you take my coffee for me and I'll meet you outside?"

"Sure," he says, taking the paper cup. He looks irritated.

God, I can't win with anyone today.

By doing a balancing act over the toilet I manage to relieve myself. I'm disgusted by the place and just want to get back on the road. I exit the coffee shop and see Milly and Brad hugging. Thank the Lord. She looks happier.

She sees me and breaks away from Brad. "Hey Stevie, you ready to go?" Her voice sounds so much better.

"Yes," I say, smiling. *Glad to have you back.*

The guys get into Shane's truck, followed by Sara, who has already started singing again. I can't help but laugh. I walk up to Shane's window and do a roll-down motion with my hand. He rolls the window down and glares at me.

What the hell? "I want my coffee," I say frankly.

He hands me the cup, looking hurt. Before he has a chance to pull his hand back inside the truck I grab it and pull him toward me. I give him a big, wet smooch on the lips. "Please don't be mad?" I beg after releasing him. I flutter my eyelashes at him in a comical way.

Shane relaxes and smirks at me. "I can never stay angry at you, Stevie," he says, now grinning from ear to ear. "You can make it up to me later," he whispers a little too loudly.

"Ew!" I hear Sara jeer from the back seat.

My face suddenly feels like it's burning. I laugh nervously. *'You can make it up to me later'*—great, another thing I can add to my list of things to worry about. I shake my head, willing the thoughts to escape.

Shane is staring at me, waiting for a response. I don't want him to know I'm anxious. I try and fail miserably to give him a sexy wink. I imagine I look more like someone who is having a stroke.

He bursts out laughing. "God, you're cute, Stevie," he says and pulls me back toward him for another quick kiss.

"Any day now," I hear Milly shouting from the car. That's my cue to leave.

"Sara *please* make sure your cocky brother doesn't speed," I plead. Sara salutes me as I back away.

I walk toward my car, hearing Shane's engine start behind me. He does a burn-out on the gravel as he speeds away. I whip around and glare at the tail end of the truck.

The remainder of the drive is pleasant. Milly has returned to her usual self and she even answers some of the questions that are unnerving me. I now know what *other things* means. I can't help but feel kind of grossed out. People actually do that? Seriously, those things should only be done by porn stars. Milly goes into great detail. I almost think that she's trying to scare me. I'm probably blowing it out of proportion, though. She's just being honest—a little too honest for my liking. I have so many unsettling images in my head right now. Thank God we're almost at the house so I can focus on something else.

The mountains are now a backdrop to a beautiful locale. As we pull onto the long gravel driveway to Milly's parents' vacation home I start to get really excited. I push all of the nasty thoughts from my head. I really shouldn't psych myself out.

The evergreens lining both sides of the driveway give way to an open area with a spectacular view of the lake. As we pull up to the house, maybe a one minute walk from the water, I'm in heaven. How could this place only be used as a vacation home? I would never want to leave. The house itself is a huge two-storey log home with a three car garage, and it also appears to have a basement. Despite its size it has a very rustic feel to it. I would love to come back here in the winter. I imagine hot cocoa next to the fireplace, cuddled under a blanket with Shane.

Speaking of Shane, it looks like he has already found a place to park, so I pull my car up next to his truck. He has already unloaded the luggage and has placed it near the front door. I didn't think we were that far behind him.

Milly and I get out of the car and stretch in unison. I chuckle as she smirks at me.

Sara bounds toward us from the side of the house. "About time you two got here!" she teases. "Oh Stevie, you have to come look at the lake—it's gorgeous, and there is a dock we can tan on!" she exclaims, jumping up and down. "Come on, I'll take you." She takes hold of my hand and pulls me toward the lake.

I roll my eyes at Shane, who is laughing at me as I get dragged away, almost tripping over my feet.

Sara is right; the view is gorgeous. The huge A-frame windows of the house look over the lake. What a sight. She leads me up a few steps along the side of the house to a massive deck at the rear. Putting our backs to the large windows, we look out over the lake. The deck is a hexagonal, with a covered Jacuzzi on the right-hand side. There is a barbeque set up on the left and a beautiful aluminum patio set next to that. Stairs situated between the Jacuzzi and the barbeque lead down to a long dock.

"Breathtaking, isn't it?" Sara asks in awe as we reach the end of the dock.

"It really is," I say. I feel at peace in this moment. I am very relaxed. A light breeze wafts my hair gently over my face. I take a deep breath and exhale slowly. I love it here; I'm very happy that I decided to come after all. Looking around the vast lake I see a few other houses, but we are pretty secluded.

I'm about to get lost in a daydream when loud music emanates from the house. So much for the serenity; I guess the party has started.

"I picked a bedroom for us," Shane says as he meets me on the deck. The double glass doors leading into the house are now open. "Come on—I will show you around." He takes my hand to bring me inside.

My heart palpitates. *Chill out,* I tell myself. *He's not going to do you right now.* I make a guttural sound and Shane looks at me questioningly, but I ignore him.

The main floor of the house, with its exposed wood beams and the twenty foot-high ceiling, is breathtaking. The living room is the first part of the house we walk through. There is a light-stone fireplace in the centre of the room that separates the spaces. You can see the dining room through the fireplace. It's very elegant. There are two sage-coloured leather sofas in front of the fireplace and a marble coffee table between those. We walk around the fireplace and into the open plan kitchen and dining area. The marble counters and central island in the kitchen match the mocha colour of the coffee table. There is an exquisite dining table with intricate flowers hand-carved into the wood. I almost get a headache trying to take in all the details of the room. It's beautiful.

Shane leads me back through the living room and up the stairs on the right that lead to the upper floor. I pause at the top of the staircase and take in the entire room below. My attention is cut short when Shane pulls me up the hallway. It leads to the two main bedrooms, and the family bathroom.

"That's the master bedroom." Shane nods toward the closed door at the end of the hallway. "Milly and Brad are staying in there. And that door just before it is the bathroom."

"Where are Sara and Calvin sleeping?" I ask.

"In the basement. There's a pull-out sofa."

I forgot that Shane knows the house well. His and Milly's parents are long-time friends and often came up here together for family vacations. I feel a twinge of jealousy, but it passes quickly. He stopped coming up here after we started dating.

We walk into the bedroom on the left. It's a quaint little room, all light purple walls and white linen. There's a double bed with an old chest at its foot and a small antique dressing table in the corner. This cozy room is much different from the room draped in red velvet with throw pillows on the floor that I'd envisioned. I roll my eyes at the thought.

"What, not to your liking?" Shane asks, staring at my bad poker face.

"It's better than I was expecting," I reply. "It's perfect, Shane." Wow, I actually said that with a straight face. Not a hint of anxiety, not a break in the sentence. I mentally high-five myself.

Shane smiles. "Good, that makes me happy. I'm going to grab our things and get comfortable."

I can't believe he's not making any moves yet. Maybe he's as nervous as I am.

"I can't wait for *later*," he whispers in my ear as he passes me to leave the room.

Oh God. What the hell am I going to do? I am *so* not ready for this. Maybe I can pretend to get my period or something? No, he will see straight through me. I can't lie. I slow my breathing and try my best to calm my rapid heartbeat. I need to get out of this room. I can hear Shane downstairs; he'll be up here any second with the bags.

I dart to the bathroom and close the door. I lock it and stand with my back to it.

"Stevie, you okay?" Shane asks through the door a moment later.

"Yeah, I'm good; be out in a minute."

"Okay, well, Sara wants you to go with her to help grocery shop while I take Calvin to buy us liquor, so meet us out front."

"All righty!" I say, sounding a little too bubbly. "Be right there." My voice cracks.

I walk up to the sink and turn on the cold tap. I really don't want to wreck my makeup, but my cheeks are burning. I find a facecloth and hold it under the tap, then carefully dab the cold water on my cheeks and forehead. It cools my face only a little, but it will have to do. I look in the mirror. I look frazzled. I force a smile to my mouth and leave the bathroom.

oOo

Sara has me laughing the whole time we're walking around the grocery store and it's doing wonders to dispel my tension. I really am going to miss her next year when she moves to France—she and Calvin plan to spend the next two years travelling to different countries. France is first on her list and after that, the United Kingdom followed by South Africa and then Australia. They really want to travel the world before settling down and having a family. I wish I had the money to do something like that. I only now realize that this will be the last time we will all be together. Sara kept bugging me to get a laptop so we could video chat, but I just can't afford it.

Tears burn in my eyes. I run up to Sara and surprise her by hugging her hard.

"Whoa Stevie, what's wrong?" Sara asks.

"I'm just going to miss you, is all," I say, snivelling into her neck. "I don't want you to go."

"Oh Stevie...I'll be back before you know it. I am going to miss you so much."

I feel a tear hit my shoulder and I know she is crying too. What a sight we must be, standing in the middle of the frozen food section, crying.

"It might be less than two years, Stevie," she says, trying her best to reassure me. "Now I have to ruin my surprise for you because you're all upset."

"Surprise...what surprise?" I ask, releasing her from the bear hug. "Did you cancel the trip?"

"No, we can't cancel. The tickets are non-refundable," she answers, slicing my high hopes into pieces. "I've organized a delivery in two weeks, on the day we get home from this trip."

"What kind of delivery?" I ask perplexed.

"Well, when you get home there will be a shiny new laptop waiting for you on the doorstep." She smiles proudly.

"Oh my God, Sara you shouldn't have!" I say, though I'm ecstatic, and hug her again. "You really shouldn't have; those things are so expensive. I can't thank you enough."

"Writing to me whenever you can will be thanks enough. You're welcome, sweetie," she says, beaming at me. "and don't you dare try paying me back; it's a gift."

I have a skip in my step as I follow Sara through the rest of the store. The guys are probably wondering what's taking us so long, but I don't care. I'm going to spend every precious moment I can with her.

Shane and Calvin meet up with us as we're standing in the checkout lane. We have enough food to last a month. Then again, I've seen Shane eat; we might only last the week.

We get to the truck and I open the cab doors. "Holy shit," I say, bemused. "What are we, getting booze for a frat house or something?" There is so much alcohol in the cab that there's nowhere for us to sit.

"Do we have to hitchhike back?" Sara asks, looking as shocked as I am.

"Of course not. We didn't want it all to get stolen," Calvin says. "I'll put it in the back with the groceries."

I look at Sara and shrug. I guess the guys plan on being wasted the entire trip. That might actually work in my favour.

Back at the lake house, I help the girls unpack the groceries while the guys start up the barbeque. I'm famished, but nervous. Night is creeping up on us.

"Babe, can you bring us a cold one, please?" Calvin calls to Sara through the open patio door.

"Coming right up!" Sara says happily, and goes to the fridge.

"What's up with you?" Milly asks when Sara is out of earshot. "You seem jumpy."

"Just a little too much excitement for one day," I lie. I never lie to Milly but for some reason I get the feeling I can't trust her. "I'll make a salad," I offer. I really do not feel like being scrutinized right now, and I want to keep my mind busy.

Making the salad takes all of six minutes, and that was with me trying to dawdle as much as possible without looking like an ass who doesn't know how to throw leaves in a bowl. I take the dish outside and put it on the table. Sara has already set out plates, glasses, and cutlery. The guys are having a heated debate on the best way to cook a steak. I sit down because I don't know what else to do. I can hear a blender running inside, and Milly and Sara joking around in the kitchen. Their voices become muted as I stare out at the lake. I wonder how Mom is doing. I should text Greg tomorrow and ask. She'll be at work then and he'll know.

"Tequila shots!" Milly shouts.

I swing my head to look in her direction; she's carrying a tray with six shot glasses on it. This can't be good. I have never drunk hard liquor.

"And strawberry margaritas!" Sara says, sashaying after Milly with three massive drinks.

Milly hands out the shots. I take mine with an unsteady hand. She smiles down at me, but it doesn't reach her eyes. What is she doing? She knows I don't drink.

"I just wanted to make a toast," she starts.

Oh. Now there's no way I'm getting out of this. I can't offend her by not drinking it. I take a sniff and I can feel my gag reflex twitching.

Milly pushes her chest out and raises her glass. She is always so composed when she speaks publicly. All eyes are on her now. "Sara and Calvin, we are all going to miss you while you're away on your long adventure. This will be the last time we will all be together until you guys decide to come home and make some babies." She winks in their direction. "Sara, I have known you since I was born. You are like a sister to me. Life is not going to be the same without you. Here's to a great trip and lasting memories. Calvin, keep her safe and bring her home in one piece. I love you guys. Cheers."

I slug the drink back with everyone else and regret it the minute it touches my tongue. I close my eyes and force myself to swallow. "Yuck!" I say, blinking watering eyes. I look around and the only other person making a face is Sara. Thank God I'm not the only one.

"Good job," Shane says and leans in for a kiss. The scent of tequila on his breath almost makes me gag into his mouth. He grabs one of the margaritas from behind me. "Here, wash it down with this."

I take a big swig of the drink. It tastes like heaven compared to the shot. "Thanks." I smile at him.

"What's in this, Milly?" I ask. "It's delicious."

"Tequila and vodka," she answers.

"I would never have guessed. I can hardly taste it."

"We'll have to make the next one stronger then," she says.

Way to dig your own grave Stevie. I really need to learn to keep my mouth shut.

"Food's done," Bradley says, bringing the steaks, hotdogs, and burgers to the table.

I stand up to clear a space on the table and the whole world spins. Shane grabs my hand to steady me. "Whoa, lightweight," he says jokingly.

I feel my ears go red. How embarrassing. I can't even have one shot without feeling tipsy. I hear Milly scoff. "I'm fine," I say. "Just a head-rush from standing up too quickly."

"Oh good, then you can drink more. I've always wanted to see you wasted," Shane says, grinning at me.

Yup, digging my own grave.

I laugh it off and sit back down. The smell of the food is tantalizing. I look around as I devour two hotdogs and a burger. Everyone is laughing and joking. It's nice to see the smiles and love in our little group. I feel Milly's eyes on my every move. Then Shane's hand is on my leg. Does she know he's caressing my thigh? What difference does it make if she does? I finish my food and excuse myself to use the washroom. I'm feeling a little less tipsy when I get up.

When I finish my task and return to the patio I see that the table has been cleared and everyone is waiting for me.

"Ready for some drinking games?" Milly asks, grinning at me devilishly, as if there's some kind of unspoken competition between us.

I don't know why I feel the need to show everyone that I'm not a lightweight, and win this weird battle Milly seems to be trying to start. I take a seat next to Shane. "Bring it on!" I say loudly, and I glare at Milly, trying to be intimidating.

Milly throws her head back and laughs.

That is the last thing I remember.

CHAPTER THREE

THE ROOM IS SPINNING. My eyes are still closed but I feel like I'm on a swaying boat. I pry them open and sit up. *This does not feel good.* The room doesn't stop twirling around me. I push my fingertips into my forehead and try to remember what happened last night.

I hear a groan next to me and look over. Shane is lying on his stomach, facing away from me. The blanket is wrapped around his legs and all he is wearing are his white boxers. I want to appreciate the glorious sight in front of me, but I desperately need the toilet. I stand up and the room goes black for a second. I stumble to the side and grab the dressing table for support. Shane groans again, but does not wake.

In the mirror I see someone standing in her bra and panties. *Wait, isn't that my underwear?* I look down. *Where the hell is my clothing? Why am I half naked?*

Oh no-no-no.

I rub the sleep from my eyes and focus my attention on the disaster that is me. There is dried up *something* on my chin. I don't even recognize myself. My makeup is smeared across my face and my hair is tied back in a messy braid. I didn't braid my hair yesterday. What the hell happened last night?

I rummage through my bag and grab clean underwear, a black tank top, and some jeans. The clothing I wore yesterday is nowhere to be seen. I hang onto the walls as I walk to the bathroom. I feel like I am still drunk and I feel—

Oh no—

I run to the bathroom and barely make the toilet before yesterday's contents come pouring out of me. Why did I have to eat so much? I'm paying for it now. I have my head buried in the bowl when I suddenly get hit with a memory: Sara holding my hair back while I vomit. Where was Shane? How much did I drink last night? Answers to these questions I surely will not get from asking myself. How am I going to face everyone when I don't even know how I acted last night? I need a shower, badly, and coffee—loads and loads of coffee.

I spend at least an hour in the shower, unable to coax myself to move a muscle, but I am feeling slightly better when I get out. I don't feel like I'm going to vomit again and the room isn't spinning quite as badly. If only I could hide in here forever.

After drying off I get dressed and sneak back into the bedroom to hide my dirty laundry. Shane is still asleep and snoring slightly. I am dreading learning the answer to the question you see in movies all the time: *Did we have sex?*

Surely I would feel different if we did. Milly said it hurts like hell the first time, and you bleed. I am not bleeding. Apart from this killer headache and an empty, sick feeling in my stomach, I feel fine—and so do my girlie bits.

Shane rolls over and I quickly disappear from the room. I'm not ready to face him yet. I hear a rattle in the kitchen below and wonder who it is. I was hoping to be the only one up. I don't even know what time it is. My cell phone is nowhere to be seen and I still haven't found the clothing I was wearing last night.

I find Bradley in the kitchen as I sheepishly step around the fireplace. He's pouring coffee into two mugs, but turns around when he hears me.

"Hey..." I say shyly.

"Good morning, Stevie. You had quite a night." He half smirks at me.

I feel my face flush as I settle on one of the bar stools. "I'm afraid to ask," I say. "Is anyone else awake?"

"No, just us."

"That's good." I sigh in relief.

"Coffee?" he offers.

"Please."

Okay, this isn't going anywhere. *Come on, just ask him what the hell happened last night.* It doesn't look like he's going to freely give me the information. I meet Brad's eyes as he hands me a cup. "Bra—" I stop when I hear footsteps coming down the stairs.

"There you are."

Brad looks over at Milly. She stalks past me as if I'm not there and stops at the fridge next to Brad. She whispers something to him but I can't hear her.

There goes my chance to get some answers. I can feel the tension. "I'll take my coffee outside," I say, and leave the kitchen as fast as my wobbly legs can carry me.

I try to get as far away from the house as possible, but only make it to the stairs leading down to the dock. They look like they're moving. I decide this is as far as I am going with this hangover. The cold morning air nips at my bare arms, and I suddenly feel extremely irritable. I can't go upstairs because of Shane, and now I can't go inside because Milly is obviously peeved at me. And to make things worse, it's freezing outside, and I forgot my sweater. *This is so annoying!* This morning can't get worse. At least I have my coffee. I take a sip and spit it out. "Dammit!" I sputter. I forgot to put cream and sugar in it. I take that back—this day *can* get worse.

Screw it, I'm going back inside. I need to man up and face whatever it is that Milly is pissed off about. I roll my shoulders back and lift my head up high.

Sara is awake and sitting in the living room when I enter. I can't see Milly or Brad, but I can hear the shower running upstairs. *Good.*

"Stevie!" Sara says merrily. "Come sit." She pats the sofa next to her.

She does not seem to be angry so I sit down.

"Oh my God, Stevie, you were ca-*razy* last night!" she exclaims.

"Sara, I don't remember anything. The last thing I remember is sitting down to play some games."

"I have never seen anyone so skinny drink so much!" She gives me a look of amazement.

"I feel like a piece of shit this morning, so I believe you. Hey, do you know why Milly is ignoring me?"

"Oh, she's just annoyed that you can drink more than her. You know how competitive she is."

That's it?

"And Shane was okay?" I ask.

"Yeah; he was drunk, but seemed fine. He looked after you all night."

"I thought you did."

"No, I just tied your hair back and went to bed; he said he was fine to watch you. I know better than to argue with him. I mean, Calvin would look after me if I was *that* drunk." She laughs.

So my faint memory wasn't Sara. *Oh no—Shane saw me puke!*

"I am so embarrassed," I say, holding my hands over my eyes.

"Don't be. It happens," she assures me.

"Are you sure that's all Milly is angry about?" I ask, because I feel like something is being left out.

"I may have heard her and Brad arguing, but I can't say for certain. You'll have to ask her. I'm going to go check on Calvin, bring him coffee."

"Okay. Well thank you for letting me know. I thought Milly and I had a fight or something."

"No, I think you guys are cool," she says, and gives me a half hug before getting up. She skips cheerfully around the fireplace and into the kitchen.

I have the nagging feeling that Milly is mad about something else. So what if I can drink more than her? That's a ridiculous thing to be angry about. I'm just going to pretend nothing happened. That won't be hard, considering I can't even remember.

I go into the kitchen after Sara disappears downstairs and decide to cook breakfast for everyone—a peace offering of sorts. I put another pot of coffee on, then get started on the feast. No one comes into the kitchen while I cook.

I set the table and leave the food on the bar, buffet-style. Then I find a tray in the cupboard under the coffeemaker and set it up with Shane's breakfast: coffee, orange juice, a huge helping of scrambled eggs, bacon, hash browns, and toast. I owe him that much for looking after me last night. I give the breakfast setup one last look. The smell of the bacon is bound to bring everyone here soon. No one can fight that urge, especially after the night we had. Or the night I think we had.

As I tiptoe upstairs I can see the steam coming out of the open bathroom door. Milly's door at the end of the hall is closed. I'm proud that I haven't dropped the tray of food, especially since my hands are shaking, as you'd expect from someone who drank all night and has no idea what the hell she did.

Shane is awake and lying on his back when I enter the bedroom. He has his hands behind his head as he regards the ceiling. "Good morning," I say with a timid smile. "I made you breakfast." I lower the tray a little so he can see.

"Mmm, smells delicious," he says as he sits up.

I can't stop staring at his naked chest. The glasses on the plate start rattling as the tremor in my hands increases. *Move your ass, Stevie!*

I take a tentative step toward Shane, then move around to his side of the bed. I place the tray on his lap.

"Where's yours?" he asks.

"I already ate," I lie. I really don't want to go back downstairs for a while.

"Well, at least sit with me while I eat," he offers, and shifts over so I have room to sit.

I gently sit down so I don't bounce the tray off of his lap. I look toward the window. "Shane...I can't remember what happened last night. Sara said you looked after me?" I ask, still staring at the window. I can't bring myself to look at him. I need to ask questions and his body is overwhelming my thoughts.

"Yes, I did," he says between mouthfuls. "You were hilarious last night. Well, until all the vomiting..."

"Oh God, Shane," I say. All I want to do is cry. "I'm so sorry. I have never drank before, and I obviously overdid it. I am *never* drinking again."

"Stevie," he says, wiping a tear from my cheek. He tugs on my chin to make me look at him. "Don't be upset; it happens to the best of us. I was pretty wasted myself, so it wasn't that bad. I hardly remember the vomiting, okay?" he says tenderly.

I know he's lying to make me feel better. Bless him. I smile at him and brace myself for the biggest question of the morning. "Umm...did we...you know...*do it?*" I quickly pull my hair over my ears to hide the redness.

Shane inhales a mouthful of orange juice. I grab the tray quickly to steady it while he has a coughing attack.

"God, no, Stevie!" he says after he stops choking. "What kind of guy do you think I am; someone who would take advantage of my very drunk girlfriend?"

Good going Stevie! The last thing I wanted to do was offend him. "Shane, no-no-no, that's not what I was even implying," I say as the tears start rolling down my face again. "Please don't take it that way." I reach over to touch his face and he pulls away from me.

"How the hell other way should I take it, then? I spent all night babysitting you. Stayed awake to make sure you were breathing. I held your hair back while you puked your guts out. And you ask me that fucking question! I am not some dick, Stevie. How could you think that of me?" He looks at me sharply.

Ouch. "I had to ask, Shane. Please...can we just forget about it?" I look at him, feeling ashamed that I have hurt him.

"Fine," he says after a moment. "I'm not hungry anymore." He pushes the tray away.

"I can take that," I say, and rise to place the tray on the dressing table. I stare down at it. I can see Shane's reflection in the mirror as he gets up from the bed. He stands in the doorway. I can't bring myself to say anything.

"Your clothing is in the washing machine in the basement. You vomited all over it, so I undressed you and put you to bed," Shane says coolly.

I turn around to say thank you—to say something, *anything*, but he has already left the room.

I am such an ungrateful bitch.

I spend the remainder of the day pretty much by myself. It's cooler than yesterday so everyone stays either indoors or in the Jacuzzi. Calvin is really hungover, even worse than me. The only time he's come upstairs is to use the bathroom. Sara has been at his beck and call all day. I am apparently in ignore-mode with everyone else. Shane must have said something. Even Brad is giving me the cold shoulder. Sara has been too busy with Calvin for me to get a word in. This day has been a total train wreck and it's all because of me. If this is the damage I can do when I'm drunk, I'm keeping that promise to never drink again.

Late in the afternoon I'm feeling steadier and decide to take a walk. I leave the house and descend to the beach. There is not a person in sight. I think the houses here are mostly vacation homes that stand empty for most of the year. All I can hear are my feet scrunching on the sand and a few birds singing. A light breeze brings the smell of a campfire, but I don't see any smoke nearby. I find a log that is perfect to lean up against. I wiggle my butt into the sand and get comfortable. I forgot to grab my cell phone in my rush to leave the house. I will have to call Greg about checking on Mom when I get back. I wish I'd brought a book to read.

Is this how the rest of the vacation is going to be? Me, by myself? I sigh. That is a very sad thought. Hopefully Calvin will feel better tomorrow and Sara and I can hang out more.

I slide further into the sand until I'm almost lying down. It's not the most comfortable angle for my head but I don't care. The clouds above me look like they are threatening to pour rain at any second; I ignore the threat and try to form pictures out of them. I'd deserve to get drenched right now.

How did things get so out of hand? Maybe I should leave tomorrow. That option is very tempting. I can't, though; Sara would be shattered and that might cause the end of Shane and me. I think about that for a while, wallow in the sadness it brings. No, Shane and I will be fine. We love each other; he will forgive me—I'm counting on it.

I see a chubby cloud and decide it looks like a cat, and I think of Charlie. *Oh Charlie, how I wish you were here with me now...*

I don't know how long I slept but when I wake up I'm freezing and my neck hurts. How do I manage to fall asleep in the most uncomfortable positions? It's very dark out, but that's not what I'm worried about. Why hasn't anyone come looking for me? Aching muscles protest as I push myself up from the sand. I feel like a decrepit old woman.

I stomp my feet as I walk back to the house. I am cold and sore and angry. What kinds of friends just leave you alone to rot? I could have been kidnapped or raped or something and they don't even care. I stomp all the way up the back stairs and onto the deck. I stand alone next to the Jacuzzi, staring through the living room window. They're all there, just sitting around having a good time without me. Milly is on the phone, pacing back and forth.

Pacing?

I blink again and clear the rage from my mind. They are not sitting around having a good time. Anger has clouded my judgement. Milly is on the phone—mad? No, not mad...worried. She is screaming demands into the phone. Shane has his arm around Sara, who is crying.

Shit, what happened? I don't see Calvin or Bradley anywhere. *Oh God, I hope they're okay.*

I run to the door and as I do Sara swings her head around. Shock and relief flood her face. Milly says something into the phone and hangs up.

Shane is the first to burst through the door. "Where the hell have you been, Stevie?" he says, running up to me. "You've had us all so worried."

Sara hugs me tightly and sobs onto my shoulder. "We...we looked everywhere for you. Where were you? Milly's been on the phone with the cops, and the guys are out searching—why would you do that to us?"

"I fell asleep on the beach," I mutter. "I went for a walk and fell asleep."

"And you didn't think to tell anyone where you were going?" Milly shouts at me. "Jesus, Stevie, I almost had a search party come here to find your ass."

"I'm sorry...I didn't mean to get you all worried. You didn't check the beach? I was lying there in the open...well not exactly in the open. I was behind a log." *Crap.*

"*Behind a log!* What person in their right mind would disappear for hours without telling anyone where you were going?" Milly fumes.

"Back off, Milly!" Sara says. "She is safe. That's all that matters. I am so happy you're okay, Stevie," she says, looking at me. "Please don't leave again without taking one of us with you."

"I won't. I really am sorry. I didn't mean to fall asleep." I look around at each of them, finally stopping at Shane. He's angry, really angry. "Shane," I start.

"Don't, Stevie," Shane says. "Just don't." He turns around and enters the house.

I race after him, leaving Sara and Milly on the deck. Maybe Sara can calm her down a bit. I need to focus on Shane right now. I follow him all the way to the bedroom and close the door behind us.

"Shane, would you please look at me," I plead, and he turns to face me. He is seated on the bed. I kneel in front of him, wrap my arms around his hips, and lay my head on his lap.

"You had us all so scared for you, Stevie," he says as he rubs my head. "We thought the worst."

I look up and stare into his eyes; they look as if they might tear up. That's the worst thing ever. He is always so strong and confident, and now I've almost made him cry. I am a terrible person.

"I'm sorry I got so angry earlier, Stevie. The thought of upsetting you and then something happening to you almost destroyed me," he says, and lifts me up to his lap.

"Oh Shane I never, ever, in a million years *ever* want to hurt you! Please forgive me, Shane, *please*," I beg, and hug him hard.

We sit like that for a long time while he cradles me. I think I'm forgiven. I hope I am. I never want to see him like this again.

There is a knock at the door, and we both turn toward it. I wipe the tears away from my cheeks.

"Yes?" Shane says coolly.

"It's Milly," she says through the door. "Can I come in? I want to talk to Stevie. I owe her an apology."

I nod to Shane, who lifts me up and places me on the bed. He tucks my hair behind my ear and kisses me on the forehead. "Come in," he says, and makes no effort to leave.

"Umm, Shane, can we have some privacy?" she asks as she walks in.

"It's okay," I say to him.

Shane glares at Milly as he walks past her. She looks like a child who has been scolded, and I can tell it hurts.

Now you know how I feel.

Milly closes the door then sits next to me. She takes both my hands in hers. "Stevie, I want to apologize for the way I acted last night," she says.

Huh?

"And for the way I've been acting today toward you." She looks down at our hands.

I wait for her to finish. That wasn't really an apology, was it?

"Stevie, I got jealous of you last night," she says.

Okay seriously, huh?

"We were all having such a good time and everyone was laughing and joking around and I shouldn't have said what I did." She glances at me, then her eyes return to our hands.

"Milly, I have no idea what happened last night. I don't remember anything," I say.

She looks at me again. "You don't?"

"No, Milly, I don't." *Let bygones be bygones, make peace.* I want to be the bigger person. I need to be for the sake of our friendship. After all, what you don't know won't hurt you, right?

"Look Milly, whatever was said and done was probably because we were both wasted out of our minds. I don't want to know what you said, or what happened after that. Can we just call a truce and leave it at that? I would hate to see our friendship go down the drain because we are both idiots who don't know when to quit."

We regard each other for several seconds. *Please accept, Milly, please!*

"I could not have said it better myself," she says quickly. "Thank you, Stevie, thank you." She leans over and hugs me. "I don't want to fight anymore, okay? I have been such an ass since we left for this trip, and I promise tomorrow will be better."

"I promise too," I say, smiling at her.

We hug again and it feels like a weight has been lifted off my shoulders. Happy Milly is always better.

oOo

What a difference I have seen in everyone. The trip has gone from a nightmare to a dream come true. We are having a blast. My little mishap has been forgotten. The days have been sunny and I had a chance to wear my skimpy bikini. I will never forget the look on Shane's face. *Thank you, push up bra!*

I am still nervous every night when bedtime approaches, but Shane has not made one move on me. Not one! Am I disappointed? Not really. I'm kind of relieved, actually. I think I scared him off with my stupid "did we have sex" question. I am so naïve.

We are ten days in now. It's going by way too fast. Milly and I are on good terms again. There is still something "off" between us, but we are both making an effort to push it aside and enjoy the time we all have together before Sara and Calvin leave for their trip. We have all calmed down with the drinking. Well, I have, anyway. No one is getting belligerently drunk, just drunk enough for me to enjoy watching how silly they can get. Sara teaching the guys how to booty shake—that was a priceless moment. Who knew watching people get tipsy could be so entertaining. I have kept my promise and haven't had a sip of alcohol—unless you count the residue on Shane's tongue.

I phoned Greg a few days ago to check up on Mom. He said she's been fine. He's been over for dinner a couple times. She didn't ask, he insisted. I thanked him graciously for that. It's good to know someone is popping in to make sure she's okay and eating. He's a great guy. Why can't she see that?

"Hey Stevie, you coming, or what?" Shane shouts.

I groan as I rise from the Muskoka chair I've been lounging in on the dock. I am trying desperately to get a tan. I look for Shane and see him sitting on one of the Jet Skis. I pause to admire his bare chest. *Yum!* He looks happier than a kid riding his first bicycle. How could I say no? "Alright, *alright*," I say, "I'm coming."

Shane beams at me as I carefully get on the Jet Ski. I wrap my arms tightly around his waist. "Please, not so fast this time, okay?" I beg.

"Don't worry babe, I got you." He laughs.

"More like I got *you!*" I yell as the Jet Ski accelerates and we shoot forward. I don't think he can hear me over the sound of the engine.

We are really moving, skimming over the water. It's exhilarating. The mist is spraying over my face. Shane spins the Jet Ski in circles so we can bounce back over the waves it makes. He is having a blast. I'm holding on for dear life and thanking the life vest for staying on me. We are somewhere close to the opposite side of the lake when he cuts the engine. He's breathing hard, as if he's just run a marathon. I can't imagine how sore his arms must be from holding onto the handles, if mine are killing me from squeezing him.

"Ready for a walk?" he asks, looking over his shoulder at me.

"A walk where?" I ask.

"You'll see; it's a surprise." I can hear the joy in his voice.

I hate surprises.

We get off the Jet Ski and Shane ties it off on a nearby tree. He takes my hand and leads me into the forest.

"Is it safe in here?" I ask, worried.

"Of course it is. Will you just trust me?"

I smile at him. He leads me farther into the woods. After about ten minutes I hear rushing water. We walk through a clearing in the trees and suddenly I'm looking at the most beautiful waterfall I've ever seen. It's not huge or anything, but the pool at its base is so crystal clear that I can see the bottom of it. Shane turns to me, grinning.

"Oh my goodness! Shane, it's stunning," I exclaim. "How on earth did you find this place?"

"Milly and I found it when we were kids. We used to come swimming here. It was like our little hideaway from the adults," Shane says.

"Oh," I reply with less enthusiasm.

"No Stevie, it's not like that; we were just kids," he says in response to my hesitant voice. "Come on; please, I want to make this our special place. Forget about Milly."

I stare into his eyes for a minute before I answer. "Count on Milly being forgotten," I say. He is so damn happy I don't want to disappoint him. Plus I like the sound of that: our special place. It makes me smile.

"Let's go for a swim," he says, and drops a small fanny-pack on the ground that I hadn't seen him carrying. He picks me up and swings me into his arms as if I weigh nothing, and carries me into the water. I imagine a groom carrying his bride over the threshold.

Hmm, this is romantic.

Well, it was romantic until he decided to toss me into the water.

"Ahh!" I scream as I surface. I splash water in his face. "It's freaking cold!" I squeal.

Shane laughs. It's a beautiful sound. He is so full of joy. I wish the whole trip could have been as wonderful as it is at this moment. We are both carefree and happy, giggling like small children, splashing and dunking in the water. I love today. Today will stay in my memory forever.

The water only comes up to Shane's chest so it's easy for him to stand and rest. Not so easy for me. If I stand on the bottom all you can see are my eyes and forehead. If only I was a couple of inches taller. Shane picks up on my weariness; he grabs me just under my butt and brings me close to his body. I wrap my legs around his waist and my arms around his neck. His head is resting on my chest. This reminds me of our last day of school, before Milly rudely interrupted us. I push her from my thoughts.

Our special place now.

"You are *so beautiful*, Stevie," he says, looking up at me. "You have no idea how beautiful you are."

"*Stop*—you're making me blush," I say playfully. I can feel my cheeks heat.

"Well you are, babe; just thought you should know." He pulls me closer and kisses my collarbone.

I inhale sharply as he trails kisses all the way up my neck, under my chin, and finally to my mouth. There's an intensity in his kiss that wasn't there a minute ago. He lets my body slide further down his so that we're face to face and I don't have to strain my neck. His tongue overwhelms my mouth with need and desire. The cold water does not feel cold any longer.

Our special place...

In what way did he mean that? I *was* thinking "special" as a place to escape everyone back at the house, to be alone and enjoy each other's company without someone always being just around the corner, eavesdropping. *Like Milly.*

I did not put too much thought into his words, but as he slides his hand under my bikini top and cups my breast I have a *you're a total idiot* moment and realize what he actually meant.

Shit.

Is this seriously going to happen right now? I am not even on birth control! This can't happen, then. Maybe he just wants to do other things. *Other things...* Horrific images pop into my head. *Thanks a lot, Milly!*

My heart rate goes up but Shane doesn't seem to notice. He's breathing hard, and I'm holding my breath. He is so in the moment that he can't tell I'm freaking out. He can't see my bad poker face when his eyes are closed.

Dammit!

He pulls away, but only long enough to carry me out of the water. He smiles at me—a sexy I-want-you-now smile—as he lays me down on the shore. How long can I do this for? How long before he notices that I'm panicking, that I am not enjoying myself? Maybe I'm a better actress than I thought possible. Oh, there goes my bikini top, tossed to the side. I am lying in the dirt topless with Shane panting on top of me. This is not how I pictured our first time. Shouldn't I be happier? Shouldn't I want this more?

I can feel him pressing against my girlie bits. I can feel him harden. I am still calling my bits *girlie bits*, shouldn't that be an indication right there that I am *NOT READY?*

"I love you so much, Stevie," he whispers in my ear, and gently nibbles on it.

That felt good—but no, I need to control my hormones. Now is not the time and place for this. Maybe in his head he's been building this up all day. Or maybe this was his plan all along. No wonder he hasn't made any moves on me until now. This is what I get. This is why I hate surprises. The least he could have done was maybe...oh I don't know, tell me! Hint at it or something—anything!

He reaches over my head and grabs that little black bag. That bag that I really don't care to know what it holds. That damn bag. What's in there? He unzips it and pulls out a small silver foil packet.

Oh fuck. Of course there are other forms of birth control out there. *You idiot, Stevie!*

I must look like my dead cat showed up and started speaking Spanish to me because Shane falters. Whatever spell is cast on him fades for a second. I smile weakly at him.

Why are you smiling you retard! Shane smiles back at me. That is not what I wanted. *Can't you see the fear in my eyes, Shane?*

He takes his board shorts off.

I guess he can't.

He effortlessly rips the packet and slides the condom on. I have never seen him naked before. I am frozen, just staring at him. I have so many emotions running through my brain: fear, confusion, anxiety—why are there no good feelings? I should be feeling *something*.

Shane unties my bikini bottom and throws it in the direction of the discarded top half. "God, you're gorgeous," he says as he looks me up and down. He lowers himself onto me and starts kissing my neck again. I would be totally embarrassed that I am lying in the nude, but I can't seem to comprehend what's about to happen. I know what's about to happen but I can't comprehend it. Nothing is making sense! He wiggles his hips, pushing my legs apart. Our parts meet.

"NO!" The words escape my mouth and I push Shane with all of my might. I did not mean to sound so vicious.

Shane's eyes widen. He gapes at me like I'm speaking another language. "What the fuck, Stevie!" he blurts.

"Get off of me, Shane. I can't do this!" I squirm from underneath him and scramble for my bikini.

"Are you fucking kidding me right now?" he screams.

"No Shane, I'm not. I thought I was ready but...but I'm not," I cry.

"You're something, you know that?" he yells, and gets up. He pulls his shorts back on. "I don't get you, Stevie—one minute you're fine, the next minute you're acting crazy. What the hell is wrong with you?" He lifts his hands into the air.

"Shane I'm s-sorry," I sob.

"Don't give me that, Stevie, not now," he says, infuriated. "You know what? To hell with you. Find your own way back!" He turns and leaves, disappearing through the trees.

I sit there weeping in the dirt with my bikini clutched to my chest. What just happened? He's leaving me here? What kind of person does that?

What kind of person leads a guy on and turns him down at the last second? I have royally fucked up this time. I pull my bikini on as fast as I can and run after Shane.

"Shane!" I scream, "Shane, please don't leave me here!" I'm really bawling now. I have no idea where I'm going. I hear an engine start up and I run in that direction. *Oh, you asshole!* He really is going to leave me here. I run faster, willing myself not to trip on the exposed tree roots.

I stumble to a stop on the shore of the lake. The water is still rough here, and I can hear the Jet Ski in the distance. He left me. He actually left me here. I can't believe it. My knees feel weak; I crumple to the ground. I cry and I cry and I cry some more. My heart feels as if it's been ripped from my chest. This is surely the end of us.

"No, Shane...I'm sorry," I sob. "Please, please come back."

After a long time the sun starts its slide behind the mountains and darkness creeps around my sad soul. I'm sopping wet, and I don't have a towel. I am cried out, hurt and confused. I have to get back before I freeze to death, or worse, get eaten by a wild animal.

I pick my sorry ass up and begin to walk.

My feet feel like they are bleeding by the time I arrive at the dock. I'm shaking uncontrollably from the cold, or my nerves—probably both. My heart literally aches. Who knew heartbreak actually really hurt your heart? I'll tell you who. Me. *And* I found out in the most horrible way. *And* it's my own damn fault. I feel like a broken, pathetic excuse of a human. I should have just let Shane have me. We would be so happy right now. *Way to make a mess of it, Stevie, when things were just getting brighter.* How am I going to explain this to Sara and Milly?

I wish that I'd left my keys in the car so I could slip away silently. I could hide out for the rest of the summer and maybe it would all blow over by the time school starts. The keys are in the bedroom, though. The bedroom I share with Shane. We still have four more days here.

No, I can't do it. I won't do it. I need to run in, ignore everyone, get my shit, and leave.

Run in, ignore everyone, get my shit, leave.

Run in, ignore everyone, get my shit, leave.

Run in, ignore everyone, get my shit, leave.

I repeat the mantra in my head until I finally get the courage to walk up the back steps to the deck. I pray that no one is in the living room. *Please God, just answer this one prayer.*

I creep up to the back window. I guess God has better things to do than waste his time on a pitiful person like me. Shane and Milly are sitting on the sofa next to the fireplace. He has his hands over his face and Milly has her back to me. She's sitting a little too close to Shane for my comfort.

He's not mine anymore, I remind myself. No, neither of us actually said the words "I am dumping your ass," so it's not true. I won't believe it.

Milly moves her hand and places it on Shane's leg.

Oh, you bitch!

Just as the words form in my mind a lightning bolt hits the lake behind me. I jump, almost stumbling. Thunder follows, a huge crash, and then the rain starts beating down.

That got their attention.

What a sight I must be—soaking wet, dirty, bloody knees, my hair hanging like dreadlocks around my face, and rage in my eyes. *And* the lightning zigzagging behind me—I probably look like some deranged psychopath out of a horror movie.

Milly flinches, then realizes it's me. Shane knew straight away. He says something to Milly, then rises and storms off up the stairs. Milly comes running out the glass doors.

"Omigod Stevie, are you okay?" she exclaims, looking genuinely shocked.

"Do I look okay to you?" I snap.

"Get in here now, before you get hypothermia!"

I look around frantically.

"Don't worry," she says. "Everyone is downstairs."

I walk into the house and she lifts a blanket from the sofa to wrap around me. I sit by the fireplace, hoping to get the feeling back in hands and feet. I will never get it back in my heart. I sit there for a while before I notice my bags are packed and waiting by the door.

Milly sees me looking at them. "We all agreed that the best thing right now would be for me to drive you home," she says.

I nod at her. I have nothing to say right now. Home sounds good to me.

"Everyone is going to stay here a few more days," she says.

I rise from the ledge around the fireplace and walk over to my bag. I pull out a black hoodie and some jeans and pull them on over my bikini. I retrieve the car keys and toss them to Milly. She catches them with ease. "You better drive; it's raining and too dark for me to see," I say to her, my voice emotionless.

"Alright. I'll grab your stuff, meet you in the car, okay?" she says sympathetically.

After seven long minutes—I know because the only thing I could focus on was the time on the dashboard—Milly gets in the car and starts it up. The rain isn't easing up at all. I put my head against the window as she pulls away from the house. I watch it get smaller and smaller in the side mirror, and then it disappears as we reach the road and turn.

We drive in silence. I was right when I said today will stay in my memory forever, because I can't seem to shut my brain down. It's like an irritating song that gets stuck in your head and you can't shake it off.

I don't know how Milly drives so well in this weather. I can't see three feet in front of the car. I look over at her and she looks like she's straining, but I don't think it's because of the weather. There's something on her mind, she's just too afraid to ask.

"Just ask me already," I say after a while.

"Stevie, whatever happened between you and Shane is your business," she says.

"Well, it didn't look like *our business* when you had your hand on his leg!" I bark at her.

"Stevie, I was consoling him," she says. "Don't be ridiculous!"

"He's obviously told you what happened; I mean, it took me over an hour to walk back from that fucking waterfall," I say sharply.

"Waterfall? What waterfall?" she stammers.

"Oh, you know, the one you guys played in when you were kids."

She breathes in sharply.

Hah!

"He took you there?" she says incredulously, and glances quickly at me before turning her attention back to the highway.

"Yes he did, and then he came onto me," I say. She might as well know the truth. Who knows what lie Shane told her.

"That's not what he said. He said you led him on, took off your clothing, then left him hanging like some tease. His words, not mine," she adds, holding up a placating hand.

"Are you seriously messing with me right now?" I exclaim. "*He came on to me*, I said no, he *left* me in the woods to find my own way home and then he *lies about it!* What the fuck, Milly, you actually believe him?" I slam my hands on the dashboard and begin to cry. "I thought you were my friend."

"I *am* your friend, Stevie. I'm just trying to put two and two together," she says. "What you're trying to tell me is, he took you to a place that means a lot to him, unbeknownst to me, and he thinks this would be the perfect time to take your relationship to the next level. You turn him down, flat out, so he gets mad and leaves you there?" She shakes her head. "You know what, Stevie? I was right in what I said on the first night of the trip, when he was at your side, helping you when you were sick, being the total gentleman that he is—you *don't deserve him!*"

And there it is. A flood of memories come back. *Milly in her skanky sleepwear, Shane helping me to bed, the room spinning, and those words, those damn words echoing in my head: "You should be with me...Shane, I miss you...She doesn't deserve you."* And Shane's response: *"Shut up, Milly... long time ago...over."*

There are a few holes in my memory, but I get the gist of it. I shake my head to try to control the flashback. I'm overtaken with feelings of jealousy and resentment; they consume my soul and make me do the unthinkable.

I turn and lunge at Milly.

CHAPTER FOUR

THE CAR IS SPINNING out of control. It all seems to be happening in slow motion. I grab whatever I can to brace myself. Milly is screaming her head off as she desperately tries to steady the car. I look over at her and see the panic in her face; her knuckles are white on the steering wheel. I am whipped forward as we hit something. There's a loud crack from the front of the car.

The first thing I feel is a deep, fiery pain in my neck.

The vehicle finally comes to a complete stop. "Oh, thank God," Milly says between gasps.

We sit there, stunned. Breathing heavily. My heart feels like it's about to explode out of my chest. I gaze down at my shaking hands, trying to comprehend what I'd just done. I can't wrap my head around it.

I feel the car teeter forward. I look through the windshield and see the other side of the canyon illuminated by the headlights. That doesn't make sense—unless...

This can't be good.

The car groans and screeches briefly. I have no idea how high up we are on the mountain—I can't tell because the rain is beating down on the windshield, and apart from the small circles of light hitting the mountain on the other side of the canyon, everything else is black. The cracking sound I heard as I was thrown forward must have been the car crashing through the guardrail—the only thing that keeps vehicles from sliding down the steep mountainside into the ferocious river below. I wish I knew how far over the edge we're actually hanging. Maybe if we work together we can get out of this alive.

I hear a click, and then the sound of a seatbelt retracting.

"No, Milly, don't!" I reach over and grab her hand.

"Don't fucking touch me, you crazy bitch!" she screams, and swats my hand away.

I recoil from her, which makes the car slant forward. "Milly, put it back on," I beg.

"Don't you tell me what to do! I'd rather take my chances out there on the highway than in here with you. You almost killed us, you psycho whore!"

"Milly, call me whatever you want, but do it after we—"

She cuts me off by reaching for the door handle. The weight shift caused by her erratic movement tilts the car right over the edge.

The car slams over bumps, throwing Milly up and down like a ragdoll. We are both shrieking and crying as we careen down the mountain slope. I am trying desperately to grab ahold of her seatbelt to put it back on her, but every time I think I have a grip on it the car hurtles over rocks and debris and I lose my grip. Milly seizes the steering wheel to try to stop herself from thrashing around the cab. She clutches it at the wrong angle and spins the tires to the side, and the car is thrown over.

I feel the roof touch my head; it compresses with every revolution. We spin over one last time and stop suddenly when the car strikes something with mighty force. My body is thrown forward and because I was looking at Milly the right side of my face slams into the dashboard. I hear a crunch and then intense pain shoots through my temple. My right eye feels wet and I can hear my heartbeat thumping in my ears. There's a high-pitched squeal that overwhelms my thoughts, and the world turns black.

oOo

I'm running through a forest and I don't know how I got here. I can hear the rush of a waterfall close by, seemingly right in my ear, but I can't see it. "Shane!" I scream. "Shane, please come back! Don't leave me here, Shane— don't you dare leave me!"

I stop, panting. The giant trees around me are dark and gloomy. I feel unsafe here and my heart begins to pound. I don't know which direction to run.

A leaf crackles behind me and I spin around. "Charlie. Oh Charlie! I never thought I'd see you again. This is where you've been hiding."

Charlie tilts his head to the side and then runs past me. "Where are you going, Charlie? Come back!" I stumble after him as he weaves through the trees. I push my way through hanging branches that look a lot like the weeping willows I have at home. "There you are, Charlie!" Relief floods my nerves. He doesn't turn around to look at me. He is staring into the distance, a tranquil river flowing past his paws.

"What is this place? Oh! A special place for us? The river is beautiful, Charlie. Oh, and the sounds of the birds singing...how nice... Can we stay here forever?" I walk up next to him and I reach out to stroke his back. Just as my fingers graze his fur he turns his attention to me and hisses. His eyes are fiery red. He pounces into the river.

"Charlie, where are you going! You can't swim. Don't be stupid! Come back here, Charlie!" I scramble to the edge of the river and reach into the water. Long hair wraps around my fingers and I quickly pull my arms back out of the water. "Charlie!" I scream. "Charlie, where did you go?"

The river gurgles at the spot where Charlie disappeared. It starts to bubble. I hold my breath and reach into the river again, but I can't feel anything. The water stills and I pull my hands out once more. I look down at them and they are covered in blood.

oOo

That was the weirdest dream. I try to open my eyes but only the left one obliges. My vision is blurry; I can't make out a thing. I close my eye again and listen. I can hear a river rushing by, and...birds? Yes, birds chirping. They sound odd. My memory is foggy, although I do remember the accident—how could I forget that!

I pray that I'm in the hospital. I'm not in enough pain to still be in the car. I feel like I'm in a dream; it must be the medication making me feel this way. I'm suddenly tired, and close my eye to sleep.

The birds are getting louder, and the sound startles me awake. I force my eye open. I can barely make out Milly's auburn hair.

"Milly?" I whisper hoarsely; my throat feels like it's clogged with sandpaper.

I try to move my hand to her but it's stuck. That was nice of the nurses, to put us together in the same ward, but I sure wish they would untie me.

"Milly, say something so I know you're okay," I say.

I hear voices in the distance, and those damn birds. Why won't they shut up? I blink a few times to get my tear ducts to work. My vision starts to clear. It's so bright in here. Why is it so bright? Maybe the nurse can shut the curtains.

"*Over here!*" someone shouts in the distance.

Yes, over here. Of course over here; where else would I be? I try to shift to look around but my neck is so stiff. I can't move a centimetre in any direction. *Wow, they really have me tied down good.*

There is an awful stench. Something I have never smelled before. Why didn't I notice that a minute ago? The tears pour from my eye and the area in front of me finally clears. I hear heart-wrenching screams. Screams that sound a lot like Mom's when she found out Dad died, screams I never, ever wanted to hear again. It takes me a moment before I realize they are coming from me.

Milly...oh God.

I am not in a hospital at all. I am stuck in this thing that can no longer be called a car. I am numb all over. Milly is a few inches away from me.

There is a branch protruding through her neck. I try to look away but I am transfixed by her face, staring into her cold, dead eyes. There is no way in hell she is still alive.

There is so much blood.

What have I done!

My screams come out raspy, barely audible now. I sound more like someone choking on a mouthful of dry dirt. I start coughing, which makes my body ache all over. It's a bearable pain, though. Why am I not hurting more?

Maybe you're paralyzed...

No, I refuse to believe that. I force my eyes away from Milly to look at my surroundings. I try frantically to wiggle out of the awkward position I'm in. I wish I could feel my legs. As far as I can see, the roof has caved in and my head is pressed against the dashboard. I can't find or feel my arms. *Oh please, let them still be attached to me.* They must be wedged somewhere; maybe my circulation has been cut off.

I really don't want to look toward Milly again but I can feel a cold draft coming from her side of the vehicle, a breeze that is bringing the stench of death with it. I start to gag and my eye waters even more. I look toward the windshield and see that we hit a tree. It went right through the glass and into Milly, harpooning her in an unnatural position. Her door is open and she is half hanging out, her feet dangling in the river. Is that why I can't feel my legs? A disturbing image comes to mind, of my legs, the flesh green and rotting from being in the ice cold water all night. *They'll have to amputate...*

Shut up! Shut up! Shut up!

My heart beats in erratically. I start to hyperventilate.

Calm down, Stevie. Calm down!

I can't calm myself. I'm sobbing and wheezing and gagging. I try to call for help but nothing comes out. I make a silent plea instead. *Please, God, save me. I'm sorry; please forgive me for what I have done. Keep Mom safe if I should die. Please...I don't want to die.*

My eyelid gets heavy, my blinking slows. All I want to do is let sleep take me. I try desperately to stay awake, fight the urge. I am terrified I will never wake up again. With every flutter of my eyelid it gets harder to open it again. I use the last ounce of energy I have and pry it open one last time.

Milly is gone. There is the image of a man in her place. He is wearing white and there is a glow backlighting him. I can't see his face. "Everything's going to be okay," he says as he brushes my cheek gently. "Hang on child, hang on."

"*Dad?*" I whisper as the darkness swallows me.

oOo

I'm on a cloud. I feel warm all over and the pain is gone. I must be dead. This isn't actually that bad. I wish I could have died on the way down the mountain—before seeing Milly's face. Oh crap, what if she's here with me. She will be so angry! No; you can't be angry in heaven, can you?

Beep-beep-beep-whoosh.

That's a weird sound.

Beep-beep-beep-whoosh.

Okay, well, it's definitely not as annoying as those birds. Thank goodness they finally shut up. Will I ever hear birds singing again, though? I hate them and their chirping, but the thought of never hearing them again scares me.

Beep-beep-beep-whoosh.

I'd rather hear the birds than that irritating beeping sound for all eternity.

"She stirred."

Who said that? Wait. Who said that! Why can't the words come out of my head?

"Why is her heart rate going up, Doctor?"

Doctor? Wait...I'm not dead? Oh God, I'm in a coma, or worse...limbo. Please, no! I can't bear the thought of watching everyone around me grow old and die.

"Stephanie, can you hear me, honey?"

No one calls me honey. That sure sounded like Mom's voice, and she definitely has never called me honey. Whoa, bright light in my left eye; what the hell. That hurts too much to be heaven. Why can't I see out of my right eye?

"Her pupil responded to the light and it looks like she is breathing on her own. I'm going to remove the ventilator," a male voice says.

"What if she stops breathing again?" Mom says.

I stopped breathing? I am in a coma! My heart feels funny. I'm panicking. I can't be stuck like this. I am so thirsty. All of these thoughts—I do not want to be trapped inside my own head forever.

Wake up, damn you! WAKE UP!

I gag and feel my entire body go rigid. The pain hits me a second after and I cry out.

"Doctor!" Mom screams.

Within a minute I have the mysterious-man-voice at my side, but now I can see him. I try to talk but the words come out in an incoherent mess.

"Try not to speak, Stephanie. You've been through a lot," the kind doctor says.

I look at him and try to nod, but apparently that's not going to happen either. I can't move.

"Stephanie, I'm Dr. Haroldson. You were in a terrible car accident. Do you remember? Blink once for yes, twice for no."

I blink once.

"Okay, good. I need to check a few vital signs now. It will only take a few minutes, alright?"

I blink once again.

Dr. Haroldson gets to work checking my blood pressure, temperature, and other things I don't understand. He checks the machines that I'm hooked up to and looks over my injuries.

I frantically look at him, hoping he can read my mind and tell me what's going on. Mom is holding my left hand. She seems to have aged about five years in the last two weeks.

Or maybe it has been five years. No, no, no! This is crazy. I need answers. I look toward Mom again. "Water," I croak.

Mom glances at Dr. Haroldson for approval.

"There is an ice machine down the hallway. Only a couple, though," he says.

A couple? I feel like I could drink ten litres right now. I recall something about vomiting after anesthesia. Right now that's the last thing I want to do.

Mom scurries off and is back in a flash. I have never seen her so accommodating. I open my mouth greedily and she pops a small ice cube in. It feels like paradise on my tongue and throat. I open my mouth for another. My lips feel terribly chapped when I rub my tongue along them.

"How long?" I say after a minute. My throat burns but it's nice to be able to talk.

"Only a day; you've only been unconscious for one day," Mom answers, and pats my hand.

There is so much worry on her face, and something else I haven't seen. I will decipher that later. Right now all I want to know is if I am paralyzed. "Injuries?" I ask, and look toward the doctor who is still prodding me. I flinch when he hits a nerve on my leg.

"In layman's terms, please," Mom says.

"Well, Miss Martin, you have three bruised ribs on your left side where the seatbelt dug in. They will take, on average, three to four weeks to heal, but we are certain they will heal completely. They will be tender to the touch and will probably hurt when you breathe, laugh, cough, etcetera. I have prescribed pain medication that you need to take three times a day.

"You suffered a bad concussion on the right side of your head. We will need to run further tests, now that you're conscious, to determine the severity of brain trauma. Considering your motor skills are fine and you are aware of your surroundings, I believe you will be okay, but I do need to run the tests regardless.

"You are very badly bruised along the right side of your face from impact with the dashboard. The roof of the car was caved in and you were wedged in the vehicle for about eight hours. You suffered from mild hypothermia as a result of being in the cold and rain for so long. The swelling around your right eye will get better over the next couple of weeks. You will need to put warm compresses on it when you get home. For now, only use cold compresses.

"You suffered from whiplash and will have to wear a cervical collar for seventy-two hours. After that we will give you exercises and show you how to move your neck so you can make a full recovery. Other than that, you are healthy." He pauses and regards me solemnly for a moment. "Miss Martin, you are incredibly lucky to be alive. We need to keep you here for four to five days for observation, and if you are doing well we can discharge you." Dr. Haroldson smiles at us.

That was a whole lot to take in. I hope Mom was paying attention. Five days in the hospital. This is a nightmare. *At least you get to come out of this alive.*

I'm surprised they haven't brought Milly up; probably because they don't want to distress me while I'm still recovering. Mom is looking down at me sadly. I can tell she wants to say something, but she's hesitant. I can't blame her. How do you tell someone their best friend died? I can't expect her to say it first; not after having dealt with the death of Dad. Maybe that's why she's looking at me differently, in a way I can't identify. There is something in her eyes...could it be appreciation? Love?

I look around the small hospital room and see a vase of flowers— daisies. Did she honestly think I was going to die? I never, ever wanted to see daisies again after what happened.

Mom notices the shock on my face as I gaze at the flowers. "Stephanie," she says, taking my hand in both of hers. "When I got the call that you were in an accident my whole world fell apart. It was as if I was reliving George's death all over again. When I got to the hospital and saw you here, looking the way you do, I realized all the wrong I have done. I have not been there for you, honey. I've been stuck in such a deep, dark depression. I didn't appreciate the fact that I still had a part of George in you. The only part of him that still lives is inside you. If I lost you, I would lose him completely." She stops and looks down.

So it's not about me at all? Well, I'm not going to argue with her. This is the most touching thing she has ever said to me; I'm not going to dismiss it. We might be able to finally heal, now that she's had this breakthrough. Who would have thought my near-death experience would have some good come out of it?

"What I am trying to say," Mom continues, "is that I love you, Stephanie, and I never intended to cause you harm in any way. I'm sorry for turning into the monster I did when all you were trying to do was make me a garden. I am still very ashamed of the way I acted, so the daisies over there...well, when I found out you were alive, I wanted to bring them so that they can signify life and not death."

I feel a tear falling down my cheek. All I ever wanted was Mom to love me, so we could have that mother-daughter relationship you hear about so often. Not to say I think it will all be flowers and rainbows now, but

I am positive there will be some improvement. "I love you too," I say to her, and she leans over and kisses me on the forehead—on the side that isn't bruised.

There is a light rap on the doorframe and we look over—well, my eye does; I can't turn my neck while wearing this stupid, uncomfortable brace. It's already annoying me.

Sara is standing in the doorway. She bursts into tears when she sees me. Mom gets up and leaves the room, whispering something to Sara as she passes her. Sara nods.

"Oh Stevie, oh my God, you look terrible. Have you seen yourself? Wait, don't answer; don't, okay? I know you can't talk very much." She's talking a million miles an hour. "Stevie, thank God you're alive. Milly was supposed to call us when she got home safely—oh no, you don't know yet, do you..." Sara chokes loudly and cries harder. I grab for her hand and she takes mine, clasping it way harder than Mom did.

"I remember," I say. "I remember the accident."

"Stevie, I can't take it; everyone is in so much shock. I can't imagine the pain you are in, and seeing her like that... The police won't give us any details. And her parents...they're just...I don't even know. Stevie, what happened? How did this happen? Shane is beside himself; he's blaming himself for the fight you guys had. He didn't go into too much detail about it, but he keeps saying over and over again that it's his fault. There's nothing I can say that will make him feel better and it's killing me. Please, Stevie, tell me what caused the accident. The only thing the police said was that Milly wasn't wearing her seatbelt when they found you. That's not like her to not wear one." Sara looks at me expectantly.

I haven't even got my story straight yet. I can't tell everyone I caused the accident and am really the one to blame for Milly's death. I don't want to go to jail. I have to lie. I need to put this off somehow so I can lay out some kind of scenario. I decide to cough, which I know is going to hurt like hell, but maybe—just maybe—it will work.

I cough and feel the pain ricochet through my body. The agony courses down my throat, up into my brain, and through my ribcage. That had to be one of the stupidest ideas I have had lately. My throat was already so raw that the one cough felt like a thousand razor blades scraping the inside of it. I wheeze and cry as if I'm being tortured, and my whole body goes into spasm. Sara screams for the nurses and they rush in. One nurse puts something into my drip and the other checks me over.

Whatever she put in the drip feels amazing—man, does it feel good. It's like there's liquid heat streaming through my body, relaxing it. I feel like I'm floating again, and the room around me goes silent. I can still see the nurses' mouths moving and Sara crying, but it looks so comical and exaggerated that I start to laugh. Sara looks confused; the nurse says something to her and Sara nods, then smiles down at me. She is so beautiful, even in this state. I close my eyes and drift off to a more serene place where Milly isn't dead and Shane and I are together again, happy and in love.

∘O∘

I spent a total of five days in the hospital. The only visitors I had were Mom and Greg. The police visited on the third day, but I would hardly call them visitors. How could I forget that interrogation? Mom and Greg stuck by my side through the whole thing. I told the police what I finally told everyone else:

"Shane and I had an argument; I wanted to go home early because I didn't want to spend any time in the same house as him. Everyone was still enjoying the trip so I thought it was unfair for the whole thing to end. Milly agreed to take me home. I couldn't drive because I was upset and it was dark and stormy out. When we were driving down the mountainside the vision was very limited. We hydroplaned on a puddle and the car spun out of control and hit the barrier. Milly panicked and took her seatbelt off without realizing that we were hanging over the edge, and that caused the car to tumble down the mountain."

The police asked me to repeat the story a bunch of times, and because I had rehearsed it so much in the previous two days, I got it right every time. Eventually they were satisfied and left me alone. I had not heard from Sara, Shane, or anyone else—and that was a relief. Shane is the last person I want to see right now.

The medication they had me on in the hospital made me pretty loopy, so I slept a lot. The neck brace was taken off a day before I was discharged from the hospital. It was so nice to get rid of that thing. I can barely move my neck, but the exercises they gave me will help with that. My ribs really hurt. I am taking shallow breaths and trying not to cough or sneeze. Greg showed me this cool trick to stop the sneeze when you feel a tickle: you press a finger just under your nose. It works every time. He said it is a pressure point.

Greg was nice enough to give me a lift home from the hospital while Mom's "getting the house ready," whatever that means. I obviously will not be driving for a while; firstly I am shit-scared to, and secondly my car is in a nasty heap somewhere in the mountains. I wonder when that will be retrieved.

The drive home is pleasant enough until I—without thinking—look into the passenger vanity mirror. I hardly recognize myself. The left side of my face is as close to normal as it could be. The right side makes me feel like vomiting. My eye is pretty swollen. I can slightly open it and have partial vision. It looks like I was in a boxing match and lost terribly. I'm black and blue and *hideous.* I start to cry. I know it's vain and selfish to cry, but I couldn't care less. I lift my hand to touch my face and wince. It's very tender. I slap the mirror closed and sigh.

"It will heal fine," Greg says reassuringly. "You'll be back to your beautiful self in no time." He glances over and smiles at me.

"Thanks," I say shyly.

"Stephanie, I didn't want to bring it up around Denise—you know how she is with any mention of funerals..."

"Milly's funeral?" I ask.

"Yes. It's tomorrow. Sara stopped by your house yesterday to let me know. She's been doing everything to prepare for it. Milly's parents are not functioning, with good reason, obviously," he says. "No one expects you to go. They know you're injured and you have been through a lot."

"Of course I *have* to go," I say. "I can't *not* go. She was my best friend."

"Denise is not going; she just can't. But I can accompany you if you want," he offers.

I look gratefully at him. "Greg, that would mean a lot. I have a feeling I'll need the support."

"You seem to be taking all of this really well," he says. "I don't think I've seen you cry once. You are a very strong woman. You should be proud of that."

"I've had my moments. But they kept me really drugged up at the hospital, which made me feel pretty numb to the whole thing," I say. Greg nods sympathetically.

Should I be crying more? Maybe I am stronger than most people. Or maybe it just hasn't had time to sink in yet.

When we reach my house, the smell of food hits me as soon as we get in the door. Mom's been cooking. As soon as she hears us come in she hurries over and gives me a gentle hug, trying to be mindful of my injuries. "You must be starved. Come eat," she says, and gestures toward the kitchen.

I stand there stunned for a moment, looking after her as she bustles away. Greg snorts at my confused expression and motions me toward the kitchen. I look at him and see him grinning. I wonder what's up with those two. The energy in the house is different—happier, but awkward. This is definitely going to take some time to get used to. I pray it's not going to be a novelty, that things will go back to the way they were before the accident.

I get to the kitchen as Mom is taking a big casserole dish of cottage pie from the oven. There are cheese scones on the counter, and cupcakes for dessert. Mom seems frazzled and energetic—is that a good combination?

Greg pulls a chair out for me to sit down. The table has been set for three people so I take it he will be joining us for dinner. This should be interesting. I'm used to eating alone, so having Mom and Greg here will be...entertaining.

Greg takes the seat to my left and watches Mom with admiration. I never took notice before, but Greg is really handsome in a George Clooney sort of way; a classic handsome that you don't see very often anymore. His hair is golden-brown and tinged with grey near his sideburns, and he has pale blue eyes. I didn't realize I had completely zoned out and have been staring at him until he looks over at me and smiles. I jerk my head away to conceal the blush and yelp in pain. *Damn this neck!*

"Are you okay? That looked like it hurt," Greg says, trying to look concerned, but he's smirking.

I was caught staring. How embarrassing. My cheeks feel hot. I try to pivot the stool to face forward. "Yes, I'm fine, just keep forgetting I have to take it easy," I say, looking straight ahead to avoid seeing his face.

I hear him chuckle, which makes my face get hotter. Why couldn't he have sat on the other side of me—my damaged side, where the bruises would conceal my humiliation. I bite my inner cheek nervously.

I *plan* to get through dinner as fast as I can without totally scorching my tongue on the hot food. All I want to do is go hide in my bedroom. You never really appreciate your body until you've hurt it and can't do simple things—like feed yourself. Trying to eat when you can't tilt your head to look down is a real pain in the ass. Mom offers to hand feed me but I just can't. That is taking this whole "new her" a little too far, even for me. I battle through the meal and even get up by myself to clear my plate. "I'm going to go run a bath and then sleep, okay? Thank you both for everything; it means a lot," I say.

"Let me run your bath, Stephanie," Mom offers, and she jumps up and leaves the kitchen before I can say no.

I hear the water running through the pipes a minute later. "Is she always going to be like this?" I ask Greg.

"I hope so," he says with optimism and longing.

I leave him to daydream and make my way upstairs. Mom is pouring bubbles into the bath as I pass the open door on my way to my bedroom. I turn the light on and notice a big box on my bed. I totally forgot Sara bought me a laptop. I feel panicky when I remember that she can't cancel her plane tickets and is leaving soon, but when? I don't even know what day it is. I go to the side table to get my cell phone—where I usually leave it to charge—but the table is empty. *Of course it's empty, idiot.* My phone is somewhere lost in the ravine. *Damn.*

Maybe the mobile company will give me a new one, considering the circumstances.

I grab a pair of my old button-up pajamas. They have teddy bears printed on them. I don't want to have to pull anything over my face just yet. That would hurt too much. I go back to the bathroom while Mom is turning the taps off. There is a fresh towel laid out for me. "Thank you," I say to her as she walks past me. "Oh, Mom?"

"Yes honey?" She turns around.

I am still not used to this "honey" business. "What day is it? The date, I mean," I ask.

"July twenty-first, why?"

"Sara and Calvin are leaving on the twenty-eighth." I sigh.

She doesn't register what I'm sighing about. I don't think she even knows who Sara is, even though I've known her for a long time. "Let me know if you need anything else, okay?" she says.

"I will—thanks." I close the door behind her and place my pajamas next to the sink. I strip from the mismatched clothing that Mom had brought to the hospital for me and turn around to look in the mirror. My face hasn't changed in the last two hours. I didn't expect it to. My ribs have seen better days. The doctor mentioned that my ribs were bruised but failed to mention the massive seatbelt mark across my chest. *Gross.*

I thought I was skinny before, but this week has wasted away the last bit of fat I had on my body. I still have over a month before school starts; that will give me time to heal and get some weight back on my bones. Feeling sick from the sight of myself, I tear my gaze away from the mirror and carefully step into the bath. I sink down into the water as far as my neck will allow, and relish the soothing warmth.

I don't know why bathing always makes me feel like a new person, but it does. I feel good all the way back to my room. There is a glass of water and my pain medication on the side table next to the bed. Mom's really going all out. I peer out the window and see that Greg's car is still here. He must have moved the laptop box because it is now sitting on the chest of drawers. I decide to wait a few days before opening the box, or at least wait until Greg can help me set it up. I am clueless when it comes to any kind of electronic device. I'm surprised I even know the word: electronic device.

The photos of Shane and I that I'd displayed in pretty frames on the chest of drawers have been moved; they rest one on top of the other in a neat pile to one side. I reach for the top one and look at it. I can't hold back the emotions when I see the photo of us sitting on a park bench. I have my head resting on his shoulder and he's smiling broadly at the camera. It was one Sara took of us.

The fight we had comes back to me full force, and I feel like I've been punched in the gut. I take a step back and sit on the bed, frame clutched to my chest, and let the tears stain my cheeks. After everything that has happened I know in my heart that we will never get back together. Our group has been torn to shreds and it's my fault. If only I had just let Shane have me, we would never have fought, Milly and I wouldn't have argued, and I wouldn't have...I wouldn't have...*killed her.*

How am I going to face everyone tomorrow? They'll see right through me. I need a mask to cover my non-existent poker face. What if someone asks me if I caused the accident? Will I smile and agree? Shit, what am I going to do? I can't even bring myself to cry for her death. Maybe the blow to my head did do some damage. What if I never feel emotions again? No, I'm being dumb—I just cried for Shane. I'm still crying now. I think I'm still angry at Milly. *I think* that the anger is overwhelming the feelings of regret and guilt. I need to come to terms with this.

Milly is dead and you caused it. Nothing. I don't feel a hint of anything. I get images of her dead eyes staring through me, the tree through her neck, the dried blood all over her chest, her limp body hanging halfway out of the car. She was too young to die. She had so much left to do in life. Why can't I feel anything for her?

I give up for the night. I need to take the medication and sleep. It's going to be a long day tomorrow. I will deal with this later.

I take the photo of Shane and me—and the rest of them—and slide them into the top drawer. I don't want to throw them out completely, just in case there's the smallest chance we will get back together. I miss him terribly, and I can't help but feel sad that he's probably thinking he's the one who caused everything. I plug my alarm clock back into the wall and set the time. I really need to get a cell phone again—I feel lost without it. Not that anyone wants to talk to me anyway.

I walk across the room and pop two pills into my mouth. That should help me sleep. I'm only meant to take one but I want my brain to switch off. I need to be fully rested for tomorrow. I get as comfortable as I can, which is hard when you're not used to sleeping on your back, then reach over and fumble for the light switch on the lamp. I wish I could curl into a fetal position which is the usual way I sleep, but that would kill me. *Kill—murderer... you don't deserve him...*

Yes, pleasant thoughts to fall asleep to, but thanks to Dr. Haroldson, the pills kick in and the thoughts melt away.

oOo

My eyes pop open at ten in the morning. I got a solid eleven hours sleep. I don't think I've ever slept that long. I didn't dream at all, which is wonderful. I decide to skip the morning painkillers because I don't want to be groggy for the funeral. I'm dreading facing all those people and not knowing how they're going to react to me.

After using the toilet I peek in the mirror while I wash my hands. I'm looking a little better. My eye is not quite as swollen, and the bruises are slightly less black; they almost look olive green now. *Ew!*

I go downstairs to make some coffee and am surprised to see Greg sitting at the table with a cup already in hand. He's wearing a black suit and looking very dapper. I stand there and look at him quizzically. "Good morning," I say, and walk past him to pour some coffee of my own.

"Good morning, Stephanie, how did you sleep?" he asks.

"Really well, thank you. *And you?*" I squeak out, then clear my throat.

"Stephanie, I *did* go home last night, if that's what you're wondering."

I put my hands up in an it-doesn't-matter-to-me sort of way and smile at him.

"You know we have to leave in an hour. I got here early to explain to Denise a few things she needs to do at the store today. She's covering for me so I can take you to the funeral," he says.

"Ah, that's why the suit. I was totally confused," I say.

Greg laughs and shakes his head.

"I guess I'll go get ready," I say, and pick up the mug. "Thanks again for taking me."

Greg sure is chipper this morning. He is probably trying to lighten the mood a little. He doesn't have any kids of his own and definitely is not used to teenage hormones, let alone female teenage hormones, so he's treading lightly. I would do the same thing in his position.

I go to my closet and reach into the far back corner to pull out the only black dress I own. Well, technically it's Mom's dress. It's the one she wore to Dad's funeral. I found it in the trash one day and for some reason felt the need to keep it. It's been "hiding" behind the rest of my clothing ever since. Now that I know Mom will be away from the house all day, I can safely wear it.

I have no other option but to pull it over my head. It's a little tight going on and scrapes across my face in an awful way, but I finally manage to squeeze into it. I look in the closet's full length mirror. The little bit of weight loss helped me fit into this dress—I can't believe Mom was smaller than me. I guess mourning will do that to you. There is no way I would have gotten the zipper on the side to go up a week ago. The dress is almost skin tight and stops just below my knees. It has a scoop neck and three-quarter sleeves. I take a step back so I can see the bottom of the closet without bending my neck, and scope out some black ballet flats—those will have to do. There's no sense in me trying to wear heels today, plus these are easy to slip on without me having to lean over to pull them on.

I search the bathroom for any kind of makeup. My makeup, along with my good clothing, is long gone. I hope I can get some of it back. I can't afford to go shopping right now. Chances are they are all toast. Milly had put my bag in the small compartment under the hood of the vehicle. We were lucky—well, I guess I was lucky—that Fiero engines are in the back of the car. We hit that tree so hard that I doubt my stuff survived, but the engine being in the back prevented the car from blowing up.

I finally find some ChapStick. My lips are really dry so that's just fine with me. I brush through my hair with care—bristles and tender bruises do not go together well. I still look like shit, but it's a funeral, not a runway show.

I hear Greg calling me from downstairs. I take a deep breath in and leave to join him.

We arrive at the church on time. People are still parking and there are small groups standing outside the building, chatting and consoling each other. Greg finds a spot and pulls in.

"Are you sure you want to do this?" he says after he cuts the engine.

"I don't have a choice. Could you imagine what people would say if I didn't come?" I say.

"I guess you're right. I'll stay by your side as long as you need me to."

"Thanks, Greg." I open the passenger door.

We walk up to the church as people are ushered inside. It's a quaint little church that can probably hold about one hundred people. The sun streams through the purple and blue squares of the stained glass windows, bright points in the dark brick walls. Orange upholstery cushions the wooden pews. Milly's casket is on the dais at the front of the church. Its polished cherry wood is draped with purple and green flowers. The casket is closed. I don't think even the best mortician out there could make her look good now. I stop my brain from going down that nasty path and look at the easels that have been set up around the casket. The pictures on them are way better to remember her by than what lies in that box. Way better than what I will always see her as now. Every time I think of her face all I see is her eyes staring lifelessly at me. I pray that will change over time. There are school photos from different grades, photos of her with family, photos of her as a child, and others of her just being her beautiful self.

The room has become awfully quiet while I stand staring at the many photos. I hear whispered conversations and try my best to ignore them. I feel as if they're talking about me.

I see Sara walking down the aisle toward me; she is dressed in a fitted black suit and heels. "Stevie," she says, and hugs me. "I didn't think you would make it."

"Of course I would. Where are Milly's parents? And Shane?" I ask.

"Her parents are sitting in the front pew, and Shane is over there." She nods to the middle of the church. "Listen, I have so much I have to do, so please just find a seat. It's really good that you came, Stevie. It's nice to see you on your feet." She leaves us to help others find seats.

I feel Shane looking at me and glance in his direction. As soon as our eyes meet he looks down at his hands. His eyes look swollen and he too has lost a bit of weight. Greg puts his arm around my back to guide me toward an open seat on the opposite side of the aisle, nearer to the front. I am grateful for his choice. I have no other option but to look ahead—away from Shane.

I want to scan around to see who else is here, but my neck restricts me. On the way in I had noticed a few people from school, and other members of Milly's family. The church is almost full. Milly was a popular girl, with a lot of admirers and people who loved her. Speaking of admirers, I haven't seen Bradley anywhere. Then, as if he knew I was thinking about him, a second later he appears. He sits down in the pew ahead of us and turns around to see me. He looks like he is sleep deprived, but other than that he looks normal. Maybe I'm not the only one that this hasn't hit yet. He's about to open his mouth to say something to me but gets interrupted by the pastor.

The funeral service begins and the room falls silent. The pastor reads a number of passages, and family members say what they feel needs to be said. Milly's parents rise to light a candle and say a few things. Mrs. Shepard breaks down on the dais. That gets me. I can't stop crying after that. Soft weeping and sobs rise from the pews. Sara rises and talks about her and Milly's friendship, with some anecdotes about growing up together. When the short service ends people rise, preparing to go to the nearby cemetery. I hope no one is angry that I didn't say a few words at the service, but how could I?

I've zoned a lot of everything and everyone out. A couple people come up to me in the time between the church service and the burial, but I'm deaf and mute to them all. Greg answers with what he can and I'm mostly left alone. I think everyone is either afraid of me or pities me. I still need to pluck up the courage to speak to Mr. and Mrs. Shepard, but that can wait for the "light snacks and refreshments" that we will be having at their house. How people can eat after funerals is astonishing to me.

At the burial site more prayers are read, more tears shed, and I stand there numb. I notice that Bradley too is stone-faced. I don't know why it makes me feel better that I'm not the only one that isn't crying, but it does. The pastor announces that everyone will be gathering at the Shepards' house in memory of Milly, and people begin walking away.

The funeral and burial went without a hitch, but that's not the part I was worried about. The "gathering," where I will be stuck in a house with Shane and people that think I'm the one who *should* have died is the part I'm panicking about now; mostly I'm freaking out about being in a house with Shane. I'm going to try to avoid him and get through the day. My neck is hurting and I regret not taking the painkillers.

Greg and I get back into his vehicle and wait for everyone to leave ahead of us. I didn't have to ask him; I think he knew I wanted to wait as long as possible. The longer we wait here, the less time we have to spend *there*. He finally starts the engine and gives me one last look that says *We can still back out*. But I can't, so we drive in silence to Milly's house.

CHAPTER FIVE

WE'RE THE LAST TO arrive at Milly's parents' house. I think in some ways that is worse than being the first. When we enter the house all eyes are on me, and the tension is suffocating. I should have let Greg take me home. I could have thought of an excuse to tell everyone later.

"Are you okay?" Greg whispers in my ear.

"I'll be fine. Would you mind being on your own for a bit? I need to find Milly's parents," I say as we walk through the spacious foyer.

"Sure; let me know when you're ready to go home, but take all the time you need."

"Thanks, Greg." I give him a half smile and walk slowly away from him, passing through the double doors to the living area and kitchen. That seems to be where people are gathering.

Milly's house usually feels very welcoming, but today I couldn't feel more out of place. I spot her parents quickly; they are sitting on a peach-coloured sofa with their arms around each other. Milly's mom— Penelope—is trying to put on a strong face, but you can see right through it to the pain inside. Her dad—Nial—looks dead inside. He's staring blankly at the room in front of him. Milly, unlike me, was definitely a "daddy's girl." He gave her the world, anything her little heart desired, including happiness and promises that he actually fulfilled. I often felt envious of their relationship. Nial is the fun-loving, carefree, Best Dad award type, so it's unnerving to see him the way he is now.

Penelope has always been a soft-spoken and kind woman, a mother I would have loved to have. She desperately wanted more children. Milly was a miracle baby. Doctors had told them for years that she was not going to be able to conceive, and then one day—*boom*—she was pregnant. After Milly they tried to have more kids, but it never happened.

Now here I am standing in front of them—the cause of the loss of their only child, their miracle baby, their pride and joy and maybe even their only reason for happiness—and I am expecting sympathy. I'm a fool. What am I even going to say to them? I put a brave face on and step in front of them. "Mr. and Mrs. Shepard?" I say, and hold my breath.

"Stephanie!" Penelope says, and stands up so quickly the motion looks blurred.

Oh boy.

Penelope embraces me and bursts out crying. Nial gets up swiftly to stand next to his wife, and places his arm around her. I know I should feel relieved that they are not trying to kill me, but I'm not—not at all. I notice that the room has gone quiet and everyone has stopped whatever they were doing to observe us.

"I'm *so sorry*," I cry out to both Nial and Penelope. I look from her face to his. "I tried to save her, I really did. The car...it was out of control...I am so sorry." I don't know why I had to blurt this out. Why couldn't I have said the usual "I'm sorry for your loss" speech, hug them both, and leave the house?

Nial tears me from Penelope's arms and takes me by the shoulders so that I'm staring into his eyes. "Why did you make her drive you? Why?" Nial yells and the pain contorts his face in an unusual way. "Melissa would still be here today if you hadn't *begged* her to take you home. You are so selfish, Stephanie!" he screams, and the anger makes the veins in his forehead bulge.

I am taken aback and can't seem to blink. I feel tears burning the edges of my eyes.

"Nial *please!*" Penelope shrieks and pries Nial's fingers from my shoulders. "Haven't we all gone through enough?" she snaps. "Look at the girl, look at what she's been through!"

I stand there stunned, speechless. Nothing I say will make either of them feel better, and I deserve all the anger of the world on me. Nial stalks from the room. There are whispers all around us, but I refuse to turn around and acknowledge them. I don't care what they are saying.

"I am *so sorry*," I finally say to Penelope. "I never intended to come here and cause any further pain. I loved Milly, she was my best friend. I feel lost without her and there is nothing I can do to bring her back. She wanted to take me home that night. I tried to say no—but she insisted," I lie. "I wish I could have driven myself, I really do. You know how stubborn she was. She always got her own way." The tears roll freely down my cheeks. I must sound genuine enough because Penelope wraps her arms around me, and rubs my back. Her tight hug hurts my bruises, but I don't flinch.

"I know, Stephanie, I know. That was our Melissa. She had a very strong personality, just like Nial. Please don't take what he said to heart. He is grieving in his own way. Who would have thought I would be the stronger one out of the two of us. No one blames you, okay?" she says earnestly, and pulls away to look down at me. "I'm just happy we didn't lose you both."

I snivel and pull her in for one last hug. I can't think of anything else to say, and I don't want to say something that will make her regret her choice in not blaming me. I give her a kiss on the cheek and turn to try to find Greg. I want to leave. I've said my piece and there's nothing more I can do.

"Oh, Stephanie?" Penelope puts her hand on my shoulder to stop me.

"Yes?" I say, without turning again.

"If you go up to Milly's room there is a box on her bed that has some things I know she would have wanted you to have. Please don't forget to take it. I don't know when I'll see you again."

"Thank you," I say, and give her a small smile.

I feel like Moses parting the Red Sea when I go in search of Sara, except it's people making room for me to walk, not the ocean. I guess they all heard what they needed to hear from me, and they're not going to try to pull me into conversation.

Thank God.

I finally find Sara in the dining room. She's picking up plates and tidying up after everyone. She looks worn out. I can't believe she is leaving for her trip so soon, *and* has taken on the huge responsibility of doing all of this for Milly's parents. That's what friends are for, I suppose. At this moment I feel like a useless piece of crap. I should be doing more.

"Sara, can I help you with anything?" I offer.

"You should be resting, Stevie; have you seen yourself?" she says.

"Well, I've been trying to avoid mirrors," I say. She smiles wanly at me. "Um, well...I guess I am feeling kind of sore. If you don't need anything I might head home, if that's okay."

"Of course it's okay, Stevie," she says, and stops what she's doing to look at me. "I think I have everything under control here. No one will judge you if you leave early. One look at you and they can tell you've been through hell and back."

"Alright, thank you...for everything you've done here. Milly was lucky to have you as a friend," I say.

"You were her friend too, Stevie," she says. "Milly loved you like a sister, and so do I."

"I love you too." I smile. "I will be at the airport on the twenty-eighth, okay? Two p.m., right?"

"Yes, 2:00 p.m.; our flight leaves at six, but we have to be there four hours early." She rolls her eyes.

"I'll see you then," I say, and give her a hug.

I see Greg as I make my way up the stairs to Milly's bedroom. He's in conversation with a short, plump lady that I recognize from one of Milly's family get-togethers. Her aunt, I think. He's too absorbed in conversation to see me, so I slip past him. I walk to the end of the hallway, where Milly's room is. Well, it had been her parents' room, but she wanted the master bedroom. Whatever Milly wanted, Milly got. She complained about not having enough space for her clothing and the master bedroom has a huge walk-in closet. It's almost the size of my bedroom—the closet, I mean. The actual room is way bigger. We spent countless nights having girlie sleepovers and watching chick flicks in her room. I stand in front of the closed door remembering all of the good times we had in there. I can almost still hear her giggles. Our friendship was so good, until it all turned to shit. *What happened, Milly?*

I turn the door handle and step into the room. The lights are on but the curtains are drawn. Shane is sitting on the edge of the huge king-size bed. He is hunched over and looking down at a frame. I see the box I'm meant to take sitting open next to him. He didn't hear me come in. I close the door behind myself with a loud *click,* and he jerks his head up to look at me.

"Sorry," he says, and puts the frame back in the box. He wipes his eyes and stands up to leave.

"No, Shane, please wait," I plead.

"Stevie, I can't..."

"I really need to talk to you, Shane. I beg of you, please, just...don't leave."

Shane sighs heavily, sits back down on the bed, and pushes the box aside to give me room to sit. I pull a chair from the dressing table and sit in front of him instead—I want to look at his face, not the side of his head. I take his hands in mine but he pulls them away. I hope I didn't offend him by not sitting next to him. We stay silent for a while. I have a million things I want to ask him but I don't know what to say first. I wish he would say something, but he's in his own world. He looks extremely uncomfortable. I don't blame him. The last time we saw each other was at the waterfall. The thought makes me feel sick. I start crying before I can stop myself.

Shane finally looks up at me. He examines the bruises on my face and his eyes wander down to my chest—not in a good way; the seatbelt mark can be seen clearly. He looks back up to my face and wipes a tear away from my cheek. I lean my head into his hand, which hurts my neck, but I need his touch right now. I need the familiarity of it. There has always been something so comforting about his warmth.

"It's not your fault," I whisper. "The accident—no one could have foreseen that. If anything, it's my fault. Shane...I shouldn't have pushed you away. That was cruel and unfair of me. You don't push away the people you love."

Shane inhales sharply, as if I have hit a nerve, and abruptly rises. I grab for his hand to stop him from leaving but he diverts it. He's always been good at that; it's what makes him a great rugby player. I scold rugby in moments like this. He can always seem to plan out the perfect escape route—something I am now only learning how to do.

I hear the doorknob squeak as he turns it. I hear him exhale. It feels like a lost cause to try to stop him, so I choose to let him leave. It's a day for mourning, not fighting.

"You're right, Stevie," he says. "You don't push away the people you love."

And with that said, he opens the door and walks out.

What's that supposed to mean? I thought he loved me. Isn't he doing exactly what I said—*and* he just said—not to do? He's pushing me away. Right now, yes, I admit I deserve it, but it still stings. I don't know what I was expecting when I asked him to stay. Is he trying to tell me he doesn't love me? I ponder that for a few minutes and conclude that there's no point in thinking about it now. It's been a long day, and I just want to go home.

I rise and step toward Milly's bed to lift the box. My foot hits the corner of something under the bed. I want to think nothing of it; people keep stuff under their beds all the time. But curiosity gets the best of me.

I look toward the door to make sure it's closed. I get down on hands and knees, ignore the ache in my body, and lift up the bedskirt. I see a beautiful wooden box that looks out of place, under there in the dark. A box this pretty should be on display. There has to be something of interest inside if it's hiding under there. I pull the box out for closer inspection. I stay on the floor in case someone walks in—I can quickly shove it back under and pretend I dropped something, like an earring.

I let my finger trail over the box. It has delicate flowers carved all around it. They look like orchids. I flick up the latch and pray it's not a music box. I don't want something so innocent to give away my intrusiveness. I listen for footsteps and hear nothing. Holding my breath, I open the lid. No music. *Phew.*

There is a small fluffy pink book on the inside with a lock on it. *Milly's diary.* I hold it in my hands, feeling the fluff on my fingertips. This is so bad of me. I stare at the diary for a long moment.

No, I should leave it where I found it. I bite my inner cheek and am about to put the book back in the box when I hear the squeak of the door handle turning. I reach up and throw the diary into my cardboard box, shove the wooden box back under the bed, and reach for my ear. My body screams in agony at the rapid movements. I didn't think I could move so quickly in my present condition.

"What are you doing?" Sara asks.

"Dropped my earring," I lie, and pop it off quickly without Sara noticing. "I found it, though." I hold it up to show her.

"Oh. Well, Greg's looking for you," she says.

"Okay, I'll be down in a minute. Penelope wanted me to take this box of stuff; that's why I'm in here." *Not stealing Milly's diary or anything...*

"Alright, let me help you up," she offers, and saunters toward me.

Shit. I really hope she doesn't look in the box. *Damn Milly and her taste for bright things!*

"No, no, I'm okay," I say, and reach for the side of the bed to pull myself up. I close the box and pick it up before Sara gets a chance to see inside it. Pain pulses through my entire body; I've overexerted myself today.

"It's weird, being in here," Sara says as we walk to the door. "Knowing Milly will never be here again, it feels so *empty.*"

"It does," I agree.

We take one last look around Milly's room, one last look at all the good memories we had in here. And we say goodbye.

I meet Greg downstairs. He looks uncomfortable—or is it embarrassed? I can't really tell. "Let's get out of here," he says as I walk up to him.

I don't ask any questions. Greg takes the box from me and I follow him back to his car.

"Milly's aunt sure is *welcoming,*" Greg says on the drive home.

"What happened?" I ask.

"She is very *forward*...is that a word you kids use?"

"She was getting frisky at a funeral!" I say, amused and shocked at the same time.

"Let's just say if it wasn't for Sara walking past us, I would have ended up in the coat closet—against my will—playing seven minutes in heaven with her," Greg says, and over exaggerates a shiver.

"Oh, gross! More like seven minutes in hell!" I squeal, and Greg bursts out laughing.

The rest of the drive home is happy and lighthearted. You would never guess we'd recently attended a funeral.

"Do you need help inside?" Greg asks as we pull up to the house. "I have to get back to the shop to check on Denise and help her close up."

"I should be fine, the box is light," I say, and shake it. "Thanks again for taking me today."

"No problem. You handled everything like a champ," he says, and gives me a warm smile.

Like a champ? I smile at him and get out of the car—box in hand, diary in box, and shame in my heart. I should feel guiltier about this, but maybe I'll get some answers about why Milly was acting so weird on the trip. That is, of course, if she even still wrote in a diary. I could have a book filled with childhood memories, something her parents might have wanted to keep. *Shit. I am a horrible person.*

I put the cardboard box on my bed, greedily open it, and pull out the fluffy pink diary. Why should I postpone the inevitable? *Who am I kidding? I knew I was going to read it—might as well get it over and done with.* I settle in the wicker chair and stare out the window, caressing the fluff on the book. I have second thoughts. Maybe I should return it somehow. Or burn it in the fire-pit.

OR! I could read it, then burn it. Hmm. I prefer the second option.

Here goes nothing. I try to open the diary, totally forgetting the damn thing has a lock on it. *Eff! That's annoying.*

I take the diary to the kitchen, find a steak knife, and put the sharp end into the lock and twist it. With a little *click*, it opens. That was a lot easier than I was expecting. I take it back upstairs and sit down in the wicker chair. I wonder when Mom will be home. I don't want any interruptions.

I take a deep breath and flip through the pages. The diary is about half full. I notice the dates are recent and release the breath I was holding. My hands start shaking involuntarily. Am I seriously this nervous? It's not like Milly can catch me reading her diary, and if Mom or Greg saw it they would think nothing of it. I tell myself to relax and start from the beginning.

oOo

Dear Diary entry 1
New school year, new diary. I should probably be calling you a journal by now but journals are so...manly, plus they don't come in fabulous colours like you! Summer is over and Grade 11 has started. What an awesome summer it was, until the end of it, that is. I mean, it sucked breaking up with Richard but whatevs, it's not like he could ever live up to my expectations. I needed him to pass the time. Plus he was starting to annoy me with his "When can we have sex, Milly blah blah blah." Don't these guys know by

now that they are not good enough for me? There is only one guy out there for me... Why doesn't he want me anymore? I'll tell you why, my dear little diary. It's because of HER!!!

oOo

Her? I try to think who she could be talking about. I always wondered why she and Richard broke up. I thought it was his doing. She told me she *had* slept with him. She was never shy about throwing that detail around. Why would she lie? I browse through the next couple pages and they ramble on about school and her parents—who are actually not as happy as they pretend to be. They should get a standing ovation for their performance. Milly gets one too for being a great actress, because this is definitely news to me. And here I thought she told me everything. I mean, she didn't even tell me she treats her diary like a real person. How weird is that? I roll my eyes and scan the pages for more interesting finds.

oOo

Dear Diary entry 7
I hate this. I swear he is doing this to me on purpose. Why must he kiss her like that in front of me? I get so angry; doesn't he see that I still love him? That I want him back? That he is killing me!

Dear Diary entry 10
I met someone. His name is Bradley. He is gorgeous and smart and is going to school to be some kind of shrink. I have been going about everything the wrong way, I realize that now. I've been trying so desperately to get him to notice me, but I've been dating losers. How will he ever be jealous if the guys I go for don't come close to being comparable to him? Well, this time I figured it out. Bradley is by far the nicest guy I've dated. This has to work! I feel slightly bad for Bradley; he has no idea that I'm using him. Oh well, I have to look at the bigger picture here. There is only one person out there for me. I love you. I

wish I could scream that at him. I LOVE YOU!!! LOOK AT ME!!! NOTICE ME!!!

oOo

She's nuts.

I hate that she keeps referring to this *mystery guy* as "him" or "he." Why can't she just say his name? Poor Brad...I can't believe she was using him to make this other guy jealous. The thing I don't get is, what other guy is she around when she's around Brad? Brad doesn't go to the same school as us and the only other guys she hangs out with are Calvin and Shane.

My heart starts beating fast. She was in love with one of them. But who?

oOo

Dear Diary entry 15
I am stoked! My parents said we can use the lake house this summer for a couple weeks. OMG! I am so excited!!! This is it! This is when I can finally let him know how I really feel. If I can just get him alone... That might be hard with HER in the way. She is so stupid. She actually thinks we are friends. Friends don't date your exes, you BITCH! Well, technically we were never together as a couple...only at times when we needed that certain release. I need to get him back to where this all started. Maybe then he will remember how great we were together. I need to get him back to the waterfall. That's where it all began.

oOo

Oh fuck! No, this can't be happening.

Our special place now...

My breathing becomes rapid, and my chest throbs with pain. I can't tell if it's the ribs aching from me inhaling too hard, or if it's my heart being torn to shreds. They slept together. I can't believe it. I've been misled. My world feels like it's falling to pieces around me. I sob out loud and force myself to keep reading. I have to know more, I just have to. With trembling hands I turn the page.

oOo

I knew that day that I would do everything in my power to be with him. That summer before ninth grade was the best summer of my life. Everything was perfect until SHE came along. Poor her with her dead father. Everyone PITIED her. He just tossed me aside like I was nothing. Like losing our virginity together was like changing the tires on his truck. He said it meant NOTHING to him! He said that he didn't care! But even after he started dating that bitch he still kept coming over to be with me. It was like our little game, to make each other jealous. I would date different guys and he would stay with her, then we'd screw on the side. It was like a drug, an adrenaline rush. It all changed, though.

This last summer before starting Grade 11...everything changed...I broke up with Richard to move onto the next guy who thought he had a chance with me, but he said enough was enough. That he was actually falling in love *barf* with HER! Are you fucking kidding me!!! Little-hurt-virgin-girl??? Give me a break! HE needs a real woman, dammit! The nerve of him. He told me we had to stop seeing each other. That he wanted to give her a real chance. That SHE had RESPECT for herself.

I threatened that I would tell her. That I would tell everyone. But he did the unthinkable. He punched me in the stomach. He told me that if I ever said a thing to anyone he would do a lot worse. And I believed him. The strange thing is, though, even after he hit me I still never stopped loving him. He did that out of anger. I deserved it. This trip will show him that I'm the one that deserves him, because I know the person he truly is. I will show him. We WILL be together again.

oOo

Furious, I throw the diary against the wall and run to the bathroom. I feel sick to my stomach. I start dry heaving. This all seems like a nasty trick. I turn the water on in the sink and splash cold water on my face.

I brace my hands on the countertop and lean over the sink. *Get a grip, Stevie.* But I am livid. Our whole relationship was a lie. My "best friend" was a lie.

It was all a lie.

I can taste bile in the back of my throat and I swallow to keep myself from retching. Turning the taps on in the shower so that Mom can't hear me when she comes home, I curl up on the floor and sob uncontrollably.

oOo

I wake up on my back, tucked into bed. That's odd. I don't remember leaving the bathroom. Looking across the room, I read *3:00* on the alarm clock. My body feels stiff all over. I push myself up into a sitting position and swing my legs over the side of the bed.

There is a glass of fresh water on the side table. I haven't taken any pain medication today. I'm supposed to take it three times a day, and I'm paying for skipping it now. I take a swig of water and one pill. I wonder if it's too early to drink coffee.

I stand up to go to the closet to get my winter coat, and realize I'm still wearing Mom's dress. *Shit!* This isn't good. I hope she never saw it. That should have been the first thing I did when I got home yesterday—take off the dress, not dive into the diary. I unzip the dress and take it off. I scrunch it into a small ball and throw it toward the back corner of the closet, replacing it with black sweats and a green, long-sleeve shirt. I also find my winter coat. It's a hideous knee-length, burnt orange beast, but it will keep me warm.

I carry it to the kitchen and toss it on the table. I turn the coffee pot on and wait for it to brew.

There is a creak on the staircase as someone tries to tiptoe downstairs. I turn. "Greg?" I whisper as he reaches the bottom. He looks like hell.

He walks into the kitchen and sits down at the table. I point at the coffee and he nods. "I thought I heard you up," he says.

"Um, what are you still doing here?" I ask apprehensively.

"Denise found you on the bathroom floor," he says, and shakes his head. "She thought you were dead."

"Oh shit," I say. "I just...broke down when I got home. The day was overwhelming. Is she okay?"

"It took me a while to calm her down after I made sure you were okay and got you into bed. You were passed out cold, but breathing fine. You scared the hell out of us, Stephanie."

"I never meant to—"

"I know, I know." He waves his hand to cut me off. "I told her not to be mad at you, that it was a rough day, and she seemed to understand. She took her sleeping pills and asked if I could lay down with her until she fell asleep."

"Did she say anything about the dress?" I ask.

"What dress? The one you were in?"

"Yes...it was the one she wore to my father's funeral. I didn't have anything else to wear."

"No, I don't think she noticed. As soon as she saw you curled up on the floor she screamed for me. I think your safety was the first thing on her mind, not a piece of fabric," he says dryly.

"Greg...before the accident, before my near-death experience, *that dress* would have been the first thing she'd have noticed," I say, and look away from him.

I pour our coffees without another word between us and leave his on the counter. I put the winter coat on, slip my feet into my gumboots, and take my drink outside.

The cold night air hits me and it's refreshing. I needed this. After everything that's happened in the last few weeks, I don't know how I'm still sane. I sit on the bench in *my* special place and am very happy that I never shared this spot with Shane, Milly, or anyone else. My whole life feels tarnished. I can't go anywhere without having a bad memory attached to it, but here there are no bad memories, only good ones. This is the only happy place I have left.

I hear footsteps on the gravel and I know they're Greg's. They're approaching. *Oh please, go away!* I sit absolutely still and slow down my breathing, I don't want him here. *Please don't find me...*

I hear him walk around, sigh, then get into his car. I exhale in relief as he starts the engine and backs down the driveway. I shouldn't have said what I did to him. I regretted it as soon as the words left my mouth. The candle he holds for Mom burns so brightly. Who am I to be the one to blow it out? I will apologize when I see him—that is, if he ever comes over again. *Poor Mom.*

I hope she will be okay. I feel like such an idiot for not taking the dress off. I pray Greg was right when he said she didn't notice it.

I feel a warm haze take over my body as the medication kicks in. I relax against the wooden post and finish my coffee. This is my thinking place, but the only things I have to think about are bad. I try to piece the last year together in my head, trying to look for signs that things were awry. Shane has always been affectionate with me. Yes, I admit grade eleven *has* been different. He has been a lot more lovey-dovey. I just figured it was because he knew that I was almost ready to have sex. I mean, we never really talked about it before; he never pushed it on me before grade eleven.

Because he was getting it from Milly...

It's a disgusting thought, but I don't cry. It's weird that this medication can make me feel numb. I can still think, but my emotions are different. They are not all...*emo...*

Did I notice a big change in Milly from grade nine to grade eleven? She always dated a lot of guys; she shared a lot of information. If I think hard about the times her and I were alone, could they really all have been fake? We had a lot of good times—sleepovers and shopping trips. Did she have an ulterior motive the entire time? Her diary would say yes, but she—as she was on a day to day basis—said no.

She could have only been my "friend" so that she would know what Shane and I were up to when *we* were alone. She did seem relieved that we were not doing anything more than kissing each other, and the whole second base thing—which was like child's play in her eyes. She might have seemed awkward on the last day of school when she caught Shane and me making out in the hallway. She sure didn't stick around for long. She did say, "You guys will have plenty of time for that at my parents' lake house."

She didn't mean it, though. Now that I recall it, there was not a hint of happiness or enthusiasm in her voice. It was dull.

And the drive to the lake house—who could forget that? She scared the living shit out of me with all of her intense details about sex and other things. She did that on purpose. She *was* trying to scare me. I have no doubt in my mind about it. She wasn't angry with Brad at all. She didn't even want to be with Brad. No wonder he looked so sullen the whole trip. She was obviously not giving him anything; she was saving it all for Shane. She was pretending.

When Shane and I had the fight at the waterfall, which he failed to mention was the same place he'd had sex with Milly...how sickening is that? How could he expect me to lose my virginity in the exact place he lost his to Milly? How could that ever be *our* "special place" when he had already shared it with her? No wonder she was so upset when I mentioned that on the drive home.

When I got back to the lake house after my long trek through the woods after the whole Shane ordeal and she was there "consoling" him, I wonder what she was really saying to him. That she would take me home and come back the day after? That she would make him forget about me? That she was the only one that *deserved* him? I was gone a long time. So much could have happened. He still looked really upset when I got back to the house and everyone was there. Well, they were hiding in the basement, but I doubt that they slept with each other in the time it took me to get back from the waterfall.

I shouldn't be thinking like that. I should only think about what I know for certain. Milly and Shane had sex behind my back. It went on through-out grade nine and grade ten. He stopped it just before grade eleven. She wanted Shane; she dated Bradley to make him jealous. She had a plan to get us to break up on the trip. Although she died, her plan worked. If she were here now I would pat her on the back.

And kill her all over again.

"Whoa, where did that come from?" I exclaim. Would I really kill her, knowing everything I know now? Is it so easy for me to take a life like that? No—I don't think it would be. Maybe I would beat the living shit out of her, but actually kill her?

You did kill her.

"No, I didn't," I say to myself.

The tree through her neck killed her. Her taking her seatbelt off killed her. I didn't push the car down the mountain. If we had worked together we could both be alive today. Do I regret lunging at her? Maybe I did at first, but after finding all of this shit out, I would do it again—a thousand times over.

The dark thoughts I have take me by surprise. I blink a few times to clear my mind. This is a bad road to travel. It needed to be traveled, but it's taking a turn in the wrong direction. I shouldn't live with this much hate in my heart. I need to take the rest of the summer holidays to clear my head. If I'm like this when school starts it's not going to be good for anybody.

Damn this small town! There are no other high schools around that I can switch to. What am I going to do? I don't have any support; I'm not going to have anyone to sit with at lunch. I'm going to be a loner. One more year—I just have to get through one more year.

oOo

The next five days go by in a flash. It's all mostly blurry. I have the chance to apologize to Mom. Greg doesn't come over for a few days after Mom's little breakdown, and my outburst, but I'm really happy to wake up today and see him and Mom laughing in the kitchen. She has such a beautiful laugh, something I've missed hearing since Dad died. It changes her whole face. She is so beautiful.

I smile fondly at the memory but my smile fades when I think about Sara and Calvin leaving today. I wish she could stay. I still have not set up the laptop. I've been too depressed to even think about it. I mentally tell myself to ask Greg to help me tomorrow, if he's around.

He kindly offered to take me to the airport today, and gave me money for a taxi ride home. I felt guilty taking the money, but I would have felt even guiltier asking him to wait around while I say goodbye to Sara. I want to spend a couple of hours with her before they embark on their journey. France is the first stop. This time tomorrow she'll be sipping red wine and staring up at the Eiffel Tower—well, that's what I think of when I think of France; they'll probably be sleeping and jet-lagged from the long flight.

I say thank you again to Greg as he drops me outside the International Departures door. The building is huge; how will I ever find Sara and Calvin? I walk through the big automatic glass doors and scan the huge terminal. There are people scurrying around like ants, some laughing, some panicking, some crying—it's overwhelming. I add this to my list of places I hate, along with hospitals, the school library (because it's creepy), the lake house, the waterfall, public washrooms, and malls. I have a good list going.

I look up at one of the screens hanging from the ceiling that display departure times, flight numbers, gate numbers, and so on; I know her flight leaves at 6:00 p.m. and it's only two-fifteen. I watch the ever-changing screen for several minutes. I keep thinking I see the flight I'm looking for, and then the damn screen flips over. I read more quickly.

"There!" I blurt without thinking. The lady standing next to me jumps. "Sorry about that," I say, and walk away quickly, stifling a giggle.

I'm still smiling when I see Sara and Calvin checking in their bags. I wait for them to get tags on their carry-ons before I announce my presence. They turn around and see me straight away. Who wouldn't be able to see me? I look like hell. I did try to make myself look presentable this morning. I put on a pair of black skinny jeans, a pretty white blouse, a light beige cardigan, and white flip-flops. I'm still uncertain about putting makeup on, because right now it would probably make me look worse.

Sara runs toward me with Calvin trailing behind her carrying the bags. No sign of Shane anywhere—that's good. I thought he was driving them today but he must have changed his mind when he found out I was coming. Sara sees the concern on my face. "He's parking the truck," she says, and waits for my response.

"Oh…" I sigh. "Well, this day is not about us, it's about my two best friends leaving me for *two* years!" I say, and force a grin. Sara looks instantly relieved.

"Hi Calvin." I wave at him. He looks terrible.

"Hey, Stevie," he says nervously.

"Ignore him," Sara says, and jabs him in the side. "He's not a good flyer." Calvin winces and shrugs.

"What better way to get over the fear than to travel across the world?" I say enthusiastically. "You'll be a professional flyer when you get home."

"I just wish I could knock myself out," he says.

Hmm. I reach into the small purse I'm carrying and lift my bottle of medication for Calvin to see, shaking it like a rattle. I smile mischievously at him. "If Sara doesn't mind flying without you clinging to her for dear life, you can take my last two pills. They'll knock you on your ass." I wink at him.

"You don't need them?" Calvin asks hopefully.

"No, I've been feeling a lot better this week; I don't need them. My neck's even doing better, see?" I slowly turn my head from side to side.

Calvin looks hopefully at Sara.

"Fine! Take the pills, you big baby." Sara laughs. "It will be nice to read my book in *peace*, without you constantly asking me how it's going." She rolls her eyes, puts her arm around my shoulder, and kisses me on the cheek. "I am going to miss you, you little weasel!" she jokes. I laugh.

We walk in search of a place to kill time. Shane joins us after about fifteen minutes and we end up sitting across from one another in a booth at one of the airport restaurants. Sara orders us a round of water and coffee. Why he has to sit directly in front of me is a mystery. I ignore the tension, push all of the ill thoughts aside—the ones that make me want to reach across the table and strangle the life out of him—and sip my coffee. I keep my attention on Sara and Calvin as they tell us their plans for France and all the places they want to see there. I find myself nodding a lot and laughing when everyone else laughs, but I'm mainly just sitting there fighting my internal demons. I have my fist clenched under the table. We sit there for what feels like hours.

Calvin looks at his watch. "We should probably be getting to our gate. We still have to go through security," he says, rising.

"Boo," Sara says, and pouts.

I follow them as far as I am allowed. Calvin puts the carry-ons on the ground and hugs me. It takes me by surprise. "Look after yourself, okay?" he says.

"You look after my best friend!" I say. "I'm going to miss you guys. Hope the pills work for you—well, I know they will. Maybe only take one. You don't want to be comatose when the plane touches down," I tease.

"Thanks again for those. Are you positive you don't need them? I'd hate to take medication from a cripple like you," he quips.

I snort and push him on the shoulder. "I think I'll survive."

Calvin switches places with Sara, who has finished saying goodbye to Shane. "Don't you dare make me cry, Stevie!" she says as she squeezes me.

"It's too late, Sara, you're already crying," I say when I feel her body shudder. "I'm going to miss you terribly. Promise me you'll write often, okay? I'm going to set up the laptop tomorrow."

"Oh, that reminds me." She reaches into her jacket pocket. "My e-mail address." She hands me a small piece of paper that I tuck into my purse.

"Thanks; when I set up an e-mail account you'll be the first person I write to," I say, then snuffle. "Get out of here before I kidnap you and take you back home, okay?"

"We'll be home before you know it," she says, and hugs me again.

I kiss her on the cheek and wave at Calvin, who has already joined the line. Sara joins him and turns to blow me a kiss. I blow one back to her and wave again. They disappear through security and I am left standing next to Shane. I didn't think that far ahead. I forgot that at some point we would be alone today. I glance at him and he's staring at me. *Calm yourself, Stevie, calm yourself.* I do not want to cause a scene in the middle of a crowded airport. "See ya," I say, and walk away as fast as I can. I won't wait around for him to say anything back to me. Crisis averted.

I get outside and sit down on one of the smokers benches. There are stinky ashtrays to my left and right and an older gentleman is enjoying a cigarette next to me. He offers me one but I kindly refuse. "Just getting some fresh air," I say.

The man laughs at me and shakes his head. "Can't get fresher than this," he says, and takes a puff. He stubs the smoke out and walks back into the airport.

I sit there wondering where the taxis are. I might have to walk to the Arrivals section. Where is that? The sound of a horn interrupts my thoughts. I look up and see Shane sitting in his truck on the road in front of me. He must have paid for parking and decided to drive back around to find me.

He rolls down the passenger window. "Need a lift?" he says, and reaches toward the passenger door. It swings open.

Say no, Stevie, just say no and walk away.

I look around to see—by chance—a taxi, but there are none in sight. Someone honks behind Shane's truck. He's in a "drop off only" area. I panic, ignore my subconscious, and climb into Shane's truck.

CHAPTER SIX

THE FIRST THING I think is, *Have you completely lost your mind?* and the second thing is *HAVE YOU COMPLETLEY LOST YOUR MIND!*

As soon as I buckle the seatbelt Shane steps on the gas. I don't have the time to second-guess myself and hurl my ass out of the vehicle. *What am I doing? Am I crazy? This is a bad idea.* It will take at least thirty minutes to get home, which is thirty minutes I'd rather not spend alone with Shane. *The lying, cheating, asshole!*

I clench my purse until my knuckles hurt and the veins show through the skin on the back of my hands. I stare straight ahead at the traffic.

Traffic!

This is a nightmare. We are moving at a snail's pace in five o'clock bumper to bumper traffic. I sure hope he knows a shortcut, because if he doesn't this is going to take hours. Why did I have to panic and get in the truck? *Worst idea ever!*

I sigh and bite my inner cheek. I am not going to be the first one to speak. I pray he's thinking the same thing. We can get through this ride in silence.

Shane reaches over and my breath hitches. I think he's going to put his hand on my leg, as he used to when we drove together, but his hand moves to the radio, and he turns it on. Is he trying to give me a heart attack? I scowl and look out the passenger window. Just then Shane slams on the brakes and I'm jolted forward. The seatbelt digs into my already tender bruises. I yelp as pain courses through my chest and neck.

"Prick!" he shouts.

The car in front of us is inches away; we almost rear-ended it. I rub my neck to get the burning sensation to stop. That was the last thing I needed, especially since I gave my last couple pills to Calvin.

"Dick," I mumble. Shane thinks it's directed to the car in front of us, but it's actually to him. He clearly was not paying attention to the road in front of him. I wonder where his mind is at this moment. Is he thinking of me—or Milly?

"What are your plans for the rest of the summer?" he asks suddenly.

The traffic is at a standstill. I can see him staring at me from my peripheral vision, but I don't give him the courtesy of turning my head to look him in the face. Instead I turn and look through the passenger window again. *Screw you, Shane!*

"Does it make a difference to you?" I say emotionlessly to the glass.

"No, I guess not," he says.

I don't ask him what he's going to do, because I really do not give a shit. I sit staring blankly at the red car next to us. Whoever designed this three-lane mess of a highway deserves to be shot. I snort.

"What are you thinking about?" Shane asks.

"If I wanted you to know I would have *thought* it out loud," I say sarcastically.

"Jesus, Stevie, what happened in the last few days? You were trying to apologize to me at Milly's funeral, and now you're giving me the cold shoulder," he says unhappily.

The traffic starts to move and I'm doing a happy dance inside. Shane has to keep his eyes on the road now; it gives me the chance to straighten my throbbing neck.

"Well?" he pushes.

"Well what, Shane?" I say coolly.

"Stevie...I just want to talk."

"Well talk then; no one is stopping you."

"How can I when you're acting like this?" he says.

"Acting like what, Shane? How would you propose I act?" I scoff.

"What have I done to you to deserve this?" he says.

"Shane, please, *don't* get me started. Can you just take me home—or better yet, stop the vehicle and I'll hitchhike."

"I am not leaving you here on the highway, Stevie."

"You left me at the waterfall." My voice is full of venom. I glare at him.

"What do you expect, after the way you acted?" he snaps.

"I expected you to at least come back for me. You left me there in the fucking *dark*, Shane. Who knows what kind of animals were out there? I could have died!"

"At least—" He stops.

"At least what, Shane? At least *what!*" I yell. "At least Milly would still be alive? Is that what you're trying to say? If I got eaten in the woods *at least* Milly would not have had to drive me home? Tell me, Shane—*tell me!*" I scream at him.

"Forget it, Stevie. Please, forget about it," he pleads.

My heart is beating way too fast against my chest; I cross my arms and fume. The traffic is moving at a steady pace now. From the looks of it we're about twenty minutes away from the exit for NorthBerry Hill. It's taking everything for me not to lunge at Shane and cause another accident. Although he never finished the sentence I know exactly what he was thinking—you can see it in his face.

We don't say another word to each other for the rest of the drive.

Shane pulls up the driveway and parks the truck in the spot where I used to park my car. Mom's not home. It's the first time I actually wish she was. I unbuckle the seatbelt and take a twenty dollar note out of my purse. I leave it on the dashboard. "For gas," I say. "Thanks for the ride."

"I don't need the money," he says, and pushes the note toward me.

"And I don't need charity," I snap. I turn to open the door. He seizes my upper arm. "Shane, let go of me!" I shout, and jerk my arm to loosen his grip.

More bruises...yay. Nial already left some on my shoulders when he dug his fingers in at the funeral. Why does everyone want to hurt me?

"Seriously, Shane, let go!" I say, and try to wiggle away from him, but he doesn't budge.

"No," he says. "Not until you tell me why you're treating me like this."

"You're hurting me, Shane," I say, and try to pry his fingers off my arm.

He punched me in the stomach. Milly's written words pop into my head. Would he really do that to me? Images fill my head of him strangling me to death. I force myself to relax. I breathe out slowly and turn toward him. "You really want to know?" I pause. "I will *tell you* if you *let go* of me," I say through clenched teeth.

Shane studies my face to see if I'm speaking the truth. He squeezes my arm harder, then releases me. I take that as a warning. My skin feels like it's pulsing, I rub my arm to soothe it. *Don't cry, Stevie, don't cry—don't show weakness.*

"Shane, did you cheat on me with Milly?" I blurt. I *know* he did, but this approach seems better than me throwing accusations at him. Reading Milly's diary revealed he has a mean streak—although I had never glimpsed it until the waterfall incident, and now with him trying to intimidate me. Mom's not home, and I don't have a cell phone to call the police if he loses his temper. I'm already battered and bruised; I do not want to add *beaten* to the description.

"What the hell would make you say that?" he says. "I am not a cheater, Stevie."

You must be a good liar, then.

"So you guys never hooked up," I say, more as a statement than a question.

"No," he says. "Why would I do anything to hurt you?" Shane reaches over and brushes my hair behind my ear. "I love you, Stevie."

Oh, you fucker. I can't believe he's trying to play that card. If only he knew how much I actually knew. I shy away from him and he looks like he's been stung by a bee.

"Don't pull away from me!" he barks.

My heart skips a beat and I start to panic. "Shane please, just let me go inside, okay? We have both been through a lot and I don't want you to do something you might regret tomorrow," I say breathlessly.

"What are you talking about, Stevie?" he says, and the anger is evident.

Please come home, Mom, please!

"What do you mean, something I would regret, Stevie?" he pushes.

I look into his eyes—the beautiful, dark eyes that I used to love staring into for long periods of time, the eyes I thought would only see me with affection and kindness. Now they're the eyes of something foreign. There is no life in them, no sparkle—it's scary as hell. I feel flustered and my palms are clammy. I want out of this truck and I can only think of one way to do that.

"Here Shane," I say, and open my purse again. Before Greg took me to the airport, I tore the bad pages out of Milly's diary—the pages all about her and Shane's affair—and I hid them in a small pocket inside the purse, on the slight chance that I happened to be in the very predicament I'm in now. I was planning to destroy them when I got home because I didn't believe it would actually happen, but here we are.

"What *is that*?" he spits.

I pull the pages from their hiding place and unfold them. "Here," I say, and shove them into his hands.

He looks down and quickly scans them. His expression goes from pure rage to complete shock. Anyone who was Milly's friend would recognize her perfect writing straight away. "Stevie, I-I—" he stutters, and looks at the pages again.

"So are you still trying to tell me you never hooked up?" I hiss, and open the passenger door.

"Stevie, wait! I can explain," he says, and gets out of the truck in a flash.

"Explain what, Shane?" I say as I back carefully toward the front door of the house—I don't want to take my eyes off of him. "Explain how the first two years of our relationship were a lie? Explain how you lost your virginity to Milly at the waterfall? Explain that you tried to *get with me* in the exact same place? Or explain how you expected me to just ignore the fact that you're a *lying—cheating—asshole!*" I scream.

My heel hits the first of the steps up to the porch and I spin around to run up them. I stumble and Shane grabs me by the back of my cardigan with enough force to fling me backward, and I almost fall down the stairs. Somehow I manage to squirm out of the cardigan. Shane looks at it dangling in his hand, then throws it on the ground. He looks furious that I escaped him. Something flashes in his eyes and it terrifies the living crap out of me. I have never seen him so livid. His hand balls up into a fist.

Oh fuck!

What Shane didn't expect was me dodging his swing. How would he have known that I could predict he would even try something so violent? Milly's diary saved me there. I don't give him a chance to hit me. I see his fist move slowly from his side—I think it was actually moving at lightning speed—but I somehow sidestep out of the line of fire.

Confusion floods his face and I take that opportunity—that mere second—to kick him as hard as I can in the shin. He keels over in pain and falls backward down two steps, landing on his backside on the gravel path.

"Don't you ever talk to me again, Shane!" I scream as I look down at him. I run up the remaining steps, fumble for the spare keys Mom gave me, and open the door. "If you ever *try* to come after me I'll call the police!" I threaten, and slam the door shut. I lock it behind me, and burst into tears as I crumple to the floor.

In between gasps and sobs of frustration I look down at my feet—somewhere between Shane's truck and the front door I lost my flip-flip. Why couldn't I have worn pointy-toed heels today? That would have hurt him more. I think I might have broken my toe because the pain is coursing right from it up my leg. I catalogue it with my other injuries and hope it's only a sprain.

Shane's obscenities filter through the door as he gets back into his truck and slams the door shut. He starts the engine and peels out of the driveway. I hear the gravel kick up onto the porch. My heart is pounding a million beats a minute. That went horribly.

I pick myself up off the floor before Mom gets home; she could pop in at any minute, or not be home for hours—who knows, with her. I don't want her to find me curled up on the floor again. I peek through the peephole in the door to double-check that Shane really is gone. There's no sign of his truck or him. I unlock the door and go outside to retrieve my flip-flop. I find it in the sad garden bed—it must have fallen off when I kicked him. My cardigan is lying in a heap on the gravel—thank God for its looseness or I would never have been able to wriggle out of it.

I pick up the flip-flop and cardigan and limp back inside. My toe is already feeling better so it must only be a sprain. That's a relief. I don't want to go back to the hospital again. I carry my belongings to my bedroom and throw them on the floor. I find Milly's diary and throw it in the box—that I still haven't gone through—along with the framed photos of Shane and me from the top drawer of my dresser. I carry it all downstairs and put it on the kitchen table. I go through the kitchen drawers like a scavenger dumpster-diving for food, looking for a lighter. I finally find one and put it in my jeans pocket.

Time for a little bonfire.

A few minutes later I park my butt on the bench in my special place and set the box next to me. I should have burned all of this crap days ago, but then I would not have had the proof I needed to make Shane 'fess up to the truth. There was no other way I could have done it. I feel relief as I start taking the frames apart to gather up the photos, leaving the diary and the stuff from Penelope in the box for now. I burn the pictures one by one, cautiously holding each by a corner. It's liberating, watching the flames slowly crawl up the photos. I throw them into the fire-pit before the heat reaches my fingertips. I am feeling better and better.

Goodbye, Shane.

I don't feel a hint of sadness as I banish the last photo of us to its fiery death. I feel...powerful. Who needs someone like that in your life, anyway? I make a silent promise to be a stronger woman in grade twelve, to not let Shane take advantage of me—or any other guy, for that matter. *Screw men!*

Next I tackle Milly's diary, ripping the pages out, scrunching them into little balls, and throwing them into the fire. I light the edges of others and watch them curl and burn to ash before dropping them. It was a diary full of lies and deceit; no wonder it burns like it's in hell. In a matter of minutes the diary is reduced to smoking ashes. I'll have to dispose of the cover another way—the lock on it won't burn. I can bury it in the woods somewhere.

Now for the box of stuff. I peer inside. The top picture—the one I assume Shane was looking at on Milly's bed at the funeral, before I interrupted him—is a picture of Shane with Milly and I standing on either side of him; he has his arms over our shoulders and a big, goofy smile on his face. I'm looking straight ahead, and Milly is smiling up at him. I decide to burn this one last. It will be a final goodbye to both of them. I leave it in its frame and put it on the bench next to me.

I again look into the box. It looks like Penelope already did me the favour of taking the rest of the photos out of their frames. Maybe she thought I'd want to keep the one of the three of us on a shelf somewhere, so she left it intact. I burn more photos of Milly and me. There is a really nice one of

Sara and I that I keep, and another one of Sara and Calvin that I put aside. I need *some* photos to put back up on the dresser.

The stuffed panda-bear was a birthday gift I bought for Milly in grade nine. She loved pandas. *I don't want this thing.* It will make a nice companion to the diary cover. I hope no one finds me burying a stuffed panda and a diary cover. How would I explain that? *He died and this is his pillow...* If I was younger that would be cute, but I'm not, so it would definitely be creepy.

My sleepover pajamas are in the box as well. They have mermaids on them. I love these, they're one of my favourite pairs. I must have forgotten them at her house the last time I spent the night. I'm happy to have them back.

There is nothing else in the box so I put the pajamas back into it, along with the few pictures I chose to keep. I pick up the frame holding the picture of Shane, Milly, and I and stare at it. Now that I know the truth I can see right through Milly's smile: *Look at me. Notice me.* Shane's face looks happy. *What guy wouldn't be happy with his girlfriend and mistress under his arms?* He had it so good, didn't he? He had the cutesy-pure-lovable girlfriend who put him high up on a pedestal, *and* a slutty lover on the side to satisfy all of his dirty desires and needs. *Now look at you—you have nothing!* The thought makes me smile.

I look at my face. I'm totally oblivious to it all. *Hey, wait a minute. What's this?* There is a big thumbprint over my face. I usually would have ignored something this small, but I'm becoming very observant lately— no stone unturned. I place my thumb over the print without touching the glass. It's definitely bigger; must be Shane's. Why was his thumb over my face? I place my thumb on the glass over my face and look at the picture again. Was he covering me on purpose? If I study the photo now, it looks like a picture of a happy couple—Shane grinning at the camera and Milly beaming up at him. He was definitely covering me up.

You don't push away the people you love.

He did love her. He *was* talking about her. In a fit of anger I throw the frame into the fire-pit and the glass cracks—right between Shane and me. I scream at the photo and pick it up, cutting my hand on one of the sharp edges. I ignore the blood and pick my way through the shards to get to the photo, then tear it up and light it on fire.

Leaving the fire-pit to get a shovel from the house, I walk as far as I dare to go into the woods to bury the panda and the fluffy pink cover from Milly's diary. When I'm done, glad to be done with it all, I return to the house and lie on my bed, trying to absorb everything, trying to forget the nightmare that has been these past few weeks. I think it will be embedded in my mind forever, though. I wish there was a way I could erase the memories. I wish I'd hit my head harder in the accident.

I wish, I wish...

What will grade twelve be like? Are people going to judge me, blame me, or feel sorry for me? I hope and pray that I don't have any classes with Shane, but the school is small, so that hope is burning to nothing just like the photos did.

There's a knock at the front door. I get up to look out the window. *A police car? Oh crap, they know I caused the accident. Oh shit-shit-shit!*

I scan for Mom's car and it's not parked in the driveway. Did Shane call the cops on me after our little dispute? No, why would he? He would have more to lose than me.

I must look terrible. I dart up the stairs and into the bathroom to fix my hair and wash my hands. I must smell like smoke. I scan the counter, then spritz some perfume on. It mingles with...ugh, yes, I smell like smoke. *Way to look conspicuous.*

They knock again, louder this time. "Coming!" I shout, and run down the stairs. "Who is it?" I ask, so it doesn't look like I was spying through the window.

"It's Officer Sheldon of the NorthBerry Police Department," a deep male voice says.

I calm my shaking hands and open the door. "May I help you?" I say, and smile.

Officer Sheldon must be about six-feet tall and is one of the darkest men I have ever seen. He doesn't smile back at me. "I need to speak with a Miss Stephanie Martin," he says professionally.

"That would be me," I squeak.

Did they think I was going to put up a fight, so they sent the scariest man I have ever seen? He has no emotion on his face. I sensed a slight accent; could be Jamaican or African—I am not good with accents at all; he could be Scottish for all I know.

"We retrieved an item from the accident and I need you to identify and sign for it," he says.

No wonder he's upset. He could be crime-fighting instead of playing delivery man. I relax a bit. "Sure, I can do that."

Officer Sheldon walks to his car and comes back with a box. He pulls out a Ziploc bag.

"My cell phone!" I exclaim, relieved. "Does it work still?"

Officer Sheldon stares at me and doesn't answer.

"Um, that's okay, I can check," I say.

"Sign here." He passes me a clipboard.

I sign and take the bag from him. "Was there anything else?" I ask.

He looks over the clipboard and flips the page. I watch his eyes move back and forth as he reads over the lines. His eyes are almost as dark as his skin, which makes the whites in them very prominent. He looks up at me and I shudder.

"No, everything else was destroyed. Have a pleasant evening, Miss Martin." He smiles, which does nothing to brighten up his face. If anything, it makes him look demented.

"Th-thank you," I stutter. I wave him off as he leaves down the driveway and then I walk back into the house, locking the door behind me.

I sit on the living room sofa. It feels strange sitting in here, but I'm too eager to turn my phone on and my legs are feeling too weak to make it back up the stairs. I unzip the bag and take out the phone. I hold down the top button. Nothing happens. I hold it down again. Nothing.

Feeling frustrated, I toss the phone onto the couch beside me. I usually don't give up that easily, but it's pointless to try again. The phone is dead and I don't have a charger for it anymore. There is so much I need to replace: my cell phone—if in fact it's broken, rather than the battery being drained—makeup, clothing, car...

I need a job.

Greg's offer might still stand. If I can get a part-time job there when Mom isn't working it could possibly work out fine. I'm not babysitting again. I don't have the patience to look after kids right now, and I don't really trust myself with them at the moment. I seem to be developing a temper. I've never been physical with anyone before and now look at me:

lunging at Milly, kicking Shane, throwing and breaking things. No, I am *definitely not* babysitting.

I realize I'm going to have to take the bus to school again. "Ugh!" I exclaim. *This royally sucks.*

The front door opens, making me jump. Mom and Greg walk in, laughing. Mom looks surprised to see me.

"Hey," I say, and stand up.

"Hi Stephanie," Greg says, and gives me a wide grin.

"Hi hon," Mom says, and looks embarrassed.

"Where have you two been?" I ask.

"We went out for Chinese food; brought you leftovers," Greg says, and holds up the bag."

"Great! I'm starving," I say.

"Did Sara and Calvin get off okay?" Mom asks.

"Yeah, they did." I'm stunned that she even knows their names.

"Good," she says, and takes the food from Greg. She walks past me into the kitchen. I hear her opening the cupboard a moment later.

"Look what the police dropped off," I say to Greg, holding up the cell phone.

"Wow, they must really have nothing to do, if they took the time to come drop it off," he says.

"Yeah, that's what I was thinking," I say. "Pity, though—it doesn't work. I think the battery is dead."

"Here, let me see." He holds out his hand. I drop the phone into his palm and watch him study it. "You know, my charger might work in this phone. It looks like it uses the same plug," he says, and runs out the front door.

I watch him through the open door as he leans into his car, then turn away because I'm looking right at his ass, and it makes my cheeks heat. I leave him rummaging through his vehicle and join Mom in the kitchen, sitting down at the kitchen table until the microwave beeps. Mom brings the leftovers to the table. "Thanks," I say.

"You're very welcome," she says, and smiles at me.

Her smile warms my soul. I look down at the food, grateful that I can look down now. It smells delicious. I have chicken chow mein, sweet and sour pork, and fried rice.

Greg walks in with a grin on his face. He holds up my phone with a cord dangling out of it. "Let's see if this works," he says.

"Fingers crossed," I mumble around a mouthful of rice.

Greg plugs the charger into an outlet above the kitchen counter. He looks at the phone and holds down the power button. "Voila!" he says proudly.

"Oh my gosh, you are a lifesaver!" I crow.

"I would let it charge overnight before playing around with it," he says.

"Oh, you don't mind me hanging onto it for the night?" I ask.

"I have two: one for my car, one for home. You can have this one."

"Wow, thanks Greg!" I say. "At least I can mark that off the long list of things I need to replace."

"What else do you need, Stephanie?" Mom asks.

"Well...a car, for starters." I laugh and roll my eyes. "I think mine is beyond repair."

"Okay...what else?" she says.

"Um, makeup and clothing. All of my good stuff was in the car. The cop told me it was all destroyed. Since my cell phone was in the glove box, it survi—um, didn't break," I say.

I don't like the word "survived" anymore. It seems wrong to say it when referring to inanimate objects. People survive, objects don't. If Milly had survived I would not have said, "she didn't break," although I would have ended up breaking certain parts of her—like her nose—if she had survived.

"Well Stephanie," Mom says, breaking my train of thought, "I have the day off tomorrow; we can go to the mall. I can buy you clothing and makeup; the car will have to wait until I can afford it."

"Really?" I say disbelievingly, and tilt my head to the side. Mom and I shopping...like mother and daughter. I look toward Greg. He shrugs. "Okay..." I say, looking back at Mom. "Sounds like...fun."

"Be up and ready by ten then," she says.

"I will," I say. "Oh Greg, before I forget, Sara bought me a laptop and I have no idea how to set it up. Do you know how?"

"As a matter of fact, I do," he says. "Where is it?"

"It's on my dresser. I'll go get it."

"No, no, sit—you shouldn't be carrying heavy things yet. I'll be back in a minute." He leaves the room.

"What a guy," I say to myself.

"Yes, he's quite something," Mom says, staring after him.

"You seem really happy, Mom. It's nice to see."

"Hmm," she says, and clears my plate.

I shouldn't push the subject. I can tell she really likes him but she is still deeply in love with Dad. How does that work, anyway? You love someone your whole life; they die before you and go to heaven; you meet someone new, fall in love with them, they die, you die; when you're in heaven you're faced with two men that love you, and you love them. Who do you spend eternity with? That's something I hope I never have to face.

Greg saunters back into the kitchen with the laptop box. He looks cheerful. He has something to do now that gives him more time to spend with Mom. I'm pretty sure he was going to go home.

"This is a great laptop, Stephanie, top of the line. Your friends must really love you," he says while he opens the box and slides the laptop out.

"They do," I say, smiling. "OMG, it's pink!" I squeal.

Greg snorts and shakes his head. "Such a girl, getting so excited about the colour instead of the hardware."

"Shush, you," I say, and nudge him in the shoulder.

Greg grins and opens the laptop's lid. I slide my chair over next to him for a better view. I can't contain my excitement. It seems to take forever to power on.

"That's interesting," Greg says.

"What?" I say.

"It looks like it was already set up for you. Sara must have had that arranged. Well, that makes my job easy," he says, and winks. The screen is displaying the logon box for a password. "You wouldn't happen to know the password, would you?" Greg asks.

"No idea." I tap my finger on my chin.

"There's a hint here," Greg says, and hovers the mouse over the question mark icon.

"Who is your bestest friend in the whole wide world?" we read in unison. I roll my eyes. *Oh Sara, how I miss you already.* "Try Sara: S-A-R-A."

Greg types it in and the screen goes black for a second.

"Did I break it?" I say.

"No, it's loading," he replies.

A minute later the desktop appears. The background picture is a photo of our little group, from the trip. *How in the hell did Sara manage that?*

I look at all of our happy faces; we are sitting jam-packed in the Jacuzzi. I look happy, really happy; I look...wasted. It must have been our first night at the lake house. I don't remember getting in the Jacuzzi.

"How..."

Greg answers my unspoken question. "She must have sent the company a photo while you guys were still on the trip, and forgotten about it."

He must sense my discomfort because he shifts uncomfortably in the chair. "I can take this photo off for you if you like," he offers.

"That would be great, Greg. Thanks," I say.

Greg opens a few windows on the screen and changes the background to a picture of an orchid.

"Um, can you change that one too?" I ask.

"You don't like orchids?" he says.

"Not anymore." Milly's wooden box of secrets killed *that* flower for me.

"How about a goldfish?" he says.

"Perfect." I smile. "Thanks Greg."

"Anytime," he says. He glances at the time. "Shoot, we're going to be late for our movie!"

"You never said you guys were going to a movie; I would have asked you to set up the laptop another night. Sorry!" I say.

"It's okay, hon, we'll still make it," Mom says.

I forgot she was standing there. Or maybe she was in the other room. She *is* great at her disappearing acts. "Well, get going then," I say. "I can take over from here."

"We'll be home late, Stephanie; don't wait up," Greg says.

"Have fun!" I say as they rush out the front door. I burst into tears as the door slams shut. I didn't expect them, they just came pouring out. I'm going to need to take control of these breakdowns before school.

Seeing that photo was a shock. It was the last photo of us all together. We'll never be a group again. It was the last time we were all happy. I wish I could remember that night better. Or maybe I don't. I pull myself together and close the laptop. I unplug the charger attached to my cell phone from the wall, set it on top of the laptop, and carry it all carefully to my bedroom.

Setting the laptop on the bed, I walk over to the side table to plug in the charger. It's so nice having my cell phone back—I sure hope it works properly. I am tempted to turn it on and explore, but I should make an e-mail account to see how Sara is doing first. I retrieve the small piece of paper that she wrote her e-mail address on from the little purse I was carrying at the airport. I unfold it. *Bootylicious_songstress?* "Wow," I say, and laugh.

I sit cross-legged in front of the laptop and open the lid. It powers on faster this time. I type in the password and am greeted by the happy goldfish. He makes me smile. I connect the laptop to the wireless modem. For some reason, when we moved here the Internet was already hooked up. Since we're not paying for it, Mom didn't bother getting it turned off. I don't even think she knew about it. The only reason I did was because my cell phone would prompt me to log on to it. I never did, though. I never had reason to. Now I do.

I scan for the Internet icon. I'm not totally technologically challenged—we have some computer courses in school, not that I paid attention one hundred percent of the time, and I watched Milly use her laptop a bazillion times, so that's a plus. I look down at the bit of paper that Sara gave me and type the name of the e-mail server into the search engine. The site comes up. "That was easy," I say. "There is still hope for me after all."

I make a new account and add all of my personal details. The site prompts me for a username. *Hmm, Bootylicious_songstress is already taken—damn!* I chuckle quietly to myself and think. Why is something like picking a stupid username so hard?

What to do, what to do...

I type *what-to-do* in the space. "Taken," I read as the red letters appear at the top of the screen. "Are you serious?" *What a dumb username.*

I try *My-life-is-a-mess-and-I-am-a-horrible-person.* "Ha! That one *is* available," I say happily. *No, I can't use that.*

My brain is getting tired. I try one last thing: *I-love-charlie* and it works. *Yay!*

That took way too long. I go to the Inbox and there is one new e-mail. It's a welcome to the site e-mail. I delete it, click on the Compose button, and type in Sara's e-mail address.

Subject: Sara it's Stevie

I miss you so much already. I hope you arrived in France safely and that Calvin wasn't too much of a mess. Sorry about that. Hopefully the medication didn't turn him into a complete zombie.

I'm not sure what the time difference is there, but I assume there is one. Don't worry about writing to me straight away. You are probably jet-lagged or partying or just having the time of your life and I don't want to interrupt you guys. You better be buying me a ton of gifts. On that note, WOW, I love this laptop. Thank you so very, very much. You are seriously the BEST! I am really and truly grateful for it. I don't know what I would do if I couldn't talk to you.

I will keep this e-mail short so I don't run out of things to say. Send me a line to let me know how you are, no rush though.

I love you!

Stevie xox

I press Send and the e-mail is off to France. *Easy as pie.* I put the laptop back on the dresser.

The clock tells me that it's ten-fifteen. No wonder I'm exhausted. It's been another long day. When will my life slow down...maybe tomorrow? Shopping with Mom is going to be interesting. I am actually looking forward to it—bonding time. I'm not getting my hopes up though. It might end up being a disaster. I set the alarm for 8:00 a.m., I throw on the mermaid pajamas, and curl up in bed.

oOo

It's dark and cold. I know I'm in my bedroom—I can see the outlines of the furniture. I reach for the bedside lamp, but it's not there. I look for the glow of the alarm clock on the opposite side of the room; it's not there either. I sit up and reach down to remove the covers from my legs, but my fingers touch nothing but my bare skin. I touch my chest; I can feel the sequins on the mermaid's tail applique on the pajama shirt I put on before bed.

I am walking now to the window in the corner of the room. I don't remember standing up. I place my hand on the glass and peer out. Not even the moon is shining tonight—I can't see a thing. Something furry rubs along my leg and it makes me jump, but when I recover and look down there is nothing but the wood floor.

I hear a faint meow and turn from the window to see where the sound came from. Charlie?

I rub my eyes to force them to adjust. The bedroom door is open. It was closed a minute ago. In the glow coming from the hallway I see the silhouette of a cat sitting by the door. "Charlie, is that you?"

He purrs and pads down the hallway. All I hear are the gentle pats of his paws on the hardwood. I follow him but my footsteps are silent, which is weird, because I am so much heavier than he is.

The glow barely illuminates the staircase. All I can see is the sparkle of Charlie's eyes at the bottom of the stairs. He's waiting for me. I glide down the stairs as if they were an escalator—I can't feel the steps under my naked feet. I want to reach out and touch him, pet him, rub his furry belly one last time. I almost do, but as soon as my fingers come within one millimetre of him, he turns and bounds through the front door.

Through the door, as if he were a ghost.

I reach for the door handle and my hand passes through it. I try again with the same result—it is the strangest sensation.

I hear a meow from outside. I hold my breath, close my eyes, and jump forward. I open my eyes and I'm standing on the porch. I am so cold. I don't understand why I can't feel the ground beneath my feet, but I can feel the coldness of this black night.

Charlie wraps himself around my legs like he used to do when I made my morning coffee. He's purring fervently. I crouch down to pick him up but he runs away from me again.

"Charlie," I say after him. "Charlie, come back."

He disappears behind the weeping willow tree. I run after him, passing through the branches, over the stepping stones, and into the gazebo. There is a fire burning in the pit and Charlie is resting on my favourite spot to sit. I look at his eyes and see a reflection of the flames in them; the colours match the amber and red tones of the fire.

Without warning he leaps into the fire-pit.

"Oh God, Charlie, no!" I scream, and fall to my knees. I reach into the flames and scorch my hands. The heat radiating from the pit draws beads of

sweat to my face. Charlie is howling in agony as the fire consumes him. The howls stop for a split second. For that one split second the world is silent, as if it's been put on Pause. Then the unearthly shrieks resume—but they are no longer those of a cat burning to death, but a thousand souls boiling in a fiery pit of hell. Charlie is no longer within my reach—he has disappeared. I scream relentlessly and try to scramble away from the pit—but a hand reaches through the flames and clutches me by the wrist. I yelp and pull at the fingers, but they grip harder. They are not fingers at all! They are talons, bloodied from tearing through the flesh on my wrists, and they're holding on for dear life—my life! They want my soul.

Something changes; I can sense it in my heart and on my skin. I feel cold again. The heat from the fire has dissipated. I watch as the talons turn from claws to a normal hand. I look up to where the fire should be, and the flames are no longer flames, but auburn hair. The world around me fades away and I am not in the gazebo anymore. I am in my old car.

"Why..." I hear. "Why..."

The hand holding my wrist lets go and goes limp. My eyes travel from my wrist up the lifeless arm and stop at Milly's face—Milly's face above her harpooned neck, with blood pouring out of the gaping hole. She is staring at me and her mouth is twitching.

"Why," she gurgles as the blood bubbles from her mouth. "Why!" she screams. Eyes bulging, she reaches for me, the hole in her neck tearing wider and the blood flowing heavier.

I try to get away but I'm trapped. I can't feel my feet. I look down and my legs are gone.

A voice somewhere says, "They'll have to amputate..."

I scrunch my eyes closed and scream.

oOo

I scream myself awake. I'm sitting up on my bed with my hands gripping the duvet cover. I tear the cover away."Thank God," I breathe as I touch my legs. The sheets are drenched in sweat. I feel my pajama bottoms and they are dry—I didn't pee myself.

It was just a dream.

I'm trembling violently and my heart is beating like a drum in a punk-rock concert. Mom must have heard me screaming. There's no way I was completely quiet through *that* nightmare. I squint at the alarm clock. It's seven-fifty in the morning.

Where the hell is Mom?

I lift my cell phone from the side table and hold down the top button. *Come on, come on, please work!* "Yes!" I say as the phone comes to life. "Sixteen missed calls?" My heart begins to race and I think of all the terrible things that could have happened to Mom and Greg: car accident, murder, the cinema collapsing on them. I flick through the menus on the phone to reach the Missed Calls page. I look at the dates. These are all from the day of the accident. The missed calls are mostly from Sara, and there are a couple from Greg. My phone only allows three voice mail messages and they are full. I press the # key to get to the messages.

"*You have three new messages,*" the robotic woman-voice says cheerfully. "*Message one.*"

"*Stevie, it's Sara. Where are you guys? You should have been home an hour ago. I can't get hold of Milly. Please call me when you get this.*"

I delete the message to move on to the next one.

"*It's Sara again. Stevie, it's been hours since you should have gotten home, and we are all worried. Calvin is calling the police. Milly's phone is dead; I can't get through to her. Stevie, please call us.*"

Little did she know Milly was dead too. Hearing the panic in Sara's voice makes me feel really horrible. That message was left at 12:13 a.m. I delete the message and move to the last one.

"*Stephanie, it's Greg. It's five-thirty in the morning. The police are searching for you and Melissa. Sara called us. Denise is beside herself. Please, if you guys are fine and you're...I don't know...please just call. Call Denise—*"

The phone alarm starts up and I can't hear the rest of the message over the "Birds Singing" tone. Birds singing—they sound exactly like the ones I heard after the accident. It must have been the alarm going off. It all makes sense now. The birds singing right in my ear was just the alarm going off in the glove box. Milly must have put it in there, because I sure don't remember doing it. I change the ringtone to a boring one that I hope won't haunt me in the future. I still can't believe I survived the accident. If my alarm is set for 8:00 a.m., I was in the vehicle for over ten hours—that's a long time to be stuck in that position.

I think of Milly in the car, and the dream I had. I know the first half of it was a dream, but the end? Was that a dream, or a memory coming back to me? Was Milly alive for a couple minutes when the tree went through her? No, that would be impossible...wouldn't it? The thought makes me shiver.

I clear all of the missed calls from the phone. I don't want to remember anything about the accident from this day forward. I dial Greg's number and shut my eyes tightly. The phone rings and rings and rings. *Doesn't this guy have voice mail?*

"He-hello," Greg croaks.

"Greg, its Stevie. Are you guys okay? Where's Mom?" I ask.

"Stephanie? What time is it?" he asks.

"Greg! Come on, just answer me," I say sharply.

"She's here, Stephanie, at my place."

"*Oh?*" I say. "Why is she there?"

"The movie ran later than we thought it would so she spent the night here; it was easier than dropping her off at 2:00 a.m. You know the theatre is an hour's drive away," he says.

"Okay...well, a call would have been nice," I say indifferently.

"Sorry, my alarm must have not gone off. I did plan on dropping her off at nine for your shopping trip today."

"Well, where is she now?" I ask.

"She's in my room—wait, that sounded bad. I slept on the sofa, and gave her my bed," he says.

I laugh. "Nice save, Greg. I'll leave you two alone then."

"I'll have her home by nine-thirty, okay?"

"Sounds good. Bring coffee," I demand.

"If it puts me back on your good side then your wish is my command," he says, and chuckles.

"Oh Greg, there is nothing you could do to get on my bad side. See you at nine-thirty," I say, and hang up. I have a huge smile on my face when I leave the room to get ready for the day. Mom is safe, Greg is happy, and I get to go shopping.

CHAPTER SEVEN

I CAN'T DESCRIBE THE dread I feel today. Summer went by way faster than I could have anticipated. I don't want to go to school. But it's too late to turn around now—Mom is driving and she would never turn around anyhow, not even if I suddenly came down with a cold. I suck at playing sick.

Mom spent way more money than I think she could afford on clothing for me. She wouldn't take *no* for an answer. The day out with her was one of the best days we've ever spent together. I hate shopping, but with her it was painless. When I used to shop with Milly and Sara we would spend hours upon hours trying everything on. Mom let me pick and choose what I wanted, and I got to avoid the changing rooms. I know my size well; it's been the same for years.

I flip open the vanity mirror in the car. It's nice to be able to look at myself without cringing. The bruises are all gone, even the ones on my chest and ribs. I'm not in pain anymore *and* I am having a good hair day. *Bonus!*

I played my eyes up with a dark brown eye shadow and the blackest-black eyeliner today—Mom went all out on the makeup as well; I have an arsenal of it. It's a lot darker than I usually wear my makeup, but the effect is astonishing, in a non-gothic way. I guess I was going for the "piss off or

I might hurt you" look. I might have screwed it up and made it look slutty. Whatever the case, I look a lot different than I did leaving grade eleven. I have grown up quite a bit in these last two months.

My hair is resting just right; there are no fly-aways, and it hits my hips perfectly. I have it parted to the side and swooped over my left shoulder. I painted my nails a deep red and the top I'm wearing is a dark blood red; it's low cut and has lace on the straps and along the bustline. I bought a fabulous push up bra that makes me look like I have boobs—I can't believe it gives me cleavage. The jeans I chose to wear today are black, hip-hugging skinny jeans. I finished the first-day-of-school look off with grey, knee-high boots and a grey cardigan. All in all I think this look is more of a "fuck you, Shane, look how great I can be without you" look. I have a dark side and I am not afraid to use it. No one is going to walk all over me this year. I made that promise to myself, and I am going to keep it.

"We're here," Mom says. "Are you sure you're going to be okay?"

"I'll be fine. Thanks for the ride." I smile reassuringly. "See you later."

"Call me if you need anything," she says.

"I will." I get out of the car and wave after Mom as she drives away. I throw my head back slightly and look at the clouds. *Lord, give me strength.*

I turn and face the school. *One more year. You can do this.*

I feel vulnerable all of a sudden, not the confident person I was a minute ago. Can I really do this? Can I really face all of these people and be strong?

"Hey Stephanie," a girl behind me says.

I turn around and can't remember her name. *Big boned. Brunette... Bianca something?* "Hi," I say.

"I wanted to say sorry about Melissa. And...I'm happy you're doing well," she says.

"Thanks," I reply. "Hey, do you know what home room we have to go to?"

"Three-A," she says.

"Thanks," I say, and leave her.

I'm not here to make friends. My trust in everyone and everything is dead. I walk quickly to the front doors of the school, avoiding eye contact with everybody I pass. A few students try to get a word in with me, but I leave them open-mouthed by blatantly ignoring them. I hate being snubbed myself, but I don't want to get a million questions and apologies from people who never gave me the time of day before. I don't need their sympathy. I push my way through the doors and into main hallway of the school. The whispers begin. I do my best to disregard them and keep pushing forward toward my locker. I'm stop suddenly when I almost trip over a huge mass of flowers, notes, pictures, and students huddled around Milly's old locker.

Give me a break. If only they knew her true colours.

I can see my locker from where I'm standing but I can't get through the crowd. "Excuse me!" I say boldly. "You guys are blocking the hallway."

The girls crouched on the ground jerk their heads toward me, glaring, until they realize who asked them to move.

"Oh, Stephanie!" a girl named Chanelle says, rising. She's a short little blonde thing who comes up to my chin. She has always annoyed the shit out of me.

Little brown-nosing bitch.

"Can you guys *please* move out of the way so that people can get by?" I ask firmly.

Her two companions stand next to her and glare at me. You can tell they want to say something, but they choose to say it with their eyes instead of their mouths.

"Stephanie," Chanelle says.

I put my hand up to hush her. "Chanelle, I don't care what you have to say. Get out of my way."

"Stephanie, I can see that you are mourning and you have every right. It's *okay.*" She puts her hand on my shoulder. "You can take it out on me if you wish. I just want you to know I'm here for you if you need a shoulder to cry on. We'll be praying for you," she says super-sweetly, and removes her hand.

I want to punch her in the face. We have caught the attention of almost everyone in the hallway. I stare straight into her eyes and lean in closer to her so the only people who can hear me are her and her two sidekicks. "Get the *hell* out of my way, because if you *don't,* the only person you'll need to pray for *is you,*" I hiss.

She steps back, shocked, and I push between her and her four-foot posse. "She must have brain damage," Chanelle says. "We'll just pray harder for you, Stephanie," she shouts after me.

The crowd around me disperses and I finally reach my locker. I enter the combination. I can't believe I just said that to Chanelle. I am shocked at my boldness. If people think I have brain damage, maybe they'll leave me alone. I chuckle and shake my head as I unclick the lock and open the locker door. My smile fades. The locker is covered in photos. I forgot all about these.

The first bell rings throughout the hallway. *Shit.* I don't have time to take all this crap down. I grab my satchel and close the locker. I make my way through the scurrying students and up to home room on the third floor. I take a seat in the back, near the window and stare blankly out at the cars in the parking lot. The day is cloudy; it might rain. I am not looking forward to taking the bus home. Mom had to work today.

I wish I was working instead of sitting here. Greg said I could have a job at the art store on a trial basis, and only on the weekends he needs me. I've already worked three weekends, shadowing him. It's going to take me a long time to save up for a car.

I scan the parking lot and spot Shane's truck straight away. There are other black trucks, but his is the only one decked out with chrome rims. It's not hard to find. He will be in the same home room as me—he might already be here. I turn away from the window and look around the room. The second bell rings. Shane is nowhere to be seen. Maybe he broke his neck on the way up the stairs. I can only dream.

The chair in front of me has a big red-headed guy in it. I can see the freckles on the back of his neck. I can't see the person in front of him—he obstructs the view. Shane is taller than this guy so I would be able to see his head. The seat to my right is empty, and there is one more chair near the classroom door that is empty too. I will be *so* pissed if he comes in and sits next to me. My heart begins to race in an uncomfortable way.

"Welcome, students," Mrs. Perkins says. She's an average-looking woman in her mid-fifties. She usually teaches English. She has a large head—like a bobble head doll—and she makes it look even bigger with the bulky amount of white hair that is curled around her face. She always wears floor-length floral dresses. I think she makes them herself.

"After a short announcement from Principal Harling I will be handing out your class schedules and we will begin the year," she says cheerfully. There is a rap at the door and Mrs. Perkins puts down the paper she is holding. "Excuse me," she says, and walks to the door. She opens it a crack and peeks through. "Mr. Jakeson, tardy on the first day of school? Not a good start," she says.

It's weird hearing Shane's last name. I was so used to calling him one thing that I almost didn't know who she was talking to. It took me all of a second to figure it out, though.

"Please come in and take a seat," Mrs. Perkins says to Shane. "Principal Harling will be making an announcement shortly and I don't want any more interruptions," she says to him, then sits down at her own desk.

Shane is looking right at the empty seat next to me. He seems to be frozen in place.

"Mr. Jakeson, *please*," Mrs. Perkins says. "There is a seat *right* in front of you."

He looks at the empty chair and relief floods his face. He hastily sits down without looking my way again. I turn my attention back to Mrs. Perkins, but instead of seeing her I see Danica Evans sizing me up. I have a hard time remembering names, but hers is *not easy*—unlike her—to forget. She is the school slut, to say it matter-of-factly. She went through puberty at a very young age. It did not go unnoticed by anyone. She was blessed with curves galore, long, silky blonde hair that always has that tousled, sexy look, and an ass that could kill. I hate her. She can have any guy she wants and right now she has a sly grin on her face. She obviously saw Shane's internal struggle as clearly as I did. I can almost read her thoughts: *He's mine now, bitch.*

News travels fast, especially in a small school like this. Shane might as well have had a note on his forehead saying *Ripe for the picking*, with that look he gave me before sitting down. Usually he would never have hesitated in parking his perfect hiney in an empty seat next to me. Now I have Miss Whore-bag licking her lips in anticipation. I have no doubt she is going to dig her claws into him the first chance she gets. *You can have him!*

The intercom hisses and emits static for a second. Danica spins around to pay attention.

"Students of NorthBerry High School," Principal Harling says over the intercom. "Welcome to another year, much to your dissatisfaction."

Ha-ha. I roll my eyes and zone out through the window. Principal Harling goes on about exciting events taking place in the school, and the rugby team hopefully winning another season against the competing school from one town over—boring stuff that I tune out.

"I am sure most of you have heard of the unfortunate loss of one of our most-loved students, Melissa Shepard."

That gets my attention. I notice that a few students glance over at me—even Mrs. Perkins looks up from her desk to peep at me. She gives me a kind but sorrowful smile. Shane twitches and puts his hands over his eyes. A guy sitting behind him pats him on the back. I am grateful the guy that's sitting ahead of me is too large to turn around in the tight confines of the desk. I'm surprised he could even get into it in the first place. I'm beyond arms reach of anyone else.

"If anyone needs counselling to help you cope with this unforeseeable tragedy, please don't hesitate to see the guidance counsellor, Mrs. Phillips. Let's all have a minute of silence to remember Melissa Shepard."

I take this minute to study Shane. I slowly gaze over the tops of the bowed heads and finally meet Shane's eyes. *Shit, he's looking right at me.* He took the minute to do the exact same thing.

Our eyes lock. He actually tries to smile at me—it's a tiny smirk that only turns up the very edges of his mouth. What is that, an apology? Does he expect me to come running back into his arms? Does he think his half-assed attempt at a smile would make me fall to my knees and beg him to take me back?

Honestly. I snort out loud and look back at my desk. *What a joke.*

The minute of silence ends.

"I will call you one by one and you can come up to take your first semester's schedule," Mrs. Perkins says. She opens a binder and retrieves the schedules.

I wish my last name began with an *A*; then I would be the first to be called. Danica will leave before me so that's good; Shane will leave before me as well. *Hallelujah!*

I watch the students get up one by one to accept their class schedules. I know I'll end up with a few classes with Shane, like English and Mathematics. We'd picked what we wanted during the summer and I'd tried to choose wisely. I want to be as far away from Shane as possible if I can help it. He's predictable so I know he'll go for electives like Strength Training and Auto Tech. I just hope he never chose any of the classes I did—Drawing and Painting, Biology, Carpentry, and Foods. I picked wildly for the first half of the year.

"Miss Martin," Mrs. Perkins finally calls.

I get up and walk slowly to her desk. She hands me my schedule but doesn't release the paper when I go to pull it away.

"I'm very sorry for your loss, Stephanie," she says, looking up at me with big eyes. "I know how close you and Miss Shepard were."

"Thank you," I say.

"If you need *anything*," she offers.

"You'll be the first to know, Mrs. Perkins, Now if you don't mind I need to get to..." I look down at my schedule. "Physical Education. What the fuck—I mean sorry, there's a mistake on here." I yank the paper out of her hands.

She gapes at me, speechless. I turn and walk quickly out of the room before she can stop me. I just swore at a teacher—a little old lady—what is wrong with me? I don't have gym clothing with me, and I am definitely not working out in this outfit. I am not in the mood to go fight with the office to change the schedule. I look at the paper again. Physical Education, Mathematics, Break, Drawing and Painting, Lunch, English, and Carpentry. Then it rotates the next day: Biology, Foods, Break, English, Lunch, Mathematics, and History. I never picked History, either. Okay, History, although extremely boring and tedious, I can deal with. Physical Education is going to be a pain in the ass. I need to change that. My only option right now is skipping first period and dealing with the office during lunch—it's not like I'll have anyone to hang out with anyway.

I sneak to the girls' washroom on the second floor—which is really the first floor, because what the school calls the "first floor" is actually the basement, which is halfway underground—and hide in one of the stalls. The first bell rings, and then the second one. I have not been spotted. I silently open the stall, walk to the window and stealthily open it. There is just enough room to squeeze through. I scan the school grounds. No one in sight. This washroom is situated at the back of the school. There is a tree line about one hundred steps away from the window. *I can make it.*

I throw my satchel through the window first, then pull myself through. I slither down like I'm going headfirst down a park slide to the ground. I do a weird handstand and realize I am staring right into the library. I am upside down though, and I can see the school librarian at her desk. *Shit, shit, shit.*

My arms begin to ache as they hold up my entire body weight. My wrists get weak and I fall to the ground, landing on my side—so much for being graceful—and get up as fast as I can to bolt across the field and into the forest. Once I think I'm at a safe distance and I'm concealed by the trees, I dust the dirt from my hands and jeans and let out a sigh of relief.

Now what?

I have about forty-five minutes to kill before going back in for Mathematics. I'm not looking forward to seeing Mr. Clarke again, especially after our last incident, and Shane will be in that class as well. "Oh, joy," I say to myself.

It's peaceful in the woods. I make myself comfortable on a fallen tree. This might work as a hiding spot so I won't be deemed a loner in the cafeteria. I could eat here every day, even if it's raining—the trees do a pretty good job at stopping the droplets. I lay along the log with the satchel under my head and stare up at the rays of light shining through the leaves and branches. I hear a bird singing a cheerful song in the distance. It is the first day of school and I have already had a confrontation with the four-foot posse, I swore at a teacher, *and* I skipped my first class. *I am on a roll.*

The warning bell rings in the distance, just when I'd started to doze off. I push myself off the log and stretch my limbs, then pick up my bag and walk briskly across the field toward the school. There are six minute intervals between each class so you have time to go to your locker and get the books you'll need for the next period. I slow my pace once I get back into the school. I don't want to be the first one in the room because that would give Mr. Ostrich a chance to make small talk with me. Is there any point calling him Mr. *Ostrich* now? I have no one to laugh about it with, no one to gossip to, and no one has my back—Milly did have her good qualities.

I walk slowly past Milly's locker with its memorial. So many people loved her; even now there are a couple of students nearby holding back tears. I don't understand. I never saw her talking to any of these people, but then again, I did not know her as well as I thought I did.

I manage to sneak all the way to the third floor unnoticed—or I just wasn't paying attention—and blend in with a small group walking into the same room. There is an open desk at the back of the room against the window, and I am thankful for it. I walk over to it and am about to sit down when an immaculately manicured hand slaps the desk, halting me. I don't understand how girls can do anything with such long nails. The only thing I can see them being good for are back scratches and picking your nose. I look up the dainty wrist, past the many chunky bangles, and into Danica's face.

What now?

Danica is staring at me with a devious look in her eyes.

"What do you want, Danica," I say coldly.

The corner of her mouth twitches into a crafty half smile. "It's true, isn't it?" she says.

"What?"

"You and Shane broke up?" She raises her eyebrow.

"What difference does it make to you?" I say.

Danica giggles, rolls her eyes to the side, and twists her fingers through a strand of hair. She looks back at me and bites her lip.

Man, she's good. I try not to scowl at her. "If it's permission you're asking for, you don't need it," I say, and drop my bag down on the seat to claim my desk.

"Oh Stephanie, silly girl, I don't need your permission. I can have anyone I want. I just wanted to make sure you wouldn't get in my way," she says, and smiles brightly at me.

You fake bitch! I know exactly what she's doing. From the corner of my eye I can see Mr. Clarke studying us, and I can see Shane, seated on the opposite side of the class at the back of the room, also watching us. She's trying to make it look like she's having a friendly conversation with me, when in actuality she's trying to make me lose my temper with her. Her main goal is obviously to make herself look like a good person, and make me look bad.

Two can play at this game. I pull her in for a hug, which totally throws her off, but she accepts it. I put my mouth to her right ear—the side of her head that neither Mr. Clarke nor Shane can see. "Danica, you can have him. You two deserve each other," I say, and pull back from her. I hold her by the shoulders and smile devilishly at her.

Danica stumbles backward then turns and walks to the front of the class. She sits down and turns her head to the side to look at me. She looks confused. That was not the response she was hoping for. She's the kind of girl who basks in other girls' misfortune. She loves the thrill of stealing boyfriends—her and Milly had something in common.

I remember last year when she stole Chanelle's boyfriend, Travis. Chanelle—like me—is a virgin. Her boyfriend and her are both very churchy, do-gooder types. "God's match," Chanelle used to say. Danica tainted that big-time. Travis and Danica were caught in the girls' locker room—Danica on her knees, Travis on his feet; you get the picture. I have no idea how she didn't get suspended from school—maybe she was screwing the principal too. Travis, on the other hand, was sent to an all-boys Christian school a province over. His parents were less than thrilled that he tarnished their righteous images. Apparently Chanelle knew they were hooking up, or at least that was what she told everyone. She was trying to "fix" him; she said he had a sex addiction or some crap. It was too late, though; after Travis got caught in that embarrassing moment, there was nothing Chanelle could do to keep him in the same school. Chanelle still tells everyone she's standing by him, that she never lost faith in him, and he is a changed man. Whatever. I know in my heart that people don't change. Not fully.

"Miss Martin," Mr. Clarke says.

I am jolted to the present. I didn't realize I had totally zoned out. I'm standing staring blankly out the window. Class has started and everyone is looking at me. I didn't even hear the second bell.

"Can you please take a seat," he says, and raises his eyebrows.

"Yeah—I mean—yes...sorry," I say, and sit down. *How long was I standing there for?*

"Miss Martin, if you will please see me after class," he says, and turns to face the blackboard.

I bite my inner cheek to stop myself from screaming. I look down at my notebook and doodle.

Despite my boredom, class is over before I know it. I blanked the whole thing out. I wait for everyone to leave before I stand. What could Mr. Clarke possibly want now? There is a fifteen minute break following this class and the last thing I wanted to do was spend it here with *him. Gross.*

Mr. Clarke closes the classroom door and heads toward me. "Take a seat," he says, and sits down at the desk next to mine.

I do as I'm told. "Did I do something wrong?" I ask.

"No Stephanie, I just noticed that you are a bit distracted today. What's going on?"

Like you care. Aloud I say sarcastically, "Well if you haven't heard, my best friend died, *remember*? So excuse me if I *seem* a bit *distracted.*"

"I don't appreciate your tone, *Stephanie*," he sneers. "If it was up to me I would send you to the office, but I think detention will suffice."

"No, it will not *suffice,* because I will not be staying here for detention. You can send me to the office instead," I say confidently, and stand up.

"Sit down, Miss Martin," he demands.

"Oh, back to Miss Martin now?" I say boldly, and loom over him. Mr. Clarke's face turns bright red. "Take it up with Principal Harling. I'm sure you'll find that they are not going to do *anything* about it. After all, *my best friend died.* I watched her bleed to death in the seat next to me. So if you think about that, and what I went through, maybe you will *think twice* before threatening me with detention. It's pity Stevie week, haven't you heard?"

Mr. Clarke's clenching his teeth so hard, it looks like his jaw's going to crack into a hundred pieces. I turn on my heel and leave the room. The door is locked when I reach it. That strikes me as odd. It locks from the inside so I have no problem unlocking it. Why would he lock it? My heart is pounding in my chest and I feel shaky about what I just did. I'm not going to get away with this act forever. Eventually people are going to stop pitying me and expect me to get over it. Little do they know I *am* over it; Milly being dead doesn't weigh on my shoulders.

I make Art class just in time and enjoy the period—I get to doodle some more and not get disciplined for being "distracted." Mr. Clarke will, with any luck, back off a bit now. My heart still feels like it will leap out of my chest when I recall how impolite I was to him. But really, what can he do?

I roll my eyes as the lunch bell rings. *Locker re-haul time.* I am not looking forward to this. My locker is on the second floor and Shane's is on the third floor. I used to hate that we were so far away from each other, but now it's fortunate that we are.

I pull a trash can along the hallway to my locker and set it next to me. I enter the combination, take a couple of you-can-do-this breaths, and open the locker door. There are a few students here and there, but most are in the cafeteria, so there won't be any prying questions about what I'm doing. And I'm avoiding the cafeteria from now on. I'll pack a lunch. Unfortunately I forgot to today, because I'm quite hungry; being mean to people sure works up an appetite.

I start at the top of the locker door, peeling off photos and dropping them into the garbage can. The only one I want to keep is a photo of Charlie; he's my strength, and his cute little furry face is the only thing that makes me smile. I peel off the photos of Shane and me, the ones of Milly and me, even the photos of Sara and Calvin—when I see Sara I think of Shane, and get angry. I need calmness at school. Today is definitely proof of that. I've been going bat-shit crazy on everyone who crosses my path. When I'm done I regard my locker. The door holds a photo of Charlie and a makeup mirror. *There, that's better. What more does a girl need.*

"What are you doing?" Shane says from behind me.

I didn't hear him sneak up on me. I spin around to look at him. He's holding the photos I've just thrown in the bin. How did I not hear him rummaging through the garbage to retrieve them? I was too much into my own world.

He's looking down at the photos in confusion and sorrow. "So that's it?" Shane asks, looking up and searching my eyes. "You're giving up on us?"

"What did you expect, Shane?" I say, fighting the urge to cry, or worse, get angry.

"I don't know," he says, and holds his empty hand to his forehead. He shakes his head slightly, as if he's suddenly developed a headache. "I guess I just thought, once school started, we could go back to the way things were. I miss you, Stevie. I don't have anyone. I realized a lot the day after I took you home from the airport." He drops his hand from his head and flips through the photos. "I want us to go back to being like this." He holds up the photos of us hugging. "Please give me another chance," he begs, and looks at me with puppy-dog eyes.

Usually that would make me melt—actually, I'm having a hard time fighting the urge to drop to my knees and grovel for him to take me back— but I'm stronger than that. I will fight tooth and nail to keep my promise: *be a stronger woman; don't let Shane take advantage of you.*

"Shane...I can't do this," I say softly. I don't want to make him as angry as he was a month ago.

"Please, Stevie, I've changed. I promise you that. I'll never do anything to hurt you," he says desperately, pulling at my heart strings. "Stevie, I love you." He pulls me in for a hug. He holds me tightly, but I leave my arms limp at his sides. I am not reciprocating, because if I do he'll have false hope. He pulls away and holds me at arm's length. "What do I have to do, Stevie? What can I do to make you take me back? Do I have to beg on my knees?" He picks up my limp hands and holds them.

"Fine, I'll beg on my knees!" he shouts, which gets the attention of a group of students that are hunkered down near their lockers.

Fuck! "Shane, please don't," I say calmly, but inside I'm shrieking.

"No Stevie, you have to see how much I love and need you," he says loudly, and kneels in front of me without letting go of my hands.

"Get *up*, Shane!" I say firmly, but he doesn't budge. *Oh God, what do I do?*

We have caught the attention of quite an audience. This is not how I wanted my lunch break to go. What other harsh thing can I add to the "I'm crazy; leave me alone" list for today? I can't believe he is the one grovelling. I never expected this. I thought I made it pretty clear the last time we were together that I wanted *nothing* to do with him.

"Shane, let go of me," I say.

"Never, never again, Stevie," Shane says, holding my hands tightly.

This is so humiliating.

Humiliating. Yes. If someone is extremely humiliated, the first thing they would want to do is run and duck for cover. How can I embarrass Shane enough to leave me the hell alone?

"Shane!" I say loudly so that everyone can hear. I notice people peering at us from all corners now. "Shane—*I. Don't. Love you!* Now get off of me!" I push him away with more force than I intended. He tumbles back onto his rear.

Yup, that should do it.

Various emotions flood his face. Shock is the first one, then humiliation as he realizes we're being watched; embarrassment follows, then anger. And worst of all, his pride is wounded.

I went too far, even I realize that. I didn't have to push him. I was just so angry. I just want to be left alone. Can't anyone see that?

Shane wobbles to his feet and gives me a hostile look. Now it's my turn to cower. He leans into my ear like I did to Danica. "You are going to regret that," he whispers, then walks away.

I look from face to shocked face. The hallway goes from dead quiet to laughter and snickers and whispers—back to normal. They don't dare come up to me and offer compassion or a friendly shoulder after what they just witnessed. The only person getting that will be Shane. If anything I will be getting dirty looks until we graduate. I will be left alone—I got what I wished for.

oOo

The rest of the week goes by smoothly. Shane skips English class on Monday, so I don't have to deal with him right after our confrontation, and he pretty much pretends I don't exist for the rest of the week. I think I feel him watching me a few times, but every time I look over he's doing something else. My mind is playing tricks on me. I don't get called into the office to be reamed out for being disrespectful to Mr. Clarke or swearing at Mrs. Perkins, so that's a plus. Mr. Clarke doesn't ask me questions in class, and when he's doing attendance he stumbles over my name—which thankfully is back to "Miss Martin." I hate it when he calls me Stephanie. Teachers should not have that right. I would never call him by his first name—even if I knew what it was.

I can't get switched from Physical Education. I tried my hardest and they refused. So I played a different card—the sympathy card: "Please, I don't have it in me to have P.E. every second day. I'm still recovering from the accident. I shouldn't really be pushing myself—I could reinjure my ribs." That got them. I weaseled my way into getting a free period, under one condition: I spend it in the library. I'll take that. I'll be happy to slack off in the library every second morning.

The remainder of the week goes by so effortlessly after that first day from hell; quite pleasantly, in fact. I'm left alone; I have lunch in the woods by myself, no one talks to me in class. I'm a ghost in the hallways and a recluse on the school bus to and from school. And now it's Saturday and I'm enjoying a cup of coffee in my special place. I have to be at Greg's Fine

Art Supplies in an hour. I'm working the afternoon shift today. It's nice to keep busy. I find my mind wanders too much when I have the time to let it.

I have been writing to Sara once a week. She replies to almost half of everything I write to her. She and Calvin are having a good time. She is already homesick, though. I tell her there is nothing worth missing here right now, and she always replies, "There's you," which makes me smile, but it also makes me sad. I do miss her a lot, but I know that even if she did end her trip early and come home, things between us would not be the same. I could never be around her family or hang out at their house. She would have to pick sides between Shane and I, and I would never expect her to pick mine. Shane is her brother and the saying is true—blood is thicker than water.

Right now we have it good; I can keep pretending that things are going wonderfully with me and I'm doing okay—I can write whatever I want to her and she can't see the emotions on my face that give the lies away. I lie to her so she doesn't have to worry about me. I want her to have an amazing time wherever she is. It would be unfair to lay so many burdens on her. I can't talk badly about her brother, either, and I can't tell her everything I know about what happened between Shane and Milly. I'm not like that. It would be unfair for me to stain the good memory she has of Milly. No one deserves to feel hate for someone they once loved. It's not my place to say anything.

Sara didn't even know that Shane and I broke up until I told her. He has not said a word to her which is crazy, because I know they talk all the time. They are very close. She was mortified when she found out, but she understood. She said I should give it time and that things will fall into place; that maybe we just need some distance for now and it will all work out in the end—the usual things a friend would say to another friend. She also said that Shane talks about me all the time, as if we were still together. That scares me, but he could also be doing what I am: making Sara happy so she enjoys her trip, by giving her hope that everything is fine at home. It's something a brother would do. At least that's what I tell myself.

I've been paranoid every night since Monday. His threat is always playing in the back of my mind. I have been trying to watch my back at school. I've made sure the front door and kitchen door are locked every night at home, that the windows are shut tightly and the curtains are drawn in my room. I think it was an empty threat—the only thing that helps me sleep at night is telling myself that before bed.

A honk from the driveway makes me twitch; I recognize it as Mom's car. She did the morning shift at the art store and she is taking me to work for the afternoon shift with Greg. Greg has been working overtime lately. I believe he wants to open another bigger store a few towns over. I have not asked too much about it. I go to work, do what is needed, and come home. I don't get involved in business matters.

I walk up to Mom's silver Toyota Camry and she has a smile on her face. She is always smiling lately. I have Greg to thank for that. "Hi Mom," I say as I get into the car.

"Hi," she says, all bubbly.

"You're sure chipper today," I say, and grin at her.

She smiles at me and drives down the driveway.

"So are you going to tell me what's going on or do I have to beg?" I ask as we get close to the art store.

"Oh, sorry honey, of course," she says. "I'll let Greg tell you though, so wait until we get to the store."

"*Okay...*" I frown. *Are they getting married or something?*

Mom walks with me into the store and Greg is waiting like a kid hopped up on Halloween candy. He is almost bouncing with excitement.

"Hey Greg!" I say.

"Hi Stephanie. I have some great news!" he says.

"Yes, I can tell—you and Mom both look excited about something," I say.

"We got approved to open another art store in St. Chalmers. Denise and I are going to be business partners. We're going into this together!" he says ecstatically.

I look over at Mom and she is beaming with joy. "That's like a four hour drive away," I say. "Don't get me wrong, I am so happy for the both of you—this is huge—but what about this store?"

"Greg is keeping this store as well. For now, that is. This is not a fast process, Stephanie. It'll take at least a year before it's up and running," Mom says.

"You will have a chance to finish high school," Greg chimes in. "And then we will be selling this store and we'll all move to St. Chalmers together. There is a great college there."

"It will be a new start for all of us," Mom says, and walks over to Greg. She puts her arm around his waist.

"Wow," I say. "Just...wow. This is a lot to take in."

"Take all the time you need. Well, take a year and figure it out, but I honestly think it will be the best thing for all of us," Greg says, and pulls Mom in for a kiss on the cheek.

"So you guys are...together now, I take it?"

"Yes. We have been for a while, Stephanie," Moms says. "With everything that happened over the summer we didn't want to throw more fuel on the fire so to speak, but Greg and I are happy. I am happy. It doesn't mean I have forgotten about your father. This is what he would have wanted," she says, but a shadow crosses her eyes.

Dad would turn over in his grave if he saw her with another man.

"I am so happy for you guys," I say, and smile brightly. Which is honest; I am thrilled for them. They make one of the cutest couples. It's been years since Dad died. Mom deserves happiness. Why should she be alone for the rest of her life?

"And Stephanie," Greg says, "I need you to work next weekend alone. Think you can handle it?"

"Sure, but why?" I ask.

"There are some final touches in the contract that we have to go through, and both Denise and I have to be there for it, so we thought, hey, why not make a weekend out of it. Do you think you'll be fine to open and close the shop next Saturday and Sunday?"

"I'll need a key, but yes, you can count in me," I say.

"Great, then—it's settled!" Greg says.

I smile at the both of them, and walk to the storage room. I need some air. Not that the storage room has any—it's more like a closet than a room, and it's muggy—but I couldn't very well walk outside, that would be too obvious. I pull the string that hangs from the ceiling to turn on the light, and close the door behind me.

Moving, going into business together, college...

I should be happier, but I'm not. St. Chalmers is four hours away. That is four hours away from Shane and away from all of the bad memories. I should be jumping for joy at the thought of leaving this place. What is wrong with me? I wonder if we can take the gazebo with us. I wonder if there will be another special place I can hide in to have morning coffee, a place to free my thoughts. That's why I don't want to leave. I have a weird attachment to that damned gazebo. That was the last place I saw Charlie—one of my only happy memories. What if we move and Charlie comes back? Where will he go, who will look after him?

Deal with that when the time comes.

There really is no point in me freaking out about this all now. A year is a long way away. So much can happen in that time. If life can change drastically in a few months, imagine an entire year. And seeing Mom so happy—I can't be the one to put a stop to that; that would be selfish of me. I've done enough selfish things to last me two lifetimes.

"Stephanie, we have customers," Greg says through the storage room door.

"Be right there," I say.

"Everything okay in there?" he asks.

"Yup, just noticed we were running low on those little angle brushes so thought I would grab a few," I lie.

"Okay, well, hurry it up," he says lightly.

I grab a handful of paint brushes and walk out of the storage room. I put them in a jar on the counter. Greg is helping an older couple pick out a canvas. I desperately need to do some research on art supplies. I wing it most of the time. Without Greg here next weekend I won't have someone to answer my million questions. I don't want to let him down.

I walk behind the counter and put my access code into the computer. The older couple pay for their canvas and even purchase a few brushes from the jar I put out. I grin at Greg as they leave. "Impulse items," I say, and wiggle my eyebrows at him.

"Good thinking!" Greg says, and laughs. "So are you really fine to watch the shop next weekend?"

"Yes...I mean, I am a little nervous; it's a lot of responsibility. I'll try not burn the place down while you're gone," I say.

"If you do we have insurance, but try not to," he says.

"I'm really happy for you guys," I tell him.

"I know you are."

oOo

I am always more cheerful after working a weekend with Greg. He makes it fun, and doesn't seem like a boss to me. I feel really good because every day I work, I am that much closer to getting a car. I can't handle riding the bus to school. The kids will go out of their way to not sit next to me. Like this morning—the bus is full but I have enough room for two skinny students or one bigger one to sit next to me, but no, they choose to stand, or sit on their friends' laps. It's not like I bite, or someone that stinks. *Whatever. It's what I wanted...to be invisible.*

I splurged a little yesterday and bought an mp3 player. It's small enough to fit in my pocket. I filled it up with a mixture of different songs. I never listen to the radio so I don't entirely know what's popular, but who cares—it's not like I'll be sharing my music with anyone. I turn the volume up as loud as my ears can handle without bursting an eardrum, and close my eyes. The bus ride is about twenty-five minutes every morning and afternoon. Instead of spending that time listening to gossip about who is dating who, what chick is getting fat, or how much people miss Milly, I can tune it all out and focus on other things—like getting through another week.

CHAPTER EIGHT

I WALK ALONG THE school hallway without interruption, go down the stairs without a sideways glance from anyone, and into the library with no questions asked. I greet Miss Tinsley, the school librarian, and walk to a small row of computers that are out of sight from her. The computers are limited in what you can do on them; you can't check e-mail, go on social network sites, or look up pornography, for instance, which is good, because what kind of freak would do *that* in school? Not this freak.

I settle down and start researching different art supplies. After ten minutes I am bored. I tap the desk lightly with my finger. Miss Tinsley is stacking books on different shelves. I'm all out of options for things to look up. I wish I could log onto my e-mail account and spend this time writing to Sara. I wonder what she's doing at this moment. I decide to research Paris. It will give me something to write about in the next e-mail I send to her.

I am deeply focused on the task when I hear whispers behind me. I twist around to have a peek and see Miss Tinsley talking to one of Shane's rugby friends, Jared. What could he possibly want from the library? I roll my eyes and turn back to the computer. I don't flinch or look over when Miss Tinsley brings him to the seat right next to me. She helps him log onto the computer.

"Thank you, Sharon," he says.

Sharon... Since when are students on a first name basis with teachers? Maybe this is a new thing that I am not aware of. I take a peek at the two of them. Jared is smiling charismatically at her and you can tell she is trying *really* hard not to blush; she conceals it by walking away quickly with her head bowed down. I hear her wheeling the book cart down one of the aisles a few moments later. I sigh and return to my research.

Jared types ferociously on the keyboard. I wish he'd sit somewhere else; the sound is annoying me. I bite my inner cheek to stop myself from telling him to calm down; the keyboard works fine with gentle taps. The sound seems to get louder and louder.

TAP-TAP-TAP-CLICK-TAP-TAP-TAP.

It's driving me mental.

CLICK-TAP-TAP-CLICK-TAP-TAP-TAP.

Maybe he is purposely trying to annoy me. I know how these guys work. He is one of Shane's best friends. Being an ex-girlfriend to someone so popular has just about as many pitfalls as being the girlfriend of a cheater. Both situations will make you miserable.

TAP-TAP-TAP—

I slap the desk between us which makes him stop typing in mid-word and almost fall off his seat. Miss Tinsley clears her throat as a warning to be quiet.

"What did you do that for?" he whispers to me.

"Oh, I'm sorry—was that *annoying*?" I say sarcastically, and glare at him. *Calm down, Stevie,* I admonish myself.

"Yes, a little, actually," he says. "Do you mind not doing that again?"

"Only if you stop torturing that keyboard," I say, and stare down at his hands, hovering above the keys. I look back up to his eyes, raise my eyebrows, and wait for a response.

"Sorry," he says.

That catches me off guard, this tall Greek god of a guy saying sorry to me. I study his face. He has olive skin, dark brown hair that looks almost black, dark brown eyes, and a scattering of light freckles across his nose. He has that complexion that keeps a tan all year long without ever going into the sun to replenish it. Milly dated him for a few weeks, then decided he wasn't her type. *He is everyone's type.* I think our school has one of the hottest rugby teams on the planet.

"Hmm," I say, and look back at my screen. It's hard tearing my gaze off of him. He is nice to look at, but I am not like Milly, I don't ogle friends' ex-boyfriends, no matter how short-lived their relationship was, or how dead she is now.

"You planning a trip to France?" Jared asks.

I turn my head to answer him and my lips brush his cheek. I hadn't noticed him leaning in so close to my face, being nosey. I place my hand on his bicep—which feels like a rock—and gently push him back. The wheels on his chair squeak under the pressure of his weight. He is not fat or anything, just pure muscle. Perhaps he couldn't help banging on the keyboard so hard after all.

"No, I'm not," I say.

"So why you looking it up?" Jared asks.

"Not that it's *any* of your business—Shane's sister Sara and her boy-friend Calvin are there right now, so I wanted to look up places that they might visit so I know what she's referring to when we write to each other."

"You still talk to Sara?" His eyebrows crease together in confusion.

"Yes, why wouldn't I? We are still friends."

"But you and Shane are broken up."

"*So?* Why should that stop me from talking to Sara?" I say irritably.

"I dunno, it's just weird, is all."

All muscle, no brains. It's like talking to a child: "*But why, Mom, but why?*"

"Are you done with the Q and A?" I say.

"Yeah," he says.

"Good." I exhale heavily. I can't take sitting here any longer. I take my cell phone out of the side pocket of my bag to check the time. I still have twenty minutes to kill before Mathematics. I log off of the computer and stand. There has to be a corner in this library where I can hide and read a book or something.

"Hey, Stevie," Jared says, halting my escape.

"Yeah?"

"I'm having a sick pool party this Sunday. My folks are leaving for Palm Springs early Sunday morning and I have the place to myself for a few days. You're invited," he says, and flashes a perfect, straight-white-toothed grin at me.

"Well, thanks for the invite, but I have to pass. My mother is leaving for the weekend and I have to work. Maybe next time," I say, and force a smile.

"Yeah, maybe," Jared says, looking slightly wounded.

Your charms have no magic on me, buddy.

I walk to the fantasy section of the library. No jock would ever be caught dead here, so I feel safe. I sit on the floor and grab a random book to look busy. I flip through the pages pretending to read, but my mind is focused elsewhere. How could Jared expect me to go to a house party, and what was up with the nosing about in my business? *Very odd.*

Could Shane have put him up to it? He could want to see where he stands in my life without directly asking me. There is no way in hell I am going to that party. I don't want to give Shane any opportunity to catch me alone. Shivers run up my spine at the thought.

The school day ends like every other one, except for a sliver in my finger from woodwork class that is being a pain. It will have to wait until I get home and find some tweezers. I walk to my locker to sort out a few books and binders that I'll need to take home for homework.

"Hey, buddy!" a guy shouts from down the hall.

I peer around the open locker door and see Jared run up to Shane; he punches him playfully in the shoulder. I spot Danica putting on her best slutty act to get their attention, but they are discussing something that I can't hear. She creeps in closer to eavesdrop. I see a wily grin creep over Shane's face and he nods. I have the uncanny feeling that Jared is telling him about our conversation in the library this morning. Danica sees me and elbows Jared in the side, which answers my suspicions, because both men shoot a look in my direction. I slam the locker door closed before they have the chance to say or do anything. Danica's cackling laughter follows me as I ram through the front doors of the school.

I run to the school bus and climb aboard. The bus is almost full except for a seat in the back. I always sit there and it's always empty, either by coincidence or because no one wants to sit there because of me. *Maybe it has cooties.* I snigger.

As I said before, news travels fast in this little school: news of me being a bitch, pushing Shane, maybe even telling off Mr. Clarke. I'm sure teachers talk to each other, and since some teachers are obviously on a first name basis—like *Sharon* and Jared—with students that news would be told and passed on, and so forth and so on. I don't let it get to me. I'll be done with all of this drama soon. Moving to St. Chalmers is looking more and more like the solution to my problems. It might be nice to have a fresh start after all. I could make decent friends who will never stab me in the back. I could even find a nice guy.

No! No men.

I have too much healing to do before I can ever put my trust into another relationship. For that matter, I won't be looking for friends, either. *Screw them all.*

The bus comes to a halt on my road. I gather my bag full of homework and depart. I am the only one at our school who lives here. This road is usually the last stop of the day and first stop in the morning. Most of the students that go to NorthBerry High are wealthy. They live in the same area as Shane. I'm glad no one is on the bus when I get dropped off or picked up. It saves me the embarrassment of living on a farm road. I always felt inadequate dating Shane; it never fully felt right. His family is so put together and wealthy and mine is, well...half missing and living paycheque to paycheque. I don't have to worry about that now, though, since we're not together. I can be who I want and I don't have to try so hard to fit in with a crowd that I didn't belong to in the first place.

I throw my bag on to the kitchen table and turn on the coffee machine, then run up to the bathroom to find a pair of tweezers. I can't find any. Mom probably has some in the medicine cabinet in her bathroom. She's not home so I feel safe going into her room. I walk a few steps down the hall and open her bedroom door. It always feels so cold in here. It's not from lack of heat, either, because the furnace is on. The room always feels eerie to me.

I walk briskly across the room and into the en suite. I open the medicine cabinet above the sink—I hate these things; I tend to shut my eyes when I close the mirrored door because I always expect some kind of monster to be standing behind me when the door swings shut.

I survey the interior. Mom could open her own pharmacy with the amount of medication she has in here: sleeping pills, antidepressants, anti-anxiety medication, and more. I rummage through the three shelves and finally find a small pair of black tweezers. I make sure to put the pill bottles back where they belong; Mom would have a fit if she knew I'd gone through her cabinet. I squeeze my eyes shut and close the cabinet door, then turn and leave the bathroom without looking behind me.

In my room, I put the laptop on my bed and while I'm waiting for it to power on, I turn on the lamp on the side table for more light and turn my attention to the sliver in my finger. "Gotcha, you little bugger," I say to the sliver firmly gripped between the tweezers. I blow it away and put the tweezers on the side table. The laptop is on now and I can smell the heady aroma of coffee floating up the stairs.

I quickly log on and check to see if Sara has replied to the last e-mail I sent. No new emails. *Boo.* I was looking forward to some normalcy. There is nothing else of interest on the laptop so I close the lid and change into black sweatpants and a t-shirt with *Fabulous* splashed across the breast in silver italics. I wish I felt fabulous. I need a shirt that says *Lousy* or *Loser*; that would be more fitting for my present state of mind.

I walk to the kitchen and make and extra-large cup of coffee. I need it to get through the heap of homework I have to finish before tomorrow. I check my cell phone out of habit. No missed calls. No new text messages. *No surprise there.* I scowl at the phone, put it on the table next to me, and stare blankly at the English assignment.

We have to write a poem? What is this, creative writing? What the hell am I supposed to write about? I stare up at the ceiling. My mind is empty—emptier than empty; it's a hollow cavern of nothingness. *Hmm, that's actually not that bad.*

Usually I think poetry is written about something happy. That's usually the garbage the girls in class write. I don't feel happy at all. I don't want to write about love. I don't feel loved. I feel lost and lonely, hateful and ashamed.

I put pen to paper and start writing:

> Hate wanders through the uncharted forest of our lives.
> Sharp points of a thousand knives.
> Desperation, wanting, hurt and pain,
> Symptoms of a heart that only feels shame.
> Farther into the forest I crawl on bloody hands and knees.

I look up for a moment to the weeping trees.
Pity, longing, and jealousy
Is what the trees think, looking at me.
They can't raise their limbs out of the dirt,
There is no escape from being rooted in hurt.
This is no ordinary forest to start.
It's the dark, dark forest of my heart.

I sit back and examine the result. *Holy crap, where did that come from?*

I have never been a good writer, but that sounds good even to me. This whole sad, depressed state I'm in might actually work in my favour.

I make a celebratory second cup of coffee and take that along with my good mood upstairs to my bedroom. I put the coffee mug on the dresser and turn to pick out an outfit to wear to school tomorrow.

I'm *still* sleeping badly every night—I toss and turn most nights and when I do fall asleep I have horrible nightmares; it's becoming the norm. My internal clock is all screwed up. I find I manage to fall asleep—full, dead to the world sleep—around 4:00 a.m., and then when I wake up to get ready for school I'm a complete zombie. Picking out things to wear in the morning is a sure way for me to look dreadful and not put together. I now take a few moments in the afternoon to pick my next day's outfit.

I walk to the closet and swing the door open. For a split second I think I see someone standing in the doorway of my room in the mirror that's attached to the inside of the closet door. I whirl to stare through the bedroom doorway and into the bathroom across the hall.

There is no one there.

Great, I'm going to have to start closing my eyes when I open my closet now, too. I shiver with a chill but it passes quickly. Just my imagination playing tricks on me. The front door was locked when I got home and I locked it when I came inside. Mom's at work with Greg and what I thought I saw was not dark enough to be Shane. He's the only one ballsy enough to come here, and I don't think he would after I threatened to call the police if he did. It was only a glimpse; it could have been my own shadow scaring me. I laugh it off and get back to choosing tomorrow's outfit.

The weather has been getting chillier with winter's slow approach. It's too nippy for anyone else to wear shorts to school and I don't want to look like I'm trying too hard, even though all the walking up my long driveway every day sure is working its magic on toning my backside. It's almost as hard as Jared's biceps. Those were nice.

Focus, Stevie!

Shorts are out of the question. I find a pale pink, three-quarter sleeve, knee-length dress. It's made out of cotton and feels as soft as a well-worn t-shirt. It's tight fitting and not ideally warm, but warm enough. My legs never seem to get cold anymore; I think because I've felt what freezing really is. I select a black belt and the black ballet flats I wore to Milly's funeral—why let good shoes go to waste? I hang the dress on the closet door and place the shoes under it. I take a step back and visualise myself in the outfit. *That will do.*

There's a creak somewhere down the hallway.

I face the door and brace myself. I never heard Mom's car tires on the gravel driveway. I sneak to the window and look out. No car in sight.

Another creak in the hallway. Closer this time.

My heart beats like a bongo drum. Whatever is in the house is getting closer. I look inside the closet for a weapon. This is when I wish I wore stilettos; those would come in handy right now. I creep over to the bookcase and pull out one of the thickest books I have: the *New Testament.*

Seems kind of ludicrous, no? Beating someone to death with a Bible...

Shut up, brain!

I take one quiet step after another toward the door, the Bible clutched in both hands like a baseball bat I'm preparing to swing. I stop near the door, out of sight from the hallway, and take a deep, silent breath.

I hear footsteps getting closer and closer, stealthy steps, tiptoeing to be silent. Hoping the element of surprise will work, I brace myself and lunge into the hallway. "*HI-YA!*" I scream as I swing the Bible with all my force in the direction of the creaking floorboards.

Mom tumbles backward, barely missed by the blow.

"Oh shit, Mom!" I shriek, and drop the Bible to grasp for her hand.

"Stephanie, *what the heck are you doing?*" she says, baffled.

I help her to her feet. "I thought you were a robber," I say. "How long have you been home?"

"Maybe five minutes. I saw your homework on the kitchen table and didn't know if you were napping, so I crept up here to check on you," she says.

"I never saw your car outside," I say.

"The damn thing broke down," she replies, shaking her head. "I took a bus home and walked from the bus stop."

"Oh goodness, Mom. I'm sorry—I could have hurt you."

Mom looks down at that Bible and starts laughing. "A Bible, Stephanie...*really?*"

"Well, it is hardcover." I giggle.

"I'm happy to know my girl can look after herself. I'll definitely call you next time I come home unannounced—or shout from the front door that I'm home," she says, smiling.

"Good thinking."

"Let's go make some dinner," she says, still chuckling. "And I'll help you with your homework."

"Okay," I say, and follow her to the kitchen.

oOo

Another week is satisfyingly over. I seem to have acquired a shadow, except the shadow is in the form of a whore named Danica, and it's not like she's following me around per se, but every time I turn around she's scrutinizing me. I'm getting fed up with it, but I do think I've figured out why she's doing it. On Tuesday I wore the pale pink dress to school, and it was—I hate the word—*hot.* It really is a knock-out dress. There must have been comments from the guys, or Shane in particular, that Danica overheard because the very next day she was wearing a very similar—but way more revealing—copy of my dress. She wore black high heels and a blinged-out belt that made her waist look extra tiny and her boobs super big.

Then on Wednesday I wanted to prove my theory so I wore shorts—red jean shorts and a white glittery tank top with a black cardigan over it. Lo and behold, on Thursday Danica came to school in shorts that I swear could pass for underwear, a shirt that barely covered her nipples when she bent over, and six-inch stilettos. I don't know how she never got sent home to change; my suspicions of her *doing* the principal still stand. I know her parents donate a ton of money to the school, so that could be another reason she gets away with the things she does. I enjoyed watching her freeze her ass off all day, though.

I think I've figured out why she's trying to out-do me all the time. She could be extremely competitive, but if so, she's picked the wrong person because I am not competitive by nature. Or—and I think this is more likely—Shane is not giving her the attention she wants so she is trying to be more like me in her own way; the only way she knows: by showing off her goods to get what she wants. I should go to school in a bikini and see what she comes up with in response to that.

But it's Saturday now and I don't have to deal with Danica or anyone else for two days. Mom and Greg left yesterday in his vehicle and Mom gave me her car keys so I can drive myself to the shop without being late. She assured me the car would not break down again. I'm surprised that she trusts me with it. It will take me a few moments to get used to handling an automatic transmission; I'm so used to a manual one. I'm going to take extra care driving to work today. I feel a bit anxious, thinking about it. It feels like it's been years since I drove my old car, or any car, for that matter.

You'll be fine, I tell myself. I'll get an early start today so I can take it slow.

People are so rude on the road—I never realized it before. I have been known to have a bit of road rage now and then, but I have never had it directed at me. Okay, so I was going ten kilometres under the speed limit, but seriously, give a girl a break. After an intense thirty minute drive I finally made it safely to the art store. I couldn't be happier to get out of the car, or happier that I made it in one piece.

I unlock the store, deactivate the security system, pull up the blinds, and turn on the *Open* sign. *I've got this!* I assure myself. Appreciating the coffee machine in the small kitchen area, I brew a whole pot to last me the morning. I walk out of the kitchen to turn the computer/cash register on at the front counter.

I had another rough night last night. More nightmares; what else is new. I don't feel any guilt for Milly's death, but maybe my subconscious does. Every night I am bombarded with images of her dying; some nights she is half alive and clawing at me, other nights she is already dead and there are maggots pouring out of her neck wound. Worst is the one where she is both alive with maggots crawling all over her *and* she is clawing for me; I'm thankful those instances are rare. That one makes me feel sick all day. I try to read before bed, I try to conjure good images in my head, but it doesn't work like it used to—Milly plagues even the few good dreams I have.

I'm jumpier than normal today. I can't shake the feeling that I am being watched. It could be because I was alone last night, or because of the bad dreams, or it could be because...*you're a wimp?*

It could be that. Who would ever have thought I would want Mom home all the time? I feel safer with her there. She is a tough woman; I don't see anyone messing with her. She and Greg will be back Monday morning. I think they're coming straight to the shop from St. Chalmers. That reminds me, I need to make a sign letting the customers know the store will be opening at noon on Monday instead of nine. I wish I could have taken the day off school to open the shop so they could take their time.

Beep.

My cell phone is alerting me to a text message. Greg doesn't like me to have it at the register; he thinks it's rude to be on it in front of customers. That makes perfect sense, so I keep it in the kitchen. I look through the front window. There are no cars parked in the lot in front of the shop and there is a bell attached to the door, so if anyone does come in I'll hear them from the kitchen. The coffee is most likely brewed by now, so I'll hit two birds with one stone and pour a cup while I check who texted me. No one texts me anymore.

I pass through the canvas area to the small room at the back of the store that contains a little two-person table, a mini-fridge, and two counters with cupboards above them. The fridge has a microwave on top of it and there's a sink in the counter on one side and a toaster and the magical coffee pot shoved into a corner of the other. I pick a mug from the overhead cupboard and fix my coffee, then reach inside my purse, left on the counter earlier, and remove the cell phone. The tiny light is blinking red. While flipping through the different menus on the phone, I take a sip of heaven.

I don't recognize the number that texted me. The message reads: *Hey, it's Jared. Here's my address if you change your mind about tomorrow: 445 Trenasee Street. I look forward to seeing you.*

Bullshit. Jared has never been interested in me in that way, and he is one of Shane's best buddies. He's trying to get Shane and me alone. *Not going to happen!*

I hit the Respond button. The bell jingles at the front of the store. I type fervently: *Sorry Jared, have to work tomorrow and house-sit until Monday when my mom is home, thanks, but no thanks.* I press Send and put the cell phone back in my purse.

What the hell did I just write to Jared? I wonder as I walk to the cash register.

A scrawny lady with long, straggly black hair is waiting by the cash register along with a small boy who is around six years old. Her dark rust-coloured eyes follow me as I walk behind the counter.

"Good morning," I say with a smile. "Can I help you with anything?"

The woman continues to stare at me; I feel awkward and shift uncomfortably on my feet. She must have had bad acne when she was a teenager; her face is pitted with scars. She looks to be in her fifties. The little boy is cute as a button, with dusty blonde hair and a spray of freckles across his face. He must be a grandson, because he looks nothing like this shell of a woman.

I turn my attention to the boy and repeat the question in a different context. "Hi," I say cheerfully to him. "What are you looking for today?"

"Hello," he says in a tiny voice. "Mom said I can paint some pictures for my room. Do you have paint?"

"Well, you have come to the right place. Follow me." I walk along the first aisle, where Greg keeps the acrylic paints, and kneel to pull out a discount wicker basket holding a selection of colours. While searching through the paints I notice the lady's beat-up runners. I can tell she doesn't have a lot of money. The boy kneels beside me and his eyes light up. The paints are all under a dollar and are brightly coloured.

"Where is your bathroom?" the lady asks in a raspy voice.

"To the back and on the right," I say, glancing up at her. I don't trust her, not at all. This is when I wish Greg had security cameras set up. I feel a little guilty judging this woman so harshly; she could possibly be poor, but that doesn't mean she's a bad person.

I hear the bathroom door close and lock.

"Your mom is cool to let you paint pictures for your room," I say to him.

"Yeah, she is," he says.

"What are you going to paint?"

"Dragons...the fire-breathing ones."

"I thought all dragons breathe fire."

"You must not know a lot about dragons, then," he says cheekily.

"I guess not," I say, and giggle. "Well, since I don't know about dragons, you pick out the colours for them. I know a lot about fire so let's get orange, red, and yellow for that."

"Okay!" he says cheerfully, and picks out more colours: green, grey, black, gold, and brown.

The lady sure has been in the washroom for a long time. The boy does not seem perturbed about her absence so I choose to ignore it. I gather up the paints and bring them to the counter. "Do you need paint brushes?" I ask him.

"Nah, I like painting with my fingers," he says, and wiggles his chubby fingers at me.

I grin at him and ring up the paints. It comes to just under ten dollars. The boy reaches into his pocket and pulls out a twenty. He hands it to me proudly. I give him the change, which he counts, approves, and shoves back in his front jean pocket. I bag the purchase.

"Do you think your mom's okay?" I say, and nod toward the bathroom.

"She's not my mom," he says hastily.

"Oh?" I say.

"I don't know who that lady is," he says.

"Where are your parents?" I probe.

"Working. They're always working," he says, and slumps his shoulders.

The bathroom door creaks open and the lady emerges. What could possibly have taken her fifteen minutes to do in there? I hope she turned the fan on.

"Well," I say happily, now that I can see her clearly and she isn't hiding in the washroom, "I hope you have a fantastic time painting the *fire-breathing* and *non-fire-breathing dragons*."

"Thank you," he says enthusiastically.

"You're very welcome," I say.

The lady walks quickly past us and the strong smell of cigarettes follows her out of the store.

Are you kidding me?

I hurriedly pass the boy his bag of paint because I want to see if anything noticeable has been stolen. He thanks me again and leaves the store as well. I watch him until he's out of sight. What parent in their right mind would trust their child to walk the streets alone when there are people like that woman walking around? *Freaking freaky!*

I run to the bathroom to make sure it has not been vandalized, and gag on the repugnant smell of old cigarette. The butt is floating in the unflushed toilet. The toilet looks like it was only used as an ashtray. *Thank goodness.* I flush the toilet and turn on the fan. Everything else seems to be in its proper place, but that damn smell seems to be sticking to the walls. I walk to the kitchen to get an aerosol can of air freshener with the intent of draining the entire thing in the small room. I pull my shirt up over my nose and do exactly that. Satisfied with the new smell of roses, I close the bathroom door and return to the kitchen. I throw the empty spray bottle into the garbage and wash my hands.

My coffee is freezing. I rinse out the cup and pour a fresh cup. That lady was so weird. Did I know her? I don't think I've ever seen her in my life. There was something familiar about her. Not familiar in the way that I'd know her, but familiar in the way that she knew something about me. I never saw her at Milly's funeral and surely she would have said something—*anything*—to me if she did in fact know me. I'll have to ask Greg if he recognizes anyone by her description. She could be an old lover of Greg's who knows he's with Mom and wants revenge... *Come on, she's ancient!* Yes, that is unlikely. Greg doesn't seem the type to date someone like that. I stop the silly thoughts from entering my head and pick up my phone. No new messages.

I bring the mug of coffee and my phone to the front counter. Greg's not here. I can quickly hide it if a customer comes in.

I spend the rest of the day tidying up the shelves, dusting, making the sign for Monday, and doing everything I can to keep my mind busy. My phone does not beep for the rest of the day. I still feel like such an idiot for telling Jared I'm going to be alone—completely and utterly alone—the entire weekend. *Think before you speak next time!*

Jared not messaging me back is what is worrying me the most. I bet he's already told Shane that I'm by myself until Monday. It's a very good thing no one knows where I work. I don't want trouble here, and Greg has put a great deal of trust in me not to screw up.

After the long, boring day at the store I give in to my paranoia and triple-check everything before leaving. I make sure the coffee pot is unplugged, the lights are off, the Open sign is turned off, the blinds are drawn, the alarm is on, and doors are all locked. The only windows in the store are the front windows and they don't unlock, so I don't have to worry about those.

I stop at the grocery store on the way home to pick up a frozen pizza and a few cans of air freshener to replace the one I drained today. That bathroom is going to smell like roses for months.

It's already dark outside when I pull into our driveway. I park Mom's car and eye the distance to the front door of the house. I still have the car doors locked. I scan the yard. Nothing out of the ordinary there. Ever since I thought I saw someone standing behind me in my bedroom the other day, I've been extra jumpy. And now with Shane knowing I'm alone and that scary woman in the store, I'm a nervous wreck.

I get the house keys ready before leaving the vehicle. I put my purse over my shoulder and the frozen pizza under my arm. Just to be safe I take one of the three aerosol cans and put my finger on the trigger. That could do some damage to an unsuspecting assailant, couldn't it? I've caught Shane by surprise a few times now, I remind myself; I can take care of myself. I put on my big girl panties and spring out of the car and bolt for the front steps, hitting the button on the remote to activate the automatic door locks on Mom's vehicle. Her car honks, letting me know it's locked up tight, as I fly up the porch steps. I jam the key into the door lock, and turn it.

Someone is sitting on the porch swing.

I gasp and spray the aerosol can in the direction of the swing. I feel sick to my stomach. The pizza box drops to the porch. Whoever is on the swing doesn't make a sound. That spray would be as effective as pepper spray, if it hits a face. I don't understand. I'm even coughing from the blast of fresh-linen scent.

"Who's there?" I sputter.

Silence.

The mist clears and the seat is empty. It's not even swinging. If someone had gotten up from the swing it would definitely be moving. If anyone even tried to sit on it, the rickety thing would have broken and crashed to the ground, I observe.

Dammit, Stevie! I rebuke myself. *There was no one there.* I'm psyching myself out again. Trembling all over, I pick up the pizza box and walk inside the house, locking the door behind me. I put my purse and the pizza on the kitchen table and preheat the oven while I tour the house, checking each room, turning on every light. I need the brightness; nothing is going to hide in the shadows. Not if I can help it. I feel a lot better knowing that nothing is in here with me.

I check my e-mail while the oven heats up. There is one from Sara, which makes me relax instantly. Her emails are always a pleasant lift to my spirits. *Spirits...ghosts... Shut up brain!* I shake it off and open the e-mail.

> Subject: Hey Girl!
> How are things with you? I have to keep the e-mail short. Sorry I have not had a lot of time to write. Things have been crazy busy with us.
> You are not going to believe this. Calvin and I are engaged! He asked me at the top of the Eiffel Tower. I know what you're going to say—"That is so cliché, Sara" but wow, was it ever romantic. I was shaking so much I almost dropped the ring off the side. Could you imagine if that happened? Wait until you see the ring, Stevie. It's huge!
> We are leaving shortly to do a long walking tour. I can't wait to show my fiancé off. How weird does that sound...fiancé! I love it!
> Write back soon!
> Sara

I am so happy for them. I click Respond.

> Subject: OMG!
> I can't believe you guys are engaged. Well I can, because you are both so perfect for each other. I couldn't be happier for the both of you. Send me a picture of the ring.

So do you think you'll be coming home in between your adventures to get hitched? Or are you going to Vegas or something? Please tell me you're coming home. I am missing you so much.

Well, I will keep this short as well because I have the oven on so will have to go check up on that.

Write back sooner and congratulations,

Stevie

I close the laptop and put it on the dresser. Sara and Calvin engaged...I sure hope they have a long engagement. As much as I miss her, I don't want to be around her family, and by her family I mean Shane. Calvin and Shane are close; what if he makes him his best man and Sara makes me the maid of honour? We would have to walk down the aisle together, which would not be a good thing. The thought makes me queasy. It will most likely not be for another year, or after their trip. Where would they honeymoon after just travelling around the world? I guess that's not really my problem.

My stomach growls, reminding me that there is a pepperoni pizza waiting to be cooked and then devoured; I should have had it cooking this entire time. I walk to the kitchen and tear open the pizza box. I pop the pizza in the oven and set the timer on the microwave for twenty-five minutes. While I wait for the pizza to cook I walk through the house again and check that the windows and doors are all locked. One can never be too careful.

Once satisfied that no one can sneak into the house to murder me in my sleep, I take a seat on the living room sofa. How I wish we had a television set. I could waste the night away watching crappy shows. I could focus my attention on other peoples' problems and not have to think about my own.

I stare at the painting across from me and get lost in the colours. I wonder if Mom will get rid of the paintings, now that she's found happiness in Greg. These canvases are better suited to a gallery rather than our old, broken-down home. I should tell Greg to hang them in the new art shop he and Mom are opening. They might give other people inspiration. The reds, blacks, and yellows seem to move, the longer I stare into the picture; sort of like staring at yourself in a mirror too long and not recognizing the person staring back at you—it's weird how that happens. It seems that lately I hardly recognize the person staring back at me when I look in the mirror for even a second. I can see why Mom used to sit here in the dark staring at the artwork. You get lost in it.

The microwave beeps. I can't believe I've been sitting here for twenty minutes already. Time usually doesn't fly when you're bored as hell. I push myself up from the sofa and walk to the kitchen. I take a fork from the drawer and a plate from the overhead cupboard. I usually screw this part up, but I have no one to take the pizza out of the oven for me. I open the door and place the plate near the rack, stab the fork into the pizza, and slide the pizza onto the plate. *Easy peasy.*

I turn around with the dish, half expecting someone to be standing behind me, but there is no one there. I place the dish on the kitchen table and walk to the knife block. I grab the biggest one I can find and turn around wildly with it. The kitchen is still empty. Being alone in this house is making me go screwy. I shouldn't be waving knives around in the first place. I shake my head and return to cut the pizza into quarters.

I carry the entire plate to my bedroom and curl up on the bed with the pizza on my lap and a romance book in hand. This is the most relaxed I have been all week.

oOo

The morning is bright, with not a cloud in the sky, which for this time of year is unusual. I bob along to a song on the radio while I drive to work, feeling like I'm the only person awake right now; everyone else must be having a lazy Sunday. I'm not envious of them; I'm happy to keep myself busy. I must remember to put the sign up today reminding everybody that the shop won't open until twelve tomorrow.

I can't wait for Mom to come home. I never thought of myself as a wimp, but last night after I had dozed off with a full belly of pizza, I remembered that I had not turned the oven off. It must have taken me ten minutes to sneak downstairs to the kitchen. Every squeak of the floorboards made me jump, the wind through the trees outside gave me the heebie-jeebies, I refused to look at the reflection in the oven door when I turned it off, and I ran for my life back to my bedroom with the certain feeling that something was going to get me. Of course I laughed it off when I finally jumped back into bed and pulled the covers up under my chin. I slept with every light in the house on, except for my bedroom light, and I only felt safe turning that off because I locked the bedroom door, checked under my bed, and rummaged through the closet to make sure no one was hiding between the hangers. I did this all with the fresh-linen scented spray can locked and loaded under my index finger. My paranoia over Shane might actually be making me lose my mind.

I unlock the store, turn off the alarm, turn on the lights, open the blinds, and put on the coffee pot. I'm getting good at this. The store looks like it did when I left yesterday. No break-ins or fires. Greg will be so proud. I am going to do a huge cleanup today so everything looks perfect tomorrow when he gets in. I have my fingers crossed for a pay raise. Driving Mom's car makes me realize how much I miss driving my own. I don't want to spend the last year of high school taking the bus like an eighth grader.

I have almost five hundred dollars saved up in an old coffee can under my bed. I need at least two thousand for a half decent car. That will take *forever*. I might ask Greg if I can start working afternoons after school, or take over the weekends completely so he and Mom can have Stevie- and work-free time together—they might actually go for that.

I think about my proposal while I dust the shelves and straighten the supplies into neat little lines. After I finish that task I find a bottle of window cleaner and a roll of paper towel under the kitchen sink and wipe down the front windows, watching the cars drive by as I work. I think about all of the different cars I could buy with two thousand dollars. I completely zone out. The parking lot and street in front of me blur until the only thing I see is my hand holding the paper towel as it sweeps across the spray of window cleaner on the glass. It's quite therapeutic washing windows. I like the squeaky sound the towel makes as it rubs at the cleaner. It reminds me of windshield wipers that are on too fast when the rain is barely coming down. That sound would normally drive a person mental, but I like it. *Because you are mental, Stevie.* Maybe I am.

I hear a tap on the glass right in front of my face. I move the cloth down and am eye to eye with the creepy lady that came in yesterday. "Ah!" I scream, and drop the window cleaner right on my small toe.

Where the hell did she come from? I lean down to rub my throbbing toe. The nail is already bruising. *Side note: don't wear sandals to work.*

I look up at the lady and she is staring down at me. I raise my eyebrows at her in a what-the-heck kind of way and straighten to go to the door. It's unlocked, so it's not like she couldn't get in. I open it and the bell jingles. "Can I help you?" I say, leaning my head out of the store.

The lady turns to regard me, but her expression is vacant, distant, as if she is looking through me, not at me.

"Miss?" I prompt. I wait for her to respond but a response doesn't come. After what feels like minutes of us staring at each other—her blankly and me at a total, confused loss—she turns around and walks off down the street. She rounds the corner and goes out of view.

What the... I must remember to ask Greg about this woman.

I return to the safe confines of the store and, keeping a watchful eye out for that crazy old woman, I pick the cleaner up from the floor and resume wiping down the windows.

She doesn't come back for the rest of the day. The clock strikes five and I couldn't be more ready to get home. I lock up the store, triple-checking everything as I do. I wanted to take an aerosol can of air freshener home for protection but if I want Greg to pay me back, all three cans have to be accounted for. *Bummer.* Well, I could just run that old coot over with Mom's car if she springs on me.

I start the car up and take one more look at the store. Blinds are shut, the sign I made is visible, and everything seems A-okay. I look through the review mirror to back the car out of the spot. No one is standing behind the vehicle. My heart calms down a little. I am always expecting *something.* If I could drive without looking out any of the side mirrors I would be a happy girl, but that is not going to happen. *Safety first, Stevie.*

"Pfft," I say, and start the drive home.

I stop at the grocery store again on the way home, this time to buy a couple of cheap TV dinners. Should they still be called TV dinners if you don't have a TV to watch while you eat them?

The lights are still on when I get home. I figured it would make robbers think there are people home, and they wouldn't try to break in. The door is locked when I get to it which is a good sign, there is no one sitting on the porch swing when I turn the key in the lock, and no figments of my wild imagination are waiting for me in the living room after I get inside. I lock the front door and walk to the kitchen.

I throw my purse on the table and put one boxed dinner into the freezer and the other in the microwave. The smell of macaroni and processed cheese fills up the kitchen. My stomach starts to rumble. I look out the kitchen window as the sky turns from a pinky-orange sunset to darker shades of blue and purple. This is when I start getting fidgety. I keep telling myself it's only one more night and Mom will be home.

It's crazy to think how far Mom and I have come in such a short time. We are a lot closer—close enough for my comfort level. I think if we were any friendlier it would come off as fake. We have a happy medium in our relationship right now. Come to think of it, I have not heard Mom cry like she used to. I guess I had gotten so used to her weeping every night that I became accustomed to tuning it out. Good things can come from bad experiences.

As I finish the meal at the kitchen table I think about my dad. I wish we could have been closer. I think about how things would be now between us all if he had not died. I push the thoughts away because they are too upsetting. I know exactly how things would be. I would still be treated like a burden, a mistake, second best.

Throwing the empty box in the garbage, I head upstairs to my bathroom for a shower. I strip off my clothes and look down at my baby toenail; it has already gone black. *God, I bruise easily.* I toss my dirty clothing across the hallway into my bedroom then close and lock the bathroom door and turn on the shower. The small bathroom quickly steams up, fogging up the mirror so I can't see my reflection. There is no way in hell I am wiping the steam away from the glass. I know what I look like; I don't need to give my imagination a chance to spook me by placing something scary behind me. I am not a dumb horror movie victim. There has to be a way to avoid scary circumstances. *Never look into mirrors or under your bed, keep all lights on, shower with the curtain open.*

I lay a towel on the floor next to the claw-footed bathtub, and I shower with the curtain open. *Nothing is creeping up on me!*

I leave the shower determined to put all of these childhood nightmares to bed. One day...I hope.

Clad in the mermaid pajamas and my black fluffy slippers, I pick up the dirty clothes from my bedroom floor and put them in the wicker hamper near the door, then open the lid on the laptop on the dresser. I doubt I have an e-mail from Sara yet, but I have nothing else to do. While I'm waiting for it to power on, there is a loud knock at the front door.

Who could that be? I am not expecting visitors, I have no friends, and Mom isn't due home until tomorrow. I walk to the window in the corner of the room and peer out. My heart stops. It actually feels like it has given out on me, or is about to explode from the pressure. The moon shines ominously off of Shane's truck, which is parked near the front door.

CHAPTER NINE

MY HEART POUNDS AS I walk down the stairs toward the living room. I don't know why Shane is here. Ignoring his persistent raps at the door would be the smart thing to do. I pause at the bottom of the stairs and slow my breathing in an attempt to lessen the deafening beats of my heart.

"Stevie, I can hear you in there," Shane says through the closed door. "I can see your shadow through the curtains. Please...it's cold out here... let me in."

Damn these bright lights giving me away! I step down the last stair and walk slowly across the living room. I feel as if I might pass out before I reach the door. "What do you want, Shane?" I squeak, giving away my rattling nerves.

"I just want to talk, Stevie. Please open the door."

I hear the wind whisk through the trees as it picks up outside. I reach the front door and stand there for a moment, trying to quell my internal struggle.

Shane knocks again, louder this time. "Stevie, I'm freezing. I only want to talk for a minute and then I'll leave you alone...I promise."

With a sigh I open the front door and Shane falls through it. He was using it to hold himself up. The first thing I smell is the strong odor of alcohol. I should have told him to go home, I should have stuck to my gut instinct, but the good in me—the miniscule part of me that still cares for him—let him in. As soon as I smell the alcohol I know it was a bad idea. Inebriated people are irrational; look at what happened at the lake house. Things are said that you can never take back. In that case the things said were honest feelings...maybe Shane being drunk right now will be an advantage for me.

Shane wobbles to his feet and plonks down on the sofa. I close the front door and lock it. I don't know if he has anyone with him, and I might be able to handle him alone, but if he has accomplices I am screwed. I peek through the door's peephole but it's too dark to see inside Shane's truck. I turn around and Shane is smiling wickedly at me. "What are you grinning at, Shane?"

"You, in your girlie pajamas. You look adorable, Stevie," he says with that award-winning smile of his.

I wrap my arms around myself, suddenly feeling very vulnerable. He has seen me in a lot less clothing than this, but this feels so wrong.

"Come sit with me," he says.

"No. I'd rather stand, thank you."

"Don't be like that, Stevie," he drawls. "Don't you love me anymore?"

"Shane, we went through this, remember?"

"None of that matters, Stevie. The only thing that matters is that I still love you." He pushes himself off the sofa and stumbles toward me.

"Shane, please...you're drunk. Aren't you supposed to be at Jared's party right now?" I step backward until my back touches the door.

Shane stops in front of me and puts his hands on the door on either side of my head. He breathes down on me and it smells like stale beer mixed with some other liquor. I don't know my alcohols too well; it definitely smells like something a lot stronger than what he usually drinks. I have smelled beer on his breath before and this certainly smells different. "How much have you had to drink?" I ask, looking up at him.

"Not *that* much. I drove here by myself, didn't I?" he scoffs.

Good he is alone...or maybe that's bad. There is no one here to stop him.

"I think you should go then. If you were okay to drive here then you are okay to drive home," I say, trying to look stern.

"You are so cute when you're angry, but I see right through it. You want me," he says, and leans in for a kiss.

"Shane *stop!*" I say, and push him in the chest. I duck under his right arm and run behind him.

He spins around and staggers toward me.

"Shane, *please*—I really think you *need* to go home." I raise my hands, trying to halt him. I can feel tears prickling the edges of my eyes. *Be strong, Stevie, be strong, don't show weakness.*

"You have no idea what I *need*, Stephanie," he hisses.

He has never called me Stephanie before. I can't help but show the fear on my face. I start trembling all over.

"What are you afraid of? *Tell me!*" he shouts, and the veins in his neck bulge and work their way up to his forehead.

"Shane, please," I beg, and the tears roll freely down my face.

"Shane please, Shane please, *Shane please*," he mocks. "It's always Shane please *something* with you, isn't it!" he spits.

"I-I," I stutter, and I can't get anything else out.

"What? You're Sorry? Give me a break, Stevie; how many times have I heard that from you. *HOW MANY!*" he screams.

I stumble backward from the intensity of his words. I'm scared. My knees feel weak. I've lost control of the situation.

Shane grasps my left wrist tightly. His fingers claw into me like something from one of my nightmares. "You're hurting me, Shane!" I cry out. He doesn't appear to hear me. The rage has completely taken over. I start pulling and scratching at his hand to free myself, but he doesn't flinch. He starts to pull me up the stairs; my shoulder feels like it will pop out of the socket at any second. "Shane, let go of me!" I scream. He ignores me and wrenches me up the remaining stairs. I try my best to clutch the railings but every time I do he yanks me harder and I can feel the muscles in my shoulder stretching. Shane is almost double my size and has ten times the strength that I do—my feeble attempts at escape are failing miserably.

He drags me across hallway as I kick and scream like a child being punished. I am feeling weaker and weaker with each second. Every injury that I sustained in the car accident seems to be coming back with full force. I am terrified of what's to come.

We reach my open bedroom door. Shane jerks my wrist up, forcing me to stand. The room spins for a second as the blood rushes to my head. There's someone in my room! Relief floods me, but it's short-lived. Shane pushes me through the door and I fall onto the pink shag rug. I glance up in search of my saviour, but the room is empty, apart from Shane and me. It was the same shadow I have seen twice, now three times.

"Get up," Shane demands.

I feel the nylon fibres between my fingers as I push myself onto my knees. Shane takes a handful of my damp hair and pulls me to my feet. I squeal in pain as I feel my fine hair breaking in his fingers. I search the room frantically for the shadow. I beg for it, pray for it.

"Get on the bed," Shane orders.

"No Shane...you don't have to do this, please...if you go now I won't tell anyone you were here," I plead.

Shane laughs out loud but there is no humour behind it. He shoves me firmly with his hand in the middle of my back and I fall to the bed, my head jerking back like I'm reliving the car accident. I move my right hand to rub my aching neck but Shane takes hold of it before I do. He flips me over like a ragdoll and falls on top of me. I try desperately to push him off, but it's no use. I have no strength left in me; I can't do this.

I look up at the ceiling as he violently kisses my neck. I try to find a happy place deep down in my soul, a place away from here, a place where I am the most happy. My pajama bottoms are savagely torn off and thrown aside. I can see the gazebo in the distance. I am almost there. I can almost feel the breeze through the trees. Shane's mouth forcefully consumes mine and I am pulled back to reality. I am in such a drained state that I can't bring myself to think about what to do. I want to give up. There is nothing I can do; there is no escaping; no one to save me, *nothing...*

Shane sits up for a second to unbutton his jeans and kick them off, all the while holding my right hand in place. I can't even feel that hand anymore; it's numb like the rest of me. I don't see the man I used to know as I lie here defeated. How did I ever fall in love with this person who had so many secrets, so many dark desires? The tears are pouring down my face; I can feel them pooling in my ears. Shane is on top of me again, forcing me into the mattress with his weight. He pushes my legs apart with his and I hold my breath. This is not how I wanted this to happen. My last bit of innocence is going to be torn away from me.

I see movement to my left. My heart, which felt like it had stopped beating long ago, skips a beat. I look over quickly and blink away the tears.

I search for the shadow, but there is no one there. I see something glinting on the side table—the tweezers. Shane is too absorbed to realize that he failed to take hold of my left hand. It's free. I stretch my arm toward the side table, straining to reach the tweezers. My fingertips graze them.

Come on—please!

I fumble for them and finally succeed in sliding them across the table. I roll them up my palm using my fingertips and grip them tightly. I lift my arm up as high as it will go—fighting the urge to yelp in anguish when my shoulder uses its last morsel of strength. I squeeze the tweezers together to make one sharp point, and bring my arm down as hard and fast as I can. It connects with Shane's shoulder. I feel the tweezers tear through his flesh. Shane screams as I pull them out, and drops of blood hit my face.

Shane jerks back and makes a guttural sound as he rips the tweezers from my hand. The rage in his eyes is the most terrifying thing I have ever seen; more terrifying than the accident, more terrifying than Mom used to be, and more terrifying than my horrific nightmares.

Shane hurls the tweezers against the wall and backhands me across the face. "You bitch!" he shouts. He raises his hand again and I brace myself for another blow.

The bedroom light flicks on, momentarily blinding me. "Get the hell off my daughter, you son of a bitch!" Mom launches herself into the bedroom, brandishing the Bible that I had used to almost attack *her*. Shane does not get a chance to defend himself. She leaps across the room like an amazon and swings the Bible with deadly strength and accuracy. It connects with the side of his head, knocking him off the bed.

He crawls around on the floor, searching for his pants. There is blood on the side of his face where the Bible made contact.

"Greg!" Mom screams. "*GREG!*"

I hear Greg bounding up the stairs. He bursts into the room seconds later. He looks around, quickly processing the situation.

Shane tries to get to his feet and Mom jumps on his back and starts beating him down with her fists. She looks like she is going to kill him.

Greg quickly pulls her off of him. "Denise. *Go* to your daughter," he orders. "I will deal with Shane."

Mom blinks and shakes her head, her rage subsiding. I am too numb to do anything but watch events unfolding in front of me. I have my knees pulled up to my chest and the blankets clutched over them. I am rocking and bawling my eyes out. Mom comes to my side and puts her arm around me.

"Get him the hell out of here," Mom hisses. "I'm calling the cops!"

Shane is speechless. He doesn't attempt to fight Greg. What can he do? He's been caught in the act.

As my adrenaline fades my injuries become apparent. My face is stinging where Shane slapped it and my shoulder is throbbing something fierce.

"Honey, Stephanie...everything is okay. I'm here, okay? Everything is going to be fine. Did he hurt you, Stephanie? Did he—" Mom pushes my hair behind my ear and turns my chin up to look at the swelling.

I start hiccupping and can't get the words out. I lie down, resting my head on her lap, and she rubs my hair. I feel her reach into her pocket; there is a beeping sound as she pushes three buttons.

"No Mom, don't," I say before she can complete the call on her cell phone.

"Stephanie, I have to call the police. He can't get away with this."

I sit up and look at her. There is so much concern and anger on her face.

"Mom, he was drunk, he didn't know what he was doing," I say. "If you call the police my life is going to get so much worse at school. I need to finish this year. Please...please trust me. Shane has been caught; he's not going to do anything else to jeopardize his future." I stop, searching her eyes.

"I'm your mother, Stephanie. I need to protect you," she says.

"And you did, Mom, you did protect me."

"I was too late," she says, the pain evident in her voice, and looks down.

"No Mom, you weren't. A minute later and you might have been. Please just let him go. I think you scared him enough into leaving me alone."

"I think you are making a mistake, but if that's what you want..." She raises her head.

"I think life will be easier for me at school if you just let him go."

"Okay...but if he *ever* touches you again, I'll kill him, Stephanie. I swear to God I'll kill him." She's staring off into the distance, the way she used to.

I believe her.

Mom rises and walks out of the room. I stand up and pull on sweatpants. I take the mermaid shirt off and throw it in the trash, along with the bottoms. I can never wear them again. I have no more tears to shed. I am completely shattered.

I take a step toward the door and step on something sharp. I look down and see the blood-soaked tweezers. If it hadn't been for the shadow that caught my eye before Shane did the unthinkable, I would have been too late to save my purity, Mom would have been too late to protect me, and I would have been in a lot worse state than I am in now.

I am not trying to protect Shane, I am protecting myself. If I were to go to school after being the reason he got locked up, my life would be over. I can't drop out of school, not when I am so close to the end of it. I have no doubt in my mind that Shane will leave me alone now. He has to, after this. He can't be blind to what he was about to do. I don't even think he was that drunk. Anger can consume you like a disease—I've been there. How can I blame him for acting the way he did when I don't even blame myself for causing the accident that killed Milly? Anger made me do unthinkable things. Unfortunately for Milly, she did not have a saviour; she didn't have someone to protect her from me. Lucky for me I was able to stop Shane long enough for Mom to intervene.

What if Mom had never come home? No. I can't think about that. I can't.

I hold the tweezers between my fingers and move to stand near the bedroom window. I look out past Shane's truck, in the direction of the gazebo. I hear muffled shouts downstairs. Mom must be fighting the urge to call the police. The only reason she isn't calling them is because I begged her not to. I hope I never regret that decision.

Shane runs out of the house and gets into his truck. His engine starts up and he backs out of the driveway. For a few seconds he looks up at the bedroom window. I stare at him and step back slowly out of sight.

oOo

Mom made me stay home from school the entire week. She called the office to tell them I was having a hard time with what happened to Milly. They bought it and didn't ask any questions.

Greg worked double shifts the whole week because Mom refused to leave me alone for even a minute. I pleaded with her to let me go to school the day after Shane attacked me, but she refused.

My face never bruised from the slap but I do have bruises on my wrist, thighs, and knees from being dragged up the stairs. The memory, although recent, seems ancient; I've locked it up in the recesses of my brain. I can't dwell on it, which is another reason I wanted to go back to school. To be a stronger person you have to face your fears head on and show people that they don't affect you whatsoever. How can I do that from here?

It was a miracle that Mom came home early last Sunday. Their meetings went smoothly and ended sooner than they expected so they decided to come home that night so they could open the shop on time Monday morning.

It's Sunday evening now and I *am* going to school tomorrow. I can't sit here any longer. I've thought about the shadow that I've seen four times now. I haven't seen it again since last Sunday. I've been trying to see it, which is freaky because I feel like I'm going crazy. Am I that lonely that I need a shadow for a friend? I think it's more a need to understand what it is. I can't tell anyone about it because I'd be locked up and deemed schizophrenic or something. I've already started talking to myself, but what can you expect when you are a prisoner in your own home?

Mom thinks I've lost it because what person in their right mind would want to go back to a place where you have two classes with a person that tried to rape you? I've spent this whole week trying to get her to see my point of view and eventually I asked her to drop the subject. She will never understand—which is understandable to me. If it was my daughter that was in this position, no one would have been able to stop me from calling the police and getting the asshole locked up. Sometimes my rationality doesn't even make sense to me.

My plan for tomorrow is to walk into school with my head held high. I am going to wear something conservative: jeans and a plain white, long-sleeve, V-neck sweater—I can still wear pure colours. Chances are when I see Shane I'm going to be flooded with every emotion a human can have, but I will not let him get to me, no sir. That's the plan, anyway.

oOo

I sit at the kitchen table and watch the time tick by on the microwave clock. Mom is getting ready for work; she is also driving me to school today. Greg is sitting to my left, eating a bowl of cereal. I tap my finger on the table with every passing second. Greg has not brought up anything about Shane since the incident and I am grateful for it. Frankly it's embarrassing, and I'd rather forget the whole thing; he seems to understand that. I told Mom that I can take the bus to school today but she insisted on driving me. I'm afraid that if she spots Shane, she'll run him over with her car—a thought that brings a twisted smile to my face.

"That's the first time I've seen you smile all week. It's a lovely sight," Greg says. I didn't realize he was watching me. "What are you thinking about?"

"Mom running Shane over with her car," I say truthfully. Greg chokes on a mouthful of cereal and clears his throat. "Are you okay?" I ask.

"Are *you* okay, Stephanie? That's kind of a morbid thought, don't you think?" he says.

"I guess it depends on the person. In this case I think it's a reasonable thought," I say.

"Just don't let your imagination get too carried away. I would hate to see you in anymore trouble."

"How much more trouble could I get into...*honestly*?" I say, and roll my eyes. "I think I've had enough to last me quite a while, *don't you think*?"

Greg sighs. "Yes, you have. Sorry. I don't want to upset you before school."

"You haven't." I offer a weak smile.

Greg looks at his watch. "I have to get going; I have a few things I need to pick up before I go to the shop. Tell Denise I will see her around ten. You have my number, right?"

"Yes. I'll call you if I need help. Don't worry about me. I'm a lot stronger than people give me credit for," I reply.

"I know you are." He stands up and squeezes my shoulder.

I flinch, but he doesn't seem to notice. I've tried my best this week to conceal how much pain I am really in, inside and out.

I turn my attention back to the clock. A shadow passes behind me, reflected in the microwave. I almost fall off the chair when I whip around to catch sight of it.

Mom's standing behind me. I sigh, but not in relief, more in disappointment.

"Ready to go?" she says unhappily.

"Ready as I'll ever be," I say, rising.

I know she's displeased that I'm returning to school, but she can't keep me home forever.

"How about we skip one more day, hon?" Mom says as she pulls up to the curb near the front entrance of the school twenty minutes later. "We can go shopping."

"*Mom*," I whine, "I'll be okay...*okay?*"

"I worry..."

"You have every right to worry, but look around you; there are so many students here. Nothing is going to happen," I say.

"But if something does," she insists.

"It won't," I assure her.

"You have my number?"

"Mom, that's silly, *of course* I have your number. You've had the same one for years; it's embedded in my brain." I smile.

"Okay, okay," she says. "Never be too afraid to ask for help—from me, from Greg, from teachers. There are a lot of people that care about you. Promise me that if you have any issues, you will tell someone."

"I promise," I say. "Can I go now?"

"Yes—yes, go. I love you," she says.

"I love you too." I give her a quick hug.

I thought that would never end, I think as I watch Mom pull her car away from the curb. I turn toward the school. It feels as if I haven't been here in years. Everything looks the same— it's only been a week, of course it *looks* the same. But I feel apprehensive, walking up to the entrance of the school. I keep telling myself that no one is going to know what happened with Shane. He wouldn't tell anyone, and I haven't told anyone, so there's nothing to worry about. I'm going to go back to pretending he doesn't exist, and I hope he gives me the same courtesy.

I note that Milly's memorial is smaller than it was a week ago as I walk past it in the first floor hallway. Time heals all wounds—is that the saying? She is already fading from memory and it's only been a month since school started. This thing that happened with Shane is bound to do the same thing.

I keep my eyes level and walk to my locker. No one stops me; it's a miracle that no one wonders where I've been. I have a free period this morning so I dump my entire bag into the locker. I look at myself in the little mirror, put a stray hair behind my ear, and smile at the photo of Charlie, then close the door.

Danica is leaning against the locker next to mine, obviously waiting for me to shut mine so she can be more dramatic. She's wearing dark red lipstick, a black bustier that pushes up her boobs, and skin-tight white jeans. I don't bother looking at her feet to see what outrageous heels she is wearing today.

She smirks at me and flicks her hair back. "Where have you been?" She takes a nail file out of her cleavage and rubs it across her talons. I wonder what else she keeps in there.

She starts rubbing the file over her thumbnail and the sound of it gives me the shivers. It's one sound I really can't handle. Sara used to bug me all the time to go get our nails done together, but the thought of getting mine filed always stopped me. I would rather rub my teeth across cement than have my nails touched by that thing.

"Well?" she pushes, and raises her perfectly plucked eyebrow.

"Mind your own business, Danica," I say bluntly.

"It *is* my business," she says, and moves on to the next nail.

"How so?" I say.

"Well, I have to keep an eye on my boyfriend's ex-girlfriend, *don't I?*" she says.

Now it's my turn to raise an eyebrow at her.

"Oh, you haven't heard, have you?" she says proudly. "Shane asked me to be his girlfriend. Great, isn't it?" She gives me a perky smile.

I know what she's expecting me to do; she's expecting me to get upset—little does she know. If I was a nicer person I would warn her about Shane, but she's a bitch, and I am not *that nice.*

"Leave her alone, Danica," Chanelle says, and pulls on my arm.

Where the hell did she pop up from?

Danica snickers as Chanelle tugs me away. I pull my arm away from her and stalk into the girls' washroom. Chanelle follows me and closes the door behind her. I scan the room. We're alone.

"What do you think you're doing?" I snap.

"Being helpful, Stephanie," she says.

"I don't need your help, Chanelle. I can take care of myself, and since when did you give a shit anyways?"

"Since I heard what you're going through," she replies.

"What are you talking about?"

"You know...the depression from Milly dying."

"You don't know jack-shit about anything, Chanelle. Mind your own business next time!" I shriek at her.

"I was trying to be a friend," she says, and the hurt reaches her eyes.

"I don't remember us ever being friends, Chanelle. I don't want friends, and if I did, they would not be anything close to someone like you. Stop trying to make yourself look better by attempting to fix everyone around you. What good has it done for you, anyway? Look what it did to Travis. You tried to fix him too, didn't you?" I know that's a low blow, but to hell with it. It's too late to take it back now.

"Travis is none of your business," she says.

"And what I am 'going through' *is none of yours*; don't try to fix my problems when you have not even come *close* to fixing yours." I glare down at her.

"I thought we could be friends, since Danica has ruined both of our lives now. We have something in common. I thought I saw some good in you, but everyone is right—you are crazy!" she says.

"The only thing that's crazy is that you think we have anything in common. I broke up with Shane; he wasn't caught with his pants down in the girls' locker room with Danica. You and I are not going to start some kind of 'I hate Danica' club and I am definitely not joining your little prayer group, either, so just leave me the hell alone!"

Chanelle's mouth opens to say something but she bursts into tears instead. She runs out of the washroom. The door swings shut and I put my hand over my mouth, muffling a scream that I know wants to escape. I bite my inner cheek until I can taste blood. What am I doing here? How am I supposed to cope and get through the year when I can't control myself? Chanelle *was* doing me a favour by pulling me away. Danica has no idea what thoughts were going through my head, or what I am capable of. If Chanelle hadn't intervened, that nail file might be sticking out of Danica's eye right now. I should apologize to her. Make one thing right.

The warning bell rings as I walk to the sink to spit out a mouthful of blood. I've really done it this time. I turn the tap on and take a sip of water to get the metallic taste off of my tongue. I look in the mirror and stare at myself for a long time while washing my hands.

Am I crazy like everyone thinks? Do they really think that?

I dry my hands on my jeans and walk out of the washroom and down the hall and to the stairs that lead to the library. Miss Tinsley is behind her desk. I greet her with a nod and walk to the fantasy section. I slide to the floor and randomly choose a book about elves and goblins. I have no intention to read it; I want to look like I'm keeping busy without actually doing anything related to school.

I think about the shadow, I think about Sara not writing to me since the Shane incident, I think about my life and where it's going. If I keep up with this charade the only place I will end up is in a mental institution...or prison. I try so hard to keep my emotions at bay, but when I'm confronted with anything that upsets me, I can't control my anger. The words come pouring out of me before I can stop them. Chanelle did not deserve that anger, even though she is as annoying as they come. She did not deserve it. Danica, on the other hand—no, I can't think about her. My blood boils, thinking about her. I don't care that she is with Shane now, although to anyone else it would look like I'm full of jealous hate toward her. They can have each other—but don't stick it in my face. I might have had a shred of fondness left for Shane, but that was stripped away. I hate him, I really do.

I walk to Mathematics and the news of what I said to Chanelle has already made the rounds. How could anyone be so mean to someone as sweet and innocent as Chanelle? It would be like punching a kitten in the face. I hear the whispers as I pass students in their small groups. I'm getting called every name in the book. There goes the apology I was going to make to her.

Screw that noise and speak of the devil—or angel, I guess; I'm the devil now.

Chanelle and her four-foot posse stalk past me. One of them shoulder checks me and I stumble to the side, hitting a locker. "Out of the way, sinner!" she says, and they all throw their heads back in laughter.

Chanelle is definitely not getting an apology from me; I don't even feel guilty anymore. I get my footing and my fury under control, and walk into the classroom. If there were a world record for most disliked student I would win it, hands down. The absurd thing is, a lot of these idiots have no reason to hate me in the first place. They only go along with everyone else so they don't have to endure the displeasure of the popular assholes. I was one of those popular assholes last year. They must all love seeing me now lower than them on the popularity pyramid.

If someone had told me that Danica would be more admired than me last year, I would have laughed in their faces, but look at her now, sitting there being bubbly and talking to everyone as if they're her life-long best friends. Dating Shane will bump even the dorkiest student to a more popular status—or sluttiest, in Danica's case. That was my lucky break in the first place: dating him. *Now look at me.* Everyone else is.

They are all staring at me; judging me, pitying me, hating me, blaming me, and who knows what else. I can't escape the looks. I bow my head and walk to my desk in the corner of the room and sit facing the window. I can't do this. It's not even October; I'll never last another eight months. Who am I kidding?

"Miss Martin, pay attention please," Mr. Clarke says.

I look from the window to the front of the class and meet Danica's eyes. She smiles devilishly at me and moves her hair away from her shoulder, exposing three fresh hickeys on her neck. She slowly trails her index finger over them.

My heart begins to beat rapidly and the sound of it throbs in my ears. She snickers and faces frontward, but leaves her hand in place on her neck. She trails the hickeys again, but with her middle finger this time.

That bitch is flipping me off!

I stand up so abruptly the desk screeches across the tile floor. Mr. Clarke spins around and so does everyone in the class—including Shane, whom I had not seen until now. He has dark red lip marks on his neck.

"Sit down, Miss Martin," Mr. Clarke says sternly.

I look from him to Danica then to the classroom door. I ignore him and walk between the rows of desks to the front of the class. I have to walk past Danica to leave the room; there is no way around her.

"Miss Martin, I am going to give you ten seconds to sit down or you are going to get a detention," Mr. Clarke says firmly.

I give him a blank look and walk past him.

"Mr. Clarke, don't you know she's crazy?" Danica says.

"Miss Evans, that's enough," Mr. Clarke says.

"Just like her mother," Danica says maliciously.

I stop at the door and force my eyes to Shane. He's told her everything. He cowers back into his chair under the weight of my glare. I could ruin him at this very moment. I could tell everyone *everything* that he did: everything about Milly, about attacking me...all of it. I hear Danica cackle and I clench my fists tightly at my sides. *That damn cackle!*

I look from Shane to Danica, who is laughing hysterically at me.

"Miss Evans, don't make me give you detention as well. Compose yourself," Mr. Clarke warns her.

"Well, it's true," Danica says. "The apple sure didn't fall far from the tree in her case. Stevie is as crazy as her lunatic mother!"

I can't control myself any longer. Mr. Clarke sees it coming but he isn't fast enough. I sprint across the room and dive right into Danica, driving her out of the desk and onto the floor. Her head hits the tile, but not hard enough to knock her unconscious. She screams and tries to scratch me with her newly filed nails.

Should have waited to file them, bitch! I ball up my fist and punch her in the temple as hard as I can.

In the few seconds that it took me to knock her to the floor and get a punch in, Mr. Clarke makes it around his desk and pulls me off of her. I kick her in the stomach as he drags me to a safe corner. The other students watch, too dumbfounded to get involved.

"You bitch!" Danica screams, clutching her temple. "You made me bleed! You're going to pay for this." She stumbles to her feet.

Mr. Clarke pulls me into the hallway just as Chanelle appears with Principal Harling. I don't say a word to either of them.

"Stephanie—office—now!" Principal Harling barks.

I look from Mr. Clarke to Chanelle—who looks rather satisfied—and then to Principal Harling. I push through them and storm off down the hallway.

How dare Danica say anything about my mother. She has no idea what we've been through. She had no right saying what she did, and Shane telling her about my past...I can't imagine what he said to her, especially after last weekend. He could have made up a bunch of lies about me to make himself look better, to make me look nuts if ever I tell anyone about him attacking me. How am I going to explain my actions to Principal Harling? I should run, run as fast as I can and escape the questions. Surely I'll be expelled for punching Danica. Mom doesn't have the money Danica's parents have to negotiate me back into anyone's good books. *I am screwed.*

Deep down I know I wanted this. I wanted a reason not to have to come back to this place. After everything I've been through, I was living in a fantasy world, thinking I could come back to school and everything would be like it was before—minus the friends. I don't have it in me to wear a fake smile all day, and be in the same classes as Shane without it affecting me. I'm not as strong as I thought I was. *I'm pathetic.*

I reach the reception area on the first floor. "Take a seat please, Miss Martin," Principal Harling says. He greets the receptionist and walks past her and into his office. He closes the door behind him.

The receptionist, Patricia, is neither fat nor skinny, but something in between. Her hair is unremarkable and she doesn't wear makeup. She's one of the most boring and average-looking people I've ever seen. The only thing bright about her is the huge arrangement of wildflowers sitting in a vase on the corner of her desk. I've seen similar flowers growing in the forest behind my house. I have no clue what they are; I should look their names up later. God knows I'll have the time to do that if I get expelled from school today.

I can tell I'm making Patricia uncomfortable—she's been trying to move her chair slowly to the side without me noticing so she can hide behind the flowers. I smile at her kindly and turn my attention to the principal's office behind her. The glass is frosted and I can barely see his outline. He is sitting at his desk and might be on the phone. I tip my head closer to see if I can hear him. All I hear are muffled sounds. He is definitely on the phone.

Patricia's handset buzzes and she picks it up. She quickly looks in my direction and then at her computer screen. I straighten my shoulders, lean back into the chair, and look at the clock hanging above the principal's door.

"Yes, yes, okay, yes," Patricia says, and returns the phone to the cradle. "It will be a few more minutes, Miss Martin," she says, keeping her eyes focused on the computer. Is she afraid of me?

Chanelle must have barged in here like a tornado, screaming for help. I wonder what she said. Probably something like, *Stephanie's killing Danica! Call the police. Call a priest! She's possessed.* A chuckle escapes my mouth. I bow my head and conceal my face with my hand. Chanelle must really think I'm possessed.

The door to my right opens; I part my fingers to peek at who has arrived. "Mom?" I say, and remove my hand from my forehead.

"What have you done, Stephanie, that I get a call to come down here immediately? I had to leave work," Mom says, her tone conveying her displeasure.

"I can explain," I say.

Patricia stands up and knocks gently on Principal Harling's door, then opens it a crack and sticks her head inside. "Mrs. Martin is here."

I follow Principal Harling's shadow as he rises from his chair and crosses the office. "Mrs. Martin," he says, and extends his hand as he walks through the doorway.

Mom shoots me a look—she is not impressed. "Mr. Harling," she says, and shakes his hand.

I rise to join them.

"I will be talking to Mrs. Martin alone, if you can please take a seat. This will not take long," he says firmly.

I sigh and sit back down. Patricia closes the office door behind him so I can't hear what they are saying. I watch their shadows sit down. Patricia returns to her desk but positions herself out of my view. I look back at the clock and tap my foot for every second the littlest hand on it moves. Patricia's typing falters every time I tap my foot so I know it's annoying her; I tap my foot louder merely to piss her off. That's the mood I'm in today.

Minutes go by. It feels like an eternity before Mom emerges from the office. Principal Harling doesn't join her. I see him on the phone as she pulls the door shut behind her.

"Go get your things from your locker, Stephanie; we're going home," she says, and walks past me.

I grunt and stand up. I walk to Patricia's desk and look over the flowers. She recoils from me. *Seriously? What did Chanelle say?* I look down at the flowers and pluck a purple one out of the vase. I take a sniff of it—it smells like lavender—and grin deviously at Patricia, who doesn't tell me to put the flower back. I leave the office.

Mom follows me silently to my locker. I choose to stay silent for the time being. No need to upset her any more than she already is. I'm itching to know what passed between her and the principal. I'm dying to know what lies were concocted to protect me.

"All of it?" I ask Mom as I stare into the open locker.

"Yes all of it, except the school books; you can leave those here," Mom says.

"Okay." I open my satchel and take out everything that is the school's property. I retrieve my belongings from the locker: the photo of Charlie, the mirror, some loose makeup, lip gloss, and ChapStick; lined paper, stationery, and binders. I shove it all in the bag and close the door.

"All done?" Mom asks.

"Yes, I think so. Are you mad at me?" I say.

"Let's get out of here and then we'll talk," she says.

I follow her down the hallway toward the front entrance. We pass the office on the way out. Shane and Danica are sitting in the spot where I'd been sitting. Shane is closer to the door. Mom is out of the school but I hesitate before leaving. I turn around and stare into the office. Shane turns his attention to me; Danica is too busy on her phone—texting like crazy—to notice me standing there. I pull my sleeves up, exposing the bruises on my wrists that show clearly on my pale skin; they probably look worse because I am so *white*. Shane cringes and looks quickly away. The last thing I see before exiting the school is him reaching for Danica's phone, and saying something in her ear.

It was a silent threat, showing Shane my wrists. It was an "if you say anything about me I will take you down" warning. He would have to be incredibly stupid to go against me. It would be his word against the evidence Mom forced me to put down on paper and the photos she took. And I have witnesses. I don't think Shane would be that senseless.

I walk down the steps. Mom is waiting in her car, which is idling in the same spot where she dropped me off this morning. I walk along the sidewalk toward her and stop as I reach the vehicle to take one more look at the school. Mr. Clarke is staring at me from the third floor window.

"Goodbye, school," I say, and get in the car. I throw the satchel on the backseat and pull the seatbelt into place.

"Well, that was pretty much how I expected this day to go," Mom says as she pulls the car onto the street.

"I know. I should have listened to you this morning. You knew I wouldn't be able to handle coming here today. I feel so dumb," I say.

"Stephanie, it's not about listening or who was right or wrong. You are a lot like me in so many ways. I know you would rather not admit to that, but you are."

Crazy...just like her mother...

"In what way?" I ask.

"Well, for one thing, you're stubborn, you have a temper, and you don't take shit from anyone," she says.

"That was three things. And you said shit. You never swear." I can't keep from smiling. Mom swearing is like hearing a priest blaspheme—it never happens, unless she is furious.

"Well, I'm pissed off," she says. "You've been expelled. You realize that, right? You can't go around punching people. And why that girl instead of the real problem? Why not attack Shane for what he did? Why not him?"

"Because he is not the one that called you crazy, Mom," I say.

Mom turns the car erratically into a parking lot and hits the brakes so hard the tires screech. "You got expelled because you punched a girl for calling me crazy?" she asks, and holds her hand to her head. "Oh Stephanie, what am I going to do with you?"

"Lock me away; apparently I'm the one who's really crazy," I say. "I'm sorry, Mom. I had so much pent-up anger for so many different things. I cracked, okay? I cracked and took it out on Danica. She deserved it, though." I cross my arms under my chest and look down at my lap.

"Thank you for sticking up for me, but maybe next time use words, not your fists, okay?" she says.

I look up. "So you're not mad at me?"

"Yes I am, but only because I don't like seeing you hurt. You can finish high school any time; these days you can finish it at home. I wish we had taken that route instead of you going back to school and leaving the way you did. It might make it harder for us to get you into a good college, with that kind of track record."

"The last thing I am thinking about is college right now."

"That's fine, but you have to figure it out. I guess first things first. You take a break from school for now; don't think I'm going to let you off easy, though. You can pick up more shifts at Greg's store. We have to make a lot of trips to St. Chalmers within the next few months and although you getting kicked out of school is horrible and the circumstances are what they are, it happened at a good time. It's unfortunate, but we will make it work," she says, and pats my leg.

"I never expected you to understand. Thank you for that," I say. "What was said in the office, by the way?"

"Well they are not happy. That girl's family does a lot for the school. That principal of yours went on and on about how much they've donated, and blah-blah-blah," she says. "They had no choice but to expel you. Let's pray her family doesn't press charges against you."

"I don't think that will happen," I say.

"What makes you think that?"

"Well, she's dating Shane now, and Shane is not going to do anything about it, and she pushed my buttons by saying things about you. And we don't have money if she does decide to sue us. The odds are not in her favour."

"You sound sure of yourself. Let's hope you're right."

"I am, I have a feeling about it," I say, remembering the look on Shane's face when I showed him the bruises he left on my wrists. "We'll be fine."

CHAPTER TEN

IT'S ALMOST CHRISTMAS; I can't believe how fast the last few months have flown by. As I predicted, nothing came of the fight I had with Danica. I received a text message from Shane, which shocked the hell out of me, but all it said was: *Danica will not be causing you any trouble, and neither will I.* That was all it said. I never responded to it. That was a week after I was expelled from school.

I have not heard from Sara either, not one e-mail, or postcard, or anything. I continued to e-mail her—although I was not getting a response—up until November, when I finally decided enough was enough, there is only so long you can have a one-sided conversation. She was the last friend I had left; now I have no one in this world. I expected after the whole Shane incident that she would stop returning my emails. What I didn't predict was that they would stop entirely without me getting a chance to say goodbye to her properly. I contemplated dropping the laptop off at her parents' house, because the sole reason for having it was to stay in contact with her, but I decided against it. It was a gift, after all, and if she wants it back she could ask for it. This chapter of my life is closed now; I need to put it behind me. I've been trying my best to do so, but some days are harder than others.

My days are pretty monotonous. I work at Greg's store two days a week, Saturday and Sunday. I am happy to work weekends. Weekends for me are the most depressing times. They used to be the days I looked forward to the most, but that was when I had friends to look forward to them with. Working helps me fill the void that is my life. The other nice thing about working full days on the weekends is that I have accumulated a nice little cache of savings—which is still hidden in an old coffee can under my bed. Greg is going to help me look for a car in the coming weeks; I can't wait to get one. I hate having to depend on Mom for transport, and public transport freaks me out. You never know what kinds of people are on the bus with you.

People like me...

Plus, walking to the bus stop in the winter we are having is a sure way to get a cracked skull on the sidewalk. The people who salt the roads usually do our street last, and they don't take as much care as they do on, say, Sara's street. It's annoying, but hey, we *are* on the poorer side of NorthBerry Hill; maybe not the poorest side, but we are on a rural road, and most of the residents here drive tractors and four-by-four vehicles, so the icy roads are nothing to them. Greg, luckily, drives a jeep with four-wheel-drive, so he has been nice enough to play taxi on the coldest days when I can't make it out of the driveway to get to work. On the days that I'm not working, I spend most of my time alone, at home. I'm housebound if it's snowing, even if Mom leaves her car for me to borrow; I wouldn't take a chance of crashing it on the way out of our driveway.

Mom spends a lot of time at Greg's house. I can't blame her; I am not the best company most days. I don't even want to be around me, but unfortunately you can't escape yourself anymore than you can escape your shadow on a sunny day.

Speaking of shadows, I have seen nothing of my saviour—*that shadow.* I walk around the house sometimes when Mom isn't home, and talk out loud. I direct questions to whoever may be listening and wait for responses. Ridiculous, I know, but I can't help but wonder if someone might actually be listening to me. I'm lonely. I know I am lonely and I feel lonely. I wonder if this is how Mom felt after Dad died. She hid in her room, never spoke to me, avoided me, and she was angry all the time—like I am. I wait impatiently for the day when that will all change, as it did for her. Do I really need to find someone to make myself happy? How can I ever trust anyone enough to let them in? I am scared to death of that.

Death is another thing that crosses my mind a lot. Sometimes I think it would be easier to let go of this life and move on to the next, but I have nothing to die for, I have no confidence that there is anything waiting for me on the other side. I might as well stay here, if the other option is ending up even more lonesome than I am now.

I am sleeping a bit better now. The nasty nightmares I developed after the crash haunted me for months, every night, but now they only come if I am feeling particularly moody that day. So basically five out of seven days a week I have them, but it's better than every night. I *try* to tell myself that tomorrow will be better, that I will have a good day, that I will make it a good day, but when that day comes I can hardly get myself out of bed. It's a struggle every morning for me.

I try to fake a smile when I see Mom and Greg, but I am the worst actress. I seem to have switched places with Mom. I am now the one who cries almost every night, who mopes around the house staring at the paintings, the one who is on a short fuse and bitter all the time. I am in such a dark place right now, and I have no idea how to pick myself up and get out of the gloomy pit that holds me. I feel as if I have a cloud above my head that lingers from the time I get up in the morning until the time I go to bed. I read before bed to clear my mind and imagine that I am in a different place, but it only works for the hour that I'm lost in the pages of someone else's mind. Reality hits me as soon as I close the book.

You have no friends.

You have no future.

You're all alone.

Charlie is gone and he is never coming back.

You killed Milly.

Sara hates you.

Everyone hates you.

You're all alone, you have no one...

And the list goes on and on through my brain all the time. Sometimes I wish I was the one that was killed in the car accident instead of Milly. It should have been me. I think about how happy everyone would be if I was the one that had died; how much better off they would be...

"Stephanie!" Mom yells from downstairs.

"Yes?" I holler from the bathroom. I stare at my reflection in the mirror, as I've been doing for the last fifteen minutes. I have dark circles under my eyes. My hair is unwashed and unbrushed, and I am still wearing the black pajamas I wore to bed last night.

"Stephanie, where are you?" she asks, walking up the stairs.

I wipe a tear from my face and emerge from the bathroom. Mom meets me outside the doorway. "Everything alright, honey? Have you been crying?" She rests her hand on my shoulder.

"I had something in my eye," I lie, and squeeze my eyelashes between my fingers to lift the lid up. "But I got it out."

"Hmm." She studies me. "You never answered your phone."

"The battery's dead. No one ever calls me, so what's the point in keeping it charged?"

"Please keep it on for emergencies, okay?" she says.

"*Okay*," I mumble. "Why are you home?"

"There is going to be a big storm tonight, and possibly a power outage across town, so I thought I would spend some quality time with you so you wouldn't be scared. I remember how terrified you were of storms when you were little."

"Yes, I remember. Well thanks...I guess," I say. "Is Greg joining us?"

"Only for dinner, then he's going home. He thought it would be a good idea for us to have a girls' night."

"Really?" I say, and wrinkle my nose.

"Well, I thought it would be nice. We haven't seen a lot of each other since you've been home. I've been really busy trying to get St. Chalmers in order. Who would have thought opening up a business would be so time consuming? But I won't bore you with the fine details; all you need to know about that is everything is slowly coming together."

"So you picked a stormy, possibly powerless night to spend quality time with me?"

"I didn't want you to be alone," she says. "There is pizza downstairs, and a surprise for you to cheer you up. I *can't take* looking at your sullen face every time I come home. Don't think it goes unnoticed."

"A surprise? What kind of surprise?" I ask.

"Go downstairs and see for yourself." She smiles widely.

I roll my eyes at her and a small smile turns up the corner of my mouth—a *very small* one.

The smell of pizza hits me as soon as I reach the living room. And I can already hear the wind picking up outside. Greg is standing in front of the sofa with his back toward me. "Greg?" I say.

He spins around with an enormous grin on his face. "Go put your gumboots on and follow me!" he says, and walks to the front door.

I am so confused, but I do as I'm told and follow him to the door.

"Here," he says, and cups his hand over my eyes. "Trust me, okay?"

"Sure."

I walk hesitantly out the door with him. Icy wisps of wind hit me. "If I knew I was going outside I would have put on a jacket."

"We won't be out here long," Mom says from behind me.

Greg carefully leads me down the front steps. Our feet slosh through the wet snow. I'm appreciative of the knee-high socks and slippers I have on, but neither of them are waterproof. It's a good thing my legs hardly feel the cold anymore.

"Are you ready, Stephanie?" Greg exclaims gleefully.

"If I knew *what* I was getting ready for, I would say yes," I say.

"Greg, hurry up—it's *freezing* out here," Mom says eagerly.

"Okay, okay." Greg leans in to whisper in my ear, "I think Denise is more excited than cold."

"Greg!" Mom urges.

"Alright!" Greg says, and removes his hand from my eyes. "Surprise!" he yells with delight.

"Oh—my—goodness!" I squeal, and it honestly feels like the first bit of happiness I have felt in months. I spin around and wrap my arms around Mom. "Thank you *so* much!" I let her go, and bound over to embrace Greg. "It's the most beautiful thing I have ever seen!" I scream, looking over his shoulder.

A car, they bought me a car. I can't believe it! Heedless now of the snow, I skip over to the car and touch the rain-soaked pink bow that they attached on the hood.

"Here, catch!" Greg says.

I turn around as he throws me the keys. They jingle through the air and I catch them. He runs to the passenger side with as much giddy excitement as me.

"You guys are like a couple of kids," Mom says, smiling at us. "While you get acquainted with your new car, I'll set the table. Don't spend too long out here; you'll catch a cold, with what you're wearing."

"*Okay*, Mom," I say, and beep the car open. "Automatic locks!" I bounce with glee.

Greg smiles and opens the passenger door; he hops into the vehicle with me. "So, you like it?"

"Are you kidding me? It's gorgeous!" I beam at him. "What is it, how much does it cost, how much do I owe you?" I grip the steering wheel with both hands.

"One question at a time!" Greg laughs. "It's not a brand spanking new vehicle, but it's safe. I know I didn't ask you what you wanted, but that car you were driving before, well…Denise and I wanted something more reliable and safe for you. It's a Honda CR-V. It has four-wheel drive, and it's a manual transmission, just the way you like," he says proudly.

"I don't have any words right now…thank you for this, Greg," I say. "So what *do* I owe you?"

"Nothing, Stephanie; it's a gift. Think of it as your birthday and Christmas present for the next ten years," he quips.

"Oh my God, this is too much!" I say.

"No, it's not enough. You're a good kid, Stephanie, and you've been through a lot. Plus I got a killer deal on the car," he adds, and winks.

"And Mom is fine with this?" I ask.

"She wasn't at first, but I talked her into it." Greg smiles.

"This is nuts." I shake my head. "Can we take it for a spin?" I move my hands across the steering wheel, pretending to drive it.

"Maybe wait until tomorrow. That storm is going to hit any second."

"*Fine*," I say, and throw my head back.

Greg chuckles and opens the passenger door. "We should get inside before Denise polishes off the pizza without us."

I follow him to the porch and beep the car locked. "This is so awesome," I say, and smirk at him. "Are you staying the night?"

"Only for dinner, then I'll get going. I wouldn't want to encroach on valuable mother-daughter time," he says.

Greg walks inside the house but I take one more moment to look at the black Honda. It's a handsome sight that only lasts a few seconds; the rain starts pouring down, obscuring the scene. I turn to go inside the house just as lightning cracks in the distance, illuminating the night sky. For a fleeting moment I see a shadowy human form standing near the trees that frame the path leading to the gazebo, then it's gone. I stand mesmerized, staring at the trees swaying fiercely in the wind. The wind whips my hair around my face. *Come on...come on...where are you?*

The thunder roars above me and the porch vibrates. I topple backward, hitting the front door. Never closed properly, it swings open and I fall into the house and land on my rear.

"Stephanie! Are you okay?" Mom says, rising from the sofa.

I laugh out loud and get back on my feet. I close the door and lock it. "I guess I *am* still terrified of storms," I say. "It's a good thing you're staying home tonight, Mom." I rub my bony bottom. I really need to eat more. I have no cushion to break my falls.

Mom and Greg start to giggle like teenagers, and although it's at my expense, it makes me smile. I am reminded of when Dad used to laugh with her like that. Maybe tomorrow *will* be a better day.

The power goes out at 9:30 p.m., leaving Mom and I in the dark halfway through a game of crazy eight countdown. I don't recall us ever playing cards together, and if we did it was too long ago to remember the memory. Greg left us at eight—I never rushed him out; I enjoy his company, and frankly, watching him and Mom interact warms my heart. Today has been by far the best day I've had since...well, *everything.*

Mom walks out of the kitchen holding two lanterns and hands one to me. "We could finish the game, but I don't think my old eyes can handle squinting in such poor light," she says. "Is it okay if I go to bed?"

"You don't need my permission. I was feeling kind of tired myself anyway," I say, stifling a yawn. "Thank you for everything today. I had a lot of fun—and the car! Well, that had to have been the best surprise ever."

"I fought Greg on the car, but now that I see how happy it makes you, I know we made the right decision," Mom says. "Good night, honey." She leans over and kisses me on the top of my head.

"Good night, Mom." I smile after her as she walks up the stairs.

I stack the playing cards, put them back in their box, and pick up the lantern to light my way to the kitchen. I stand near the kitchen window and narrow my eyes to look outside. It's even darker than it usually is, with the power out across town. Everything looks like a black cavern. The only thing that brightens up the sky is the lightning in the distance, and even that's not happening as frequently or violently as it was an hour ago. The thunder isn't shaking the house anymore, either. I stand at the window for a few moments and in my mind's eye an image develops of someone peering at me from outside. I would not see a face against the window until the lightning shocks the sky again. I don't give it time to. I turn around and leave the kitchen. I hate that my imagination does that to me. I creep myself out way too often.

I make a pit stop at the bathroom. There is no use in brushing my teeth because when the power is out the water doesn't run. It's a righteous pain in the ass. I place the lantern on the counter and use the toilet. I notice the curtain on the bathtub is closed.

Lightning sears the sky and lights up the whole bathroom. I squeeze my eyes shut. I want to see the shadow, but not if it's lingering behind the shower curtain. I count to ten in my head and open my eyes. Reaching over, I thrust the curtain open. There's no one there. I exhale and stand up and look at myself in the mirror; the lantern makes my features look sharp and peculiar. I've lost a lot of weight since being home—well, what I would consider a lot of weight—maybe five pounds, but me losing five pounds is like a heavier girl losing twenty pounds. I didn't have much to spare in the first place. I lift my pajama top up to my bustline and pull it back down quickly. My ribs look way worse in this light. *I could wash clothing on those things!*

I need to eat more, I know I do. When I'm stressed or feeling depressed I can't eat; even a mouthful makes me feel sick. Tonight I ate five pieces of pizza without gagging. I was in a better mood tonight—mystery solved: when I'm sad I can't eat and when I'm happy I can. I need to try harder to be happy, not only for me, but for Mom too. There were so many times I needed Mom to be happy for me in the past, and I know first-hand how it feels to be around someone who is permanently in a foul mood—it's not that fun. Now here I am doing it to her, when all she is doing is trying to make me happier. How can I trick my brain into making me think I'm in a better mood than I actually am? That's the question I hope to get the answer to before I suck the joy out of everyone around me.

Without electricity there is no water, so I rinse my mouth out with mouthwash and spit it in the sink, then pick up the lantern and walk to my bedroom, closing the door behind me. Setting the lantern on the side table next to my cell phone, I sit on the edge of the bed to remove my slippers and socks. I don't even know what time it is right now. I hope I can get to sleep without having nightmares. I lie back and pull the covers up, then realize I should plug in my cell phone in case the power comes back on in the middle of the night; that way it can charge while I sleep. I turn onto my side and reach for the chord that is usually dangling over the edge of the table, but it's not there. It must have fallen under the bed.

Under the bed. My worst fear! Well, one of them...

I am not crawling on the floor to look under the bed. Imagining what might be under there, waiting for me, is freaking me out too much: clowns, monsters, dead things... *Fuck that!* Instead, rather than *seeing* what's under there, I roll onto my stomach and stretch my arm under the bed. It can't be too far, the outlet is nearby. I pat the hardwood flooring, feeling for the chord.

Great job, Stevie—wait for something to grab you and pull you under the bed. Ew, I never thought of that!

My fingers graze something—*furry.* I yelp just as the power surges on. My room brightens for a second, and this time, there is definitely someone sitting on the wicker chair near the window.

I scream.

The power flickers off once more, plunging my room into darkness again, save for the small pool of light around the lantern.

"*Mom!*" I scream. "*Mom HELP!*"

There's a rattle and a crash from Mom's room, and seconds later she bursts through the doorway in her nightgown, baseball bat in hand. "*Stephanie what, WHAT!*" Mom shrieks, eyes frantically scanning the room.

"I—I saw someone sitting in that chair." I point toward it. "I swear it, Mom, someone was sitting there."

I sit as if paralyzed on my bed while Mom searches the room with the baseball bat held ready. That was Greg's idea to get; the Bible, we all agreed, was not really a good choice of weapon.

"There's nothing here, Stephanie," Mom says. "It was probably your eyes playing tricks on you." She sits on the bed next to me.

"Mom," I say, "can you look under the bed? I felt something furry under there when I was trying to plug the phone in."

"Want me to check the closet too?" she says with a grin.

"It's not funny! I really *saw* something, and there really *is* something under my bed!"

"Sorry," she says, trying to hide her amusement at my adolescent insecurities. "I'll look."

I edge to the middle of the bed while Mom gets on her hands and knees with her lantern to look underneath.

I hear something shift, then get dragged from under the bed.

"Oh my God, Stephanie!" Mom screams.

"What! What is it!" I yell.

Mom tosses something that looks like a dead animal at me. It's orange.

"Ahh!" I shriek, and try to push it away. I leap up to stand on the bed and kick it.

Mom bursts into laughter. "Relax, Stephanie!" she says, and wipes a tear away from her eye. "It's a stuffed animal."

"That was *not* cool, Mom," I say, annoyed. "I thought it was Charlie."

Mom's face softens and she gets to her feet. "I'm sorry, hon, I thought it would be funny. That was a cruel joke. I didn't even think about Charlie."

"It's okay," I say. "Now that I think about it, it *was* a *little* funny."

"You should have seen your face," she says, and starts giggling again.

"Mom, I have no idea what Greg's done to you, but I am happy for it."

"Me too," she says. "Now, would you like me to spend the night with you in here?"

"No, that's okay, but thanks for the offer."

"Okay, holler if you need me. I'm right next door." Mom leaves the room still chuckling to herself.

She never did check the closet.

Don't be silly, Stevie; there is nothing in there.

I erase the thoughts of what could be lingering in the closet and get out of bed to dash over and snatch up the stuffed animal lying next to the wicker chair. Ignoring the chair, I leap back into bed, pull up the covers, and hold up the orange, stuffed cat. I forgot Shane bought this for me after Charlie went missing. *To remember him by.* That's what Shane said when he gave it to me. It looks exactly like Charlie. I don't know how it ended up under my bed, and how I never saw it until now. I had totally forgotten about this. I should throw it away, but I think I will hold onto it for now.

I roll over and face the bedroom door—instead of the wicker chair—and clutch the dusty cat to my chest. How on earth am I going to get to sleep tonight? I definitely saw someone, or *something*, sitting on the wicker chair. I have no doubt in my mind that it was my saviour. For a brief second I thought it was Shane, but what I saw was definitely not Shane.

What I saw was a young man around my age, with ash-blond hair and piercing blue eyes.

oOo

The power was out until around five-thirty this morning. I had forgotten to turn off the bedroom light and that woke me up when the power finally kicked back on, and I couldn't get back to sleep.

I didn't have any nightmares last night. I thought my dreams would be riddled with them after the night I had, but instead I dreamt of the blond-haired man with blue eyes. His face took on many shapes in my dreams, but I only felt happiness when I saw him. Now that I'm awake, sitting on the wicker chair—where he sat last night—all I can do is daydream about him.

Does he see me the way I see him, in flashes? The first thought that crosses my mind is *ghost*, but why now, why didn't I see him before? What has changed in the almost four years since we moved here? Could it be because I hit my head really hard in the accident? Has he been watching me like he was last night? If so, for how long? I have so many questions and no answers. I can't tell Mom or Greg; they'd think I am losing it.

"Who are you?" I say quietly, and look around the room.

I sigh heavily and stand up to retrieve my cell phone from the side table. I power it on; its battery is half full. It's 6:11 in the morning. I leave the phone to charge and move to the alarm clock to set the time on it. It's only

Wednesday. Three more days until Saturday, three whole days to fill. What can I do? I walk to the window. It's still quite dark out; the sun won't rise for another forty minutes or so. The only thing that brightens up the dreary morning is the snow. It must have snowed after the storm we had.

Mom's car is parked in her spot. *And so is mine!*

I had completely forgotten about it. My heart leaps with anticipation. I have freedom again—not that I have anywhere to go, but the thought of being able to go wherever I want, when I want, without depending on anyone is liberating. I smile at the snow-covered car through the window. "You and I are going for a spin today," I say to the Honda.

With a rush of excitement I run to the closet and open it, then jump at my own reflection in the mirror. I need to do something about that. I look in the mirror again. I look like a hobo.

I search through the closet and pick out an outfit for the day: dark-wash jeans, a plain, light blue—*like his eyes*—t-shirt, and my favourite grey hoodie. I can't walk around the house like I have been for weeks, looking the way I do. The thought of his eyes makes shivers run down my spine—in a good way. If I'm not going to know when he appears, I need to look my best all the time. You would think I'd be more frightened of seeing him, a ghost, than him seeing me, but the way I look right now is a lot scarier.

I bundle the outfit up in my arms and walk to the bathroom, closing the door gently so I don't wake Mom up; she will not be getting up for at least another hour. I turn the shower on and while I'm waiting for it to heat up, I step in front of the sink and look in the mirror.

Yup, definitely a lot scarier than a ghost.

"Are you here?" I whisper. "Can you hear me?"

No reply.

The steam from the shower fogs the mirror, and I get the wildest idea. What if he can't hear me? What if he can only see me, like I see him? I am nervous and shaky and a little embarrassed, but what harm can it do? I push my index finger against the glass and write a message on it: *Who are you?* Then I undress and get into the shower. I fight the urge to peek around the curtain to see if somehow he responded to me. *Have a little patience,* I tell myself.

I take my time washing my hair and body, then shaving. When I'm done I stand for a long time and let the water beat down on my back, until the water starts to run cooler. *That should be enough time.* I turn the shower off and reach around the curtain—without fear—to get a towel.

I wonder if he has seen me naked, I think as I dry myself. A blush creeps over my face at the thought. There's not much to see, but I wrap the towel tightly around myself before stepping out of the bathtub. I refrain from looking at the mirror, still trying to exercise patience, but also because I'm afraid of what might be on the glass. I almost walk past it and leave the bathroom, but stop myself. What am I so afraid of, anyway? *It's the living you should be afraid of, not the dead,* pops into my head. My head is right. When I thought it was Shane in my room last night I was scared shitless, but when I realized it wasn't him, I was no longer scared. I've been chasing this shadow for months now; it's time to face him.

I close my eyes and turn toward the mirror. I open them before I change my mind. The words *Who are you?* are barely visible now, muted by the steam from the shower.

And that's all that's there.

I am such an idiot! And to think I really believed that would work. I feel foolish. I take a hand towel from the rack and wipe it across the mirror, erasing the words.

He's standing right behind me.

I stifle a yelp by holding the hand towel to my mouth, and spin around, my wet hair spraying the mirror with drops of water before falling against my back like a wet mop. I am face to face with him, frozen in place, in terror.

This is what you wanted.

My eyes are burning with unshed tears, and I'm fighting the urge to run screaming from the bathroom to the safety of...where? There is nowhere to run. I hold my breath as long as I can. He's here; he is really here, standing right in front of me. If I were to take one step forward I would bump into him, or pass through him—I don't have the courage to test which. I'm trembling and my knees feel weak, but I force them not to collapse on me.

Come on, Stevie, do something!

He is studying me. His eyes are the colour of a tropical ocean. They are the bluest eyes I have ever seen. I feel as if they can see through my soul. He almost looks like he's looking through me, like I'm the one that is the ghost. He's not that much taller than me; the top of my head comes up to his eyebrows, his dark blond, messy eyebrows.

I would never have to wear heels with him. I look down and shake the silly thought my brain. *Are you crazy? He's a ghost, Stevie; there is no you and him—ever!*

He furrows his eyebrows at me, as if he's trying to read my mind. I remove the towel from my mouth and let it drop to the floor. His eyes follow the movements. I open my mouth to say something, but the only thing that escapes is a strangled gurgle. His mouth twitches.

He has gorgeous full lips. Argh! Focus, Stevie! I tear my gaze from his lips and feel a shudder course through my body. My cheeks start to burn. *No, not now, don't blush!*

The thought of blushing makes my cheeks hotter, as always. I want to look away from him to hide my face, but I'm afraid that if I do, he will disappear. I don't want him to go, not yet—not ever. I want to absorb everything I can about him—his eyes, his lips, his ash-blond hair that is short on the sides and a little longer on top, and his perfect features that make him handsome and beautiful at the same time. I need to remember him so that when I dream of him it will be of *him*, not some muddled shape that my mind forms for me.

The thought of never seeing him again pulls at my heart. I feel a tear roll down my cheek, something I can't stop. He lifts his hand and my heart starts to beat dangerously fast. He slowly brings it up to my face in an attempt to wipe the tear away. I close my eyes and wait for his touch, but it doesn't come; I lean my head to the side but his hand doesn't meet my cheek.

I know he will be gone when I open my eyes; it's a feeling I have. I keep them closed a little longer, conjuring the image of his face, and I smile. When I open my eyes he is nowhere to be seen. I feel for the counter behind me to steady myself and keep from collapsing to the floor.

And to think that actually worked!

I dress quickly and don't bother to dry my hair. I am too excited to stay in the bathroom a moment longer. I run downstairs and turn the coffee pot on. While it brews I look out the kitchen window. The sun has emerged from hiding; it looks like it might actually be a bright day. It will still be freezing out, but there are no clouds in the sky and that makes me very happy, because now I can drive, and I have a purpose. I need to find out who he is.

oOo

It didn't take long to get used to the way the new car handles, and there are not as many blind spots as the Fiero had. I feel a lot safer, riding higher from the ground. My first stop—the only stop that I can think of, offhand—is NorthBerry Hill Public Library. It's a smaller library nestled not too far from Greg's shop. We have a small downtown area in NorthBerry Hill that's sort of like a strip mall on either side of the main street. It consists of a small coffee shop, a butcher, bakery, grocery store, two gas stations, the library, Greg's store, an animal shelter, the liquor store, three small family-run restaurants, a couple of thrift stores, a tiny jewellery store, the police station that is in the same building as the city hall, and a used car dealership. There is also a home-based beauty salon, but that's situated a few minutes from downtown. If you want to get any real shopping done, you have to go to the next town.

I park in front of the library and scan the street before I get out. I'm hoping to go unnoticed as I venture into the building. It's a school day, so I should be fine. I zip the grey hoodie up and pull its hood over my head, just in case, before I get out of the car and swing my satchel over my shoulder. I walk briskly to the entrance with my head lowered, pausing as the automatic doors swoosh open. I step into the quiet of the room. It seems more silent than a library usually is, but they did just open; it's only nine-fifteen in the morning.

"Good morning," a chipper voice says.

Shit, I've been spotted. I turn my head toward the voice. *Just the librarian...phew.* "Good morning," I reply, and smile weakly at the pudgy, middle-aged man behind the counter.

He puts down the book he was reading and takes off his glasses. "Can I help you with anything this fine morning?"

I'm about to decline his offer, but he might actually be able to make my task easier. The faster I get this done, the sooner I can get home, and the sooner I might see *him* again. "Well actually, yes," I say, and smile more brightly. I push the hood back and pull my hair over my shoulder as I walk toward him.

The pudgy man's eyes light up.

"I was hoping—and I am not sure if I'm in the right place—to find information on the family, or persons, who lived in my house before me; can I find that kind of information here?"

"How long have you lived there?" he asks.

"Almost four years now, but I believe the house was empty for about five years before we moved in, give or take a few months...So I was wanting to know who lived there nine, possibly ten years ago?" I twist my mouth to the side.

"Hmm..." He taps his finger on the desk while he stares thoughtfully at me.

I bite my inner cheek.

"We can consult the census records, and if that doesn't work you might be able to get material through NorthBerry Hill's community archives, which will have newspaper articles. If your house was in the newspaper, that could be a good source of information for you. These days you can look up a lot just by searching for it on the Internet; have you tried that?" he says.

"Well, no. It was something I only thought of doing this morning, sort of a side project of sorts, so I figured the library would make a good first stop," I say.

"I will walk you over to the computer. We keep all of the census records and archives on disk," he says proudly. "It's a lot easier to search through than a stack of paper. We do only have the last fifty years on the computer, though." He rises and walks to the back of the library. "I'll get it started for you and if you need any help, you know where I am."

I take a seat in front of the ancient-looking computer. Even though he pulled the screen up for me I still have no clue what I'm looking at. *Where do I start?* I don't even know what the hell a census record is.

I click the cursor on the search area and type in my home address, since that's all the information I have right now. I wish I had a name to search on. The home address pulls up absolutely nothing. I am already getting frustrated. *Where did your patience go?* I chide myself. I sigh heavily and rest my elbow on the desk and my head on my fist to stare at the screen. The librarian told me that this search engine would explore every census record and archive—including newspaper articles—from the last fifty years. That's all that's documented on the computer. If I want anything older than that I need to go to the stacks, but he doesn't have the key to that room. Just my luck.

I sit for what seems like hours searching through pages and pages of newspaper articles and obituaries from the last ten years. I stop when I see a very familiar one: my dad's obituary. I feel a tug at my heart and exit the screen straight away. But it's too late, my mind is already straying. His is the only familiar face I saw throughout the hundreds of lost souls...why does that word come to mind? *Lost souls*...is Dad lost like *he* is—my shadow? Does he wander around aimlessly looking at Mom while she moves on? Or is he trapped in a place that he can't escape, like the street where he died?

No!

I tell myself not to go back. I need to focus on what I came here to do... what can easily be done at home. I have the Internet there, too. I should have done that in the first place. But then, if I can't find anything here, where all of this town's and the surrounding area's records are, what makes me think I'll find anything by searching the Internet at home?

I feel defeated, but I'm not going to give up that easily. I pack up my belongings and thank the pudgy man as I exit the library. Outside, I stand on the sidewalk for a few minutes, weighing my options. I could go to the city hall and see if I can dig up anything there, or the police station...they'd probably tell me to stop wasting their time. It's worth a shot, though.

I leave my car parked in front of the library and walk down the street toward the police station. Greg's store is in the opposite direction, so I won't have to explain to him or Mom why I'm wandering around downtown. I have no explanation that would suit this particular situation. *Oh, I'm trying to find out information on the dead boy I see at home.* Somehow I don't think that will go down well.

I cross the street to the police station, grateful that the road is salted well here, so I don't slip. I walk up the ten steps to the entrance but hesitate as I grip the door handle. I feel tense all of a sudden. I can see my reflection in the glass doors, but I can't see through them. Do I really want to go in there? What if they start asking me questions about Milly again? What if I falter this time and they sense that I am lying? I can't even remember the full story that I came up with in the hospital to save my ass. Even looking at my reflection in the door glass, I can tell I look guilty, and I haven't even said anything. I let go of the handle and walk back down the steps.

"Miss Martin?"

I recognize that deep voice behind me. *Ugh—eff!* I grit my teeth and slowly turn around, forcing a smile to my face. "Yes?" I say through clenched teeth. The cop that returned my cell phone to me is standing on the top step with his foot wedged between the door and the jamb to keep it open; he looks about twenty feet tall from where I'm standing. I feel as tiny as a toddler.

"Was there something you needed? You stood here for a long time without moving. Is everything alright?" he asks, wearing that smile that does nothing to soften his face.

"I changed my mind; sorry for interrupting you," I say.

"Well, come on in out of the cold and we'll talk." He pushes the door wider open with his foot, then steps inside and waits for me.

I slump my shoulders and walk back up the stairs and into the station. It's dead quiet in here and I feel extremely uncomfortable. I can't for the life of me remember the cop's name. I take a tentative step past him and he lets the door fall shut.

"Why don't you step inside my office," he suggests.

"Am I in some kind of trouble?" I ask.

"No."

That doesn't make me feel better. I hate one-word answers. I bite my inner cheek as he leads me down the hallway. We pass a few other offices, all empty. This place is dead. Nothing really ever happens in NorthBerry Hill, so it makes sense that they don't have many policemen on duty. We walk to the fourth doorway and I follow him inside and sit down in the chair facing his desk.

The room is neat and organized. There is a gold-rimmed nameplate sitting near the edge of the desk that displays the name *Sheldon*; that will save me the embarrassment of asking his name when he so clearly knows mine.

Officer Sheldon takes a seat behind the desk and I notice an African mask hanging on the wall behind him. It prompts a funny thought of him wearing it and dancing round in nothing but a beaded loincloth. I hide my growing smirk under my hand and silence the laugh that wants to escape with a cough. He looks at me suspiciously and I straighten my posture.

"Had a tickle in my throat," I say.

"Would you like a glass of water?" he offers.

"No—no, thank you," I say.

"So what brought you in here today?"

"You did," I say cheekily.

His jaw clenches and then relaxes. I shouldn't push his buttons.

"I was watching you through the glass doors. You must have come here for a reason, then changed your mind. So please: go ahead, Miss Martin," he says.

"Well," I rub my fingers across my eyebrows, "I want to know who lived in my house before me, around ten years ago. I went to the library but I couldn't find anything, so I thought maybe there would be records that were not released hidden somewhere here." I wave my hand around the room.

"If they weren't released, there would be reason for it," he says coldly.

"Yes, that's what I realized, which is *why* I turned away to leave," I lie. "I'm sorry for wasting your time. Can I go now?" I stand up to leave.

"Hold on," he says. "Let me check the database, see if I can pull anything up."

"Okay..." I hesitantly sit back down.

He types rapidly on the keyboard. I can't see the computer screen from where I'm sitting, only a tiny glow from it reflected in his dark eyes. I watch him intently, hoping to catch a glimmer of anything in his stone-cold face. He stops typing and his eyes move back and forth slightly as he reads what's on the screen. I hear his finger working the wheel on the computer's mouse as he scrolls down, and watch his eyes moving down the screen. He stops scrolling and his eyes move back and forth once again. His expression changes from stone-cold and irritated to confusion, and then to shock. His eyes dart to mine and in that split second—where the whites of his eyes show the reflection of the computer screen—I see an image of *him*, of my shadow, of my saviour.

CHAPTER ELEVEN

"**WHAT—WHAT IS IT?**" I say and stand up quickly to lean over Officer Sheldon's desk.

Officer Sheldon turns the screen off before I can see what's on it. "Nothing that concerns you," he says, but he looks worried.

"What do you mean, nothing that concerns me?" I yell, and slam my fist down on the desk. The nameplate rattles, then topples to the floor.

"Miss Martin, control yourself," he warns.

I lean down to pick up the nameplate and put it back on the desk. "Look, I'm sorry for the outburst, it's just that I need to know who lived in the house before me. I can't explain why," I say, trying very hard to control my emotions.

"There is nothing you need to know," he says firmly.

"But I saw the shock in your face! What is it? Please...please tell me," I beg.

"This is a confidential matter, Miss Martin. You need to find something else to fill your time with. Don't push the subject. I can't help you any further. If you please..." He waves his hand toward the door.

I huff loudly and storm out of the office before I lose control of my temper and wind up locked in one of the cells. If it is confidential, as he put it, there's not a damn thing I can do about it. Maybe that's why I couldn't find anything about the house in the archives at the library. Was something covered up? If so, why?

I leave the police station with more questions than answers. As I reach the bottom of the front steps the snow starts to come down in gentle, fluffy flakes.

"Getting into trouble?" a male voice I recognize says.

I turn around and see Bradley smiling widely at me."Omigosh, Brad!" I step toward him. I can't tell if it's a hug or handshake moment, considering the last time we saw each other was at Milly's funeral. I smile weakly at him, pondering my next move.

"It's been ages," he says, and pulls me in for a hug.

I hug him back, then take a step away, keeping my hands on his shoulders. He looks about the same, except for the incredible tan that he did not have the last time I saw him. His hair is sun-bleached, and from the feel of his muscles under my hands I can tell he has bulked up a bit. "Brad, you look great," I say, and release his shoulders. I feel my ears warming up under my hair. "Where have you been? I haven't seen you since..."

"The funeral," he says, completing my sentence. "I know." A wave of sadness crosses his face.

"Sorry, I didn't mean to bring it up," I say. The wind picks up and I shiver as it reaches my skin through the thin hoodie I'm wearing. I cross my arms over my stomach and rub my hands up and down my upper arms. I wait for Brad to respond.

"What are you up to right now?" he asks. "Why were you in the police station?" He jerks his head toward the station.

"I was doing a little research, trying to dig some stuff up about my house."

"What for, a school project?" he says.

He must not be talking to Sara or Shane, either. I let out a snort and roll my eyes. "No," I say. "I don't go to school anymore."

"What? Why?"

"Long story," I say, and quirk my mouth to the side.

"Are you in a rush, or do you have time to grab a coffee to catch up?" he asks.

"Um...what time is it?"

He pulls his phone out of the pocket of his blue parka and flips it open. "It's two-twenty," he says.

"Already?"

"Why, is there somewhere you need to be?"

"No, I just don't want to be downtown when school gets out."

"Ah," he says. "We have forty minutes to catch up. Come on. I'll buy." He winks and smiles brightly. I can't say no to that.

We walk to the closest coffee shop. It's nice to get out of the cold; the snow is coming down in flurries now. I choose a table next to the window so I can keep an eye out for people I may have to avoid. We are the only customers in the little coffee shop. I cup my hands over my mouth and blow into them to warm them up. Brad walks over with two steaming cups of coffee. He puts them on the table.

"Thanks," I say, and wrap my hands around the cup. I lift it up and smell the coffee. "Mmm."

Brad takes his jacket off and hangs it over the back of the chair. He is wearing a pale blue V-neck t-shirt. I chuckle.

"What's so funny?" he asks.

"We're matching," I say. I zip down my hoodie, exposing my blue t-shirt. "I wish I had your tan, though; the shirt looks *way* better on you than on my pale skin."

"Thank Mexico for that," he says. "I'm surprised the tan has lasted this long."

"I didn't know you went. Wasn't Mil—" I stop.

"Milly supposed to go with me?" he says, finishing my sentence again.

I sigh heavily. "Sorry—again. I have no filter, *apparently*."

"It's okay. The tickets were non-refundable, so I brought a friend with me instead. I should be the one apologizing. I never called you when I got back, and never really said goodbye to you after the funeral. I wanted to, but after running into Shane I figured you wanted to be left alone as much as he does."

"You ran into Shane? When?"

"Let's see...it was after school started. In October, I think...somewhere then. I actually ran into him downtown as well. He was with some girl. I asked about you and he said he doesn't talk to you anymore. I didn't poke any further; he looked uncomfortable at the mention of your name, so I wished him well and went on my way."

I scoff and shake my head. "Yeah, I don't see anyone anymore either. How is school going for you, by the way?" I ask to change the subject.

"It's never-ending, but I'm in for the long haul. That's one reason I'm in town right now. I'm mentoring in NBHI."

NorthBerry Hills Institution, I realize. "The mental hospital?" I say, surprised.

"Well yes, if you want to put it that way. My father is a clinical psychologist there, so I have been mentoring under him whenever I have any free time, to get a better understanding of everything. It's a great opportunity being there, being able to work hands-on. I still go to class during the week; this is just something extra to help with grades."

"Hmm," I say, and nod.

"That boring, huh?" He laughs.

"No, not at all," I lie.

"I'm training to be a clinical psychologist, Stevie; I can tell when you're *lying*," he says, and laughs again.

"A four-year-old could tell if I was lying," I quip, grinning.

We both laugh for a while and then fall into an awkward silence. I have the unnerving feeling that he has things he wants to ask me, but he doesn't have the courage. I tap the side of the ceramic cup with my thumb and gaze out the window. The snow is already starting to cover my car. I take the last gulp of coffee and put the cup down. "I should probably get going."

"Yeah, me too; I have a ton of homework. I guess you don't miss that," he says.

"No, not really."

"Why aren't you in school? I thought this was your last year." He sounds concerned.

"I was expelled, for numerous reasons," I say.

Brad squints at me, pressing for more of an answer than I gave him. I sigh heavily and lean back against the chair. "That girl you saw Shane with—was she a tall, blonde, busty girl?"

"Yes, she was," he says with a sparkle of interest in his eyes.

"Well...she said something horrible about my mother. So I kind of—attacked her." I look down at the empty cup and run my index finger around the rim. When I look up at Brad he has a grin spread across his face.

"Jesus, Stevie, a tiny thing like you?" he jokes.

"Yes, a 'tiny thing' like me." I giggle. "She pushed my buttons, and after everything I've been through...I snapped." My smile fades.

"We've all been through a lot," he agrees, and shifts in his seat. "Well, Miss Feisty, as much as I would love to sit here all day, I should get going. The only reason I'm in town today is to pick up an assignment I'd forgotten at the hospital. It's already past three and I'm sure you want to get going yourself. If you ever want to grab another coffee or talk—here." He pulls his cell phone out. "What's your number?"

I give him my number and he puts it in his phone.

"It was really great seeing you, Stevie," he says, and rises.

"Don't I need your number to call you?" I say.

"Give it a minute," he says.

I give him a confused look and then my phone beeps. I smile. "Thanks," I say. I take the phone out of the satchel and save his number into my contact list. "Call me as well, if you need anything, alright?"

"Thanks, Stevie," he says. He lifts his coat and swings it on. "Want me to walk you to your car?"

"Nah, that's okay. I'm not parked too far away," I say.

"Alrighty. See you," he says brightly.

"Bye, Brad." I remain seated and wave at Brad as he walks past the coffee shop window. That was strange, running into him, but it was nice to feel normal for a bit, and talk to someone that isn't Mom or Greg. *Or your imaginary friend. What would Brad say about that?* I squelch that question before it evolves into another inward battle—I don't have time to argue with my brain right now.

Rising, I scan the street through the window as I put the cell phone back into my bag. Not recognizing anyone, I leave the coffee shop and start walking back toward the library and my car, constantly scanning the street. I make it without being seen or stopped by anyone I know.

On the drive home I think about Brad's offer to talk; I will most likely not seek him out again. Bringing people from my past back into my life—especially ones that deal with crazy people—sounds like a bad idea, even to me. Who knows if he was even telling the truth about not talking to Shane anymore? Just because I'm a bad liar doesn't mean he isn't a good one. There are lots of things I don't know about Brad, and a lot more he doesn't know about me, or what I've done. I can't divulge any information to him—after all, I'm the reason his girlfriend is dead.

I park in my usual spot at the side of the house. The first thing I do is delete Brad's phone number and the text message he sent giving me his number, before leaving the car. I don't want it to be easy to get in touch with him when I have an impulsive moment.

The dashboard clock tells me it's almost three-forty. Mom's car is here but that doesn't necessarily mean she is home. I lock my car up and walk past hers; from the look of the snow on the windshield she has not driven it today. I press the Lock button on my key and hear the car beep behind me as I open the front door of the house.

"Mom, you home?" I call out. "*Mom?*"

No answer.

I walk to the kitchen and throw my car keys on the table. I fill the coffee pot with water and ground coffee and turn it on, then snag a banana and carry it to the window to eat it while looking out at the darkening sky. *That's really going to put the weight on!* I think sarcastically as I peel it. I roll my eyes. Something is better than nothing.

Officer Sheldon's reaction to whatever he read on his computer keeps replaying in my head. If only I was a little faster, I could have caught a glimpse of the screen. Now, thinking back, I don't even know if it was *his* face that I saw reflected in the officer's eyes; it could have been anything.

Maybe I should go to our neighbours and ask them if they remember anything from ten years ago. I'd considered that option before, but I don't know the neighbours at all, and I don't have the guts to go over and knock on strangers' doors. Searching the Web already sounds like a lost cause; if someone has gone to this much trouble covering up whatever happened in this house, I highly doubt I'll find anything on the Internet. I give up before even trying.

The only way I am going to get answers is to ask the only person who has to know something. It's *him* I need the information on, so go to the source—but how do I summon him?

I open the cupboard under the sink and get a plastic bag, then pour a cup of coffee and take both out to the gazebo. I wipe as much snow off of the bench as I can with my hand, then put the plastic bag down to sit on so my pants don't get wet. I sigh and look around. *Heaven, that's what this place is.*

It looks like heaven from where I'm sitting. The trees are frosted in snow and the lake in the distance looks like a sheet of ice. The only sounds I hear are the crackles in the frozen branches surrounding the gazebo as the wind curls lightly through them. I could sit out here all night if I wouldn't freeze to death. Now that I think about it, this place would be a nice place to die. If I could choose somewhere to have my last breath it would be here, sitting with my back against the post, feet up on the bench, and a steaming cup of coffee in hand. *Ideal.*

I take a sip of coffee and breathe out, the hot air escaping like a billow of smoke before it drifts off—a lot like *him.*

"I wish you were here," I whisper, eyeing the steam floating up from the mug. "I wish I could see you again." I look around the gazebo and into the forest, bidding him to appear, imagining his face, his eyes, his lips. I want him here so badly it hurts, and I have no idea why this wanting feels more like a need than a desire. I need to see him again. I need him.

I leave the gazebo after finishing the cup of coffee and mope all the way back into the house and to my bedroom. This feeling of defeat is pissing me off. There has to be a way that I can see him again. Maybe I can't find out what happened in this house, but maybe I *can* find out more about spirits and how to speak to the dead. I feel a little moronic thinking like this, but I am desperate. The desperation might also be a longing to find out if I'm seeing something that's really there, or if I am possibly going mad.

I sit on the wicker chair with the laptop resting on my thighs and start the search for anything related to spirits that bear a resemblance to *him.* I spend hours upon hours going through what seems like hundreds of different websites. I watch videos from people who have experienced ghostly encounters and digitally captured their images. Nothing comes close to what I experienced. I could see him clearly, so clearly that I swear I could touch him if I'd had the courage to lift my hand when he was right in front of me. These videos show ethereal forms and floating "orbs," as they describe them—*he* definitely was not floating around me like some kind of dust molecule that the light reflected off of, making it look bigger in a photo than what it actually was. What I saw was real; *he* is real. Every photo that I go through shows almost the same thing: a blurry white image of a person that has no similarity to what I saw.

I glance at the clock in the bottom corner of the laptop screen. I've been at this for almost three hours. *Where does the time go?* I close the screen and return the laptop to the dresser. I'm all out of options now, and I've wasted my entire evening.

I check my cell phone. There's a text message from Greg telling me that Mom and he are having a date night and that she is spending the night at his house, and also to remind me that it's Saturday tomorrow and I have to work. I am grateful for his little reminders; if not for them, I would never know what day it was. I send Greg a smiley face emoticon to let him know that I received his message.

It's almost nine already; no wonder I'm starving. *What shall I eat tonight? Chicken or beef?* I twist my mouth in concentration as I stare at my only two options in the open freezer. I settle on Chicken Penne. I pop it in the microwave, then lift it out three minutes later. "Hot-hot-hot," I say as the heat reaches my fingertips. Instead of putting the food on the counter while I close the microwave, like a logical person would, I use my head to close it. The door clicks shut. I straighten my neck and stand frozen, staring at the reflection in the microwave door.

He's back.

I spin around so fast the box flies right from my fingertips toward him. "Watch out!" I scream as it soars across the room.

He stands there watching the box as it cuts right through him and lands just outside of the kitchen, splattering across the hardwood. I look from the splattered food to his face. He has the slightest smile turning up the corners of his lips. I put my hand over my mouth to hide the horri-fied expression on my face. Did that really just happen? My dinner passed through him. Like a—*yes, dumbass, we've already come to this conclusion...*

"*Ghost,*" I mumble into my hand. "Oh God, I am *so* sorry about that," I say, dropping my hand and taking a hesitant step toward him. "I didn't mean to throw my food at you, and then call you a ghost. I mean, you *are* a ghost, but you don't need me to tell you that. Did I burn you with the food? Wait—of course not. You don't even have a drop of it on your clothing. Oh

God, I'm rambling..." I feel the heat flowing over my face and lift my hand to my cheek to conceal the blush, breathing deeply to calm my nerves. "I'm just going to take a seat, down over here." I point toward kitchen table, then do so, shoving the chair next to me out from under the table. "Um, you can sit if you like. I don't even know if you can hear me. This is crazy. What the hell would Mom say if she walked in here and saw me talking to myself?" I look down at my hands and shake my head.

From the corner of my eye I see movement to my right. I don't hear his footsteps, but when I look up he's sitting on the chair that I pushed out for him, and he's staring at me. His eyebrows are slightly drawn together, as if he is deep in thought.

"You and I both," I say, and nod at him. I smile slightly and gaze down at his lips. *I wonder what they taste like.* I inadvertently bite my lower lip. His mouth twitches and I look away, my cheeks flushing wildly.

Can he read my mind? Oh shit, did he just hear what I thought about his lips? Could I be any more obvious? I squeeze my eyes shut, then pop them open. He's still here. I grin like an idiot at him. *Good going, Stevie; way to play it cool.*

"Can you hear me?" I blurt.

He tilts his head to the side and his eyebrows draw together again.

"I guess not," I say, disappointed.

My emotions are all over the place. I am happy that he's here, but I am also terrified, excited, worried, and fighting the logical side of my brain that is telling me that this is impossible. I sit for a while, absorbing the flood of emotions and trying to rationalize this extraordinary situation.

Sitting here like this is not doing either of us any good. An idea materializes in my head and I pop up from the chair. "Come with me!" I say as I pick up the car keys and stride away from the table. I turn as I reach the kitchen door; he's right at my heels. "You really need to work on that; you're going to give me a heart attack." I smile. He doesn't understand. This is going to be frustrating, but I hope my idea will work.

I take a random coat from the back of the kitchen door and throw it on. We leave the house with him walking beside me; every time he falls behind I wait for him and point to the ground next to me. He seems uncertain of me, a reservation we share. I wish I could read his mind; his face gives nothing away. Unlike me, he has an amazing poker face.

We reach my car and I unlock it and get into the driver's seat, pushing my satchel from the passenger seat into the footwell before turning the overhead light on. Then I look around. "Where did you go?" I look through the window to my left, scanning the yard, then through the windshield, and finally the passenger side—where he is now sitting. My heart leaps and I jump, hitting my thighs on the steering wheel. "Ouch!" I yelp, and rub my legs. "Seriously, we *really* have to work on that," I say to him. A grin spreads across his face. He has perfect white teeth.

I shake my head at him and giggle. "I'll have to hurt myself more often if the end result is me getting to see you smile." I blush. "Now to do what I came here to do." I lean over him and reach into the satchel. I take a peek up at him as I rifle through the bag. His head is tilted to the side as he watches me intently. I am surprised that he is this trusting of a complete stranger. But maybe I'm not a stranger to him; who knows how long he's been watching me, and I was just unable to see him until now. I smile nervously at him and finally find what I was searching for. I pull a notepad and a pen from the bag. I take another quick look at him; comprehension floods his face.

"Okay," I say, as I flick off the lid of the pen using my thumb. I tap the pen against the steering wheel while I think about what to ask first, but I'm stuck with questions I am asking myself: *Am I really sitting in a car with a ghost? And am I seriously about to ask this ghost questions? And where the hell did my confidence come from?*

Any normal person would be running, screaming, to telephone an exorcist or something, but not me—*no*, I sit in my car *with* the ghost, comfortably contemplating a list of questions to ask him, to get to know him better. *Maybe I am crazy...*

It's taken me months to come to the conclusion that the assholes at school were right, and therefore were maybe not assholes to begin with.

He leans over the gearshift to look at my face—which has been staring down at the blank paper while I zone out. I look up at him and smile kindly, nod, then put pen to paper. I write the word *Yes* on the top left of the paper in big, bold letters, then on the right side I write *No*, equally large. I circle both words. My heart starts to race with giddy little thumps as I write down the first question on the same piece of paper.

Do you speak English, or did you?

I hold the paper up so he can see it. I watch as his eyes move across the question. A small smile tugs at his lips; he lifts his hand and points to the *No*. I slump my shoulders and twist my face in confusion. He still has a small smile on his face.

I support the paper on the steering wheel to write: *How did you read the sentence if you can't speak English?* I hold the paper up to him again.

His smile extends across his face and he starts lightly bobbing up and down. "You're laughing at me, aren't you?" I say. "I guess that was a stupid question, considering if you didn't speak English you wouldn't have been able to read the question." I roll my eyes at him and mouth, *"Sorry." I sure wish I could hear the sound of his laugh.*

I snatch the paper back and write: *Can you hear me, when I talk?*

He reads the question but doesn't answer straight away. I watch as his cheek curves in.

Is he a cheek biter like I am when he's nervous? The very human mannerism makes me feel warm, a lot warmer than what I should be in this cold car.

Finally he points to the *Yes*.

"You can hear me?" I squeak. "Why didn't you say so, then?" I wait expectantly for him to answer me, but he only shrugs. "Can *you* speak?" I ask.

He shakes his head.

"So you can hear me but you can't speak, correct?"

He nods.

"So I guess we don't need this after all," I say, crumpling the paper up and tossing it over my shoulder to the backseat. "Well, let's go back inside then. It's getting cold in here." I open the door and stop. "Can you read my mind?"

He shakes his head.

"Thank God!" I say happily. "Not that I'm thinking bad things about you. I prefer to keep my thoughts to myself, when I can."

He grins and shakes his head.

We walk side by side to the house and back through the kitchen door. I glance at the clock on the microwave; it's almost eleven. I never did eat anything, but the hunger has faded. I don't want to waste even a second stuffing my face when I could be asking him more questions. I should get ready for bed, though; I have to be up early tomorrow for work. It's the first time I actually don't want to work; I want to spend all of my time with him. I might not see him again after tonight. What if tonight is all we get?

"*So,*" I say.

He turns and stops in front of me, inches away. I nervously look up at him. He tilts his head in that adorable way that reminds me of a puppy. I want to squeeze him. He raises his eyebrows at me.

"Would you like to, um, go upstairs?" I look down anxiously and fidget. His hand appears under my chin as if to raise my head. I look into his eyes—those pale blue, crystal clear eyes—and I feel my whole body relax. There is something about the way he looks at me that's comforting, heart-warming, and—well, right. I catch my breath. "You know, I don't know when I will see you again, and this might sound strange since you are, well, a spirit or whatever, but I want to stay up with you as long as possible. I feel incredibly close to you for some reason. I can't explain it. I've been searching for you for months, and now that you're here, I don't want to let you disappear again."

He nods reassuringly, his expression warm and kind. I smile at him and lead him upstairs.

"You can sit on the bed if you like; it's more comfortable than that chair," I say, nodding toward the wicker chair.

He walks across the room and sits on the edge of the bed. The mattress doesn't move under his weight. It's a weird sight.

"I need to put my pajamas on, but I don't want to leave the room, I don't know if you will be here when I get back," I say, and rock back on to my heels. "Have you seen me naked before?" I blurt.

He looks shocked; he shakes his head, looking hurt.

"I'm sorry, I didn't mean to assume, I just have no idea how this thing works—me seeing you and you seeing me. I didn't mean to jump to conclusions." I kneel down in front of him. "Please don't be mad," I beg. *Please don't leave.*

He lifts his hand and shields his eyes. I'm confused for about ten seconds, then I realize he's covering his eyes so I can change into my pajamas without worrying about him seeing me, or him disappearing if I leave the room.

I run to the closet and frantically search for pajamas that are not child-ish. I rummage through the shelves and find a pair of pink flannel shorts and a white tank top. I change into them and turn to the mirror to fix my hair and give the outfit a good look. *Crap, my nipples are showing!* I glance behind me; he's still sitting facing the door, with his hand covering his eyes. I take my favourite grey sweatshirt from the closet and throw it over the tank top. *That should do.*

I turn the bed lamp on and run across the room to turn the overhead light off. Then I turn to him. He looks like an angel sitting on my bed, not creepy at all—maybe he is an angel. I never took notice of what he was wearing before; I was too consumed with his beautiful face. I finally give him a good once-over while he still has his eyes covered. He's wearing black sweatpants, a white crew-neck shirt, and no shoes—not really angel attire. I look at his skin. It's pale but not ghostly pale; nor is it glowing angelically. It's simply normal, pale skin—like mine.

"All done," I say as I walk back to the bed. I sit next to him with my back against the headboard.

He drops his hand and shifts so he's sitting cross-legged on the corner of the bed, facing me. He looks very innocent, sitting like that.

Without wanting to waste even a second, I start asking him random questions that can be answered with yes and no answers. We talk for hours—well, I talk, he gestures—and it only feels like minutes have passed. Somehow through the hours we end up lying facing one another—I'm leaning on my right side and he is leaning on his left. If he could breathe, I would feel the air on my face. I look down at his chest and notice it moving up and down. He is breathing. Do dead people even take breaths? I will probably only find that out when I one day die.

I have no clue what time it is, but I feel my eyes getting heavier and heavier. I'm struggling to keep them open. He, on the other hand, does not look tired at all.

"I want to know your name," I say sleepily, and blink. My eyes feel as if they have mini weights attached to them. "I bet you have a beautiful name, a beautiful name for a beautiful man," I mumble. *Did I just say that?*

I peek out of one eye and he's smiling. His pale cheeks look slightly rosy in the dim light coming from the lamp. "Will I see you again?" I whisper.

He nods and brings his hand to my cheek, but I can't feel the touch. How I wish I could feel his skin and his warmth. "Good," I murmur, and close my eyes once again.

Sleep has won this battle. I fall asleep to the image of him smiling kindly at me, and the whisper of the name *Nicholas* drifting gently into my dreams.

oOo

Waking up with a smile on my face and a very real feeling of happiness after a night that was not filled with nightmares is a start to the day that I never would have thought possible. Even as I roll over and place my hand on the cold, undisturbed comforter where he lay last night, I swear I can still feel his presence. I know in my heart that what I felt and saw last night, what I found out, was not an illusion conjured by my mind.

Nicholas...

I had almost forgotten the name that came to me as I was on the brink of sleep; the name that was whispered to me like a small gust of wind wafting through an open window. I can't be certain that Nicholas is his name, but it's another thing that feels right to me. How I heard his name is a mystery, a lot like he is. Unless he can talk and he is hiding it from me, but why hide it? How amazing it would be, to be able to communicate with him, to hear his voice. What if he isn't talking because he has a high-pitched feminine voice and he's embarrassed by it? I giggle at the thought and hope that's not the case; a squeaky girlie voice from someone so handsome would definitely ruin his image.

No...not my Nicholas.

He must have another reason why he won't speak to me. Everyone has their secrets; he may not trust me enough to let me in on his.

On the drive to work I go over everything I managed to find out last night, everything that I thought would be safe to ask him without frightening him away. I don't want to have that effect on him; I've lost too many people in my short life, and I don't want to lose him as well.

The details I know so far: he's twenty-one years old; he didn't have any siblings when he was alive; his favourite colour is green; he didn't go to NorthBerry High—he was homeschooled; and his favourite season is autumn. Getting that small amount of information from him was very time consuming. I wanted to ask so many more questions: about his parents—are they still alive?—how he died, if he'd died in our house, how long he'd lived there, and so on, but I couldn't. Questions like that can't be answered with a shake or a nod of the head; they require longer answers, better explanations—I need him to talk.

The day passes so slowly. I have never been antsier than I am today. I want to go home. I know that you shouldn't watch the time when you want to be somewhere else because it makes your day go slower, but I can't help it. I look at the clock when I think an hour has passed and it's only been ten minutes. I keep busy by stocking the shelves, cleaning, pacing, counting the cash, recounting the cash, restocking the shelves, organizing every little thing I can get my fingers on. I even mopped the floors and meticulously made signs saying *Wet Floors*. When that was all done I started to pace again. The storage room is looking more and more inviting as a place where I can hide and take a quick power nap, but I can't take the chance of someone coming in to Greg's store and stealing stuff, so I do the next best thing to taking a nap—I drink a whole lot of coffee to ward off the sleepy haze that wants to overwhelm me. How on earth will I manage to stay up tonight if Nicholas decides to grace me with his presence again? He showed up at around nine last night. I finish work at five. *Hmm...*

I plan to rush home after work, have a bite to eat, shower, and then nap. I'll set my alarm for 8:45 and pray that he waits around for me. It sounds like the perfect plan to me.

Finally five o'clock rolls around. I close the store in record time, even with double-checking that everything is in order for tomorrow. I lock up, climb into my car, start the engine, and look over the building one more time to be sure the *Open* sign is off and the blinds are drawn properly. I never take chances with the shop, especially now that Greg and Mom are going into business together; if anything happened here it would slow the process of opening the other store in St. Chalmers right down, and they need to sell this place first, so I always take precautions.

The parking lot is usually empty at this time of day so I glance in the side mirrors to make sure nothing is obstructing the car, and start backing up. I turn my head to look out the back window as I slowly reverse, and slam the brake pedal down hard to stop the car.

It's that creepy old lady again; she's standing right behind the car.

I turn the engine off and jump out of the vehicle. "Are you crazy?" I yell. "I could have run you over! What are you doing, standing behind my car?" I slowly walk around to where she is standing. "Hello?" I say, and wave my hand in front of her face. She gradually turns to meet my eyes. She reeks of cigarette smoke and her long black hair is lying in thick, dirty tassels down her back. Her eyes look barren and cold. "Listen lady, I'm not sure exactly what you're doing. Do you need help or something?" I ask.

Please say no, I just want to go home!

She makes a rumbling sound in her throat and a small amount of air escapes her mouth. I gag involuntarily when the smell reaches my nose. I hold my hand up to my face and my eyes start to water. She smells as if she is rotting from the inside out. "Look, I'm sorry," I say through my hand. "I can't help you." I take a step back toward the car door without taking my eyes off of her. I turn as quickly as I can and open the door, jump in, and slam the door shut behind me, then lock it. Feeling panicky, I watch her in the rearview mirror. I can't go anywhere with her standing behind the car. *What the hell is she thinking?*

She sluggishly walks around the vehicle to the driver's side window. I watch through the mirrors and look away as soon as she reaches me. I hear a tap-tap-tap on the glass.

Oh my God, I don't want to look.

I clutch the steering wheel tightly with my left hand, put the key in the ignition, and start the engine. The sound of rubber squeaking on glass comes from where she is standing and I can't *not* look at what is making the sound. Bracing myself, I glance over. She is leaning in close to the window with the tip of her nose pressed against it; she has a wicked grin on her face that exposes her yellow, smoke-stained teeth.

"Oh my fuck!" I scream. I throw the car in reverse and slam my foot down on the gas pedal. The tires screech loudly and smoke pours over the windows from the rubber burning on the cement. I forgot to release the engine brake. I do so and the car lunges backward; I spin the wheel and the vehicle whirls around. I must look like some kind of bank robber when I leave the parking lot. I hurl a look left and right for oncoming traffic, then glance in the rearview mirror. The lady is nowhere to be seen. I burn rubber out of the parking lot and onto the road. Greg's going to have a fit when he sees the tire marks that I left right near the entrance of his store. I'll explain the situation to him.

I had completely forgotten about this lady until now. What the hell was she doing? I have not seen her since that time she scared me outside the store window when I was cleaning the glass.

I slow down as I pass the police station on the way home and contemplate stopping to make a report, but what good would it do? What can I really say to them? She did not appear to have any weapons, she didn't threaten me in any way, she only stood there looking weird. They wouldn't do a damn thing about it. I don't even know her name, and could only offer a vague description of her. I continue the drive home without stopping. I try desperately to calm my nerves but my mind keeps presenting the look in her eyes. There is something chilling yet very familiar about them. I can't put my finger on it.

Home is a welcome sight when I pull into the driveway. My schedule has only been altered by about fifteen minutes, but I need to add one more thing to my list: I must phone Greg before I forget again. I leave the car running so the heat continues to pour from the vents—we're a week away from Christmas and winter is in full swing. I dial Greg's phone number.

"Hi Stephanie," Greg answers on the fourth ring. He sounds out of breath.

"Hi Greg," I say, "am I interrupting something?"

"No, no," he says. "Denise and I are painting the new shop and moving things around. I'm not as young as I once was; the phone ringing was a welcome sound and a needed break." He laughs. "How may I be of service?" he jokes.

"I didn't even know you had the keys for that place yet," I say.

"We got them last week. Things are really moving along nicely now. Denise didn't tell you?"

"She said something along those lines, but never said you were actually in the building, fixing the place up."

"Well we are, and it's going great. I can't wait for you to see it."

"I can't wait either," I say. "So when do you think we'll be moving?"

"Not until the summer. We still have to sell the store in town and find buyers for my condo and your house. We're in the midst of talking to realtors—but don't worry about all that grown-up stuff."

"Mmm," I groan. *What about Nicholas?*

"Was that the only reason you were calling?" he asks.

"I wish—no, there is something else I forgot to tell you."

"What is it?"

"When I first started working for you, a woman came into the store who gave me the creeps. I've seen her twice after that, hanging around, acting like a weirdo. She was behind my car today when I tried to reverse, and she wouldn't move out of the way."

"Why didn't you tell us sooner?"

"Because things happened at school and I never saw her again until today—it slipped my mind."

"We've definitely had some characters over the years. What did she look like?"

"She has long black hair, bad skin, and she's kind of scrawny and poorly dressed. The first time I saw her she looked a little better than what she does now. Now she looks...diseased or something."

I can hear Greg breathing. "Nope, can't say that whoever you're describing has ever been in or around the shop while I've been working," he finally says. "Want me to ask Denise?"

"I guess it wouldn't hurt."

"Okay, hold on for a minute."

I peer out the car's windows while I wait for Greg to return to the phone. It's already dark out. *Why am I waiting in the car again?* I turn the engine off and get out of the vehicle with the phone pressed against my ear. While opening the front door, I beep the car to lock it.

"Hi, sorry," Greg says as I lock the front door.

"No problem. So what's the verdict?"

"Denise said that she *has* seen a lady that fits your description a few times, hanging around the parking lot, staring at her. It's the first I've heard of this. She said the lady left her alone though, and never came close to the store or entered it, so she never felt the need to tell anyone. She's probably some homeless lady looking for change."

"Yeah, probably," I say. "When was the last time Mom saw her?"

"Not for months," he says. "If you see her again and she comes close to you please let us know, and we'll go down to the station and make a report."

"Sure, Greg," I say. "I hope I never see her again in my life."

"I hope not too. We'll see you on Monday, okay?" he says.

"Alright, see you then, and thank you," I say, and hang up.

I walk to the kitchen and put my phone on the table. There is no time for everything I have planned before I hope to see Nicholas again. I decide to skip the shower and have a quick bite to eat. I need to take a nap; I've been stifling yawns all day, and with another long work day tomorrow with no reassurance that that crazy lady won't show up again, I need to be as awake as possible.

The coffee pot is calling my name but I ignore it. A caffeine boost is the last thing I need right now; maybe after my nap, but not right now. I devour two bananas and a toasted blueberry jam and cheese sandwich. That's the most I have eaten in one sitting in a long time. Feeling full and more than sleepy, I double-check that the doors are locked before going to my bedroom.

I set the alarm across the room for 8:45 p.m. That will give me a solid two hours of sleep, if I manage to fall asleep this early in the evening. In bed, I close my eyes and bring Nicholas's face to mind; I make him smile that gorgeous toothy grin of his, and I comfortably and happily drift off.

CHAPTER TWELVE

"YOU'RE HERE," I SAY sleepily, and force my eyes to adjust to the darkness. I can't see him, but I can feel his presence, and his eyes on me.

I stretch out on the bed and hear my back click all the way down from my neck to the bottom of my spine. I push myself into a sitting position, smooth out my hair, and turn on the lamp. He's sitting in the chair near the window. I smile shyly at him. "Hi," I say, fighting the massive grin that wants to take over my face.

He smiles at me and stands. I move over to the middle of the bed, leaving room for him to sit, but he perches on the corner of the bed instead. I try not to look hurt.

"Did you have a good day? Wherever you were..." I say to break the silence. He's staring out the window toward the moonlit sky. He turns to look in my direction and a flash of sadness crosses his face before he smiles and nods. "That bad, huh?" I say. "My day was pretty interesting too." He cocks his head and raises an eyebrow. "It's nothing to worry about; work stuff, you know?" I smile.

The alarm goes off on the other side of the room. I almost ask him to reach over to turn it off, then remember that he can't. I crawl across the bed and stretch my arm across the gap between the bed and the dresser to turn it off, not thinking about how on earth I'll get back to the bed safely.

The distance is a little farther than I anticipated. I feel like a bridge. I push off of the dresser to spring my body back to the bed, but the dresser tips backward and I crash to the floor. "Ahh!" I yell as I hit the floor. I flip over onto my back and see him leaning over the side of the bed, regarding me. I can tell that he's trying really hard not to laugh. "Go ahead, you can laugh," I say, and giggle as I replay in my head what I must have looked like falling off the bed. "I am not the most graceful person."

He grins and extends his hand to help me up. I reach for it and our hands pass through each other.

"Oh right," I say, grasping the foot of the bed to heave myself up. "It's easy to forget that—"

He nods grimly at me and I don't need to finish the sentence.

"Well, I for one need coffee. So let's go do that," I say, to change the subject.

"Can I ask you something?" I say to him minutes later, as the coffee brews.

He nods.

"I really, *really* want to know your name. It would be nice to put a name to your face—" I chuckle. "It usually works the other way around. If I guess it, will you let me know?" I bite my inner cheek and look up at him. "You can say no if you want."

He taps his finger against his chin and his mouth quirks up.

"Is that a yes?" I say eagerly.

He grins and nods.

I clap my hands together happily. I already know what his name is and I have a feeling he can talk, but something is stopping him. I don't want to scare him off by saying "Nicholas" outright, so I'll play this little game for now. "I don't want to do this here, though. Let me pour a cup of coffee and then I want to take you somewhere I have never *ever* taken anyone. Not even my mother." I get up without waiting for his answer, pour the coffee, and take a thick winter coat from the back of the kitchen door. I pull on my floral gumboots and open the door."Oh, it's really dark out there," I say. "I have a lantern in my room; I'll run up quickly and grab it. You can come with me if you'd like...or wait here."

He follows me to my room. I find the lantern and press its switch. It doesn't work. I shake it and try again. "Ugh. The battery must be dead.

Mom might have one in her room from when the power was out." I put the lantern back on the table and we walk down the hallway toward Mom's room. I open the door, turn the light on, and walk in.

Nicholas is no longer by my side. I turn around to see where he went and he is standing in the hallway, frozen in place. His skin blanches before my eyes as he looks around the room. "Are you okay?" I exclaim, and walk toward him. *Can a ghost that doesn't look like a ghost be as pale as if he's seen a ghost?*

He is visibly shaking. He wrenches his blue eyes away from the room and there is the smallest glint of a tear in the corner of his eye as he looks at me.

"You don't have to go in there," I say, and close the door behind me to block his view. I stand against it. There are so many questions screaming through my head; there is so much I don't know about him, but right now is clearly the wrong time to ask any of them. "Wait downstairs, okay?"

He blinks the unshed tear away and turns toward the stairs.

"I'll be right down," I say after him.

What the heck was that all about? He must have seen something I can't see. Or maybe he has a memory of the room that scared him. I have no clue.

I go back inside Mom's room and quickly spot the lantern. I've never stayed in here too long because I do get a sick feeling from this room. I never put too much thought into it, but maybe this whole time I was picking up on something that happened in here before we lived here. Shivers run up my spine and I leave the room as fast as possible. I close the door and almost run down the stairs.

He is waiting in the living room, examining the painting across from the sofa.

"Found it," I say, and hold up the lantern.

He turns around and I'm glad to see the colour has returned to his face, but his eyes are begging me not to ask about Mom's room. I smile at him and push the questions to the back of my mind.

"Interesting painting, huh?" I say. He scrunches up his face and looks back toward the painting. I stop next to him. "It's meant to signify going through the darkness to get to a happier place or something; I am not really sure. Different meanings for different people, I guess." I twist my mouth to the side and sigh. "Well, shall we go to my secret place?" I wiggle my eyebrows at him.

He grins and nods.

There's that smile. Focus on that, Stevie; don't ask about that room. Don't do it.

We walk across the porch and down the front steps. My boots crunch in the snow on the way to the gazebo. I stop at the hidden entrance in the trees and look at him. He is still wearing a white t-shirt, black sweatpants, and no shoes. "Oh my God, I am so rude!" I say, shocked. "Are you freezing your ass off right now?" I look down at his feet. They still have colour in them.

He wriggles his toes in the snow, but the snow doesn't move. I view his face and he's smirking. He shakes his head.

"Thank goodness," I say, relieved. "I would have felt like such a bitch...I mean...*horrible* person. I am all cozied up in my winter gear and you're dressed more for... the gym, or bed...or whatever you're dressed for." I crinkle my nose at him. "Never mind." I laugh.

We continue through the trees and over the stepping stones.

"This," I say, and sweep my hands in a big wave across the gazebo, "is my special place." I position the lantern in the middle of the fire-pit to light up the surroundings, then pick up the plastic bag that I had left on the bench and shake the snow off of it. "I guess you don't need one of these to sit on?" I ask, and show him the bag.

He shakes his head and sits where I usually rest my feet. I place the bag next to him and sit on it. Taking a big sip of coffee to warm up my insides, I turn my attention to him. "I sure love it here. It feels like I'm the only person on this planet when I come here. I wasn't lying when I said I have never brought anyone here. And I'm happy for it. It never felt right sharing this place with anyone...until now." I smile over the cup at him and take another sip.

His eyes are focused on the piece of mug that I wedged in the crack between the fire-pit bricks—the one with Charlie's face on it.

"That's Charlie; well, that was what he looked like. He went missing shortly after we moved here. Do you like cats?" I ask.

He looks from the bit of ceramic to my face and nods.

"You would have loved him, then—he was the best. I only wish I knew what happened to him." I sigh.

He lifts his hand to cup my cheek. I lean into it again, but this time I stare into his eyes. I know I won't feel his touch, but sometimes seeing something can trigger your brain to believe that it can actually happen. I do almost feel the warmth from his hand, but it's only my cheek reddening from the thought of him touching me. I smile softly at him when he looks down at my lips. I feel my body tremble. This would normally—key word *normally*—be the perfect moment for a first kiss, but we are far from normal right now. The moment doesn't pass, but we both seem to realize that we are limited in what we can do. He sighs without sound and looks around the gazebo.

"Did you come here often when you lived here?" I ask.

His eyes light up and he nods.

We sit in silence for a long time while listening to the sounds of the woods and looking at the stars. Bringing him here was an easy decision; like so many other things about him, it felt right.

"*So,*" I say to break the quiet, "can I start guessing your name now?"

He rolls his eyes at me and grins.

"I love your smile," I say. "It makes me happy." A touch of pink traces his cheeks, a lot like it did the first night he stayed up with me. *Ghosts blushing; who would have thought?*

"Anyways," I say before I get totally sidetracked, "I'll go through the alphabet; nod when I get to the letter your name starts with."

We both turn and sit cross-legged on the small bench, face to face. It's uncomfortable for me, but the closeness it allows makes me forget the pain in my ankles where the bench is digging in.

I start from the beginning of the alphabet and watch him intently as I say every letter. I take it really slow, not because I have to, but because the longer I drag this on, the longer I can stare in to his eyes. He must sense what I'm doing, but he doesn't stop me—maybe he wants to stare at me too. The thought elates me.

After minutes I finally reach the letter *N* and his face twitches ever so slightly—if I wasn't watching him as diligently as I have been, I wouldn't have noticed the small change in his expression. He doesn't nod.

Hmm... I furrow my eyebrows and squint at him. "It's *N*, isn't it?" I say softly. "You don't have to be afraid." I hover my hand above his knee, trying to assure him that he can trust me. "I promise you that I won't ask for your last name, if that's what you're worried about. I want to know your first name, that's it. I have secrets too, ones you could never imagine by looking at me, ones that would most definitely make the police want to lock me up and throw away the key." I look down at my hand.

He puts his hand over mine and I meet his eyes. He mouths the word *okay* to me.

"Okay," I whisper. "I'll continue then, the same way as before." I look back into his eyes. "Is it Ned? Napoleon? Neo?" I start.

He shakes his head and raises one eyebrow in a look of distaste.

"Thank God." I laugh. "Those are horrible names. Hmm, let me think." I tap my coffee mug with my nail. "Nathan, Nathanial...um...Noah, Neal, Nick—"

He holds his hand up, stopping me.

"It's Nick?" I ask.

He moves his hand side to side.

"You know this would be *a lot* easier if you could talk," I say, and curl my mouth to the side. "So it's maybe Nick?"

He nods and puts his hands together as if he is praying, then moves them apart slowly.

I tilt my head to the side, knowing damn well what he means, but I don't want to reveal that I already know his name. "Longer?" I say.

He beams.

"Is it—Nicholas?"

He nods enthusiastically.

"Well gee, why didn't you say so?" I joke. "Nicholas, it's nice to finally know your name. And you must already know my name is Stephanie, or Stevie for short." I extend my right hand in a greeting and he places his close to mine; we move them up and down. It feels weird shaking hands without actually touching, and I start to giggle.

"What are you doing?" a voice says from outside the gazebo.

In a second Nicholas disappears and I abruptly turn around, almost falling off the bench. I pick up the lantern and shine it in the direction of the voice. "Who's there?" I say, and walk forward out of the gazebo and across the stepping stones.

"Stephanie, do you have any idea what time it is?" Mom says.

"Mom?"

"Yes, Mom, who else would it be? Stephanie, I've been looking for you everywhere."

I meet her at the end of the stepping stones. "What are you doing home?" I ask.

"What are you doing out here in the freezing cold at one in the morning?" she retorts.

"I—I was...I couldn't sleep," I lie. "How long have you been home?"

"For a couple hours. I told you I was coming home tonight."

"I don't remember you saying that, Mom."

"Well, I did. Who were you talking and laughing with?" she asks.

"Um—no one."

"Stephanie, don't lie to me. The only reason I found you out here was because I heard you giggling. I went to check on you before bed and you weren't in your room. I searched *everywhere*. Then I came out here to check inside your car and heard you laughing in the bushes." She looks bewildered.

"I don't know what to say." I shrug and pull my mouth to the side.

"Well, get inside and go to bed; you have to work tomorrow." She storms off through the trees.

I stand there for a moment until I hear the front door slam. "Nicholas," I whisper. "Nicholas, are you there?"

Silence.

I gather the mug and walk back to the house. Mom is nowhere to be seen once I get inside. I wonder what happened, and why she's home early. I would have remembered if she had told me she was coming home a day sooner. Maybe something happened with her and Greg; she does not handle stress well.

Mom's door is closed when I walk past it. I put my ear up to the door and can't hear anything. I continue to my bedroom, knowing that when she is in one of her moods, it's best to steer clear of her.

Nicholas is not in my room when I get to it. Mom must have scared him off for the night. I get ready for bed and lie down. My heart is still jumping all over the place; how on earth am I supposed to fall asleep like this? Every time I pull the image of his face to the front of my mind I feel like I'm melting all over. I hope he doesn't think I'm some kind of dork for making him "shake" my hand. I thought it was funny. I roll my eyes and turn onto my side.

Nicholas is lying next to me with a smile on his face. I swat at him and put my hand over my mouth to stifle a laugh. "You're going to get me into *so* much trouble," I whisper. "My mom must think I'm nuts, talking to myself in the woods." I chuckle quietly. "Thanks for coming back, though." I smile.

The corner of his mouth turns up. He lifts his hand and moves two fingers over my eyes.

"Yeah, you're right, I should sleep. Maybe with you here now, I can. You have a calming effect on me when you're around. Can you stay with me until I fall asleep?"

He mouths the word *okay* and leans up on to one elbow. He peers down at me and slowly brings his face to my cheek. I close my eyes and imagine the kiss that he leaves there.

"Goodnight Nicholas," I say softly.

oOo

Mom is making breakfast when I reach the kitchen. I am showered and dressed and ready for work.

"Good morning, Mom," I say cautiously. *Please don't be angry.*

Mom turns around with a smile on her face. "Good morning, hon; want breakfast?" She holds out a spatula with a piece of French toast on it.

"Yes please." I take a seat at the kitchen table. She seems awfully chipper this morning. I probably shouldn't even mention last night, unless she does first.

"Thanks," I say as she hands me a plate with two pieces of French toast on it.

"Coffee?" she asks.

"Yes, thank you," I say.

She pours two cups and then joins me at the table. We eat in silence for a while. The sun is shining brightly through the kitchen window. I smile fondly at the memory of falling asleep next to Nicholas for the second time in a week.

"It's Christmas tomorrow," Mom says, disturbing my daydream.

"Already?" I say.

"I know, it's come up fast."

"Do you and Greg have any plans? I mean, I know I was already given my gift so I'm not expecting anything."

"Well, the shop will be closed tomorrow, as you know, and his parents want to fly us out to see them. He hasn't seen them since last Christmas. That is actually why I'm home—so I could pack a few things. I knew you wouldn't mind, since we don't usually celebrate Christmas. You don't mind, do you?" She looks concerned.

"Of course not, Mom," I reply, laughing. "Christmas is more of a kid's thing. I'll be fine."

"Great," she says. "Well, the flight leaves at noon and we'll be back late Tuesday evening. Greg asked that you make a sign saying we will be closed on Monday and Tuesday."

"No problem; I love making signs."

"Good then, it's settled."

I finish breakfast and look at the time on the microwave. "I should get going. Don't worry about the dishes; I'll do them when I get home." I stand up. "Have a good trip, and thanks for breakfast." I smile.

"Alright, hon, we will see you on Tuesday, if you're awake when we get back."

"Alrighty." I smile.

That was strange, I think as I leave the kitchen; *there was no mention at all of why she was in a foul mood last night.* Perhaps there was nothing wrong and she was only upset that she couldn't find me. I should cut her some slack.

The drive to work is uneventful; the snow isn't too bad today and there is hardly any traffic. I pull into the parking lot and there is no creepy-ass lady waiting for me. My nerves are a little on edge, being here alone today. I have my fingers crossed that I scared her off yesterday. I do a thorough search throughout the store to make sure she's not hiding somewhere, although I'm sure I would smell her if she was. That smell makes my eyes water even today, thinking about it. Shivers surge up my back, but I shake them off. I need to keep my mind off of her.

I can't believe it's Christmas tomorrow. Mom and I stopped celebrating after Dad died; it wasn't the same without him. In some ways I think it was better without him. Christmas with my parents was a happy occasion—for them. They would give me gifts, but you could tell it was just to keep me busy so they could shower themselves in presents and love and whatnot. Christmas was never about me, it was about them. I wonder what Christmas was like for Nicholas when he was alive. I should do something special for him, to show him that I care about him. I *do* care about him, more than a little. I'm going to plan something amazing; hopefully he'll show up for it.

The day holds no surprises and I arrive home with a box of items I picked up from the grocery store for Nicholas's gift. I have a lot of work ahead of me tomorrow. I'm very excited. With Nicholas being a ghost I can't necessarily give him a gift he can keep, but I can give him a memory to cherish.

I hide the box of things in my closet and smile at myself in the mirror as I close the door. Now the only thing to do is wait for him to visit me tonight. I kill the hours by cleaning the house top to bottom, then shower and put on black sweatpants and a white tank top—I think it will be funny. It's nine o'clock when take a book from the shelf—romance novels don't seem so scary and depressing to me now—and get comfortable on the wicker chair. I try to concentrate on the pages but I keep looking up to see if Nicholas has materialized. After an hour of that, he still hasn't shown up. I put the book on the windowsill and rise to look out the window. Nothing out of the ordinary out there.

I go to bed at twelve with worry in my heart. I hope nothing has happened to him. It would be impossible, wouldn't it, for him to disappear after disappearing? I try to think positively. I hadn't seen him in all the years I've lived here; maybe he doesn't visit every night.

I roll over to the empty side of the bed; if he does materialize, here I'll be, lying right on top of him. The thought makes me blush. *Ugh! Now I'm never going to get to sleep.*

I toss and turn for what seems like hours, feeling flustered and annoyed at not being able to fall asleep—until a yowling screech shatters the silence downstairs. It sounds exactly like what Charlie sounded like when he used to get into cat fights.

"What the fuck?" I yell, and my heart instantly pounds as if it's about to pulsate out of my mouth. I bolt out of bed and run down the stairs, stopping on the bottom step. *Where could it be coming from?*

The shriek stops. The air in the living room feels icy cold. I feel a draft coming from my left. The front door is open. A sick feeling clutches my gut. That shriek—what if someone is hurt? I take a deep breath to steady my nerves and run out onto the porch.

There is a red glow shining through the trees. *The gazebo.*

The front door slams behind me with enough force to knock me down the stairs. *What the hell is going on!* I don't want to go near the gazebo, but the light is drawing me to it.

The scream again. Louder and shriller this time.

Without a second thought I run toward the gazebo. The cold night air stabs through my skin and into my heart. I'm breathing heavily, panting.

Branches rip at my hair and face as I push my way through the trees; they wrap around my ankles and force me to the ground. I kick them away and push myself up. The red glow is coming from the fire-pit and Nicholas is here.

"Nicholas, get away from there!" I scream.

He is standing motionless, staring into the glow that is now pulsating in red, orange, and gold tones, the colours reflecting off of his ashen skin. He is mesmerized by it.

"Nicholas, please!" I beg. I run to him and try to grab his arm to pull him away, but my hand flies through it. "No!" I say. I try again and again to get his attention, but my attempts fail. He does not see me, he does not flinch; he only looks into the fire-pit, unmoving, cold, and lifeless.

That's when I hear it—the gurgling sound, like someone choking on thick tar. It rises from the glow, getting louder and louder.

"Nicholas," I beg one more time. "We have to go. Now!" I reach for him again, and this time I come in contact with his skin. My first instinct is to pull my hand away at the touch because it feels so cold and foreign, but I don't let go. Instead I shake him as hard as I can. "Snap out of it!" I yell, and yank his arm again.

He blinks and looks at me, disoriented. "Stephanie?" he whispers. He trembles as he searches my face

My heart stops beating for a long second at the sound of his voice.

"Stephanie, help me!" he cries as he is jerked to the side, toward the pit.

The gurgling is louder and with it comes the smell of death. The fear in his eyes is making me lose concentration. I don't know what to do. I feel helpless and scared.

I grasp his wrist as tightly as I can as he's dragged to his knees. I pull, terrified his arm will break from the force.

His cries for help are tearing a hole through my heart. Flames rise out of the pit, their red glow shining brightly through the cracks between the bricks. The gurgling sound is very loud now, as if it's right here with us. I couldn't see what was pulling him before, but now I can. *No, not again!*

Two slender hands grip his arm, working their way up it like a mime pulling an invisible rope, but this is not miming, and the rope is Nicholas's arm. I would recognize those hands anywhere; they have been plaguing my dreams for months now. But this is real.

But how is this real? My mind wants to reject what my senses confirm is happening.

I smell burnt flesh. Nicholas's arm is burning; I can see the skin melting before my eyes. I swallow bile as it burns the back of my throat and I pull on his arm harder, the adrenaline coursing through my veins. I don't care if his arm is torn from the socket now, as long as I can save him. Having one arm is a lot better than what awaits him in *there*. I brace my feet against the bricks and I can feel the heat through the soles of my shoes.

"Milly, let go of him!" I plead.

Hearing her name brings Milly's head up through the flames. Her eyes are hollow and the flesh has melted away from her mouth, leaving her teeth bare. The only recognizable thing about her is her auburn hair, which seems to be entwined in the flames. She opens what is left of her mouth and tries to speak. Blood pools at the back of her throat and the words are mere gurgles, stopping her from forming a sentence. The blood gushes down her neck. She watches me with hollow eyes and turns her head in a choppy, unnatural way. I can't tell if she is smiling at me or laughing when she turns her attention back to Nicholas.

He is wrenched toward the fire again. His fingers slip through mine and released, I hurtle backward into the wooden bench. He's screaming as Milly wraps her arms around him and the fire consumes them both. She drags him into the flames and the fire disappears along with the reverberations of Nicholas's screams for help, and my name.

I shriek his name in return, over and over again as I drop to my knees and dig through the ashes, digging until my fingers bleed, but I can't reach him, I can't get him back.

I bring my ash-covered hands to my face and weep. "Nicholas, I'm so sorry, please forgive me," I say into my hands. *I never got the chance to say I love you.*

Stephanie...

I can still hear the whisper of his voice.

Stephanie...

There's a flash, so bright it hurts my eyes. I shut them tight and feel warmth all over my body.

"Stephanie!"

I open my eyes to my bedroom; there is a small amount of light seeping through the window. I'm trembling violently with cold sweats. *Wait—I don't understand. It's morning? Already?*

That couldn't have been a dream, it was too real. It's not possible. I don't remember falling asleep.

I wipe the tears from my eyes with my left hand and look down. There is a hand hovering above my other hand.

"Nicholas!" I wail. "Oh my God, I thought I had lost you!" I start crying again. "I'm sorry for being like this. I had a nightmare that I thought was real." I snivel and cry harder, but it's more from relief now.

He leans in and hugs me. I wrap my arms around him even though I can't feel his skin.

His hand! "Can I see your left hand?" I say quickly, remembering the flesh being melted off it.

He looks confused, but shows it to me. It's perfect, untouched by flames.

"That was by far the worst nightmare I have ever had—because you were in it. Wait, that sounded wrong."

He smiles, but worry still plagues his eyes.

"What I mean is, you were hurt in this nightmare. And that is what made it the worst. I never want to see you get hurt. I never want to lose you." I pause to catch my breath. "There was one good thing about it, though—I felt you...and...I heard your voice." I twist the comforter between my fingers so that my hands don't shake. "Nicholas, I heard you when I was already awake, as well." I gaze up at him.

His eyes dart from left to right and he shifts uncomfortably.

"I'm not saying you have to say anything to me, I just want you to know that you really can trust me. That nightmare made me realize how much I actually care for you, and I never want to hurt you or see anything bad ever happen to you...ever."

I look at the alarm because I feel too shy to look at his face. It's almost nine in the morning. "How are you still here?" I ask when he doesn't say anything. "Not that I'm unhappy about it—you saved me from that nightmare."

A shadow passes across his eyes but he covers it up with a grin that makes me melt, makes me forget that something could be wrong, makes me forget about the nightmare altogether. "I really love it when you smile," I say, and smile bashfully. "Will I see you tonight? I have something for you; a present, sort of..."

He nods and cups his hand at my cheek. I lean into his hand and meet his eyes. "Merry Christmas, by the way," I say coyly.

"Merry Christmas, Stephanie," he whispers, and disappears.

CHAPTER THIRTEEN

THE GAZEBO IS DARK and cold. I sit on the bench with an extension cord on my lap and my finger on the switch. There are notes around the house for Nicholas, telling him to meet me outside. I spent the day tweaking his gift and I hope all of my efforts will pay off.

It's the first time in many years that I'm actually feeling extraordinarily happy on Christmas day. And it's not because I will be getting any gifts (because I was already given the car), and it's not because I'll see Mom and Greg, as they are spending Christmas with Greg's parents. The reason I am feeling this happy is because in the last few days I have spent every nightly hour I possibly could with Nicholas, and on this particular night I am as happy as can be because I have the promise to see him again and now we can actually talk to one another, voice to voice.

I take a good look at the area to make sure everything is perfect. The fake candles lining the stepping stones are all lit, there is not one flake of snow on the benches (who knew a hairdryer would have another use) and my makeup is pristine, as is my hair and dress—which is gorgeous, to say the least. It's a fitted, knee-length, deep burgundy cocktail dress with a square neck. I was worried that the satin material would make my bony hips more pronounced, but I seem to get away with it. I'm wearing simple black ballet flats with it, and feeling thankful again that my legs don't feel the cold. I did borrow one of Mom's black shawls to drape over my shoulders, but I only plan on using it after Nicholas sees me in the dress.

I used extra care in applying my makeup, though I went with more of a natural look: light brown eye shadows, a thin line of black eyeliner, and mascara. I braided my hair loosely over my left shoulder and I added a glittery black hairclip behind my ear. All in all I think I look great.

I see movement through the trees. I don't know if I'm shaking from my jittery nerves or from the cold, but when I see Nicholas walking across the stepping stones with that gorgeous grin of his, my whole world warms up. I stand up quickly before he speaks, and flick the switch on the extension cord. Hundreds of white twinkle lights sparkle around the gazebo. They are wrapped around every post in tight spirals. I stand back in awe at how gorgeous this place now looks. I drop the cord to the ground and watch Nicholas's expression. He is in as much wonderment as I am. I didn't think it was possible for him to look any more handsome, but in this light he is.

"Merry Christmas...*again*," I say shyly.

"Merry Christmas, Stephanie," Nicholas says nervously, and closes the distance between us. "This is amazing." He gestures at the lights. "You did this all for me?"

"Yes." I blush. I feel tongue-tied. For someone who has been wanting him to speak, and who has been doing most of the communicating, I can't seem to get more than three words out.

We stand for a while looking at the lights and how they reflect on the satellite that makes up the roof. It's our very own light show and it's magical. For the moment it feels as if we have been transported into a different world, where we are the only two people that exist.

"No one has ever done anything like this for me," he says, and takes a seat on the bench.

I mentally pat myself on the back and sit down next to him. "Well, I think you're worth it." I smile, glad that I'm finding my voice. "I wish I could do more for you."

"You've done so much already." He takes one last look around the gazebo, then turns his eyes to mine. "You look really beautiful tonight."

"Thank you," I say, looking down at my fingers. I pick up the shawl and fidget with it.

"I love it when you get shy," he says, and moves his hand under my chin.

I open my mouth to say something but only a small giggle escapes me. Nicholas smiles kindly at me. "I never thought I would ever meet anyone like you," he continues. "No one has ever seen me before, but out of anyone on this planet, I'm glad it was you."

I still can't seem to form a sentence in my brain so all I do is smile and blush.

"I was surprised at first," he says. "You can imagine my shock the first time I thought you saw me—I must have been as scared as you. There were so many times you would look right at me, then you'd look away a second later. But after that evening I was sitting on the porch swing—"

"It was you!" I say, cutting him off and making him jump.

"Yeah." He laughs. "It was me; I didn't mean to surprise you so badly. It's a good thing I can't smell, because I'm sure you would have poisoned me with that air freshener."

"Oh God." I put a hand over my eyes. "I'm so embarrassed."

"Don't be. I would have done the same thing if I were in your shoes."

I shake my head, recalling the memory. "Well, if it's any consolation, I'am sorry for trying to suffocate you with a fresh-linen scent." I laugh.

"Apology accepted." He smiles. "As I was saying, after that time on the porch swing I knew for sure that you could see me, and after that I tried to figure this thing out, figure out why you could see me when, say, your mom or that other guy—Greg is it?"

"Yes, Greg."

"When Greg couldn't," he finishes.

I nod. "I've often wondered the same thing." It doesn't make any sense at all.

"Don't be mad, okay?" he says after a minute.

"I could never be mad at you. Why would I be?"

"I said don't be mad because after getting confirmation that you saw me on the swing I spent weeks trying to get your attention. Sometimes I would stand right in front of you and wave my hands back and forth, but nothing. You would stare right through me. But other times there would be a look in your eyes that said maybe, *maybe* you could glimpse me. I tried desperately for months," he adds with a smirk.

"Wow," I say. "That's so weird, having someone watching you when you can't see them. Don't worry, I'm not angry about it. It's comical, in a way. I think if the tables were turned I would do everything in my power to have even a second to catch your eye."

Nicholas's cheeks turn a rosy pink and he grins. "What did you see when you looked at me, or thought you saw something?" he asks.

"Shadows, mostly; sometimes a flicker of shapes. I thought my mind was playing tricks on me. The first time I actually saw you for what you are was that night the power was out, and you scared me half to death. That time I thought you were someone else."

"You thought I was *him*," he says, a hint of venom in his tone.

"Yes, I did, but only for a moment. Only at the moment it happened. But after I had the time to calm myself I replayed your appearance in my head and you obviously were not him." Thinking about Shane tonight is the last thing I want to do. I stay silent for a moment, planning my words carefully. "You saved my life. That night he attacked me. If it wasn't for you, I don't know what kind of person I would be today."

"That was one of the worst nights of my life—or death, I guess; however you want to look at it. I wanted to kill him. I tried to kill him. I have only felt anger like that once before. You have no idea how much I wanted to help you. And when trying to get him off of you failed I prayed, harder than I ever did in my life. I prayed that you would see me—"

"And then I did," I say. "I *did* see you. You saved me. There is no amount of thank-yous I could say to make up for it."

"I don't know what I would have done if he did anything to you. I guess there's not much I could have done."

"Let's not think about that. The fact is, you protected me the best way you could. Thank you for preventing something that could have ended a lot worse than it did. I used to call you my saviour before I knew your name."

"Really?"

"Yes, because that's what you were to me."

"'Were?'"

"Well, I like to think you are more than a saviour to me now. You are my friend, and I think that if we *were* normal, you would be a lot more."

"Like a boyfriend?"

"I'd like to think so."

"I think you would have made a great girlfriend." He smiles.

My heart feels giddy again and the thoughts of Shane and that horrible night dissipate. It feels like years ago; it was another life when that all happened, another time. All that matters is now being here with Nicholas. In a way he still is my saviour, because without him I would still be lost. Without him I would have no reason to keep going.

"Not to ruin the moment or anything," he says, bringing my thoughts back to the present.

"What is it?"

"What do you dream of when you have nightmares? You seem so afraid, and in so much pain. I tried many times to wake you when you were having one, but I never could, not until the other night."

"Well..." I fall silent and fumble with the shawl.

"You don't have to tell me if you don't want to," he says kindly.

"No, it's fine, I trust you." I smile weakly and exhale. "I'm not sure if you know this, but I was in a car accident in the summer. My friend Melissa died right next to me." I sigh.

"I was wondering what happened when you left for those weeks. They were the longest weeks of my time here. I didn't know if I would ever see you again. And then when I saw your mom break down before my eyes after you were found, I thought you had died. Then I heard her talking with Greg about the accident and that you were in bad shape, but you were alive. I—" He bows his head.

"You were worried about me even back then?" I say, bending over to see his face.

"Yes, more than you know." He looks up, a haunted look in his crystal-blue eyes. "When you came home all beaten up and bruised I was scared for you, but I knew what a strong person you were. I knew you would get better. I stayed by your side every night after the accident to watch over you."

"You did?"

"Yes, I did." He looks into the blackness surrounding the gazebo, lost in thought.

"Thank you for watching over me," I say. "You truly were a saviour, even before I ever saw you."

"I guess in a way I was," he says. "Are the nightmares a memory of the accident?"

"They were at first, but—"

"What is it?" he asks.

"I can't believe I'm going to tell you this. No one knows this." I stare into the trees, looking for eavesdroppers, and take a deep breath. *Don't hate me for this...*

"I caused the accident that killed her."

"What do you mean?"

"It's a long story, but I'll make it short. She was driving me home late at night from her parents' lake house, because I had a fight with my ex and I am kind of night-blind, so she volunteered to take me home. She said things on the drive that really upset me, and I lost control of my anger. I attacked her while she was driving and the car went off the side of the highway, down a really steep hill. She was killed on impact; a branch went through the windshield and into her neck. I think guilt has plagued my mind. I dream she's coming back for me. The nightmare I had the other night, when you succeeded in waking me up, was about her. But this time she attacked you and pulled you into this fire-pit. I couldn't save you— that's why I was so upset."

"Sometimes anger can take over and make you do horrible things. I don't believe you are a bad person. I've watched you struggle over the months."

"You're not going to run for the hills, knowing that about me?" I say, shocked.

"No, why would I?"

"Because any *normal* person would."

"Clearly I'm not 'normal,'" he says with a smile.

"'Clearly' not," I say. "I thought that was a secret I would take to the grave, but for some reason I feel I can talk to you about anything." A cold breeze from the lake makes me shiver and I pull the shawl tighter around myself.

"I wish I could do that for you—give you my coat or my shirt to warm you up," he says, trying to lighten the mood.

I smile at him. Telling Nicholas about Milly, I feel as if a burden has been lifted from my heart. I can't believe how well he took it. "Thank you for not judging me," I say.

"I would never judge you." He wraps his arm around me and I move closer to his side.

"Does your arm get tired floating, above my back?"

"No, I can't feel much of anything," he says. "I wish I could."

"Me too," I sigh.

"You know I have not spoken in nine years," he says all of a sudden.

"Nine years!" I say, stunned.

"It's been a long time." He nods, almost to himself.

"Why didn't you speak for so long?"

"Call it guilt as well, I guess."

"For what?"

"I know out of anyone you would understand, but if it's okay with you, I'd rather not relive that memory. It's taken me many years to come to terms with certain things."

"That's okay," I say, a little disappointed. I thought we were sharing, but I won't pry. He's finally talking to me; I'm not going to screw that up.

"What's the radio for?" he asks, changing the subject.

"Oh crap, I forgot all about it." I giggle. "It was meant to be playing music this entire time." I lean over and turn it on. "I made a playlist. I didn't listen to much music before Milly died—Melissa, I mean—but when things weren't going so well for me in school I used music to tune the nasty things people were saying about me out. It helped a little. Did you listen to much music?" I say to get off the subject of school.

"Yeah, I loved music. This is a good song," he says, catching my hint. "I've never heard it before."

"I like the guy's voice," I say. "He sounds moody, but happy at the same time."

"It's nice," he agrees.

We sit listening to the acoustic guitar while enjoying each other's company. If he was real we would look like a regular couple enjoying a romantic evening—not a girl all dressed up, talking to herself while sitting alone, leaning against an imaginary person. He's not imaginary to me, though, and that's all that matters. I want to know everything about this man, but those looks he gets in his eyes beg me not to ask what I want to. He now knows my darkest secret. I feel a little hurt that he won't share his life with me, but I understand at the same time.

"Are you getting cold?" he asks.

"A little, but I want to stay out here until I can't feel my face."

"You're funny," he says. "I really like you."

"I really like you too." I grin.

"We should get you inside before you turn into an ice cube."

"I guess that wouldn't benefit either of us," I joke. I pick up the extension cord and turn the lights off. We walk across the stepping stones and I gather the candles on our way back to the house.

"Can you stay with me again, until I fall asleep?" I ask as we get to my bedroom.

"I was planning on it," he says.

"Good. I don't have nightmares when I spend time with you; weird, huh?"

"That is strange."

"I think it's because I'm in a better mood after a night with you. You make me happy."

"I'm glad I make you happy, Stephanie. You make me happy too." He smiles.

I feel fluttery in my stomach. I know he can't touch me but I still get nervous—in a good way—knowing I get to sleep next to him again. I place the candles around the room; the box said they will stay lit for twenty-four hours, so that's good. I wish I had discovered battery operated candles ages ago. I'm always afraid I will burn the house down.

"I'm going to duck into the bathroom; make yourself comfortable," I say, and leave to change into black satin pajama pants with a matching spaghetti-strap top. I wish he could feel how soft it is. I choose not to wash my makeup off; he won't be here in the morning to see it smudged across my face.

I walk back into the bedroom and Nicholas is lying on his back on his side of the bed with his hands behind his head. *He looks mighty tasty!* I wish I could kiss him. "Hey," I say.

"Hey," he says smoothly.

I turn the overhead light off and the only light comes from the candles flickering delicately around the room. This would have been the perfect night to lose my virginity.

Oh my God, control yourself woman! I'm grateful that the dark room conceals the flush that blooms on my cheeks. I need to clear such thoughts from my mind, but the way he's lying so comfortably on the bed is so inviting. *Well, you told him to get comfortable. I guess he did.*

"Is everything all right over there?" Nicholas says.

"Yes, of course." I move toward the bed.

"Are you sure? You've been standing by the door staring at me for a good minute, with the strangest expression on your face." He laughs.

"Internal battles—that's what I call them," I say as I join him on the bed. "And the lack of a good poker face."

"Well, your face showed a lot of confusion; what are you confused about?"

"Oh nothing," I say, and smile sweetly.

He furrows his eyebrows at me, but I don't give in this time.

"So," I say to break the awkward silence, "was this your room when you lived here?"

"Yes, but it looked a lot different."

"What, you didn't have a princess bed and girlie-coloured bedding, romance novels, and a pink rug?"

He snorts. "No. You're kind of cheeky, you know that?" He grins.

"I've been told," I say, and roll my eyes. "So what did it look like when you lived here?"

He pushes himself up onto his elbows and looks around the room. "Well for starters, I had a lot more books than you." He nods toward the lame excuse of a bookshelf. "I loved reading horror stories and comic books, that sort of thing. Where your bed is now was where I had my books. I enjoyed painting a lot, too. I had an easel set up between two bookshelves, and my bed was by that window. I would stay awake sometimes and stare out into the sky. Get lost in the darkness of it." He ponders the memory for a while with a smile tugging on his lips.

"Sounds like a nice bedroom."

"Yeah, it was." Sadness touches his eyes.

"Did you have any pets?" I ask.

"No, my parents didn't want to spend the extra money it would cost to feed an animal. I always wanted a cat, though. I enjoyed yours while he was alive." He coughs, then lifts his eyebrows and looks at me. "Shoot, I'm sorry; I was going to tell you, I just didn't want to on Christmas."

"You saw Charlie after he was dead? Like a ghost cat? I mean, I always assumed he had died, I just never knew how or where."

"No, I never saw him after he died, but—" He stops.

"It's okay, I've come to terms with it. Please tell me." I sit up and tuck my legs underneath me, then wait for him to speak.

"It was about a month after you moved in; I had already become attached to Charlie because of the way he made you smile. You never showed happiness any other time, only when he was around. You were sitting in your room, staring out the window, like I did so many nights when this was my room. But you were crying and I didn't know why. I knelt beside you and so desperately wanted to wipe your tears away. You were holding that mug with the picture of Charlie on it; it was empty and you were running your finger over his face, so I knew right then that something must have happened to him. I felt sad for you, and helpless. I stayed with you that night until you fell asleep and then—I don't know what I was expecting to do if I found him, it's not like I could have told you—but searching for him made me feel like there was something I *could* do.

"You know, Charlie used to stare at me all the time. Most nights when he fell asleep on that chair, he was sleeping on my lap. Well, *in* my lap, since I'm not technically solid." He half grins. "Anyway, I wanted to do *something*. So I searched the house top to bottom, and the yard. I remembered my parents telling me never to go into the woods because of all the wild animals, but what harm could they do to me now? So I went through the trees and I searched for hours. I think if I *could* hear my footsteps I would never have heard the quiet meows that led me to him."

"He was alive?" I say.

"When I found him, yes, he was alive."

"What happened then?"

"I finally tracked him down; I walked quite a distance into the forest, following his meows. I was so busy trying to think of how I would get him back to the house that I almost fell off the edge of a cliff."

"Oh, goodness!"

"I know. It scared me, even though I knew if I fell off I wouldn't have felt anything. I didn't even know there was such a drop in the forest, but it's not as if I had ever searched before. So I stopped suddenly and looked down. The cliff is around eight storeys high, and at the bottom there is a stream. I leaned over the edge and that's when I saw Charlie. He was trapped three-quarters of the way up, on a small ledge. Something must have spooked him in the forest and he ran, and he hadn't seen the drop-off either. He didn't look like he was hurt or anything, but there was definitely no way he was going to get back up to safe ground, and the other way—well, it's too far of a drop for anyone to survive. I felt completely useless."

"Poor Charlie," I say sadly.

"I know," he says with a rueful twist of his mouth.

"So what happened to him after you found him?"

He sighs. "Well, since there was nothing I could do to get him off of the rock, the least I could do was spend time with him until he either made the dive into the water below, or attempted to climb up the side of the cliff. Both ways would have been impossible and I think he could sense that."

"Is he still there?"

"No, he isn't. I stayed with him every night; he was really unsteady the last time I visited. It was hard for me to see him like that, especially when he could see me and kept giving me that look like, 'Why aren't you helping me?' He got so weak near the end, disoriented. I was there when he ended up losing his balance, and he fell into the river. I didn't see him resurface; there was nothing more I could do. I'm sorry."

"You stayed with him every night, so that he had company. Nicholas, that is...you are...*amazing* for doing that. Knowing now that you were there with him, it makes me feel so much better that he was with someone that loved him when he died. Thank you for that." I wipe a tear away from my cheek. "Can you take me there, to where he died?"

"I wouldn't recommend going there at night. The nights I went to stay with him, I saw bears. It's not safe. I wouldn't even go in the daytime."

"Don't bears hibernate in the winter?"

"They do. But cougars don't."

"Oh...I forgot about those." I sigh.

"You should get some sleep," he whispers.

"Well, normally after a story like that I would definitely *not* be able to fall asleep, but having you are here with me makes me feel safe in knowing I won't have any nightmares."

Nicholas leans over and kisses me on the forehead.

"Want to know something strange?" I ask as I lie down.

"Sure," he says, relaxing next to me.

"I had a dream months ago that Charlie drowned. It was actually when I had the car accident and I was stuck in the vehicle. Weird, right?"

"Maybe he was trying to tell you something, or let you know he wasn't alive anymore."

"Maybe..." I pull the covers up under my chin and Nicholas turns onto his back. I can tell he still feels guilty about not being able to save Charlie; I wish he wouldn't feel that way.

"Good night, Stephanie," he says. "Thanks again for everything today. It really was a wonderful Christmas."

"You're welcome," I say. "Thank you for caring about me so much."

"It's not hard."

"It's not hard loving you either," I whisper.

oOo

What a night that was with Nicholas. I could not have asked for a better day myself. I mean, I know there was a bit of sadness that came along with it, but knowing how Charlie died is another burden that has been lifted from my heart. At least I now know he wasn't torn to shreds by animals and left half alive to suffer until the end. The way he died wasn't wonderful by any means, but at least he had Nicholas to watch over him.

Speaking of Nicholas, I think I told him that I loved him last night, in an indirect sort of way. Can you really love someone in such a short time? Mom and Dad did. Could it be possible for me, though? Even with Shane the word 'love' wasn't as meaningful as what I am feeling now. With Nicholas it's different. It could be because he knows so much about me and has not judged me for anything. Shane was never that understanding when we were together—like with Charlie he bought me that stuffed cat, but I think it was more of a gift to get me to shut up, like my parents used to do. I could never see Shane spending countless nights at Charlie's side—look what he did to me, and I'm a human. No, there is no comparison between the two. Shane is dirt—less than dirt. Nicholas is...he is...

I love him.

There is no question about it. I'm pretty sure he feels the same way about me, but it will never work out. A relationship between a ghost and a human—it's not possible.

I ponder the possibilities of a relationship while I make my morning cup of coffee. I can't believe it's already almost eleven-thirty. I did get to bed really late last night, though I didn't have any nightmares, as I'd feared. Nicholas is my own personal dream catcher. I have a lot to clean up today. It's bad enough that Mom caught me talking to myself that one evening; all I need is her coming home to a decked out gazebo and candles all over my bedroom.

I take my coffee out to my special place. I'm wearing more appropriate attire today: runners, jeans, and a winter jacket. It didn't snow last night so the benches are still clear. I settle into my usual spot, check my phone for any missed calls (none), and sip my coffee, gazing at the bit of mug with Charlie's face on it. I don't feel as sad as I usually do while looking at it. I smile instead; he's in kitty heaven now. All those times he slept on the wicker chair, he was sleeping on Nicholas—who would have thought? All the times Charlie would meow at nothing, was he really meowing at him? I remember Charlie purring and wrapping himself around the legs of the chair; was it really Nicholas he was rubbing himself against? I could ask myself questions all day.

I finish the coffee and put the cup on the bench. I'm not really in the mood to clean all of this stuff up, but I need to. I don't want to give my secret place away to anyone driving down the street, or to Greg. The lights make it look too inviting, and the only person invited here is Nicholas. I guess this is no longer my special place, it's ours—a place with real meaning for the both of us.

I lean down and I'm about to unplug the first string of lights from the extension cord when a bare foot steps into my field of vision. I almost jump out of my skin, but I recognize the foot, and the black sweatpants attached to it. I straighten. "How the heck are you here right now?" I say happily.

"I don't know how much time I have," Nicholas says.

"What's wrong?" I blurt, alarmed.

"Nothing is wrong," he assures me. "I've just never come here during the day, and I might not have very long. I want to take you to where Charlie was; I thought about it after I left, and it wasn't right for me to say you can't go see where he died. And if you think it will help with closure, I would be happy to take you there."

"Honestly?"

"Yes. Come, let's go quickly."

"Wait, what about the wild animals?"

"After you fell asleep last night I went into the woods to make sure I remembered how to get to the cliff—I know how to get there now. I did a quick scan this morning and didn't see any bears, so they must be hibernating. It's daytime too, so maybe less animals?"

"That doesn't sound too convincing but yes, okay, let's do this. I'm going to get a baseball bat, and the air freshener."

He grins at me. "No Bible this time?"

I laugh and shake my head.

Minutes later, with the bat clenched in my hand (I couldn't find any aerosol air freshener), I follow Nicholas into the forest. I would be lying if I said I'm not shit-scared of what lingers in here, but so far, so good. Nicholas walks a few feet ahead of me, setting a brisk pace. He stops every now and then and I do the same. I strain to detect anything abnormal, but hear nothing but the wind rustling in the trees. I don't see any other life forms.

"We're almost there," he says, turning to give me a wary smile.

I hear the sound of rushing water, faint with distance, as we approach the edge of the forest. Nicholas holds up a hand. "Slow down, okay? I don't want you falling off."

"Alrighty."

"This is when I wish I could take your hand; I would feel a lot better if I could."

He stops at the cliff edge and looks down. I step lightly among the moss and dead leaves, putting one foot ahead of the other to make sure the ground won't cave in under me, but it feels pretty solid. I get onto my stomach and army crawl the rest of the way to the edge.

"Did I mention I'm scared of heights?" I say.

"I am too, actually," he says, "but I guess I have no reason to be anymore."

I reach toward the edge of the cliff and pull myself up to it so I can peer over the edge. Nicholas does the same.

"Wow, it's actually quite beautiful up here, once I get the urge to retch under control," I joke.

"See over there?" he says, not sharing my humour. He points to a rock that is jutting out from the rock face. "That's where he was."

The rock looks barely big enough to hold Charlie. I stare at it for a long time, imagining him on it, meowing for help. I can see why Nicholas is sad; he must be seeing the actual memory of Charlie's final days. I begin to cry quietly.

"Was bringing you here a bad idea?" he asks.

"No, it wasn't." I sniff. "I'm happy to see where he spent his last days."

"Come, let's get away from the edge." He stands up and walks toward the trees.

"Can we take a slow walk back?" I ask.

"Of course."

I push myself away from the edge and cautiously get to my feet. Nicholas waits as I take one more look around. "If I knew about this place earlier, and if there weren't so many wild animals out here, I think I'd have loved to spend more time here," I say as I walk toward him. "It's peaceful out here."

"It is." He smiles. "Let's go, though; I don't want to disappear and leave you stranded out here alone."

"Thank you," I say.

"For what?"

"For being you."

We reach the house safely and I return the bat to its rightful place—Mom's room. I asked Nicholas to wait outside so I could do so—even mentioning that room makes him tremble. I will find out one day why it scares him so much, but right now I want to spend however many daylight seconds I have left with him.

We meet at the gazebo and sit next to each other.

"So, any idea of how much longer we have together?" I ask.

"It's hard to say." He grimaces.

"Well, I'm glad to get any minute I can with you," I say. "Listen, about last night..."

"What about it?" His eyes sparkle.

"I meant what I said, about...loving you and such," I mumble, and look down at my hands.

"Stephanie?"

I look up into his eyes. "Yes?"

"I've loved you for years."

My heart feels like it's going to explode with joy. He loves me, he actually *loves* me, and he doesn't even care about my flaws or my past. Like everything else, I don't know how this is possible.

"So now what?" I say.

"Now I have to go, but I'll be back tonight." He moves his hand to my cheek so I'll turn my head to face him. My shyness makes me want to look away and hide my expression, but his eyes are locked with mine. He leans forward and so do I. I know what's coming and my heart leaps again. I dare not close my eyes in case I've read the moment wrong—I don't want to be the only one going in for a kiss—but as soon as his lips meet mine I reluctantly do. I can't feel his touch, of course, but I imagine that I can.

I open my eyes a moment later to an empty space in front of me. I sigh heavily and stand up. The butterflies that were swarming in my stomach have moved down to my knees. I grip the post to steady myself. I wonder how I would react if I could actually *feel* him.

The rest of the day drags on, as it does when you are waiting for something you've waited for your whole life, but now that what I have always wanted is sitting right next to me, I can breathe and stop wishing the time away. All I actually want now is time to stop ticking; I want the moments that Nicholas and I share to never end.

"Do you think I should leave?" Nicholas says.

We're sitting on the floor with our backs against the wall between the closet and the wicker chair. We are hand in hand—literally; our hands are inside one another. It's a strange thing to look at, but I'm getting used to this whole thing.

"No!" I exclaim. "I want you to stay. Greg and Mom will be here soon, but all I have to do is go downstairs, say hi, then tell them I'm going to bed. It is almost ten anyways, so it's believable. Then I can whisper when I speak to you and they won't hear me," I say.

"Are you sure? I don't want to get you into anymore trouble with your mom."

"It will be fine, *please.*" I pout.

"Okay." He laughs. "Stop making that face; it's killing me."

I stick my tongue out and giggle. "*So*, anything you want to do tonight?"

"Hmm, I'm not sure. What are our options?"

"Well, we could watch a movie on the laptop, or talk, or...practise kissing again, like last night." I blush and bite my lip.

"We could do all three." He wiggles his eyebrows.

"Hey, that's my move!" I joke.

"I think I do it better."

"No way! I definitely do it better. See?" I wiggle my eyebrows one at a time.

"Okay, you win." He laughs. "I don't know *how* you do that."

I hear a car pull up to the front of the house. "They're back." I grimace and roll my eyes.

Nicholas smiles at me and stands up. I get to my feet and adjust my hair.

"You're so beautiful," he says.

"Don't make me blush right now!" I say, and slap him through the shoulder.

"Hey, that hurt," he says, and rubs his arm.

"Oh God, I'm sorry." I reach out to touch him. My hand passes through him again. I look at his face and he is grinning down at me. "You are such a brat!" I yell.

He bursts out laughing.

"I will deal with you later," I say with a mock scowl, which only makes him laugh harder.

"Stephanie, we're home," Mom shouts from downstairs.

"Be right down," I yell. "Be right back," I whisper to Nicholas. I stand on my tiptoes and kiss him on the cheek.

Nicholas jumps onto the bed and lies down with his hands behind his head. His shirt lifts up a little, exposing a bit of his stomach. I stand mesmerized for a second and then shake it off and walk out of the room before I get sucked into his gorgeousness, which is a very easy thing to do. Last night we stayed up for hours, talking and staring at each other, kissing and laughing at the fact that I looked like I was making out with a pillow and not him.

"There you are," Mom says as I reach the living room.

"Um, what the hell is this?" I say, staring at a huge pile of flat, unmade boxes.

"Watch your language," Mom warns.

Greg walks in carrying more boxes. "Hey Stephanie," he says happily as he adds them to the pile, then walks back outside again.

"Hey," I say. I look back to Mom. "What's with all the boxes?"

"Great news," Mom says. "We found a house in St. Chalmers."

"What? This house isn't even sold yet...or is it?"

"No, it's not sold, nor is Greg's condo. But our realtor called this morning and she's found us the perfect house. It's a rental, but that's all we'll need for now, until these places sell. The store will be up and running within the next month. I thought you would be happy," Mom finishes, slightly out of breath. She puts her hand on her hip.

"Well, I'm...I just didn't think we would be moving until the summer," I say.

"Well, plans change," she says. "We got home early this afternoon to buy boxes. The sooner we get this place packed up, the sooner we can start our new lives."

"Your new life, you mean!" I say. "I don't want to move anymore."

Greg returns with more boxes. "What's going on?" he says.

"Stephanie has decided she doesn't want to move anymore," Mom says. Greg looks at me. "I don't understand."

Mom throws her hands up and walks into the kitchen.

"This is selfish. What about what *I* want?" I say. Tears prick my eyes.

"There is nothing here for you; why would you want to stay here?" he asks, confused.

"Because I like it here, okay?" I scream. "I'm happy here!"

"Stephanie, you're being silly," Mom says behind me. "We are moving and that's final! We've already paid the security deposit on the house. Tomorrow you need to start packing up this house. We'll be packing up the shop and Greg's apartment; we don't have time to do all three. You need to start acting like an adult."

"This is bullshit, you know that? I didn't get any warning that we would be moving so soon, and now you expect me to pack up this entire house by myself. No, if you want to move that badly, do it yourself. I'm not helping."

I storm up the stairs and pause out of sight in the hallway to catch my breath and calm my nerves before seeing Nicholas again.

"I can't deal with this, Greg," I hear Mom say in the living room.

"She'll be okay, Denise; just give her some time. This is a big change for everyone, and we did spring it on her," Greg says.

I lean against the wall between two paintings and cry. *I'll never see Nicholas again. I don't believe this is happening.* I'm finally happy again. I've finally found someone who appreciates me for who I am, someone who loves me even though I have done terrible things, and now...I'm going to lose him forever. This house is going to sell and I can never come back here.

I hear footsteps on the stairs. I wipe a tear from my cheek and run to the bedroom. I slam the door and lock it behind me. Nicholas is already standing near the door, concern pinching his face. I run past him and collapse onto the bed, unable to stop the tears from falling.

"I have to move," I say between sobs. "Nicholas, I don't want to lose you. I can't—I just can't." I sit up and wrap my arms around my knees.

"It's okay," he says, trying to sound soothing, but worry seeps into his voice.

"No, it's not okay!" I exclaim. "Nothing about this is okay." I duck my forehead against my knees and rock.

"I don't know what to say."

"If this house sells, I will never see you again." I peek up at him and sniff loudly.

"We'll figure something out. I promise."

"What options are there? Really? I can't live in the bushes; I can't drive four hours here every night and sneak into the yard. And I'm too young to move out on my own. Mom would never allow that. I wouldn't be able to support myself."

"Stephanie," he says.

I wipe a hand across my nose and meet his eyes. We are both quiet for a long time. I can see him struggling with what to say, what to do.

He finally moves his hand to my cheek. "Stephanie, look at us. I'm a ghost and you have your entire life ahead of you."

"No, don't say anything else." I wave my hand between us.

"You have to realize that there is no future for us," he continues.

"Nicholas, don't!"

"I don't have any other ideas. I have to go now. It's for the best." A tear trickles down his cheek.

"What do you mean?"

"The only way you're going to move on is if *I* do. I've been holding onto this life for so long. For so many years I have been wandering these halls. I need to move on now. You deserve so much happiness, happiness that I can't give you."

"But you make me happier than I've ever been."

"For how long, though? How long could this really have lasted? How long before you needed more—more of me that I can't give you."

"You'll hurt me if you leave me."

"I'll hurt you more if I stay."

"So that's it?" I say. "You're just going to disappear and never see me again?"

"I don't know what else to do."

"This isn't right, this doesn't feel right," I wail.

"I'm sorry, Stephanie. I'm so sorry." He holds his hand under my chin. "I love you," he says, and kisses my lips.

I fall forward onto the empty bed as Nicholas disappears, and I cry harder than I have ever cried before. There has to be another way. There just has to. My world is falling apart again and there is nothing that I can do to change it.

I hear the front door close, then Greg's car start up. I rise and walk to the window. I see two figures in the car. I'm alone, truly and completely alone. My heart aches. I feel as if Nicholas has ripped out my soul and taken it with him. There is nothing left of me. I have nothing more to lose.

I place my hand against the window and look toward the gazebo. *This place would be a nice place to die. If I could choose somewhere to have my last breath, it would be here...*

The unspoken words hit me in a flash, and I know what has to be done. There is only one way I can be with Nicholas...here, in this house.

Forever...

CHAPTER FOURTEEN

TODAY IS THE DAY I die.

After Mom and Greg left last night I waited for Nicholas to return to me, but he never did. I walked around the house begging out loud to see him one last time. He never answered my pleas. It's a strange feeling, being this alone. I've been here before, but this feels different. I can't seem to talk any sense into myself.

Death; you think I would be afraid of it, but it's been around me for so many years—with Dad, with Milly, and even with Nicholas—I'm not afraid of what's to come. If there is even the slightest chance I will see Nicholas again, or a chance to spend eternity with him, I find comfort in that thought.

It's eight-thirty in the evening. I need to make things right with Mom; I can't leave this earth knowing she was upset when she left last night. I sit in the hallway with my back against her bedroom door and I dial her number.

"Stephanie," she answers.

"Hi Mom," I say, trying to keep my voice from trembling.

"Is everything alright?"

"Yes, everything is fine. I wanted to apologize for yesterday."

"No, I'm the one that should apologize. I should have called you as soon as the realtor called me. I was so excited and I thought you would share the excitement with me. Having a chance like this, to start over—I never thought I would have that after George—" She stops.

"I know, Mom; I shouldn't have been so selfish. I'm really and truly pleased for you and Greg. Seeing you happy is all I ever wanted for you."

"I know, hon, which is all I want for you, too."

"I will be happy. I promise...and I love you." A tear rolls down my cheek and I wipe it away with the palm of my hand.

"I love you too," she says.

"Are you and Greg going to come home at all tonight?"

"No, not tonight. Maybe in a day or two. Do you need me to bring you anything? How is the packing going?"

"I'm going to start packing first thing tomorrow morning. I'm good for groceries and stuff."

"Okay hon, I should get back to this. So much work, so little time."

"Alright, love you."

"Love you too." She hangs up.

My heart is aching after speaking to her. She only wants the best for me, but the best for her is a fresh start in a life with Greg, and without me. I will only hold her back; I've been holding her back for so long.

I check the phone; it's eight forty-five. I feel shaky and nervous as I get up from the floor.

"Nicholas," I whisper. "Nicholas, if you are listening, I wanted to say..." I hold my hand to my forehead to think. "I wanted to say that I love you, and that you mean everything to me...and I want to be with you forever. Please forgive me for what I'm about to do. I can't bear the thought of never seeing you again. You have brought so much light and happiness into my life in short span of time. That has to mean *something*. I will see you soon." I turn and walk into Mom's room and close the door behind me. Nicholas would never follow me in here, so this is where I'll have to do it.

I head straight to the medicine cabinet before I have a chance to change my mind. Mom's bottle of prescription sleeping pills is on the top shelf, where it usually is. I reach for it and pop the lid off. It's about half full. I turn the tap on and pour the pills into my hand. I should be able to swallow these all at once.

My heart is racing incredibly fast and my knees feel weak. *Can I really do this?*

I look into the mirror to give myself one more chance to talk myself out of this, but the person looking back at me...I don't recognize her. I don't want to be her anymore.

I lift my hand and tip all of the pills into my mouth. Then I turn on the cold water tap and fill the glass beside the sink with water and wash the pills down my throat in one big lump. My eyes run as I suppress a gag reflex. I don't know how many pills I took and I don't know how long it will take for them to dissolve. I crumple to the tiled floor, beg God for forgiveness, and weep.

I'm not sure how long I've been sitting on the cold floor before the first wave of nausea hits me. *No! I won't throw up!*

The toilet is calling my name. I reach for the sink to pull myself up. I need to get out of here. I need the cold air on my face to stop the room from moving. My arms feel lifeless and my legs feel like they weigh a hundred pounds each. It's a battle, trying to heft my body into a standing position, but I finally manage the task.

I look in the mirror. My eyes stare back at me from dark hollows in an ashen face streaming with perspiration. The room spins again. I steady myself but then fall backward out of the bathroom. I feel like I'm in the car again, when it was spiralling out of control—except this time, I will be the one to die. Blotches of red and gold float around Mom's room in between beams of light. I follow them with my eyes, but it only makes me dizzier. I gag and feel the burn of stomach acid on the back of my tongue. *No, dammit!*

I drag myself along the floor, ignoring the colours of the room. I don't want to be in here any longer. Crippling pain in my stomach slams me to the floor and I let out a ghastly scream. My body curls with the power of it. I try to get to my feet but my legs won't obey me. I drag myself farther along the floor and reach up for the handle of Mom's bedroom door before another spasm of pain twists my stomach. It takes all of my energy to pull on the handle. The latch clicks and the door opens slowly as my body slides down it. I lie with my head in the hallway facing the stairs, breathing rapidly. The distance to the gazebo is an impossible journey.

I'll never make it.

This is all wrong.

I curl over in pain again. My stomach feels like it's getting torn to shreds from the inside out. I retch, but only stomach acid leaves my mouth. I didn't eat anything today so that the pills would take effect faster, and they have already dissolved. I strain to move my body. *Just a little farther...*

If I can just make it to the stairs I can roll down them, which won't take any energy. I lift my torso off the floor and lunge forward using my last bit of strength; it only takes me half a foot farther. I collapse on the hardwood floor halfway between the stairs and Mom's room. *I can't do it. I can't go on.*

I close my eyes and bring the image of Nicholas's smile to my mind. *Let go...*

"Stephanie?" a voice says.

A small surge of adrenaline brings me back, but only long enough to see bare feet blocking my view of the stairwell.

oOo

"Stephanie—oh God, what have I done! Stephanie, wake up!"

My body convulses and I crack an eyelid open. "It worked," *I gurgle.* "You're here...I feel you."

"Oh God, Stephanie...I'm sorry, I'm so, so sorry, I shouldn't have left you. What have you done?"

"Be with you..." I mumble "...forever..." I feel my eyes roll back and close.

"Please wake up, Stephanie; don't die—you can't die!"

"Stay with me, don't leave me!"

Floating, I'm floating...being carried away by angels. Fresh air on my face...it feels so good.

"Please don't die, hold on for a little longer. Please God, don't let her die." The furtive gulps and sobs of weeping.

"I'll be back, Stephanie...I promise. Keep fighting, don't let go. I love you."

The house is silent, apart from my breathing, which is coming in slow, raspy gasps. I focus on it, wondering which breath will be the last one I take. I feel like I'm floating in a sea of darkness. The floor beneath me starts to move, rippling like gentle waves in an endless ocean, carrying me along with it—is this what death feels like? I let the water carry me for a long time as I try to think of my life, but I can't remember a thing from it, or how I got here.

An owl swoops in from the gloom and spirals above me. Its large eyes pierce my soul, but the sound coming from its beak is all wrong. I've heard the sound somewhere before, but I can't remember where. It's like...the echoes of birds singing.

Think...

Birds singing...no, not birds...too loud to be birds. It's all wrong.

The floor vibrates and the owl dissolves into the night, but the sirens still echo through my mind—yes sirens—they were not birds at all. How could I forget so easily?

The sirens fade out and I can't hear anything, not even my own breathing. Did I forget to breathe? Did I already take my last breath?

Why does this feel so wrong?

There is pressure—so much pressure on my chest. I scream for it to stop, but it doesn't. Is Death reaching into my heart to take what's left of me? Will he be disappointed when he figures out Nicholas has already taken it?

Forever alone in the darkness, unable to escape it...

The owl flickers back into sight. Its wings expand, revealing red feathers; I've never seen anything so beautiful. It loops around and dives toward me, landing on my chest. Its talons rip into my torso. My heart tightens as the claws take hold of it. I scream, but only a puff of air escapes my mouth and then it's gone. The owl grips my heart harder and brings its face to mine. The owl's familiar crystal-blue eyes reflect the fear that is in my own eyes, and in that moment I have a revelation. A revelation that...

I don't want to die...

The owl clenches again and I feel my heart burst into a thousand pieces. I try to gasp for air but nothing enters my lungs. A warm drop of liquid leaves my eye and rolls down my cheek—and then there is only blackness.

oOo

I awake to the recognizable beeps that accompany hospital machinery. I peer through a haze at the indistinct features of a room. I try to lift my hands to rub the fog from my eyes but something is holding my arms in place. I crane my neck to look down at leather straps, binding my wrists. There is an IV attached to my arm with clear liquid seeping into it. I drop my head back to the pillow and try to recall the night. My head throbs, thinking about it.

My eyes clear and I look around the room. It's different from what I remember the hospital looking like; it has a tranquil aura. The walls are painted off-white and there is a gorgeous landscape painting on the far wall. The trees look exactly like the ones in the forest behind my house, like the ones that Nicholas and I walked through to get to the place where Charlie died.

Nicholas!

Where is everyone?

I try unsuccessfully to find the button that calls the nurses. "Hello?" I croak.

This place is dead quiet. If this is the afterlife I want nothing to do with it. I wiggle my feet and realize that they too are tied down. *What is going on?*

I pull myself up onto my elbows to get a better look at the straps on my ankles. I have bruises where they are digging in; I have bruises on my wrists, as well. I twist my hands but the straps don't ease. I try not to panic. They must have me tied down for a reason. I can't remember anything, though. The bruises look days old. The ones on my ankles are worse.

I notice a tube running up my leg and under the pale yellow gown I'm wearing. *What the hell is that?* I bunch the gown up in my hands and pull it up my thighs to see where the tube leads. I scream when I realize the tube is inside me and I can't reach it to pull it out.

I continue to scream for help and finally the room's door bursts open. Two men wearing white pants and white button-up shirts rush in.

"Get that thing out of me!" I yell at them. "What the fuck is this place? Where am I?" I shriek. I can't seem to turn off my anger.

"Hold her down," a deeper male voice says from behind the two men. An older man holding a clipboard walks into the room.

The men grip my shoulders and force me to lie down. I lose control and fight against them. "Let me go!" I scream, trying to kick, but the straps just dig deeper into my ankles.

"Miss Martin, you will need to calm yourself," the older man says.

"And who the hell are you?" I spit.

"My name is Dr. Turner; I'm the clinical psychologist at NBHI, which is where you are now."

"What the fuck am I doing here?"

"It is protocol, Miss Martin. You tried to commit suicide, did you not?"

"No, I didn't," I say. "Can you please let go of my shoulders? I won't fight."

Dr. Turner studies me for a moment, then nods at the two orderlies. They release me. "Wait outside, I will call you if I need you," he orders, and the men leave the room, closing the door behind them.

"Why am I here?" I ask more calmly. Fighting is not going to get me anywhere.

"My records show that you overdosed using Denise Martin's prescription sleeping medication, since the medication had already disintegrated into your bloodstream, we cannot tell how much you ingested, only that it was enough to put you into a coma."

"I was in a coma?"

"Yes, for three days, after which you were released into my care, and you have been here for—let's see…" He flips up a page on his clipboard. "Five days now." He looks up at me to read my expression.

"What day is it?"

"It's Saturday morning, January the fourth."

"January the fourth…" I whisper. My head is throbbing. "Where is my mother?"

"You will see her, once we know you are calm enough. You have been extremely erratic, these last few days."

"How so? I don't remember anything since—" I stop and think. "Since—" It hurts too much to think.

"It's probably best that you cannot remember."

"How long do I have to be here?"

"That all depends on you, Miss Martin. Right now we need to do a psychiatric evaluation and put you on the right medication. I have a student that I would like to sit in while we evaluate you; is this okay with you?"

"Yes, whatever," I say. "Can you get this thing out of me before then?" I point down at the tube. "And this." I indicate the IV.

"Yes, I think that's safe to do, now that you are lucid."

I bite my inner cheek; there is no sense arguing. The sooner I get this over with, the sooner I can leave. Nicholas has not seen me for over a week. For all he knows, I'm dead. I was so close to death that I can remember feeling him. He was right there.

Dr. Turner leaves the room. A moment later an attractive nurse enters and takes the tube out of me. That feels so much better. She removes the IV as well, then quickly leaves the room with not so much as a word to me. I roll my eyes in her direction.

Dr. Turner arrives a moment later with his student trailing in after him. "Bra—"

Bradley puts a finger over his mouth, shushing me.

"Something the matter, Miss Martin?" Dr. Turner asks.

"Bra, I need a bra," I lie, and flush.

Bradley relaxes and stops next to his father. I didn't put two and two together until now. Dr. Turner looks like an older version of Brad. I grimace and shift uncomfortably. *This really blows.* "Can you remove these straps so I can sit up?" I ask.

Dr. Turner scrutinizes me, then nods to Brad, who walks over and removes the bindings. He gives me a warning look before returning to his father's side.

I sit up on the bed and adjust the gown at the same time. I smile weakly at the doctor. "Thank you," I say, and rub my wrists.

"How long have you suffered from depression?" Dr. Turner asks while looking down at his clipboard.

"I don't suffer from it. I mean, I have my sad days, like after my father died and after Mi—"

Bradley shoots me another look.

Jesus, give me a break! "After *my* best friend died, and I had problems at school, and so on and so on." I wave my hand impatiently.

"Can you elaborate?"

I sigh. What do I have to lose? "I was in a car accident with a friend who died next to me. I found out later that she was having an affair with my boyfriend the entire time we were friends—I found that out after she died." I look at Bradley with sympathy and he shifts his eyes away. "Um, I got kicked out of school for getting into a fight with my ex's new girlfriend, and I've been having horrible nightmares that my dead friend is trying to drag me into hell...or some form of it."

"Hmm." Dr. Turner nods. "And who is Nicholas?" He glances up at me from his notepad for the first time during his interrogation.

My heart stops. "Nicholas?" I squeak. "Haven't heard of anyone by that name."

The doctor shoots me a suspicious look. "For the last five days you've been screaming his name, Miss Martin."

"Well, out of the last five days I only remember waking up here alone... *so*?" I raise my eyebrow.

"Is he an imaginary friend? Or a voice in your head that tells you to do things?"

"I don't know what you're talking about," I say firmly.

He jots something down on his clipboard. "Have you had thoughts of suicide in the past?"

"No."

"Not even when your father was killed?"

"No, not even then. We didn't really get a long enough for me to care."

"Can you elaborate?"

I snort. "He never really showed me any interest growing up; he didn't pay me much attention...what do you want from me?"

I hear a beep and the doctor reaches into his pocket and pulls out a pager. He looks annoyed for a second. "Miss Martin, I will be back in a couple of hours." He rushes out of the room without an explanation, leaving Brad to follow.

Brad closes the door and waits a minute to see if his father will return. Then he looks at me. "Stevie, what the hell were you thinking, trying to kill yourself?" he says, walking to the side of the bed. He sits on the edge.

"I wasn't!"

"Stevie, please. I've read the hospital records, the police statements. Why—why would you try to do that? Do you know how lucky you are to be alive right now?" He looks anxiously at the door, then back at me.

I look down at the ugly hospital gown and fumble with the edge of it.

"Stevie, you can trust me, okay? I asked you to call me if anything was wrong; why didn't you?"

"I didn't know who I could trust."

He tilts his head to the side and places a hand on my knee.

"I'm sorry about Milly," I say.

"Don't be. I always knew something was up with her and Shane, but I thought it was my paranoia. How did you find out?"

"I stole her diary at the funeral."

He shakes his head. "Look, I'm sorry all of this has happened to you, but it's not a reason to end it all. You are beautiful and funny and smart, Stevie. Nothing should get in the way of that."

"Brad, that's not the reason...if I admit to trying to end my life, are they going to keep me locked up in here forever?"

"No. You might stay here for a while, but if you show that you aren't suicidal and this has not been an ongoing thing or something you've tried multiple times to do, they have no grounds to keep you. So what *is* the reason?"

"This is not the right place to be telling you this; you'll definitely want to keep me locked away."

"It will be off the record, okay?"

I look into his eyes to see if he's lying, but all I see is worry and fear troubling them. I sigh. "After Milly died and I found out about Shane and her...I confronted him. He got really aggressive with me. And then after school started he kept trying to get me back, but I pushed him away, literally...in front of everyone. He got mad...really mad, and he tried to...he came to my house late one night and he had been drinking. My mother was away for the weekend. He...he—" I look down.

"You can trust me." He puts his hand under my chin like Nicholas did so often.

"He tried to rape me, Brad," I finally manage.

Bradley pulls his hand away abruptly. "Oh my God. Did you call the police?"

"No...I didn't. My mother happened to come home early and she attacked him before he could do anything. I mean, who would the police believe anyway? We dated for three years, you know."

"I don't know what to say." He shakes his head sadly. "I can't believe he would try to do such a thing. Is that why you tried to kill yourself?"

"No. That would have been a better reason to, I guess."

"So what, then?"

"I started seeing things...more like someone—someone that wasn't real, but was real to me."

"Was it that Nicholas person?"

"Yes... He started appearing to me—he actually saved my life when Shane attacked me."

"Do you think he is real?"

"I just said that, didn't I?" I snap. " Look, I know it sounds crazy, Brad. I thought I was going crazy myself, but he was as real to me as you are right now, sitting here, except I couldn't touch him. Not until the night I tried to kill myself. He saved me again. Somehow. I don't know how...but he did. How is that possible?"

"It's not possible, Stevie."

"It is, though. I saw him. I *felt* him."

"Stevie, when the ambulance got to you, you were lying in the hallway a breath away from dead. There was no one else there."

"*He* was there."

"You were delirious; it must have been your imagination, or the effects of the sleeping pills."

"These last few months could not all have been my imagination. I saw him when I wasn't dying too. I spent nights with him, Brad, long nights, talking and laughing."

"I don't know what to say. I wish I could help you more."

"You *can* help. I tried to find out who lived in our house before us and all the records were missing. Maybe you can find out something...anything?"

"I don't know, Stevie. You should let it go."

"I'm not going to let it go!" I yell.

"Stevie, you need to keep your voice down." His eyes shift to the door.

I undo the straps from my ankles and wobble to my feet. My legs are aching and I can tell it's been days since I stood up. The room spins as blood rushes to my head. Bradley grabs me by the arm to steady me. I look at his face. "Brad, he was all I had left."

He doesn't say anything as I walk to the painting and place my hand on it. I feel the bumps of oil paint beneath my fingers and look into the deep woods that make up the canvas. There is something I had not noticed before about the painting; a small shape hidden between the trees. "What is that?" I say, and point to it.

Brad walks up next to me and gazes at the painting. "Looks like a shed to me."

"No, it's not a shed. I recognize this place. This here," I outline the shape with my finger. "I know this place. This is a gazebo."

"So what are you trying to say?"

"This is near my house, Brad!"

"That could be anyone's house."

"No, I know this place; I sit there almost every day. Where is this painting from?" I stand back and look at the picture and trail my finger down the canvas to the bottom right corner. There are faint letters painted on it. The initials *N.G.*

"All the paintings in the institution are made by the patients. Why do you ask?"

"Because Brad, this is him." I tap the initials. "This is Nicholas."

"Stevie, please. Are you trying to tell me that the person that painted this visits you?"

"That's exactly what I'm saying."

"That's impossible."

"Can you for one minute open your mind and—I don't know, hear me out?"

Brad looks at his watch. "I don't have long," he says.

"Okay, so let's just say whoever painted this was a patient here and died. Maybe he used to live in my house and *maybe* after he died, I don't know, his spirit visits the house and I just happen to see him."

"Stevie, it's impossible!"

"Why do you keep saying 'it's impossible'?" I fume, and pace back and forth.

"It's impossible because the person that painted this is *still* alive, so he can't be *your* Nicholas. Do you see how crazy this sounds?"

I stop in my tracks and my knees buckle. Brad rushes to my side and helps me onto the bed. "Are you okay?" he asks.

I shake my head. "He's still alive?"

"*That* person is." He nods toward the painting.

My head starts pounding and I lift my fingers to my temple to massage it.

"I'm sorry, Stevie." He pats me on the back and rises from the bed.

"Wait!" I say, and grab his wrist. "Can you do me one favour?" I beg.

"It depends what it is."

"The person that I see—the ghost or whatever. He is a little taller than me, with blond hair and crystal-blue eyes, and he is—or I guess was—a painter. His name is Nicholas. I don't know his last name. He told me that he had not spoken for nine years, but he speaks to me. Have you seen the person that painted that?" I point to the canvas.

"No, I don't have access to that area of the hospital."

"Why not?"

"I just don't, okay; students can't go wandering the halls. I only have access to this part of the hospital, because it's safer."

"Can you try?"

"I'm not jeopardizing my career for this, Stevie; you're going to have to give it up."

"Okay, Bradley," I say, and lie down. I turn onto my side and face the opposite wall.

"I'm sorry Stevie, I really am." He looks at the painting once more, then leaves the room.

If whoever painted that is Nicholas...that changes everything.

oOo

The silence on the drive home is welcome. Greg and Mom both spoke to Dr. Turner on the day before I was released from the hospital, so I'm spared the questions asking why I would try to commit suicide. Mom has to administer antidepressants once a day—God forbid I get my hands on them and try to kill myself again. They will never trust me after this.

I relax in the back seat of Greg's car as we approach the highway exit for home. I can't wait to see Nicholas; I wonder if he thinks I'm dead. My relaxing turns into fidgeting as we close in on the exit, but Greg drives right past it.

"You missed the exit, Greg," I say.

"No he didn't," Mom answers.

"Uh, yeah, he did," I say sarcastically

"We're not going to that house, Stephanie; we're going to our new house in St. Chalmers."

"What!" I yell, and bolt forward in the seat.

Mom cringes. "We—we thought it was best to keep you away from that house."

"What about all of my stuff?"

"We moved most of it last week, while you were in the hospital," Greg says calmly, and clears his throat.

"So what about the *rest* of it? I can help pack," I say eagerly.

"That won't be necessary. Denise is going to go back throughout the next few weeks to finish packing everything, and we're having movers pick it all up at the end of the month."

"I really don't mind helping," I say desperately.

"The answer is no. You are staying in St. Chalmers. You can help around the house there. There is a lot to be done," Mom says.

"But my car is big enough to transport boxes, at least the smaller ones."

"Stephanie, *please*," Mom warns.

I bite my lip and sit back against the seat in a huff, crossing my arms over my chest. "Has the house sold yet?" I ask.

"No, it's going on the market once it's cleared out, hopefully around February or March," Greg says.

That will give me enough time to get back there and see Nicholas.

"And my car—is it in St. Chalmers yet?"

"Yes, but you're not driving it," Mom says.

"What! Why?"

"Because the medication the doctor has prescribed is very strong," she says, and turns her head to meet my eyes. It's the first time she's looked at me since picking me up, "and he said it will take a couple months for you to adjust."

"How am I going to get around, then? St. Chalmers is *huge!*"

"I think—*we* think—it's best that you spend more time with Greg, and me when I'm home, so if there is anywhere you need to go you can ask one of us." She glances at Greg before returning her attention to the road ahead.

"So not only do I not have freedom, I have to have a constant chaperone twenty-four seven?"

"Until you can prove that you are not going to do something so selfish to us again, yes, you are going to be supervised. That's the only way we were able to get you out of that institution so soon." Mom massages her temple.

I'll never be able to escape. "What about school? I thought I was going back."

"We are enrolling you in home-school," Greg says.

All I want to do is scream at them and jump out of the moving vehicle. They are the ones being selfish right now. I clench my teeth and inhale deeply. "Alright, that's fine," I say.

Mom and Greg simultaneously relax.

This is going to be the longest four hours ever.

After many failed attempts at trying to make small talk, Greg and Mom finally give up and leave me to my own thoughts—which was probably a bad idea for them, because the entire drive to St. Chalmers, all I've been thinking about is trying to find my way back to NorthBerry Hill. I don't even realize that we've pulled up in front of the new house until Mom and Greg get out of the car and Greg holds my door open for me.

I get out of the car and give the one-storey white townhouse a once-over.

"What do you think?" Mom asks hesitantly.

"It's nice," I say. "Where's my room? I'm feeling tired, wouldn't mind a nap."

"I'll take you," Greg offers.

We walk up the cement walkway to the front door. The house has two floors if you count the carport where my car is parked; it's directly below the main part of the house and has a room to the right—probably a laundry room. It's open to the backyard in the rear. The driveway, where Mom's car is parked, slopes upward from the carport. The front garden is small and

JENNA-LEE BROWN

not very private, and the units on either side are exactly the same. Almost every townhouse is identical. I instantly hate it here.

"There are lots of teenagers living in the area. I'm sure you will make friends in no time," Greg says with a smile before fumbling with the lock on the front door. He looks nervous.

I don't answer him. He opens the door and I walk in behind him. The entranceway is small; the floor is light blue tiles and the walls are white. There is a small coat closet on the right and stairs on the left that I assume lead up to the main floor. I remove my runners and walk up the carpeted stairs. There are boxes everywhere so it's hard to distinguish what room I've walked into; I'm supposing it's the living room. There is tan carpeting throughout and more white walls.

Greg walks up the stairs behind me. "This will be the dining room, and over there is the living room." He nods toward the other side of the house. "The kitchen is over here."

I follow him across the dining room and cast a disinterested look into a small kitchen and breakfast nook. White walls, blue tiled floor. *Boring.*

"Our bedroom is over here." He walks back across the dining room to a closed door and opens it a crack. "We have our own bathroom, which means this bathroom over here is all yours." He opens the door between this room and one other room—probably my bedroom—and inside is a small, windowless bathroom with a toilet, sink, and bathtub with a shower attached—a normal, non-claw-footed bathtub. So far that's the only thing I like about this place. "And you probably already guessed the last room is your bedroom, so go have a look and call me if you need anything."

"Thanks," I say, and walk to the last room—which is the closest to the stairwell—and open the door. It's small—*really* small—with one window. There's a twin bed and a side table. My other bed would never have fit in here.

"We're putting a lot of stuff into storage until we buy a bigger house; this is only temporary," Greg calls from the other room.

"It's fine," I say. "At least my laptop is here. Is there Internet yet?"

"The cable guy is coming this afternoon to set everything up."

"Cool," I say. "Well, I'm going to take a nap, unless you need help with anything."

"No, that's fine; we have it under control."

"Alright." I close the door and lean against it. "This must be a nightmare," I whisper. I walk to the closet and am happy to at least see my clothing. I don't really care that the bed is small; it's not like Nicholas is here to share it with me. The small side table next to the bed has my cell phone and laptop placed on it. I find the chargers for both in the side table's drawer—at least Greg and Mom thought of that—and I plug them both in to charge. I lie back on the tiny bed and try to devise a plan of escape.

My car keys must be somewhere in this place. If I can get a free moment by myself I can search for them. It's going to be impossible for Mom and Greg to watch me every second of the day, and with Mom travelling back to NorthBerry Hill to pack up our old house, and Greg with so much to do here, that has to take most of their time. The only way I'm getting out of here will be when Greg's asleep and Mom's away.

If I turn up at the house when she is sleeping, the worst she can do is drive me back here the next day if she catches me, which will leave me an entire night with Nicholas. That would be one plan. The only other plan would be to gain their trust again and then get my car keys back, but that could take months, and for all I know, Nicholas might not wait that long. He might already be gone.

Sleeping is pointless right now. The curtains on the lone window are sheer and there is too much light coming through them. I get up and try to open the window, but it won't budge. I look at for an obstruction and I see the lock attached to the top of the pane. *Jesus, they really don't trust me.* I sigh and pull the curtain aside. There is not a tree in sight. I miss the woods already. I miss my special place.

There is a rap at the door.

"Come in," I say.

Mom opens the door and walks in. "Sorry hon, I almost forgot you have to take your medication." She holds out a glass of water and a small orange capsule.

"What's that?" I nod toward her hand.

"They are antidepressants," she says with an uneasy glance around the room, to avoid looking me in the eyes.

"You can leave it on the laptop; I'll take it in a bit."

"I think you better take it now, while I'm here." She pushes her hand toward me.

"Mom, seriously!" I snap.

She takes a step back and I instantly feel bad for my overreaction. "I'm sorry," I say. "Here." I hold out my hand and she drops the pill into it. I pop it in my mouth and take the water. "Happy?" I say, and open my mouth after I swallow the water.

She smiles weakly and leaves the room. I close the door and reach into my mouth to remove the pill. I'm shocked she didn't see me move the capsule between my top teeth and the side of my mouth with my tongue, but then, she was trying to avoid eye contact. *Lucky me.*

I roll the pill between my fingers. As if this is the cure to all my problems, medicating me. Look what good it did to Mom—it turned her into a zombie most days. I don't want to feel numb. I want to feel happy.

I open the closet and move the shoes to the side so I can reach the back corner. I rip the corner of the carpet up, put the pill under it, and then put the shoes back. No one would ever look there.

I wish the Internet guy would get here so I can research the side-effects of antidepressants; that way I'd know which ones to fake around Mom and Greg. That gives me pause. *Where do I get these ideas from?* I shake my head and smile as I leave the bedroom.

"Couldn't sleep?" Greg asks.

"No, the room is too bright and stuffy. It would have been nice to be able to open the window a crack to let in fresh air," I say, and raise my eyebrow.

"You can't open it?" Greg says, trying to look innocent.

"No, I can't *open it.* There's a lock on it. But you knew that already."

"I put it on, Stephanie," Mom says. "We can't take any chances with you."

"What makes you think I can't use the front door?"

"Because we're setting the alarm every night, so if you try to open it, that will go off," Mom says.

I frown. "So I'm like a prisoner here?"

"Only until you can prove that we can trust you again," she says.

Greg walks into the kitchen, clearly uncomfortable, or scared of my reaction.

"How am I going to do that if you won't even let me outside?" I say.

"I'm not getting into this with you; we have too much to do. When we think you're ready to go out, we'll decide when and for how long. End of story," she says firmly.

"Can I at least see the backyard?" I say quietly.

"There is a sliding door in the kitchen that leads to a deck. As long as one of us is with you, you can spend time there."

Oh my God. I bite my inner cheek until I taste blood and stalk into the kitchen and past Greg. I reach for sliding door. It's locked. "You had locks put on here too!" I shout, and slap my hand against the glass.

Greg reaches past me and flicks a switch up and slides the door open.

"Oh," I say. "Sorry."

"There are no locks on here, but if you open it after the alarm is set—"

"The alarm will go off," I finish for him, and roll my eyes. I step onto the deck. There are no stairs leading down from it and the deck is too high to get down from. *Dammit!*

I inhale the cold air and brace my hands on the metal railing. The back-yard is even sadder than the front. There is a small green shed in the far back corner, and a small, overgrown vegetable garden. The yard is fenced in a perfect square, like every other yard belonging to the houses on both sides of us. Past the fence there is a park with picnic benches, playground equipment, and barbeque pits—but no trees—and past that there are more townhouses. The view makes me feel sick. I want to see Nicholas; I want my special place back; I want anything but this. *There has to be a way to sneak out of this place.*

I lean over the railing to get a better view of the back of the house. There is a window on the bottom floor, and through it I can see a washing machine and not very much else—if I tilt any farther out I might fall off. I look above that window to Greg's and Mom's bedroom window. I study it for a moment. *There's no lock!* They forgot to put one on their window. So this place is not totally sealed up tight.

But there are two problems—well, maybe three. The first is going to be getting inside Greg's room at night, while he is sleeping, to climb out the window. I'm definitely going to have to wait until Mom leaves for NorthBerry Hill; she is a very light sleeper. If I can get past him and open the window without waking him up, I may have a chance in getting out of this place. The second problem is the height. If I accidently fall the wrong way I could break my neck, and I can't dive headfirst like I did from the girls' washroom at school. If I can get out the window backward and slowly lower myself down, the drop to the ground will only be about six or so feet.

That brings me to my third issue: getting my car out of the garage. Surely when Mom leaves for our old house Greg will park his vehicle behind mine, which means I have to get his out of the way so I can get to my car out.

I need coffee. My brain always works better with some caffeine bursting through it. I open the sliding door. "Is there coffee?" I ask.

"There should be some in the cupboard next to the fridge," Mom answers.

"Thanks. Do you want any?"

"Yes please, but just for me; Greg is going to check on a few things at the new art store. He'll have to take you sometime to see it; it's gorgeous." She smiles.

"Yeah, that would be great," I say as I fill up the coffee pot. Greg walks into the kitchen. "Change your mind?" I wave a cup in his direction.

"No, thank you. Just needed to grab my keys," he says, and reaches toward the cupboard above me. He opens it and there is a hook attached to the inside of the door, a hook with his car keys hanging from it. He takes the keys and puts them in his pocket.

I try not to look surprised or obvious, but inside I'm doing a happy dance.

Who needs my car when I can drive his?

CHAPTER FIFTEEN

IT'S BEEN ANOTHER LONG week. I've tried to help out as much as possible around the house to keep my hands busy and my brain from over-thinking everything, but all I'm really waiting for is Mom to leave, already. Why is she sticking around? I try not to look annoyed most days, but my patience is running thin. If this plan is going to work I need Mom and Greg to think I'm not planning anything. So I bide my time and put a fake smile on my face. She obviously isn't leaving because she is worried Greg can't handle me, but she can't wait forever.

I sit on the living room floor with a cup of coffee and flick through the channels on Greg's television. I've never really liked watching TV but there is nothing else to do.

Mom walks out of her bedroom and yawns. "Good morning, Mom," I say.

"Morning," she says groggily.

"I didn't wake you guys, did I?"

"It's okay; I needed to get up early anyway. And Greg sleeps like the dead." She smiles.

I snort and continue to browse the channels. *Sleeps like the dead, does he? Good.* I smile wryly at the screen. "There's coffee brewed," I say over my shoulder.

"Way ahead of you," Mom says, and walks back into the living room with two mugs.

"So why do you need to be up so early?" I ask.

"I'm going back to NorthBerry this morning. I've been procrastinating. I hate packing."

"I could come with you to help."

"No, we already discussed that, remember?"

"Thought I would offer," I say coldly.

"I appreciate the offer but I should be able to get everything packed up by myself this week."

"When will you be home?"

"When it's done."

"Okay," I say, and drink the last mouthful of coffee. I turn the television off and stand up. "See you when you get back, then."

"I have my phone if you need anything, and Greg will give you your medication while I'm gone. Don't give him a hard time about it."

"I won't." I roll my eyes and walk to the kitchen to put the mug in the sink. I hear Mom close her bedroom door, and then Greg's muted voice a moment after.

She's finally leaving. It's a miracle.

I walk to my room, collapse on the bed, and stare at the ceiling. My nerves feel like a tight ball in my chest. Who thought breaking out of a house would be harder than breaking into one? *And* I have to steal Greg's car. Technically it's not stealing when he is living under the same roof—or is it? *Whatever!*

I've made up my mind. I don't think I can go much longer without seeing Nicholas. I have never missed someone so badly in my life. I close my eyes and conjure the memory of us walking through the woods together, but in my mind I make us walk hand in hand, and we are both smiling. If only it were true. I turn on my side and face the window.

There is a small red light blinking in my peripheral vision. *Who could that be?* My heart skips anxiously as I pick up my phone and turn on the screen. There are seven missed calls from a number I don't recognize and two new voice mails. I've had the phone on silent, since no one calls me anyway. I only leave it charged for Mom's peace of mind. I dial the voice mail number and input my password. I don't know why I feel like I'm going to throw up, but I do.

Message one: *"Stevie, it's Brad. Where are you? I went to see you, but you had already been released, and I went by your house and you're not home. I need to talk to you. It's urgent. Call me back."*

That didn't sound good. I delete it and move on to the next message. That message was three days old; the next one was left yesterday.

Message two: *"Stevie, Brad again. You have to call me back. Call me now! I don't care what time it is. It's about Nicholas. God, I could get into so much trouble. Call me!"*

I drop the phone. "Shit!" I yell, and scramble for it. My hands feel like they have a jackhammer attached to them. I can't focus on anything and the walls feel like they're closing in on me.

There is a knock on my bedroom door. "Everything alright in there?" Greg says.

"Yes," I squeak. "Everything is fine."

"I'm going to help Denise put boxes in her car and then I'll be back," he says.

"Sure, whatever." My voice sounds way too erratic.

Greg sighs and walks away. I don't have long. Mom and Greg have stored the empty boxes in the laundry room, so they'll be outside for a while. I watch from the bedroom window until I see them both outside. Then I dial the number that the calls were placed from. It rings once.

"Stevie?" Brad answers. He sounds anxious.

"Yes, it's me, what's going on? I don't have long to talk; my mother and her boyfriend will be back soon."

"Stevie, how do I say this..." He pauses.

"Nicholas? You said something about Nicholas—what!" I say.

"Stevie you were right, I'm such an ass for not believing you."

I stay out of view from the window, but I can still see out of it to keep watch, I lean on the wall for support. "Tell me!" I urge.

"I could get into so much shit for this. Do you understand me?"

"Yes, I do."

"I saw him, Stevie. I saw Nicholas."

"What, like a ghost?"

"No, as a person. He's real."

I let my body slide to the floor. "How—how is that possible?"

"I don't know, but after I spoke to you, I started paying more attention to the paintings around the hospital and there is a similarity about them *all*. Every picture from that patient was painted in the same forest, with the same shed."

"You mean gazebo?"

"Yes, whatever—gazebo. That's not the important part."

"What is, then?"

"Stevie, there are paintings of *you, everywhere*."

Cold shivers run up my legs and down my back. "Of me?" I whisper.

"Yes, I'm sure of it. They look exactly like you, and your house. Paintings of you by your old red car; by the gazebo; in the woods—the list goes on."

"But—how?" I shake my head as the tears roll down my cheeks.

"I thought about it, Stevie. This goes against everything I'm trained for. I couldn't come up with any explanation, so I did some digging around and I found his file. You have no idea how much my career is on the line."

"Please tell me."

"I could go to jail for this," he says, more to himself than to me. He sighs. "His name is Nicholas Gilman; he has been in the institution for just over nine years. He was admitted at the age of twelve."

I do the math quickly in my head. "So he's twenty-one now?"

"Yes, he's been here for a very long time."

"Why was he admitted?"

"You're not going to like this, Stevie."

"What is it?"

The line is quiet for what seems like eternity. All I can hear is Brad's apprehension in every breath he takes over the phone. My heart starts thumping irregularly. "Bradley," I say seriously, "*what is it?*"

"Stevie." He pauses. "Stevie...he killed his parents in their sleep."

I let out a gasp. "You're lying!" I cry.

Nicholas's smile comes to my mind; his crystal-blue eyes, the look of his skin, the way he talks to me, the way he protected me.

"I wish I were lying, but I have nothing to gain by being untruthful to you. It is him, as hard as this might be for you to understand. He killed them, Stevie," Brad says, making the image of Nicholas shatter into a million pieces. "The records show that he has not spoken a word since he was admitted. Didn't you say *your* Nicholas had not spoken for nine years?"

"I did, but he speaks to me. He does. This can't be the same person."

"I visited him; he is exactly how you described him."

"Oh my God, no, this can't be true." My voice quavers. "Why did he kill his parents? Why would he *do* something like that?"

Was this why he was so scared to go into his parents' room? Because seeing it made him relive the memory? Is this why he didn't want to talk about his past? Why he wouldn't let me in?

"Sometimes anger can take over and make you do horrible things."

"You know I have not spoken in nine years. Nine years. It's been a long time."

"Why didn't you speak for so long?"

"Call it guilt as well, I guess."

Nicholas's words echo in my mind. "I think I'm going to be sick," I say.

"There's more," Brad says.

"What else could there be?"

"The notes in his file show that before he killed his parents, he used to see a therapist. His parents were worried about him because he was a sleepwalker. They were afraid he was going to get himself hurt."

"So what does that have to do with him killing his parents?"

"It doesn't."

"So why are you telling me?"

"Have you ever heard of the term 'astral projection'?"

"No, I haven't," I say.

I hear the front door open and Greg's muffled voice talking to Mom. "I haven't got time for an explanation; they're coming back in the house." I push myself to my knees and peer over the windowsill. I can't see Mom's car or Greg outside. *Shit!*

"That's the only explanation I have for it," Brad says. "What's your e-mail address? I'll send you some information...and pictures of the paintings. I took photos. I don't know how this has happened, Stevie, or how you can see him, but it's scientifically impossible."

"Well, apparently not. Listen, I really have to go. Thank you, Brad, for everything."

"You need to stay away from him," he says before I hang up.

"I don't know what I 'need' anymore."

I end the call and text Brad my e-mail address. This is way too much information to handle right now. I curl my knees against my chest and weep into them silently.

Nicholas a murderer, killing his parents—it doesn't make sense. It can't be true. I won't believe it to be true. I have to speak to him, now that I know. He has to tell me what is real. "He's real," I whisper between sobs. "He's alive."

"Stephanie, what do you want for lunch?" Greg asks through the closed door, making me jump.

"Not hungry," I say shakily.

"You have to eat with this medication," he says.

"I will, just not right now."

"Oh—okay," he says. "Let me know when you want to eat, then."

"I will."

I wipe the tears from my eyes and rise from the floor. I sit on the bed and open the laptop. There is an e-mail from Brad. *That was fast.*

Stevie, I would have emailed you sooner, but didn't know your address. I'm sorry if I upset you on the phone, but you needed to know the truth. As I said before, I don't know how this is possible, but for some reason when Nicholas astral projects you can see him. Maybe he did as a child too and that's why he used to sleepwalk—I really have no idea. This is what I found out.

Astral projection is said to be an out of body experience where the "astral body" or "spirit" leaves the "physical body" and is capable of wandering through different planes, if that makes sense? So what you are seeing—somehow—is Nicholas's spirit, not really a ghost, because he is alive.

This sounds crazy, doesn't it? That's what I thought. But when your story of him not speaking for nine years just so happened to match up to the nine years he's been in the institution, things started coming together. As for the death of his parents, he had their blood all over him and he was found out in the woods by your house. And yes, that is the house he lived in before you did, which makes the room your mother had the one where his parents were killed. That's all I know.

Things like this that involve young children aren't always reported on, so that could be a reason why you couldn't find any information about it. I feel like I'm typing a mile a minute so I hope this is all making sense to you. Please look at the attached photos and I'm sure you will believe this is the same Nicholas you see. I wasn't allowed to take my cell phone into the area where they keep him so I couldn't get a picture of him, but he looks exactly how you told me he would. He is going to be here a long time; people like him usually live their lives out in institutions. I'm sorry I can't do more; the only advice I have for you is to move on with your life and forget about him.

Bradley.

I take a deep breath and click on the attached file. The photo appears across the screen. My heart stops when I look at the picture of a girl with long brown hair wearing a grey hoodie and black pants. She is sitting on a wooden bench with her back leaning against a post with a cup in her hand. Although I cannot see her face because she's looking toward a distant lake, I would recognize this place anywhere.

There is one more attachment that I open; again it's a painting of me, but this time I'm smiling and looking toward the fire-pit—probably at the bit of mug with Charlie's face on it. There is no doubt in my mind now that the girl in these paintings is me, and Brad was telling the truth.

oOo

Two days have passed since I spoke with Bradley, and my feelings have not changed. I need to see Nicholas and find out for myself if what Brad told me is true. Somehow I don't think it is, but I know first-hand how it feels to think you can trust someone only to be horribly betrayed by them. Nicholas does not seem like the murdering type; then again, *neither do I*.

That's the other thing that has been nagging at me these past couple of days. If I could appear so innocent after causing an accident that killed someone who was considered my best friend, what makes me think

Nicholas could not have killed his parents? For all I know, they could have been child abusers or something. That would be a good reason to kill them, wouldn't it? I guess it was kind of hard to get a confession from him because he stopped talking all together, so what better way to make sure the public is safe than locking him away and hiding the whole incident?

What if he is innocent, though? What then? Did he waste away the last nine years of his life locked up in a mental institution? Where is the rest of his family? He must have an aunt or cousin that could have taken him in. Unless they know what happened and wouldn't take the chance of having him in the same house with them. I wouldn't, after hearing something like that—or would I, knowing him now? Nine years was a long time ago. There must be more to the story. There has to be.

Mom has been in NorthBerry Hill for the last two days and Greg has been here with me. He has not let me out of his sight, only when I need the washroom or when he goes to bed, which is usually around 10:00 p.m. He has been very meticulous with that damn house alarm; it's like he's terrified of disappointing Mom. It's been hard, trying to cover up the fact that I'm not taking the medication he gives me. He watches me a little closer than Mom does. I found a great trick, though. Instead of drinking water from a glass, he gives me the pill and I walk to the kitchen sink, turn the tap on, and lean down to take a drink. My hair covers my face and I let the pill drop from my mouth into the drain.

As for Greg's car keys, they're in the cupboard hanging from the hook. His vehicle has an alarm that beeps loudly when you turn it off, so that's going to be hard to get around if I want to steal his car tonight.

Not steal, borrow.

I feel bad for taking his car and breaking the miniscule amount of trust he has in me, because he is such a nice guy, and I don't want him to be on the outs with Mom. Then again, I don't have any other choices. He won't freely take me back to the old house, and he for damn sure won't let me borrow his car or let me take my own. Mom has given him strict instructions and God forbid he fails with any of them. I have to do whatever it takes to get out of this house and back to Nicholas.

I didn't want to leave the first night Mom did because I knew Greg would be extra cautious with me. I used this time to determine how deep a sleeper he actually is. I also needed to make sure he doesn't lock his bedroom door at night. The window in his room is the only means of escape for me. Last night I waited until eleven-thirty, then snuck into his room. I walked all the way to the window and unlatched the catch, and he didn't even flinch. The only thing I need to keep under control is my frantic breathing. It's louder than anything else.

It's now just after nine o'clock and I'm trying to cover up my nerves by watching the comedy channel. Greg is sitting on the floor next to me, laughing at the bad jokes. I laugh along with him and he doesn't catch on that I'm actually not paying any attention to the show; I'm counting down the minutes until he goes to bed.

Greg stifles a yawn and checks his watch. "Do you want to go see the new store tomorrow with me? I could use your help organizing things," he says, and resumes watching the show.

"Sure, it would be nice to get out of here for a few hours," I say, and smile.

"It's a date, then," he jokes. "Well, all this laughing has made me sweaty. I'm going to have a shower and knock off early."

"Okay. I'll set my alarm for early, then."

Greg stands and stretches. He walks to the alarm panel and inputs the code.

Damn!

"Good night, then," he says as he walks to his bedroom.

"Good night, Greg."

He closes the bedroom door and I wait. This is the only opportunity I'm going to get to turn his car alarm off. I turn the volume of the television down and strain my ears to listen for the flow of water. My heart is jumping erratically against my chest. My hands feel clammy. How am I going to pull this off if I'm this nervous already? *I've got this!*

The shower turns on.

Wait, Stevie...just a little longer.

The hooks slide along the bar as the shower curtain is pulled to the side.

Oh God, if I can hear that, will he hear his car alarm turning off?

My heart beats faster. I rise and walk unsteadily to the kitchen cupboard. I cock my head to listen for Greg. He sounds like he's humming a tune I don't recognize.

Do it. Now! I pull the keys up from the hook, clutch them in my hand so they don't jingle, and close the cupboard door. Then I run to my bedroom window and hold the remote up toward his car. I pause. *Shit, what if it's already unlocked and all I'm doing now is locking it and turning the alarm on?* I never thought of that. My finger is hovering above the Unlock/Lock" button on the clicker.

I can still hear the shower running—but for how long? *Fuck it.* I push the button and the car beeps loudly. I hold my breath, waiting for the shower to turn off and Greg to run out here and yell at me. I count slowly to ten in my head and pray that I unlocked the car, rather than locking it. I walk back to the kitchen and replace the keys. Greg's singing continues. He didn't hear me.

I calm my breathing and sit back down on the living room floor where I was seated before, then turn the volume back up on the television. The shower turns off and I can hear Greg shuffling around. The light from his bedroom shines under the bottom of his door. I fiddle with the ends of my hair. By eleven-thirty it should be safe to get out of here.

I turn the television off when the light under his bedroom door disappears, and I noisily get up to go and brush my teeth in my bathroom. It will make Greg think I'm getting ready for bed. I turn the shower on to cover my movements while taking off my pajamas and putting on the outfit I hid under the sink last night: my black skinny jeans, a black t-shirt, my grey hoodie, and a pair of runners. They're the quietest shoes I own, perfect for sneaking around.

After a suitable amount of time I turn off the shower and leave the bathroom—after peeking to make sure Greg's door is closed. Walking quickly to my bedroom, I half close the door behind me and check my cell phone. It's almost ten o'clock. I turn the bedroom lights off and get into bed and pull the covers over me, on the off chance that Greg comes in to check on me. I wait and wait and wait some more. I can't afford to rush things. If he's not fully asleep and he catches me climbing out the bedroom window I'm screwed—there'll be a lock on it by tomorrow morning.

My cell phone vibrates, which means its eleven forty-five. Slowly I get out of bed, trying not to let the mattress creak, then take a deep, steadying breath. Tucking the phone into the back pocket of my jeans, I tiptoe to my half open bedroom door—one less squeaky doorknob to turn—and pass through it to walk to the kitchen cupboard. Praying that the keys won't clink against the wood, I slowly open the door, grip the keys in a bunch and squeeze them together so they don't jangle against each other, and lift them gently off the hook. I silently exhale. This was the easy part. Now for the most stressful part of the night: getting out the window.

I gently take the car's remote off the keychain and put it on the countertop—I don't want to take the chance of it going off while I climb out the window—and put the keys in my other back pocket. The jeans are pretty tight, so hopefully the keys won't fall out. *Please let the car be unlocked.* If it's not, I'll have wasted the entire night and I'll have to wait outside in the cold until Greg finds me in the morning.

The short walk from the kitchen to Greg's bedroom feels like miles. My nerves are getting the best of me. I wipe my sweaty hand on my jeans, then grip the doorknob, hold my breath, and gradually turn it. The latch screeches against the metal plate as the door finally edges open a crack. I let out the breath I was holding and peek through the crack. Greg is sound asleep, lying on his side, facing the window. Another silent exhale as I push the door the rest of the way open with my index finger. Thank God this is a new house; the door opens soundlessly.

You can do this, Stevie. Just a little farther.

I walk gingerly toward the window. Greg hasn't stirred. I gently slide the window's bolt to the side and push the window up—slowly, slowly... My hands feel like they are pulsating with adrenaline. I glance at Greg, half expecting his eyes to be open and staring at me, but he is breathing deeply with his eyes closed.

The window only opens halfway; it's going to be a tight squeeze. I put one leg over first and straddle the sill, then pivot to the side and grip the windowsill with my fingers, still with one leg out and one leg in. *Don't slip, don't slip, don't slip!* I bend until my stomach is flush against the sill, one knee in my face and my other leg dangling against the side of the house. I bring my other leg out the window and slide down the side of the house until I'm hanging with my hands clenched on the sill. I look up—no Greg— then down; there's about a four-foot drop from the bottom of my feet. My hands start to ache. I let go of the sill and drop, stumbling backward onto the grass. I sit motionless, staring up at the open window. There is no movement and the lights are still off. *That's a good sign.*

Getting up and around the house to Greg's car was easy, because I don't remember doing it. The rush of the escape is taking over.

I made it out of the house. I can't believe it.

I take the keys and phone out of my back pockets, glad to see that the phone wasn't broken when I landed on it—the grass made for good padding. The house lights are still off and there is not a person in sight. With a silent plea for success, I touch the driver's side door handle. The alarm doesn't go off. The car door clicks open. *Thank God!*

Now I just need to get the vehicle far enough away from the house to start it up. I climb in and leave the car door open as I insert the key into the ignition, though I don't turn it. My foot is hovering over the brake pedal. I release the emergency brake and put the car in neutral. The vehicle slowly coasts backward down the slope of the driveway. I let it roll until the ground levels out and it stops.

No lights on in the house. Greg is still asleep.

"Here goes nothing," I say, and turn the key in the ignition. The engine rumbles to life. I bite my lip, put the car into gear, and drive a few houses down before closing the driver's side door. Looking through the rearview mirror toward the house, I notice nothing out of the ordinary; no lights are on and Greg isn't running down the street after me.

As I turn onto the road that leads to the highway toward NorthBerry Hill, I begin to laugh hysterically.

My plan worked.

CHAPTER SIXTEEN

I HAVE NEVER DRIVEN so fast in my life. After getting onto the highway I finally remembered how night-blind I actually am. What was I thinking? My plan obviously has a few flaws. The only thing that's making this drive easy is the lack of rain; if it were pouring down I would never get home in time to see Nicholas.

What if he isn't there? What if he's moved on? What if he thinks I'm dead?

There are too many what-ifs, but it's too late to turn around now. I push my foot harder against the gas pedal. So far I'm making the trip in record time. Usually it would take about four hours, driving the speed limit. I'm aiming for two and half hours. The posted speed limit is one hundred kilometres an hour; I'm doing at least one hundred and thirty, maybe more; I'm too afraid to take my eyes off the road to check. The adrenaline is coursing through my veins and my heart is racing.

What the hell am I going to say to Nicholas if he is there? I can't bark questions at him. I've worked so hard to give him space and to respect his wishes in not asking about his past. And now his past has been thrown in my face like projectile vomit—it's disgusting and way too much to handle. I feel like *I'm* going to vomit. It's all I've wanted to do since Bradley told me about Nicholas's past.

You don't know for certain that the reports were right. No, I don't know. People screw up all the time. Doctors screw up all the time: putting people on the wrong medication, misdiagnosing diseases, doing the wrong surgery because the papers got mixed up. So there is a good chance they misinterpreted the blood that was covering Nicholas when they found him—maybe it was paint; he loved painting.

No, that's stupid. Of course it would be blood, they would have checked. Could someone really kill a person while sleepwalking? That is one hell of a scary thought. His parents were found dead in their bed, but Bradley didn't say how they were killed, only that they were found covered in their own blood. *And so was Nicholas.*

There are too many questions.

"Shit, the exit!" I slam on the brakes, then pull the car to the side of the road and check the highway. There are no headlights behind me so I slam the car into reverse—which has never been my strongest driving skill—and back the vehicle up along the side of the road. I must look like I'm drunk; the car weaves left and right all the way back to the exit. I put the car in Drive and push my foot down on the gas pedal.

Almost home.

I drive slowly through town—there are more cops here than on the highway so I don't want to push my luck. The drive home feels longer through town than it did from St. Chalmers to NorthBerry Hill, but I finally arrive at the bottom of our familiar driveway; it looks eerie in the dark. My heart begins to race again with nerves and excitement and worry.

I should leave the car parked at the bottom of the hill so Mom can't hear me. What a brilliant idea! I pull the car onto the steep driveway and turn the engine off, leaving the car in gear and setting the emergency brake. With the headlights off the driveway looks even scarier. My stomach starts to hurt as my anxiety ramps up. *What's the worst that could happen? One: Mom gets angry at you—you've been there many times—and takes you home in the morning. Two: Nicholas never wants to see you again because you accuse him of being a murderer.*

No! I'm not going to accuse him; I'm going to ask him. And he would never turn his back on me. He loves me.

I take a deep breath and start the trek up the dark driveway.

I'm out of breath by the time I reach the top. I pause. Something doesn't feel right. I know it as soon as I see the lights on in the house. Mom's car is here, as it should be, but the front door is wide open and the lights are all on. I feel like I'm about to vomit as I try to decipher what is going on.

Mom could still be packing; the door could be open while she...throws things out? No! It's almost three in the morning. Mom never stays up this late! Something is terribly wrong; I can feel it in my heart—the heart that is thumping loudly in my ears. I try to move my feet but they feel as if they're wading in wet concrete.

No, not now! You've been through worse, Stevie—get it together! Everything could be fine; you're overreacting. I shake the nerves off and take the phone out of my pocket. I scan the house and don't see any shadows lingering behind the windows. I dial the emergency line on the phone but don't press Send; if there *is* something wrong at least I'll be able to call the police without fumbling for the numbers. I shove the phone back into my pocket and I force my legs to move across the lawn and up the porch steps. Tears fall down my face that I can't stop; there is a feeling of dread in my chest.

I creep across the porch and over the threshold. My shoes crunch loudly on something. I look down; broken glass litters the floor. I follow the shards with my eyes to a smashed window. I didn't notice that before. *What's happened here?*

"Ste—Stephanie," a faint voice croaks.

I turn toward the voice and see Mom lying at the bottom of the stairs, her leg is bent in an unnatural position. "Oh my God, Mom!" I whimper, and run to her side. I bend down to her level and pull the cell phone out of my pocket. The tears fall faster down my cheeks. "Mom, what happened, are you okay?" I ask quickly.

She holds a finger to her mouth to shush me and points upstairs. As if on cue, there are loud crashes as things are thrown around in one of the rooms.

"Stephanie," she gasps. Pain contorts her face. "My leg is broken. There is a lady...she broke in, she—" Her body jerks involuntarily and she lets out a strangled cry. "You have to get out of here; call the police."

"I'm not leaving you, Mom," I cry. The lady upstairs curses and I hear something smash, then more cursing.

There is movement at the top of the stairs, and my heart leaps. "Nicholas!" I shout, and then hold my hand over my mouth. I really didn't mean to be loud, but seeing him here...I couldn't help it.

He looks nervously down the hallway and runs down the steps. I hear another loud thump and a throaty scream. Nicholas looks ashen. "Stephanie, you have to get out of here; get somewhere safe," he urges.

"No! I'm not leaving my mother here," I say.

Mom looks from me to the blank space that I'm talking to, confusion flooding her face.

"Mom, I can't explain right now. Please, let me help you up. We can get to your car; I can drive us away from here," I whisper, and place the phone on the floor so I have two free hands to lift her. If I can get Mom to safety first, I can call the police afterward. If I call them now and whoever is upstairs comes down before they get here...who knows what will happen?

Mom nods curtly and I put my hands under her armpits. I try to lift her up but the pressure on her leg is too much and she screams in agony.

"I can't do this, Stephanie, it hurts too much," she cries. There is perspiration and tears running down her face.

"You don't have time for this. Your phone—call the police now!" Nicholas yells.

I fumble for the phone and turn the screen on. I press Send and hold it up to my ear. I hear the line pick up.

"Oh, the little princess came home," a raspy voice says from the top of the stairs.

I drop the phone in panic and shove it under Mom's nightgown in hopes that the person who did this to her didn't see the movement. I turn my head slowly in the direction of the voice. My heart stops. "It's you," I say. My stomach turns in knots as I meet the eyes of the lady from Greg's old art store; she is standing with her hands on her hips and her head is inclined like a vulture staring down at its prey. Her greasy black hair is hanging in long snakelike tendrils down the sides of her face. I'm too shocked to say anything else. The words are balled up in my throat. I look anxiously at Mom. I don't know what to do. Her eyes are begging me to run, to get to safety. I can't leave her. I just can't.

"Stephanie," Nicholas says, breaking me out of my mortified trance.

I blink and look toward him, then back at the woman, who is now smiling wickedly at me. She takes the steps two at a time toward me and I scrabble backward to get out of her way. My left hand presses into a piece of broken glass. I scream in pain and lift my hand; a big shard of glass is sticking out of my palm. I start to cry as the pain radiates up my wrist and arm.

The lady steps over Mom like she isn't there and starts to cackle, visibly amused that I have hurt myself, amused at how defenceless I now am.

"Who are you?" I scream as she leans over me.

"Cheeky little bitch, aren't you." She tilts her head to the side and her eyes bore into me.

I glance at Nicholas, who is sitting next to Mom with his knees pulled tightly against his chest; he is rocking back and forth. Mom is lying on her side, weeping. *God, what is happening?*

"Oh that," the lady sneers, and nods toward Mom. "She was a useless piece of shit like I assume you are going to be. Like mother like daughter; lies and deceit, they go hand in hand, don't they?" she spits.

"I—I don't know what you're talking about," I say.

"Oh, don't you now!" she screams, and spittle flies from her mouth. She crouches and brings her face close to mine. The smell from her mouth, her rotting teeth, her bloodshot eyes—everything about this woman screams death. "So like your mother, I guess you're not going to know where my money is either." She tilts her head again and looks right into my eyes.

"I, I—what money?" I snivel.

"Lies!" she shrieks. "You and your whore mother are both liars!" She grabs my left hand and holds it tightly; the blood drips from the protruding glass down my wrist and onto her hand. I start to tremble uncontrollably as she touches the glass with her other hand and stares scornfully at me. "Are you sure you don't know where it is?" she taunts, and pinches the glass with her fingers, then slowly twists it deeper into my palm.

I cry harder from the pain. "No! I swear I don't know where it is," I sob.

She wrenches the glass to the side and I shriek as I feel it break inside my hand. The room goes black for a second as the pain takes over.

No! I won't pass out!

"Help! Help us!" Mom yells from somewhere far away. I force my eyes open before the darkness takes over completely. Mom is screaming into my cell phone. "Nine seven—"

The demented lady is across the room before Mom can complete our address, and in a split second the phone hurtles across the room.

"No!" I scream as the lady raises her foot above Mom, then brings it down hard on her broken leg. Mom opens her mouth to scream but the pure pain that she must feel makes her collapse to the floor. Her eyes roll into the back of her head and she lies at the bottom of the stairs like a lifeless, broken doll.

"Mom!" I scream, and clamber to my feet.

Nicholas looks up at me in that moment, pulled from his own daze. He looks lost and helpless. I can't say anything to him—what can I say? There is nothing he can do to help us.

The lady snorts and crosses the room before I can get to Mom; she bunches up my hoodie in her hand and holds me in place. For someone so thin and frail, she sure is strong. I study her face for some kind of emotion that is not hate, something that I can twist into stopping her from doing what she's doing, and that's when I see it, the thing that looked so familiar about her the last time I saw her. I can't believe I never saw it before.

Her eyes.

It's not the colour of them, or the way they cut through me, it's the shape of them, and the way they are positioned on her face—she must have been a beautiful woman before whatever demon took hold of her and ruined her looks. I glance at Nicholas again and he's crying. The tears pool around his eyes—eyes that are the exact same shape as hers.

"Nicholas," I mutter hopelessly.

The lady shoves me against the wall. "What did you say!" she shrieks.

My vision darts from her to Nicholas, then back to her. "Nicholas...I said Nicholas. Does that name mean something to you?"

A distant look crosses her eyes, and then a shadow so dark, I swear it turns them black. "Don't *ever* say that name to me again," she hisses, unclenching her hands from my hoodie and taking a step back.

I see Nicholas hold his hands over his head as if he's suddenly got the worst headache, and then he falls to the floor. He looks like he's having a seizure. I try not to let the panic set in, but I'm way past calm. "Tell me!" I yell at the woman, "Tell me why that name has meaning to you!" The lady backs up as I walk toward her. Does this witch have dark secrets of her own? Does guilt plague her as it does me? "Tell me about Nicholas!" I demand.

"Shut up!" she screams, and puts her hands over her ears. "Shut up!" She runs to the kitchen.

I run to Mom's side and put my ear up to her mouth. Her breathing is laboured, but she is breathing. I don't bother to retrieve the phone, it's too close to the entrance to the kitchen and I don't want to waste any time on something that is surely broken.

"Nicholas." I turn to him and whisper in his ear, "Nicholas, please!" He settles and looks up at me with blue eyes aching with sadness. "You have to help me! Tell me something, anything about her," I beg, and point to the kitchen. My hand is throbbing something fierce and I'm happy at that moment that Mom has passed out; at least for now she's not feeling anything.

I hear kitchen drawers being opened and items clattering to the floor. "My money, where is it!" the lady screeches. Something else is thrown. I hear a window smash.

I look nervously back at Nicholas as dishes are thrown through the kitchen doorway. I don't want to have my back to the woman, but I have to get through to Nicholas. I have to break through whatever wall he's built around himself that protects him from his past. "Nicholas," I urge him, "tell me who she is—tell me. Please. I don't want to die; I don't want my mother to die. You have to help me."

His pupils enlarge and he finally searches my face. He sees my bleeding hand and Mom's limp body beside him. He finally breaks through and registers just how much trouble we are actually in. He closes his eyes, squeezing them shut in deep concentration, then pops them open. He reaches for my arm. "My aunt," he says, and shakes his head. "She's my aunt."

Oh my God.

"Her name!" I push as I watch him slip away. I don't want him to disappear. *Come on, don't give up on me now!*

Nicholas scrunches his eyebrows as he searches his memory. "It's Daisy...her name is Daisy."

The irony almost makes me laugh, despite my struggle not to descend into hysteria.

Daisy lets out an animal-like growl as she flips the kitchen table over.

"I need your help," I say, my voice low and urgent. "I know you're being flooded with memories right now, but this is not a good time. If you don't help me I'm going to die; my mother is going to die."

Something flickers behind his eyes and he blinks. "She killed my parents," he says. "She...I thought...she said..."

"Dammit Nicholas, what happened!" I scream, trying to get him to make sense.

"Who are you talking to?" Daisy says from behind me.

I whirl around and see that she is carrying a steak knife. She waves it toward me."No-nobody," I stutter.

"I heard you! I heard you talking away." She takes a step forward, her eyes frantic.

How is this witch related to my Nicholas, how?

I ball up every anxiety I have and take a deep breath. "Daisy. That's your name, isn't it?" I say slowly. Her mouth twitches but she doesn't answer. "I know something about you, Daisy, something you've been hiding for years. Something you let an innocent child believe for so long to be true, but it was a lie. It was all a lie." I stand up and hold my head high.

She twitches again.

"You killed Nicholas's parents, didn't you!" I scream, and take a step back, in the direction of the front door. I don't even know for sure if she did kill them, but I have nothing else to go on.

"How did you know that?" she says at last, admitting to my speculation. She moves in closer and flails the knife in front of my face. "Who told you that?" She stabs the knife toward me.

I cringe as the blade gets closer and closer to my skin. "Nicholas did. Nicholas told me!" I blurt.

"That's impossible."

"I've been hearing that a lot lately, that things are impossible, but it's not. *He told me.*"

She blinks and smiles derisively. "Then I guess he told you where all that money is hidden. Is that how you bought your new car, little princess, and how your whore mother and that asshole managed to buy that big place in St. Chalmers?"

"Those things were bought with *our own* money," I say.

"Bullshit," she says. "Everyone knows your mother is broke, and that prick barely made ends meet," she says scornfully.

I pause to think for a second, but it was enough for me to make her think I wasn't telling her the truth.

She leaps forward and holds the knife up to my throat. "What good are you, then? All the money is gone," she spits. Her left eye and shoulder spasm wildly. "You know what I'm going to do? First I'm going to slit your throat," she says in rapid succession, "and then I'm going to stab your mother to death, just like I stabbed Nicholas's parents in their sleep when *they* wouldn't give me what I wanted either."

The knife presses against my skin and I feel the warm trickle of blood roll down my neck.

"Tell her you know where the money is!" Nicholas yells.

"I know where the money is," I croak as the knife pushes harder against my throat. "I'll take you."

She pulls the knife back and bares her rotten teeth at me. "The money is all gone," she hisses. "I searched this house top to bottom before your perfect little family moved in and I've searched it again."

That's why the house was in such disrepair when we moved in. It wasn't the homeless or partyers, it was her. I panic. "No, no it's not. I know where it is. It's not in the house, that's why you couldn't find it."

She studies my face and I shudder. The fear in my eyes must be enough to mask the lie. "Take me," she demands, and shoves me backward through the front door.

Daisy holds the knife between my shoulder blades as I walk toward the gazebo; I can feel the point pushing through my hoodie. If I stop moving it will surely stab me.

"Follow me, Stephanie—I have an idea. Trust me," Nicholas says from the opposite direction. From the corner of my eye I see him disappear into the dense stand of trees. How am I going to trust him when I can't focus on anything besides the knife in my back?

"Keep moving, you little bitch," Daisy says behind me, and twists the knife a little.

"It's this way." I change direction and follow Nicholas. It's very dark under the trees, but the white shirt Nicholas is wearing makes it easier for me to follow him. Why is he leading me into the woods? Is there really money in here? What makes him think she won't kill me when she gets what she's after? There is nothing keeping me safe right now.

I trip over an exposed root, stumble, and fall to the ground. "Get up!" Daisy yells, and prods me with her shoe.

I wobble to my feet and continue to follow Nicholas through the trees. The pain in my hand is excruciating and I feel light-headed. How much blood have I lost? I hope Mom is okay. I didn't want to leave her side.

"Come on, Stephanie, we're almost there, stay with me," Nicholas says from a few feet ahead. He sounds miles away.

Where is he leading me?

I hear Daisy's ragged breathing behind me. "I think you're trying to make a fool out of me," she pants. "Why would they hide money all the way out here?" She grabs my arms and spins me around to face her.

I glance over my shoulder and can't see Nicholas anywhere. *Shit! Where did he go?* The panic I have been trying so hard to suppress starts to kick in and I feel another surge of adrenaline. She is probably going to kill me anyway; why fight the inevitable? I'm not going to wait around for her to do it. What's the point?

"Well?" Daisy says, staring up at me with unblinking eyes.

"Why is this money so important to you?" I ask suddenly. If I'm going to die tonight I might as well find out what I'm dying for, and why. I may as well find out everything I can.

She continues to stare at me for several long seconds. I stand my ground. I raise my eyebrows at her, which makes her twitch. "Daisy?" I prompt.

She blinks and absently looks at a nearby tree. "My brother had a lot of money. He was always so cheap with it," she snarls at the tree, then meets my eyes; she looks agitated.

"Why did you need the money so badly that you would kill him and his wife?"

The tic in her eye twitches and she winces. "My brother had a lot of money. He was always so cheap with it," she repeats.

"You said that already."

She tilts her head sideways and lifts the knife to scratch her wrist with the blade. I can't help but look down at the sleeve of the old sweater she's wearing. It's now spotted with her own blood. I cringe as she continues to scratch herself through the threadbare material. Does she not feel that?

She blinks and, as if reading my mind, looks from my face to her arm. She holds the knife between us and watches the blood drip from the tip of the sharp blade. I try not to look afraid. "What did you say!" she screams unexpectedly, and stabs the knife toward me, splattering blood on my face.

I stumble backward against a tree. "The money—you said your brother had a lot of it," I blurt.

"What's it to you, princess? Haven't you had enough already?" She leans in close and holds the knife to my cheek. I'm wedged between her and the tree.

"Please don't hurt me," I beg. "I'll take you to the money; it's not much farther." I glance around her for any sign of Nicholas. I can't see him anywhere.

She relaxes her grip on the knife and takes a step away. "If you are lying to me, princess...well, maybe I will leave that as a surprise." She grins. "Go!" she yells.

I fall around the tree. I've been totally spun around now; I could very well be walking back in the direction of the house. *Please God, give me a sign.*

"You have no idea where you are, do you!" she shrieks after we walk for another few minutes. "Shut up!" she screams as I'm about to answer. "Listen!" The forest is silent. I can't hear anything. Daisy starts to laugh hysterically. "Can you hear that?" she says, cocking her head. "Can you hear them calling me?"

"I can't hear anything," I say, frantically looking around.

Daisy sniffs and the sound of phlegm vibrating in the back of her throat makes me grimace. She grabs a handful of my hair and pulls me backward, bringing my ear to her mouth. "They are coming for me. You lied. I can hear them," she gurgles, then pushes her hand against my head, propelling me forward.

I land on my hands and knees. "I don't know what you're talking about!" I yell.

"Don't you? Don't you hear them? The sounds...the sounds—" She squats in front of me and puts the knife under my chin so I look up at her. "Listen!" she hisses.

I close my eyes and listen to the sounds of the woods, to my elevated breathing, to my rapid heartbeat and the distant sounds of sirens. How in the hell did she hear those and I didn't? Am I so accustomed to the sound that it's not something I would notice? My heart beats faster as realization hits: Mom is safe. And I could be too. I don't have to die like this.

"You hear it now, don't you?" Daisy rises and hovers over me.

I move to stand up and she drops her foot on my injured hand. I let out a sharp cry. "Shut up! You shut up!" she shouts, and puts her hands over her ears. Her shoe twists over my hand, grinding it into the ground as she spins around.

Ignoring the pain in my hand, I rip it out from under her foot, then leap up before she can stop me and run past her. My heart is beating so hard I feel like I might pass out. I run blindly through the trees, trying to follow the direction of the sirens, but they're echoing off the trees.

"Get back here, you little bitch!" Daisy screams behind me. "I'm going to kill you!"

Panting, I run over exposed roots and fallen branches. I can hardly see a thing. Daisy is swearing and screeching behind me, her footsteps sounding more like those of a lumbering barbarian than someone who weighs less than me. I hear my own sobs and gasps as I run with my hands in front of me to avoid slamming into trees. I keep going, pushing frantically forward. Daisy is not letting up; in fact she sounds as if she is right on my heels. I can feel her fingers brushing my back—or is that the knife? Her breathing is rapid and course and louder than mine. She is right behind me! One stumble and she'll be on top of me. I can't stop, not now.

The sirens are more distant than before—I'm running in the wrong direction! Too late to turn around now; I have to keep going. My legs start to feel weak; I'm running out of energy. How much longer can she keep this up? I don't have much left in me. The adrenaline is fading.

"Stephanie, stop!" Nicholas screams.

I come to an abrupt stop at the sound of Nicholas's voice. My arms wave at my sides like propellers as I struggle to keep my balance. My feet are teetering dangerously close to the edge of a cliff. How did I end up here? Is this what Charlie experienced before he fell off the edge—something crazed chasing *him* through the woods?

"Stephanie, watch out!" Nicholas yells.

I turn around just in time to see Daisy launch herself toward me. I dive out of the way and land facedown on the edge of the precipice. I scramble toward a safe piece of ground. "Where did she go, where did she go!" I scream, looking around wildly.

Nicholas walks to my side. He stays against the edge so that I know where the drop-off is. The moonlight is brighter here, without the trees blocking its path.

"Help me! Please help me," Daisy pleads.

I look in the direction of her voice and see only her bony fingers, clutching the edge of the cliff. I crawl over and look over the edge. Nicholas crouches next to me.

"Please save me," she begs, and looks in terror down to the river below. Her fingers begin to slip and she cries out. "I'll admit to the murder! Please, help me up. I can't hold on for much longer."

"What do you want me to do, Nicholas?" I ask softly. He doesn't answer me, just sits next to me, almost paralyzed, looking down at his aunt. "*Nicholas*," I press, and wave a hand in front of his face.

He looks up at me and with that one look I realize what he wants me to do. I don't exactly know how I know, I just do.

Daisy's legs thrash helplessly as she tries to get her footing on anything she can.

"Was it worth it, Daisy?" I ask.

"Was what worth it?" she screams.

"Killing Nicholas's parents for something as meaningless as money?"

She glances up at me and hesitates before opening her mouth to speak.

"Not quick enough," I say, and pick her fingers off of the edge.

Shock makes her eyes go round as she falls down the side of the cliff. Before she gets the chance to scream, her head hits the rock that Charlie had his last moments on with a loud crack. A second later there is a thump as her limp body meets the shallow river below. It's too dark to see her mangled corpse, and I'm thankful for that. I don't need that image to plague my dreams.

"Nicholas." I look up at him and he is crying. *Oh God, I hope that's what he wanted me to do.* I feel like throwing up all over again.

"Thank you," he says, and wipes away a tear. "Thank you for doing something I never could have done." He looks at me with his crystal-blue eyes and there is something I never saw in them before: a spark of clarity, a spark of forgiveness, a spark of liberation.

I smile weakly at him because I really have nothing I want to say. All I want to do is lie down and sleep this night away. I feel too weak and shaky to stand. I fear that if I try, I might end up next to Daisy. And I definitely don't want to die like that. I don't want to die at all.

After some time spent sitting in silence—silence that we both desperately needed—I notice beams of light touching the ground nearby. I hear my name being called.

"Nicholas," I whisper.

"Yes?" He meets my eyes.

"I have to go. But" —I place my hand close to his cheek— "I'll see you soon."

Nicholas smiles at me and, as the footsteps reach me, he disappears from sight.

CHAPTER SEVENTEEN

"COME HERE," NICHOLAS SAYS as he takes my hand. The feeling of his hand in mine is electrifying; I get instant butterflies in my stomach. I never could have imagined that we would actually be together like this. And to think I almost killed myself to be with him. Destiny had a different plan for us, though.

It's only been two weeks since Nicholas was released from the institution, and just over a month since the death of Daisy Gilman. I never told the police about the phenomenon Nicholas and I shared that led to Daisy's death and Nicholas's release back into society. Mom didn't remember very much from the night Daisy broke into the house, or if she did, she never questioned me about it. The only thing she did say was a thank you for saving her life, and for keeping my cell phone fully charged—to which I rolled my eyes, then hugged her tightly. I regained her trust in me that day.

My cell phone had captured Daisy's confession of the murder of Nicholas's parents for the police, the whole call recorded by the 911 service. We were very lucky that the phone didn't shatter when it was thrown against the wall. But the police getting to our house in the wee hours of morning was thanks to Greg, who woke up to a freezing bedroom, because I hadn't shut the window after my daring escape. He searched the house only to find both a teenager and his car missing, and called ahead to the

NorthBerry Police to let them know that I was most likely going back to the old house. He was worried that I was going to try to kill myself again.

What they found when they showed up wasn't what they had expected. It was Officer Sheldon who answered the call that night, and it was he who searched through the woods to find me sitting on the cliff edge with Daisy's corpse somewhere below me. One wave of his flashlight was all he needed to spot her body.

I was taken along with Mom to the hospital. I had to get stitches in my hand and Mom's leg was pretty mangled, but we got away with our lives and that was all that mattered. I was released from the hospital into police custody for questioning, and Daisy's body was pulled from the river when the sun rose that morning. I didn't confess to prying her fingers from the edge of the cliff, but I did tell the police the entire story from the time I stole Greg's car to the time Daisy "accidentally fell" off the cliff when she was trying to attack me, and along with Mom's muddled recollection of events, Daisy's recorded confession, and her drug abuse in the past, there wasn't anything they could do to hold me.

"It feels so good to be here with you," Nicholas says, breaking me out of my thoughts. He cuddles in closer to me.

"It's kind of surreal," I reply, and lean in to nuzzle his neck.

Nicholas smiles broadly and wraps his arm around my shoulders.

"I'm going to miss this place," I say sadly, looking around the gazebo. "For me there are only good memories here; it's a pity we can't take it with us."

"Maybe one day we will have a house of our own and we'll build a gazebo that is even grander than this one." He waves his hand with a grand flourish, which makes me laugh. "We can build new memories together," he says a little more seriously, and kisses me on the forehead.

"I can imagine our life together," I say shyly.

"What do you imagine?"

I turn to face him and I look into his blue eyes. "Things like marrying you, having a house of our own, kids..." I flush and look down.

Nicholas puts a stray piece of hair behind my ear and holds my chin up with his fingers so that I meet his eyes. "It's been two times that I thought I had lost you, Stephanie, and I never want to lose you. My life without you wouldn't be worth living. A forever with you is all I want too." He smiles.

I kiss him softly and then embrace him. I never want to let him go. I try to think about what kind of person he would be if he'd never been locked up for those nine long years, but it pains me to think about it. We probably would never have ended up together, and he's right, a life without him would not be worth living.

"Do you think you will visit this place in your dreams still?" I say into his ear.

"No. I think I kept coming back here for a reason, and now that that reason is right next to me, there's no point."

"You mean me?"

"Yes," he says, and pulls away to see my face. "I love you, Stephanie."

"I love you too."

We still don't know how it was possible for Nicholas to get himself here by astral projection, and I don't think we ever will fully understand it, but I like the way he thinks. I was surprised that he wanted to come back here, all things considered, but this place had meaning to him too, and we both wanted to say our goodbyes.

Nicholas smiles lovingly at me and rises to crouch next to the fire-pit. I frown, curious. "When this was my parents' house and we lived here," he says, and rubs his hand over the red bricks, "I used to sleepwalk every night." He glances at me to gauge my expression, then looks back at the fire-pit when I don't say anything. "I would get out of my bed and go to my parents' room. They would wake most nights, but after a while they got used to me coming into their room." Nicholas grins and puts his finger in the crack where the bit of mug sits. He pushes it and slides it out of the hole. "You should keep this." He hands me the fragment.

"Thank you," I say, and hold it between my fingers.

"They say never to wake a sleepwalker," he continues, "so my parents would let me do what I did almost every night, which was squeeze my way in between them." He smiles fondly. "They told me I would never stay long, though; I would always eventually get up and leave the room. My mother and father took turns following me every night, because *every night* I would leave the house and come out here." He gazes around the gazebo, and then looks back toward the bricks. "I was totally unaware that I was sleepwalking, of course, but as soon as I came out here I would lie down on the bench and then my mother or father would carry me back to my room to tuck me back in." He pauses and bows his head, probably thinking the same thing I am.

When Bradley told me about Nicholas, he said the police had assumed he had killed his parents. All the evidence would have pointed to that. He was covered in their blood, after all, and he never spoke afterwards. Little did they know he was just doing what he did every night as a child, except no one was there to bring him back into the house and tuck him back into bed afterwards. I don't know why Daisy didn't kill him that night. Maybe she forgot that he was in the house, or maybe she had some form of a conscience back then. I imagine a younger Nicholas, cold and alone when the police found him out here, and my heart breaks. I look at the man he is today and you would never have guessed that he'd been institutionalized for nine years for something he believed he did. The guilt that he must have felt would have been unbearable for any normal person. I smile at that, because neither of us is normal at all.

I continue to wait silently while Nicholas fights off his own memories. He gives me a reassuring smile after a moment, then focuses his attention on the hole between the bricks. He puts his finger in the crack and pulls one of the stones to the side, and then another. "My father never believed in banks. He was forever hiding his money in weird places. When my grandfather died he left everything to my father. He didn't give Daisy anything because he knew giving it to her would mean killing her—she would waste it on drugs. I guess in the end it didn't matter; the money killed her anyway—it was her fate, either way." He shakes his head.

I kneel next to Nicholas and place my hand on his shoulder in silent support, because there's nothing I can say that will make what happened to his family any easier to bear. He inhales deeply and reaches both hands into the open space he's revealed beneath the fire-pit. He heaves out a heavy black plastic bag. I don't say a thing; I only watch in amazement as he fumbles with the knot.

"Those paintings your mother would hang around the house," he says. "They have meaning to me too. For so long I have felt that I've been wandering aimlessly through darkness. I've been lost. That was until the day I saw you for the first time. Stephanie, you helped me through it, you helped me find my way back into the light." He opens the bag.

"No, Nicholas." I lift his chin gently with my fingertips and look deeply into his eyes. "You helped me find mine."

We both look down into the open bag between us. There is more money than we will ever need, but I don't care about the money. I already have what I've always wanted.

My light through the darkness.

Him.

CPSIA information can be obtained
at www.ICGtesting.com
Printed in the USA
LVOW07s0619121017
552034LV00004BA/892/P